The Collected Supernatural and Weird Fiction of Hugh Walpole Volume 3

The Collected Supernatural and Weird Fiction of Hugh Walpole Volume 3

One Novel 'Portrait of a Man with Red Hair' and Fifteen Short Stories of the Strange and Unusual Including 'The Clocks', 'The Silver Mask', 'Major Wilbrahim', 'Field with Five Trees' and 'Tarnhelm'

Hugh Walpole

LEONAUR

The Collected
Supernatural and Weird
Fiction of
Hugh Walpole
Volume 3
One Novel 'Portrait of a Man with Red Hair' and Fifteen Short Stories of the Strange
and Unusual Including 'The Clocks', 'The Silver Mask', 'Major Wilbrahim', 'Field with
Five Trees' and 'Tarnhelm'
by Hugh Walpole

FIRST EDITION

Leonaur is an imprint of Oakpast Ltd

Copyright in this form © 2018 Oakpast Ltd

ISBN: 978-1-78282-768-9 (hardcover)
ISBN: 978-1-78282-769-6 (softcover)

http://www.leonaur.com

Contents

The Clocks	7
'Enery	17
Head in Green Bronze	29
Henry Fitzgeorge Strether	32
The Silver Mask	42
The Perfect Close	55
Mrs. Lunt	65
Barbara Flint	78
Major Wilbraham	91
Field with Five Trees	104
Mr Huffam a Christmas Story	116
Tarnhelm or, the Death of My Uncle Robert	133
The Tarn	147
Nancy Ross	159
The Ruby Glass	171
Portrait of a Man with Red Hair	180

The Clocks

He lay in bed, shaking with terror. One of those strange, sudden unaccountable panics that overwhelmed him so often had seized him now. It was not only at night they came; he had known them in the daylight when the sun had been shining brilliantly on to the uneven flags of the old stone court, and everything—the dark elms, the shining borders of flowers, the red and brown of the twisted, uneven roof had stood out in sharp, brilliant outline against the bluest of skies—even then he had felt afraid.

But it was at night that it came most frequently—or in these first grey hours of the early morning, when the shadows were creeping in flocks, strange shapes and outlines, over the floor.

It was like that now; the blank, dead square of the window stared across the room at him with no expression only a dull, lifeless gaze, like the open eyes of a dead man. The room was almost dark, but the half-light gave strange shapes to the furniture; the huge cupboard against the wall by the window flung vast shadows across the ceiling; the two chairs near the door seemed to his excited fancy to move—their legs multiplied and dwindled before his eyes; now there were four and two waved wildly in the air—now there was only one, and the chair hung foolishly forward as though it was about to fall.

His clothes, flung wildly across the iron railing at the foot of the bed, were monstrous; now they were a mountain, blocking the grey window, and now, at every turn of the eye, they had dwindled to nothing at all, and the window stared at him again across the bare, uneven boards of the floor.

The door was a little open, so that a thin bar of light crept in from the passage; it was almost white against the grey, shadowy room, and it was on this light that his eyes were fixed.

He had woken suddenly with the thought that the gleam had

gone; not that the door had closed; he could see that was not so, but that someone or something had crossed it, blotting it out. To his wild brain this was no new thing; he had often watched the door with the same fear, but it was worse to wake up suddenly from a heavy, dreamless sleep and imagine it. It might have entered just before his waking—it might have been its entry that woke him—it might be in the room now; and he searched the room with staring eyes.

An old grandfather clock in the corner of the room ticked monotonously. He hated the sound of it; he hated the sound of any clock, and they had so many in the house. There was one on the stairs, with a high, shrill cry like the voice of his grandfather when he was angry, and there was one down below in the hall that came up to him, softly and mysterious, like the hum of some enormous insect.

There were others in the house, and he always thought of them as live people, quite as much alive as his aunt and grandfather, Captain Bulstrode and Lizzie; indeed, at times he thought that it was only the clocks that were alive—the clocks and himself—and that one day they would march upon him, with their terrible buzzing noise, and kill him.

And now in the perfect silence of the house, with the grey dawn in the room, their voices seemed very loud, and they hid the stir that the Thing that had entered through the door would make. He did not know where it was, and he was afraid to look, but it would suddenly creep upon him from behind the bed, and he could feel its long fingers twine about his neck and he could see its eyes gaze terribly into his.

His heart was beating so that the bedclothes shook above him and his forehead was wet; his hands had clutched the blanket and held it as though it were a talisman that would keep him safe.

Then suddenly from the courtyard came the crowing of a cock, and immediately his terror left him. That was Gabriel: he was always the first to crow. Soon there would be Hector, and, last of all, Robert; it must be nearly four, and it would soon be time for him to get up. He knew that the animals would be slowly waking, and the thought of their movements pleased him. There was company at last, and the gradually broadening light robbed the room of its fantastic terrors. He could see Gabriel, Hector, and Robert standing against the grey sky, watching solemnly the gradual approach of day. They were his best friends, kinder and more amusing than the people in the house; and he turned and fell into an uneasy, broken sleep.

When the grandfather clock wheezed out four, he jumped from his bed and began to tumble on his clothes. For a moment he looked from the window into the courtyard below. There was Gabriel standing, sharp against the sky, on a rained and crumbling wall that had once bound the garden. Already the sky was breaking, and white mists were creeping like serpents over the grass.

He stood, a wild and uncouth figure, at the window. His yellow hair, falling to his shoulders, was tangled, and yet held pieces of grass and leaves that had caught in it when he had lain, the evening before, on the hill beyond the house watching the setting sun. His head was enormous and all his features were exaggerated—his body looked as if it were of tremendous strength, his long arms shot from his miserable coat, his trousers scarcely extended below his knees, and his great fingers closed and unclosed, their muscles making reports like so many little guns. He sighed heavily, picked up the battered candlestick, on which the candle had guttered in the draught until it lurched fantastically to one side, and groped for the matches.

He found them at last, lit the candle, and crept softly into the passage. The noise of the clock in the hall stole up the staircase and surrounded him with a noise like the furious buzz of an insect.

'They're at it again,' he said to himself, cross and angry. 'They'll be up one day. They're angrier every week I haven't done anything to you,' he went on. 'It ain't anything to do with me. I'd be afeared to touch you.'

He crept, in his stockinged feet, down the stairs. He glanced furtively at the clock as he passed it and clung to the farther wall; the candle shook a little in his hand. The grey light was penetrating through the dim shutters of the house, and the dark outlines of the hall with its rows of hats, absurdly alive in the dim glow, an umbrella stand with sticks that leant rakishly to one side, the end of the cloth that had escaped its nail beating dustily against the floor, blown by the little draught through the heavy front door—all these things he faced with hurried little gasps of fright and wide, saucer-like eyes.

To his hazy impression of things, these early morning hours, when he must light the fires and sweep the house, were full of horrors, and he faced the violent scoldings of his aunt and the cursings of Captain Bulstrode with far less fear. Those things were transient and ineffectual in their consequences, but the grey, ghostly mornings spread their mist about him throughout the weary length of the day.

By seven o'clock the fires were burning brightly, the table was laid

9

for breakfast, the floors were swept, and Janet, slattern and virago, general servant and indifferent cook, was already scolding in the kitchen.

He stepped out of the house into the garden. The sun was beating down on the uneven stones of the court, and he could see Gabriel crowing for joy on the ruined wall. There were butterflies—white and red and blue—and in the corner, against the red stone of the house, a cloud of yellow daffodils were blowing gently in the little morning wind. But the moment of escape was a short one. Soon the shrill voice of his aunt called him, and he shuffled back into the house. Why was it that as soon as there were pleasant things in the world—butterflies and flowers and a warm golden sun—in an instant they were a! snatched away and the world was grey again? There were so many things that were hard to understand!

They were all at breakfast when he returned; he saw their heads through the window as he passed; the straight, tightly-bound hair of his aunt, the bald, fat head of Captain Bulstrode on which the light would shine until you could see your face in it. He crept to his seat at the bottom of the table. There were never many words wasted at breakfast time, and there was very little said now.

'Late as usual!' sharply from his aunt 'Why can't you come when it's time?'

She was a hard-featured woman who ran, on every possible opportunity, into points—her nose, her ears, her head, her arms, they all had sharp edges; and the stiff, steely folds of her black dress and the little steel reticule at her waist were in keeping. Captain Bulstrode was red and fat—his neck was short and thick, his eyes tiny, his cheeks heavy and flushed. He had, a little, the air of a navy man run to seed.

By the large white-stone fireplace sat a very, very old man—Grandfather Tackity, He was so old and wrapped so thoroughly in rugs that it was difficult to see whether he were a man at all; he had been, as it were, extinguished by his wrappings, and the only thing that remained alive was the sharp yellow tip of a nose and two twinkling eyes. Occasionally he shuffled his feet, and two very wrinkled old hands were stretched outside the rug and held tremblingly a plate on which was a very small piece of bacon as withered as the old man himself.

He muttered continually to himself, and, at times, his voice rose in shrill expostulation. He finished the tiny piece of bacon and turned the plate upside down to see whether something might have possibly clung to the bottom.

'Well, Jane, my dear, just a leetle piece more for your old father—

just a leetle,, leetle bit, my dear; your poor old father's so hungry, and it was such a very, very leetle piece and it's *all* gone, my dear, *all* gone. Deary me, the old man's so hungry—the poor old man! Just a leetle piece of bread, my dear, on this beautiful morning.'

His grandson at the table watched him, and nodded, every now and again by way of encouragement and sympathy. He was never quite sure what his grandfather might be—sometimes he was the devil, and sometimes the spirit of one of the clocks, and sometimes nothing at all—but he understood the hungry feeling, and was sorry.

The heap of rugs was violently agitated, and the plate fell with a crash to the ground.

'Dear me!' his voice rose in a little scream, his hands waved for a moment feebly in the air. Then a look of cunning flashed into the sharp eyes. Perhaps they hadn't heard at the table. The rugs were convulsed again as he tried to move his foot towards the broken plate to cover it. But his daughter had heard. She was up in a moment and had moved towards him. His eyes closed and his nose seemed to shrink; his hands crept beneath the rug.

'Come, father,' she said, 'don't be so stupid now. Breakin' good china like that.' She shook him up until he disappeared altogether, then she picked up the pieces of plate and returned to her place.

As she passed the fool at the table he had drawn his shoulders in and lowered his head as though he expected a blow, but she passed him without even glancing in his direction.

He continued to watch her furtively. There was trouble in the air, trouble on every side, and it came, he knew instinctively, from her. The clocks were always louder in his ear when danger was at hand, and now he could hear them, it seemed to him, from every part of the house.

She opened the door and called for Lizzie, the servant. They began to clear the table. She turned suddenly on her nephew:

'Well? What are you standing about fer? Haven't yer got anything to do, yer lazy lout, you? Get to work, now! Isn't it enough that we feed yer and clothe yer! Yer hulking fool that yer are!'

He stood in front of her with his head lowered and his arm up—then he moved, slouching, away.

Bulstrode stood at the window and watched the old man with a smile on his lips. The old man scarcely recovered from his shaking, was looking at the fire. Suddenly he felt that the other's eyes were upon him, He turned very slowly in his chair and faced him. The two men gazed at each other.

Bulstrode crossed the room and leant over the chair. 'Tell us where it is,' he said. 'We won't touch it but it's safer you know—much safer.'

'No, no!' The old man shook his head violently. 'Yer shan't know—none of yer. Yer think yer so clever, but yer aren't. Yer shan't know.'

Bulstrode frowned. 'You'd better, you know,' he said, softly, 'It's safer—'

Then he left the room,

Tackity beckoned his grandson to him.

'He's the Devil, you know,' he said, in a hoarse whisper. 'Such a clever devil, too! Oh! Dear me! But I'm cleverer—much cleverer!' He chuckled.

'Is he really the Devil?' said the fool looking at the door.

'Oh, dear me, yes—Old Tackity knows. He knows a thing or two.' He continued to chuckle hoarsely like a watch that had run down and was being wound.

In the things that had to be done in the morning the fool gener-ally forgot the rest of the world. The butterflies and the sun were lost behind the carrying of coals and the scolding of Lizzie and his aunt, But today everything was doubly heavy: the shadowy kingdom of his world was shot with strange colours, and the passages and stairs of the house were filled with figures that vanished mysteriously as he approached them, He had seen such shadows before—they had often met him and surrounded him in his dreams, and come to him in the first grey morning hours, but he had never known them so urgent in the glare of the daylight. From the wide window at the turn of the staircase the sun poured into the house: a great golden bee buzzed fu-riously against the pane, and a white mist of roses hung like a cloud in mid-air, with a burning sky of blue beyond. But the figures thronged the stairs and pressed upon him and touched his arm as he with his finger in his mouth watching the clock at the stair-head.

'They're up to their mischief. *They* know. They never call out like that when there's nothing the matter. You devils! You devils!' He shook his great fist at the clock; then he heard his aunt's step on the floor above, and crept about his work again.

At the midday dinner he watched his aunt and ate his food in frightened silence. They were talking at the end of the table, and it seemed that there was some dispute between them.

'No!' she said, shaking her head violently, 'There are other ways. I tell you. We'll find it out if we wait.'

'I tell you I *can't* wait,' he said, angrily, 'I've waited here long enough. You're always telling me to wait. A man would think he could spend his time hanging round and waiting—as if a fellow hadn't things to do, I tell yer I'm off tomorrow.'

Her face went very white, and she clutched his arm, 'No. You can't leave me like that. You wouldn't dare. You promised.'

'Well, and *you* promised,' he answered, roughly, 'You said I should have it.'

'*We* should have it,' she caught him up eagerly. Then she went on quickly: 'He isn't so well today. It won't be so long to wait—a week or two—'

'No!—I'm sick of it,' he said. 'Waiting and waiting. He's got the life of Methuselah,'

'Well, *he* suspects'—nodding her head in the direction of the fool. 'He's had his eyes on us this long time. He's sharper than folk know.'

'Well—he'd better not be,' muttered Bulstrode. 'That's all—he'd better not be. And what's it matter? A year or two less to his days. He's lived long enough, blast him!'

Old Tackity wasn't so well today. He wasn't so well as he'd been a breakfast. He took his little piece of beef without a murmur, finished it, and stared dismally into the fireplace. Every now and again he jerked his head round in a frightened way and glanced at the table, but he said nothing.

The afternoon was the fool's holiday. He wandered through the fields, up the hill and down into the wood. There he was fascinated—frightened. The darkness and the silence terrified, but the colours, the little wind that blew the leaves across his feet, pleased him. But today there was utter silence. The leaves hung in so thick a tapestry overhead that the sun could not pierce them, and it was very dark. At his frightened ear seemed to crowd things that he could not see; and down the long silence of the forest paths came the whispering patter of mysterious feet.

He fled back into the sunshine, fearing pursuers as he ran. He flung himself, panting, on to the side of the hill in the full glare of the sun, and watched the dark, and sinister house, the high stone wall, the clustering gables, the enclosing trees. What were they doing there, he wondered? Had anything happened? Something was going to happen. He knew—the clocks had told him. Supposing it had happened already? He drew his coat up over his collar and waited throughout the afternoon. Then when the sun grew low and the shadows slipped, like birds with trailing wings over the long golden breast of the corn, he returned.

The house, with its thick walls and small diamond-paned windows, was already dark, A fire burned in the kitchen; the room was empty. He tossed his hair back from his forehead, and groped in the cupboard; he was hungry, he had been hungry all day, and if they would not give him anything, then he must take it. But the cupboard was empty; and a sound made him draw back in sudden alarm. It was the clocks again; he could hear their beat in every part of the house. There was one in the room there with him, and he watched its round, smooth face with growing fury. It was laughing at him—he could almost see the grin, and it mocked him for his ignorance. As he looked at it, the madness surged in his brain, and, suddenly he leapt at it, and with his fist broke the face. His hand was cut and began to bleed furiously; the glass fell with a little sound like a cry to the ground. He noticed the blood, and began to whimper. His face grew white with terror, for the hands had stopped, and the great pendulum had ceased to swing.

'What will it do? What will it do?' He cowered back against the wail and stared at it. It seemed to him that its grin had changed to a frown, and its silence frightened him more than its noise had done. With trembling knees and shaking hands he crept from the room and up the dark staircase. On the landing he paused to think. He must hide somewhere, for they were pursuing him; even now he thought that he could hear their footsteps. He turned blindly to the first door that was at hand and pushed it open. As he did so there was a sudden noise from every part of the house—all the clocks struck eight.

He gave a little scream of terror; to him it sounded as though they were all calling to each other, bearing news of the thing that he had done. They knew, and they would follow him; and he stumbled blindly headforemost into the room. The place was thick with dust, so that he coughed and choked; at last he made out a dim lamp and by the side of it, sitting propped up at the table, his grandfather.

At the sound of the opening door the old man cried out; 'No, no—I tell you! It's no use your coming here! You devil! You devil! You devil!' Then he saw who it was. 'Oh, my poor flesh!' he said. It's you, is it? Oh! I'm glad it's only you. I thought it was the other. Deary me, what a shock for an old man!'

'Let me in,' said the fool, coming close to him. 'Let me in. They're after me. They're coming up the stairs.'

'Oh, they won't come in here,' said Tackity, confidently, 'I'm too

14

clever for 'em by half. They can't do anything, they can't.'

'I've killed one of them,' said the fool, shivering, 'I broke his face with my hand. See!' He held it up for the old man to see,

'That's right,' said the other, nodding his head, 'Brave boy! That's right!'

The fool crept into a corner, and at last he slept, His dreams were troubled, and he gave little cries, and he moved uneasily. Then suddenly he awoke. Someone was in the room. It was difficult to see because of the dim burning of the lamp. The old man was bending over the table, and in front of him was a great pile of round, yellow metal; he let it pass through his hands so that it tinkled, and glittered as it fell in front of him. But it was not that that had awakened the fool. Someone had opened the door. Suddenly through the mist he saw the Captain; he would have screamed had not fear held him silent. He was stepping very silently, like a cat, and his face was white and his neck bulged over his collar.

The old man had not seen him; he was still murmuring to himself with pleasure at the sight in front of him. Then something warned faint, and he turned round with a little cry.

'No! No!' he screamed, 'You devil, you—'

But Bulstrode was upon him. He said nothing at all, but he caught the skinny throat between his hands and bent over it. Another little strangled scream, then the hands beat the air wildly for a moment, the face turned purple under the light of the lamp, and the head fell right back, crookedly, across his shoulder and stared at the fool.

Bulstrode looked for a moment at what he had done, then he began furiously to pour the gold into his pockets. He filled them all, and yet there was more: he filled his handkerchief and tied it; he found a box that was on the table, and he filled that. Then he crept from the room, locking the door after him.

The fool did not move. He did not understand what happened. He sat crouched there for a long while, and then the head, leering at him so strangely with fixed and staring eyes, annoyed him.

'They're gone,' he said, in a whisper. 'They're gone, grandfather. Yer can move now.' But old Tackity was silent.

Then the fool began to be frightened, 'Grandfather! Grandfather!' he whispered. The light of the lamp jumped up and down and the shadows on the wall leaped with it. The house was absolutely still; he could not even hear the clocks. He moved from his corner and raised himself on his knees; he lifted his hand and, very gently, touched the old man's coat.

'Speak to me, grandfather,' he said, 'They're gone. He won't hurt you again. Oh! The shadows!'

The oil had nearly failed in the lamp, and the flame flared up and died down like a jack-in-the-box; the room seemed to jump with it. His hand touched the man's shoulder, and now it travelled down the sleeve. He stopped and let his fingers travel round the buttons—they were so hard and cold that he started for a moment. Then his fingers slipped off the coat and touched the back of the hand. The knotted veins stood out like iron but the flesh was clammy and warm. His own hand was suddenly frozen. He could not move it away, and he knelt there, rigid, with his eyes fixed in front of him,

The flame of the lamp gave a leap and for an instant the room was alive with light.

Everything sprang out of the darkness—the table, the shuttered windows, the dirty floor littered with papers and the unswept refuse of fifty years, and, at the last, for a moment, the white face, the crooked neck, the filmy eyes of the old man.

Then the lamp flickered out into darkness. The fool struggled to his feet, and, with little cries, his hand stretched before his face, he crept towards the door. Suddenly he stumbled. There was something in the way. He pushed it aside and knew that it was the leg of the dead man. The touch that he gave it brought it heavily to the floor.

He did not dare to move. He felt as though the body were on every side of him. He became wild with terror and there were noises in his ears. Suddenly he knew—it was the sound of the Clocks. They were coming up the stairs. The buzzing grew louder and louder. The room was filled with the sound.

He shouted 'You devils!' and stumbled to his feet. He must get out but the body stopped him—it stuck to him, so that he dragged it with him as he moved.

Then they were upon him; the room was filled with them; their hands at his throat, their cry was in his ears, their breath was on his cheek. He beat them off with his hands but they had by the knees—they dragged him down and down—

When the grim silence of the house stirred an inquisitive attention, its doors were invaded.

In the dusty room at the head of the stairs they found the dead bodies of the fool and the old man lying, in a tangled heap, together.

'Enery

1

Mrs. Slater was caretaker at No. 21 March Square. Old Lady Cathcart lived with her middle-aged daughter at No. 21, and, during half the year, they were down at their place in Essex; during half the year, then, Mrs. Slater lived in the basement of No. 21 with her son Henry, aged six.

Mrs. Slater was a widow; upon a certain afternoon, two and a half years ago, she had paused in her ironing and listened. "Something," she told her friends afterwards, gave her a start—she "couldn't say what nor how." Her ironing stayed, for that afternoon at least, where it was, because her husband, with his head in a pulp and his legs bent underneath him, was brought in on a stretcher, attended by two policemen. He had fallen from a piece of scaffolding into Piccadilly Circus, and was unable to afford any further assistance to the improvements demanded by the Pavilion Music Hall. Mrs. Slater, a stout, amiable woman, had never been one to worry. Henry Slater, Senior, had been a bad husband, "what with women and the drink"—she had no intention of lamenting him now that he was dead; she had done for ever with men, and devoted the whole of her time and energy to providing bread and butter for herself and her son.

She had been Lady Cathcart's caretaker for a year and a half, and had given every satisfaction. When the old lady came up to London Mrs. Slater went down to Essex and defended the country place from suffragettes and burglars. "I shouldn't care for it," said a lady friend, "all alone in the country with no cheerful noises nor human beings."

"Doesn't frighten me, I give you my word, Mrs. East," said Mrs. Slater; "not that I don't prefer the town, mind you."

It was, on the whole, a pleasant life, that carried with it a certain dignity. Nobody who had seen old Lady Cathcart drive in her open carriage, with her black bonnet, her coachman, and her fine, straight back, could deny that she was one of Our Oldest and Best—none of your mushroom families come from Lord knows where—it was a position of trust, and as such Mrs. Slater considered it. For the rest she loved her son Henry with more than a mother s love; he was as unlike his poor father, bless him, as any child could be. Henry, although you would never think it to look at him, was not quite like other children; he had been, from his birth, a "little queer, bless his heart," and Mrs. Slater attributed this to the fact that three weeks before the boy's birth, Henry Slater, Senior, had, in a fine frenzy of inebriation, hit her over the head with a chair. "Dead drunk, 'e was, and never a thought to the child comin'. 'Enery,' I said to him, 'it's the child you're hittin' as well as me'; but 'e was too far gone, poor soul, to take a thought."

Henry was a fine, robust child, with rosy cheeks and a sturdy, thick-set body. He had large blue eyes and a happy, pleasant smile, but, although he was six years of age, he could hardly talk at all, and liked to spend the days twirling pieces of string round and round or looking into the fire. His eyes were unlike the eyes of other children, and in their blue depths there lurked strange apprehensions, strange anticipations, strange remembrances. He had never, from the day of his birth, been known to cry. When he was frightened or distressed the colour would pass slowly from his cheeks, and strange little gasping breaths would come from him; his body would stiffen and his hands clench.

If he was angry the colour in his face would darken and his eyes half close, and it was then that he did, indeed, seem in the possession of some disastrous thraldom—but he was angry very seldom, and only with certain people; for the most part he was a happy child, "as quiet as a mouse." He was unusual, too, in that he was a very cleanly child, and loved to be washed, and took the greatest care of his clothes. He was very affectionate, fond of almost everyone, and passionately devoted to his mother.

Mrs. Slater was a woman with very little imagination. She never speculated on "how different things would be if they were different," nor did she sigh after riches, nor possessions, nor any of the goods Fate bestows upon her favourites. She would, most certainly, have been less fond of Henry had he been more like other children, and his dependence upon her gave her something of the feeling that very rich ladies have for very small dogs. She was, too, in a way, proud. "Never been able to talk, nor never will, they tell me, the lamb," she would assure her friends, "but as gentle and as quiet!"

She would sit, sometimes, in the evening before the fire and think of the old, noisy, tiresome days when Henry, Senior, would beat her black and blue, and would feel that her life had indeed fallen into pleasant places.

There was nothing whatever in the house, all silent about her and filled with shrouded furniture, that could alarm her. "Ghosts!" she would cry. "You show me one, that's all. I'll give you ghosts!"

Her digestion was excellent, her sleep undisturbed by conscience or creditors. She was a happy woman.

Henry loved March Square. There was a window in an upstairs passage from behind whose glass he could gaze at the passing world. The Passing World! . . . the shrouded house behind him. One was as alive, as bustling, as demonstrative to him as the other, but between the two there was, for him, no communication. His attitude to the Square and the people in it was that he knew more about them than anyone else did; his attitude to the House, that he knew nothing at all compared with what "They" "knew. In the Square he could see through the lot of them, so superficial were they all; in the House he could only wait, with fingers on lip, for the next revelation that they might vouchsafe to him.

Doors were, for the most part, locked, yet there were many days when the rooms had to be dusted, and sometimes fires were lit because the house was an old one, and damp Lady Cathcart had a horror of.

Always for young Henry the house wore its buried and abandoned air. He was never to see it when the human beings in it would count more than its furniture, and the human life in it more than the house itself. He had come, a year and a half ago, into the very place that his dreams had, from the beginning, built for him. Those large, high rooms with the shining floors, the hooded furniture, the windows gaping without their curtains, the shadows and broad squares of light, the little whispers and rattles that doors and cupboards gave, the swirl of the wind as it sprang released from corners and crevices, the lisp of some whisper, "I'm coming! I'm coming! I'm coming!" that, nevertheless, again and again defeated expectation. How could he but enjoy the fine field of affection that these provided for him?

His mother watched him with maternal pride. "He's *that* contented!" she would say. "Any other child would plague your life away, but 'Enery—"

It was part of Henry's unusual mind that he wondered at nothing. He remained in constant expectation, but whatever were to come to him it would not bring surprise with it. He was in a world where anything might happen. In all the house his favourite room was the high, thin drawing-room with an old gold mirror at one end of it and a piano muffled in brown holland. The mirror caught the piano with its peaked inquiring shape, that, in its reflection, looked so much more tremendous and ominous than it did in plain reality. Through the mirror the piano looked as though it might do anything, and to Henry, who knew nothing about pianos, it was responsible for almost everything that occurred in the house.

The windows of the room gave a fine display of the garden, the children, the carriages, and the distant houses, but it was when the Square was empty that Henry liked best to gaze down into it, because then the empty house and the empty Square prepared themselves together for some tremendous occurrence. Whenever such an interval of silence struck across the noise and traffic of the day, it seemed that all the world screwed itself up for the next event.

"One—two—three." But the crisis never came. The noise returned again, people laughed and shouted, bells rang and motors screamed. Nevertheless, one day something would surely happen.

The house was full of company, and the boy would, sometimes, have yielded to the Fear that was never far away, had it not been for someone whom he had known from the very beginning of everything, someone who was as real as his mother, someone who was more powerful than anything or anyone in the house, and kinder, far, far kinder.

Often when Mrs. Slater would wonder of what her son was thinking as he sat twisting string round and round in front of the fire, he would be aware of his Friend in the shadow of the light, watching gravely, in the cheerful room, having beneath His hands all the powers, good and evil, of the house. Just as Henry pictured quite clearly to himself other occupants of the house—someone with taloned claws behind the piano, another with black-hooded eyes and a peaked cap in the shadows of an upstairs passage, another brown, shrivelled and naked, who dwelt in a cupboard in one of the empty bedrooms, so, too, he could see his Friend, vast and shadowy, with eyes that were kind and shining.

Often, he had felt the pressure of His hand, had heard His reassuring whisper in his ears, had known the touch of His lips upon his forehead. No harm could come to him whilst his Friend was in the house—and his Friend was always there.

He went always with his mother into the streets when she did her shopping or simply took the air. It was natural that on these occasions he should be more frightened than during his hours in the house. In the first place his Friend did not accompany him on these out-of-door excursions, and his mother was not nearly so strong a protector as his Friend.

Then he was disturbed by the people who pressed and pushed about him—he had a sense that they were all like birds with flapping wings and strange cries, rushing down upon him—the colours and confusion of the shops bewildered him. There was too much here for him properly to understand; he had enough to do with the piano, the mirror, the shadowed passages, the staring windows.

But in the Square, he was happy again. Mrs. Slater never ventured into the garden; that was for her superiors, and she complacently accepted a world in which things were so ordered as the only world possible. But there was plenty of life outside the garden.

There were, on the different days of the week, the various musicians, and Henry was friendly with them all. He delighted in music; as he stood there, listening to the barrel-organ, the ideas, pictures, dreams, flew like flocks of beautiful birds through his brain, fleet and always just beyond his reach, so that he could catch nothing, but would nod his head and would hope that the tune would be repeated, because next time he might, perhaps, be more fortunate.

"The Colonel," who played the harp on Saturdays, was a friend of Mrs. Slater. "Nice little feller, that of yours, mum," he would say. "'Ad one meself once."

"Indeed?"

"Yes, sure enough. . . . Nice day. . . . Would you believe it, this is the only London square left for us to play in? . . . 'Tis, indeed. Cruel shame, I call it; life's 'ard. . . . You're right, mum, it is. Well, good day."

Mrs. Slater looked after him affectionately. "Pore feller; and yet I dare say he makes a pretty bit of it if all was known."

Henry sighed. The birds were flown again. He was left with the blue-flecked sky and the grey houses that stood around the garden like beasts about a water-pool. The sun (a red disk) peered over their shoulders. He went with his mother within doors. Instantly on his entrance the house began to rustle and whisper.

2

Mrs. Slater, although an amiable and kind-hearted human being who believed with confident superstition in a God of other people's making, did not, on the whole, welcome her lady friends with much cordiality. It was not, as she often explained, as though she had her own house into which to ask them. Her motto was, "*Friendly with All, Familiar with None*," and to this she very faithfully held. But in her heart, there was reason enough for this caution; there had been days— yes, and nights too—when, during her lamented husband's lifetime, she had "taken a drop," taken it, obviously enough, as a comfort and a solace when things were going very hard with her, and "'Enery pre-ferrin' me to be jolly meself to keep 'im company." She had protested, but Fate and Henry had been too strong for her. "She had fallen into the habit!" Then, when No. 21 had come under her care, she had put it all sternly behind her, but one did not know how weak one might be, and a kindly friend might with her persuasion——

Therefore did Mrs. Slater avoid her kindly friends. There was, how-ever, one friend who was not so readily to be avoided; that was Mrs. Carter. Mrs. Carter also was a widow, or rather, to speak the direct truth, had discovered one morning, twenty years ago, that Mr. Carter "was gone"; he had never returned. Those who knew Mrs. Carter intimately said that, on the whole, "things bein' as they was," his de-parture was not entirely to be wondered at. Mrs. Carter had a temper of her own, and nothing inflamed it so much as a drop of whisky, and there was nothing in the world she liked so much as "a drop."

To meet her casually, you would judge her nothing less than the most amiable of womankind—a large, stout, jolly woman, with a face like a rose, and a quantity of black hair. At her best, in her fine Sunday clothes, she was a superb figure, and wore round her neck a rope of sham pearls that would have done credit to a sham countess. During the week, however, she slipped, on occasion, into *déshabille*, and then she appeared not quite so attractive. No one knew the exact nature of her profession. She did a bit of "char"; she had at one time a little sweetshop, where she sold sweets, the *Police Budget*, and—although this was revealed only to her best friends—indecent photographs. It may be that the police discovered some of the sources of her income; at any rate the sweetshop was suddenly, one morning, abandoned. Her movements in everything were sudden; it was quite suddenly that she took a fancy to Mrs. Slater. She met her at a friend's, and at once, so she told Mrs. Slater, "I liked yer, just as though I'd met yer before. But I'm like that. Sudden or not at all is *my* way, and not a bad way either!"

Mrs. Slater could not be said to be everything that was affectionate

22

in return. She distrusted Mrs. Carter, disliked her brilliant colouring and her fluent experiences, felt shy before her rollicking suggestiveness, and timid at her innuendoes. For a considerable time, she held her defences against the insidious attack. Then there came a day when Mrs. Carter burst into reluctant but passionate tears, asserting that Life and Mr. Carter had been, from the beginning, against her; that she had committed, indeed, acts of folly in the past, but only when driven desperately against a wall; that she bore no grudge against anyone alive, but loved all humanity; that she was going to do her best to be a better woman, but couldn't really hope to arrive at any satisfactory improvement without Mrs. Slater's assistance; that Mrs. Slater, indeed, had shown her a New Way, a New Light, a New Path.

Mrs. Slater, humble woman, had no illusions as to her own importance in the scheme of things; nothing touched her so surely as an appeal to her strength of character. She received Mrs. Carter with open arms, suggested that they should read the Bible together on Sunday mornings, and go, side by side, to St. Matthew's on Sunday evenings. There was nothing like a study of the "Holy Word" for "defeating the bottle," and there was nothing like "defeating the bottle" for getting back one's strength and firmness of character.

It was along these lines that Mrs. Slater proposed to conduct Mrs. Carter.

Now, unfortunately, Henry took an instant and truly savage dislike to his mother's new friend. He had been always, of course, "odd" in his feelings about people, but never was he "odder" than he was with Mrs. Carter. "Little lamb," she said, when she saw him for the first time. "I envy you that child, Mrs. Slater, I do indeed. Backwards 'e may be, but 'is being dependent, as you may say, touches my 'eart. Little lamb!"

She tried to embrace him; she offered him sweets. He shuddered at her approach, and his face was instantly grey, like a pool the moment after the sun's setting. Had he been able himself to put into words his sensations, he would have said that the sight of Mrs. Carter assured him, quite definitely, that something horrible would soon occur.

The house upon whose atmosphere he so depended instantly darkened; his Friend was gone, not because he was no longer able to see Him (his consciousness of Him did not depend at all upon any visual assurance), but because there was now, Henry was perfectly assured, no chance whatever of His suddenly appearing. And, on the other hand, those Others—the one with the taloned claws behind the piano, the one with the black-hooded eyes—were stronger, more threatening, more dominating. But, beyond her influence on the house, Mrs. Carter, in her own physical and actual presence, tortured Henry. When she was in the room Henry suffered agony. He would creep away were he allowed, and, if that were not possible, then he would retreat into the most distant corner and watch. If he were in the room his eyes never left Mrs. Carter for a moment, and it was this brooding gaze more than his disapproval that irritated her. "You never can tell with poor little dears when they're 'queer' what fancies they'll take. Why, he quite seems to dislike me, Mrs. Slater!"

Mrs. Slater could venture no denial; indeed, Henry's attitude aroused once again in her mind her earlier suspicions. She had all the reverence of her class for her son's "oddness." He knew more than ordinary mortal folk, and could see farther; he saw beyond Mrs. Carter's red cheeks and shining black hair, and the fact that he was, as a rule, tractable to cheerful kindness, made his rejection the more remarkable. But it might, nevertheless, be that the black things in Mrs. Carter's past were the marks impressed upon Henry's sensitive intelligence; and that he had not, as yet, perceived the new Mrs. Carter growing in grace now day by day.

"'E'll get over 'is fancy, bless 'is 'eart." Mrs. Slater pursued, then, her work of redemption.

3

On a certain evening in November, Mrs. Carter, coming in to see her friend, invited sympathy for a very bad cold.

"Drippin' and runnin' at the nose I've been all day, my dear. Awake all night I was with it, and 'tain't often that I've one, but when I do it's somethin' cruel." It seemed to be better this evening, Mrs. Slater thought, but when she congratulated her friend on this, Mrs. Carter, shaking her head, remarked that it had left the nose and travelled into the throat and ears. "Once it's earache, and I'm done," she said; Horrible pictures she drew of this earache, and it presently became clear that Mrs. Carter was in perfect terror of a night made sleepless with pain. Once, it seemed, had Mrs. Carter tried to commit suicide by hanging herself to a nail in a door, so maddening had the torture been. Luckily (Mrs. Carter thanked Heaven) the nail had been dragged from the door by her weight—"not that I was anything very 'eavy, you understand." Finally, it appeared that only one thing in the world could be relied upon to stay the fiend.

Mrs. Carter produced from her pocket a bottle of whisky.

Upon that it followed that, since her reformation, Mrs. Carter had come to loathe the very smell of whisky, and as for the taste of it!—but rather than be driven by flaming agony down the long stony passages of a sleepless night—anything.

It was here, of course, that Mrs. Slater should have protested, but, in her heart, she was afraid of her friend, and afraid of herself. Mrs. Carter's company had, of late, been pleasant to her. She had been strengthened in her own resolves towards a fine life by the sight of Mrs. Carter's struggle in that direction, and that good woman's genial amiability (when it was so obvious from her appearance that she could be far otherwise) flattered Mrs. Slater's sense of power. No, she could not now bear to let Mrs. Carter go.

She said, therefore, nothing to her friend about the whisky, and on that evening Mrs. Carter did take the "veriest sip." But the cold continued—it continued in a marvellous and terrible manner. It seemed "to 'ave taken right 'old of my system."

After a few evenings it was part of the ceremonies that the bottle should be produced; the kettle was boiling happily on the fire, there was lemon, there was a lump of sugar. . . . On a certain wet and depressing evening Mrs. Slater herself had a glass "just to see that she didn't get a cold like Mrs. Carter's."

4

Henry's bedtime was somewhere between the hours of eight and nine, but his mother did not care to leave Mrs. Carter (dear friend, though she was) quite alone downstairs with the bottom half of the house unguarded (although, of course, the doors were locked), therefore Mrs. Carter came upstairs with her friend to see the little fellow put to bed; "and a hangel he looks, if ever I see one," declared the lady enthusiastically.

When the two were gone and the house was still, Henry would sit up in bed and listen; then, moving quietly, he would creep out and listen again.

There, in the passage, it seemed to him that he could hear the whole house talking—first one sound and then another would come, the wheeze of some straining floor, the creak of some whispering board, the shudder of a door.

"Look out! Look out! Look out!" "and then, above that murmur, some louder voice; "Watch! there's danger in the place! "Then, shivering with cold and his sense of evil, he would creep down into a lower passage and stand listening again; now the voices of the house were deafening, rising on every side of him, like the running of little streams suddenly heard on the turning of the corner of a hill. The dim light shrouded with fantasy the walls; along the wide passage, cabinets and high china jars, the hollow scoop of the window at the far distant end, were all alive and moving. And, in strange contradiction to the moving voices within the house, came the blurred echo of the London life, whirring, buzzing, like a cloud of gnats at the window-pane. "Look out! Look out! Look out!" the house cried, and Henry, with chattering teeth, was on guard.

There came an evening when standing thus, shivering in his little shirt, he was aware that the Terror, so long anticipated, was upon him. It seemed to him, on this evening, that the house was suddenly still; it was as though all the sounds, as of running water, that passed up and down the rooms and passages, were, in a flashing second, frozen. The house was holding its breath.

He had to wait for a breathless, agonizing interval before he heard the next sound, very faint and stifled breathing coming up to him out of the darkness in little uncertain gusts. He heard the breathings pause, then recommence again in quicker and louder succession. Henry, stirred simply, perhaps, by the Terror of his anticipation, moved back into the darker shadows in the nook of the cabinet, and stayed there with his shirt pressed against his little trembling knees.

Then followed, after a long time, a half yellow circle of light that touched the top steps of the stairs and a square of the wall; behind the light was the stealthy figure of Mrs. Carter. She stood there for a moment, one hand with a candle raised, the other pressed against her breast; from one finger of this hand a bunch of heavy keys dangled. She stood there, with her wide, staring eyes, like glass in the candle-light, looking about her, her red cheeks rising and falling with her agitation, her body seeming enormous, her shadow on the wall huge in the dickering light. At the sight of his enemy Henry's terror was so frantic that his hands beat with little spasmodic movements against the wall.

He did not see Mrs. Carter at all, but he saw rather the movement through the air and darkness of the house of something that would bring down upon him the full naked force of the Terror that he had all his life anticipated. He had always known that the awful hour would arrive when the Terror would grip him; again, and again he had seen its eyes, felt its breath, heard its movements, and these movements had been forewarnings of some future day. That day had arrived.

There was only one thing that he could do; his Friend alone in all the world could help him. With his soul dizzy and faint from fear, he prayed for his Friend; had he been less frightened he would have screamed aloud for Him to come and help him.

The boy's breath came hot into his throat and stuck there, and his heart beat like a high, unresting hammer.

Mrs. Carter, with the candle raised to throw light in front of her, moved forward very cautiously and softly. She passed down the passage, and then paused very near to the boy. She looked at the keys, and stole like some heavy, stealthy animal to the door of the long drawing-room, he watched her as she tried one key after another, making little dissatisfied noises as they refused to fit; then at last one turned the lock and she pushed back the door.

It was certainly impossible for him, in the dim world of his mind, to realise what it was that she intended to do, but he knew, through some strange channel of knowledge, that his mother was concerned in this, and that something more than the immediate peril of himself was involved. He had also, lost in the dim mazes of his mind, a consciousness that there *were* treasures in the house, and that his mother was placed there to guard them, and even that he himself shared her duty.

It did not come to him that Mrs. Carter was in pursuit of these treasures, but he *did* realise that her presence there amongst them brought peril to his mother. Moved then by some desperate urgency which had at its heart his sense that to be left alone in the black passage was worse than the actual lighted vision of his Terror, he crept with trembling knees across the passage and through the door.

Inside the room he saw that she had placed the candle upon the piano, and was bending over a drawer, trying again to fit a key. He stood in the doorway, a tiny figure, very, very cold, all his soul in his silent appeal for some help. His Friend *must* come. He was somewhere there in the house. "Come! Help me!" The candle suddenly flared into a finger of light that flung the room into vision. Mrs. Carter, startled, raised herself, and at that same moment Henry gave a cry—a weak little trembling sound.

She turned and saw the boy; as their eyes met he felt the Terror rushing upon him. He flung a last desperate appeal for help, staring at her as though his eyes would never let her go, and she, finding him so unexpectedly, could only gape. In their silent gaze at one another, in the glassy stare of Mrs. Carter and the trembling, flickering one of Henry, there was more than any ordinary challenge could have conveyed. Mrs. Carter must have felt at the first immediate confrontation of the strange little figure that her feet were on the very edge of some most desperate precipice. The long room and the passages beyond must have quivered. At that very first moment, with some stir, some hinted approach, Henry called, with the desperate summoning of all his ghostly world, upon his gods. They came. . . .

In her eyes he saw suddenly something else than vague terror. He saw recognition. He felt himself a rushing, heartening comfort; he knew that his Friend had somehow come, that he was no longer alone.

But Mrs. Carter's eyes were staring beyond him, over him, into the black passage. Her eyes seemed to grow as though the terror in them was pushing them out beyond their lids; her breath came in sharp, tearing gasps. The keys with a clang dropped from her hand.

"Oh, God! Oh, God!" she whispered. He did not turn his head to grasp what it was that she saw in the passage. The Terror had been transferred from himself to her.

The colour in her cheeks went out, leaving her as though her face were suddenly shadowed by some overhanging shape.

Her eyes never moved or faltered from the dark into whose heart she gazed. Then, there was a strangled, gasping cry, and she sank down, first on to her knees, then in a white faint, her eyes still staring, lay huddled on the floor.

Henry felt his Friend's hand on his shoulder.

Meanwhile, down in the kitchen, the fire had sunk into grey ashes, and Mrs. Slater was lying back in her chair, her head back, snoring thickly; an empty glass had tumbled across the table, and a few drops from it had dribbled over on to the tablecloth.

Head in Green Bronze

The Lord God Almighty was busy that time examining the artists. This was a tiresome and monotonous job, for He had been doing it for thousands and thousands of centuries and, with one or two exceptions a century, artists are always the same.

About Him stretched into everlasting space fields and fields of light, rather as on an early summer evening, when the harvesters have drawn away home and the sun-drenched soil is left to its own peace.

But every artist as he appeared for his examination brought with him his own personal memory and consciousness, his individual litter. . . . . It was the authors whom just now God Almighty was examining. The examinations were very brief.

Against the vast eternity of light—light upon light upon light and of a stainless purity—the impedimenta of each separate little soul seemed incredibly mean and paltry. Now, for example, there was William Newcombe with his country cottage, old oak beams, settle by the fire, flagged garden path, refrigerator and most modern bathroom. Also, his twenty-three travel books and his blank-verse drama called *Armageddon*.

'They all sold very well, I hear,' said God Almighty.

'Well,' William answered modestly, 'they did. Except *Armageddon*, which didn't sell at all.'

'Why did you write that one?' asked God Almighty.

'Because I wanted to,' said William, blinking his old eyes a little at the unaccustomed light.

'Good,' said God Almighty. 'Because of that one book you may have with you, while at work, any one of your earthly goods and chattels you prefer.'

'My dog Caesar,' William said promptly. All his impedimenta, oak beams, garden path, bathroom, *all* the travel books disappeared, and only a charming fox-terrier with engaging whiskers, frisking in the light, remained. William and Caesar, in the charge of an Archangel, passed into light.

A flock of angels cut the brilliant air like a wave breaking through mist.

'Next one,' said God Almighty.

This was Peter Bentham, whose consciousness provided him with four very thin books of poetry, a life of Rimbaud, a small painting by Dali, and a cough mixture in a dirty blue bottle.

God Almighty looked at him. 'How have you allowed your body to get into such a miserable state?'

'I never *was* very strong,' Peter answered with that rather shrill staccato little cry that had before now thrown so much terrible scorn on prosperity and success.

'I'm afraid,' said God Almighty gently (for there was something very touching about Peter), 'that you have prevented yourself from enjoying too many amusing and vivifying things.'

'That,' said Peter firmly (he was not going to be put down by a God Who, all his life, he had asserted did not exist), 'is because my taste has always been perfect. I have never been able to endure any kind of athletics, popular novels and novelists, optimistic essays and sentimental plays, patriotism, or anyone, male or female, in rude health.'

'What *have* you enjoyed?' God Almighty asked.

'My own poetry,' Peter answered, 'the paintings of Dali, Miró and Léger, the music of Tschenakivitzky, free love in Russia and a cocktail called "Flowers of Parnassus."'

'I like your honesty,' God Almighty said, 'but you are a little too serious, especially about yourself. However, what you really need is fattening up. Without your earthly clothes' (for now all Peter's worldly impedimenta had vanished) 'you are frankly a miserable object—nor have you washed as frequently as you should. However, we shall soon change all that. I shall hand you over to Henry Fielding for an aeon or two.'

And then came Margaret Cunningham, a tall, fat, red-faced woman whose teeth because they had not been kept back in childhood now protruded over a receding chin. Without her clothes she was shapeless, helpless, innocent. Her impedimenta were an untidy two-roomed flat, a tortoiseshell cat, some London chimneys, her working tools and some twenty-four misshapen clay heads with long necks leaning to right or left.

'Well, Margaret,' God Almighty said kindly, 'I'm afraid you haven't made much of a living out of this work of yours.'

'Well, no, I haven't,' Margaret said frankly in her Woman's-Club how-are-you-all-girls voice. 'Of course, there was the teaching twice a week.' She felt the light on her nakedness with so keen a pleasure that her brown-grey eyes shone with delight. 'It's like the Riviera, which I've never been able to afford,' she said.

'But this,' said God Almighty, 'has been always your secret longing'—and there, solid against the light, was the curving road, the signpost 'To Watendlath,' the newspaper placard 'Mussolini attacks Britain' and the stream, the shelving green hill, the mouse-shaped clouds watching a cat-faced moon.

'Yes,' Margaret murmured. 'That and the head in green bronze.'

'Head of whom?' God Almighty asked.

'Of no one in particular. Simply a grand head of some hero—in dark green bronze. I've imagined myself for years and years creating such a thing. I could, I believe, if I'd gone on. I was really improving. But then I caught cold and pneumonia followed—and here I am!'

'There's plenty of time,' God Almighty said. He looked at Margaret kindly. 'Here's where you've always wanted to be. You're a true artist although not as yet a very good one. Donatello shall give you a lesson or two. . . . .'

Margaret was on her bare knees looking into the stream behind Rosthwaite. Beside her was a little pile of clay.

'God Almighty thinks I can help you,' a voice said.

She looked up and saw Donatello, naked and glorious. He knelt down beside her, taking the clay in his hands.

'Now let us see,' he said. 'Head of a Hero in green bronze. . . . .'

Henry Fitzgeorge Strether

1

March Square is not very far from Hyde Park Corner in London Town. Behind the whir and rattle of the traffic it stands, spacious and cool and very old, muffled by the little streets that guard it, happily unconscious, you would suppose, that there were any in all the world so unfortunate as to have less than five thousand a year for their support. Perhaps a hundred years ago March Square might have boasted of such superior ignorance, but fashions change, to prevent, it maybe, our own too easily irritated monotonies, and for some time now the square has been compelled, here, there, in one corner and another, to admit the invader.

It is true that the solemn, respectable grey house, can boast that it is the town residence of its Grace the Duke of Crole and his beautiful young Duchess *née* Miss Jane Tunster of New York City, but it is also true that No.— is in the possession of Mr. Munty Ross of Potted Shrimp fame; and there are Dr. Cruthen, the Misses Dent, Herbert Hoskins and his wife, whose incomes are certainly nearer to £500 than £5,000. Yes, rents and blue blood have come down in March Square; it is certainly not the less interesting for that, but—

Some of the houses can boast the days of good Queen Anne for their period. There is one, at the very corner where Somers Street turns off towards the Park, that was built only yesterday, and has about it some air of shame, a furtive embarrassment that it will lose very speedily. There is no house that can claim beauty, and yet the Square, as a whole, has a fine charm, something that age and colour, haphazard adventure, space and quiet have all helped towards.

All the oldest London mendicants find their way, at different hours of the week, up and down the Square. There is, I believe, no other square in London where musicians are permitted. On Monday morning there is the blind man with the black patch over one eye; he has an organ (a very old one, with a painted picture of the Battle of Trafalgar on the front of it) and he wears an old black skull-cap. He wheezes out his old tunes (they are older than other tunes that March Square hears, and so, perhaps, March Square loves them). He goes despondently, and the tap of his stick sounds all the way round the Square. A small and dirty boy—his grandson, maybe—pushes the organ tor him.

On Tuesday there comes the remnant of an itinerant band—remnant because now there are only the cornet, the flute and the trumpet. Sadly wind-blown, drunken and diseased they are, and the Square can remember when there were a number of them, hale and hearty young fellows, but drink and competition have been too strong for them. On Wednesdays there is sometimes a lady who sings ballads in a voice that can only be described as that contradiction in terms "a shrill *contralto*." Her notes are very piercing and can be heard from one end of the Square to the other. She sings "Annie Laurie" and "Robin Adair," and wears a battered hat of. black straw. On Thursday there is a handsome Italian with a barrel organ that bears in its belly the very latest and most popular tunes. It is on Thursday that the Square learns the music of the moment; thus, from one end of the year to the other does it keep pace with musical fashion.

On Fridays there is a lean and ragged man wearing large and, to the children of the Square, terrifying spectacles. He is a very gloomy fellow and sings hymn-tunes, "Rock of Ages," "There is a Happy Land," and "Jerusalem the Golden." On Saturdays there is a stout, happy little man with a harp. He has white hair and looks like a retired colonel. He cannot play the harp very much, but he is quite the most popular visitor of the week and must be very rich indeed does he receive in other squares so handsome a reward for his melody as this one bestows; he is known as "Colonel Harry." In and out of these regular visitors there are, of course, many others. There is a dark, sinister man with a harmonium and a shivering monkey on a chain; there is an Italian woman, wearing bright wraps round her head, and she has a cage of birds who tell fortunes; there is a horsy, stable-bred, ferret-like man with two performing dogs; and there is quite an old lady in a black bonnet and shawl who sings duets with her granddaughter, a young thing of some fifty summers.

There can be nothing in the world more charming than the way the Square receives its friends. Let it number amongst its guests a duchess, that is no reason why it should scorn "Colonel Harry" or

"Mouldy Jim," the singer of hymns. Scorn, indeed, cannot be found within its grey walls, soft grey, soft green, soft white and blue—in these colours is the Square's body clothed, no anger in its mild eyes, nor contempt anywhere at its heart.

The Square is proud, and is proud with reason, of its garden. It is not a large garden as London gardens go. It has in its centre a fountain; Neptune, with a fine wreath of seaweed about his middle, blowing water through his conch. There are two statues, the one of a general who fought in the Indian Mutiny and afterwards lived and died in the Square, the other of a mid-Victorian philanthropist whose stout figure and urbane self-satisfaction (as portrayed by the sculptor) bear witness to an easy conscience and an unimaginative mind. There is, round and about the fountain, a lovely green lawn, and there are many overhanging trees and shady corners. An air of peace the garden breathes, and that although children are for ever racing up and down it, shattering the stillness of the air with their cries, rivalling the bells of St. Matthew's round the corner with their piercing notes.

But it is the quality of the Square that nothing can take from it its peace, nothing temper its tranquillity. In the heat of the days motor-cars will rattle through, bells will ring, all the bustle of a frantic world invade its security; for a moment it submits, but in the evening hour, when the colours are being washed from the sky, and the moon, apricot-tinted, is rising slowly through the smoke, March Square sinks, with a little sigh, back into her peace again. The modern world has not yet touched her, nor ever shall.

2

The Duchess of Crole had eight months ago a son, Henry Fitzgeorge, Marquis of Strether. Very fortunate that the first-born should be a son, very fortunate also that the first-born should be one of the healthiest, liveliest, merriest babies that it has ever been anyone's good fortune to encounter. All smiles, chuckles and amiability is Henry Fitzgeorge; he is determined that all shall be well.

His birth was for a little time the sensation of the Square. Everyone knew the beautiful duchess; they had seen her drive, they had seen her walk, they had seen her in the picture-papers, at race-meetings, and coming away from fashionable weddings. The word went round day by day as to his health; he was watched when he came out in his perambulator, and there was gossip as to his appearance and behaviour.

"A jolly little fellow."

"Just like his father."

"Rather early to say that, isn't it?"

Well, I don't know; got the same smile. His mother's rather languid."

"Beautiful woman, though."

"Oh, lovely!"

Upon a certain afternoon in March, about four o'clock, there was quite a gathering of persons in Henry Fitzgeorge's nursery. There was his mother, with those two great friends of hers, Lady Emily Blanchard and the Hon. Mrs. Vavasour; there was Her Grace's mother, Mrs. K Tunster (an enormously stout lady); there was Miss Helen Crasper, who was staying in the house. These people were gathered at the end of the cot, and they looked down upon Henry Fitzgeorge, and he lay upon his back, gazed at them thoughtfully, and clenched and unclenched his fat hands.

Opposite his cot were some very wide windows, and three windows were filled with galleons of cloud—fat, bolster, swelling vessels, white save where in their curving sails they had caught a faint radiance from the hidden sun. In fine procession, against the blue, they passed along. Very faint and muffled there came up from the Square the lingering notes of "Robin Adair." This is a Wednesday afternoon, and it is the lady with the black straw hat who is singing. The nursery has white walls—it is filled with colour; the fire blazes with a yellow-red gleam that rises and falls across the shining floor.

"I've brought him a rattle, Jane dear," said Mrs. Tunster, shaking in the air a thing of coral and silver. "He's got several, of course, but I guess you'll go a long way before you find anything cuter."

"It's too pretty," said Lady Emily.

"Too lovely," said the Hon. Mrs. Vavasour.

The Duchess looked down upon her son. "Isn't he old?" she said. "Thousands of years. You'd think he was laughing at the lot of us."

Mrs. Tunster shook her head. "Now don't you go imagining things, Jane, my dear. I used to be just like that, and your father would say, 'Now, Alice.'"

Her Grace raised her head. Her eyes were a little tired. She looked from her son to the clouds, and then back again to her son. She was remembering her own early days, the rich glowing colour of her own American country, the freedom, the space, the honesty.

"I guess you're tired, dear," said her mother. "With the party tonight and all. Why don't you go and rest a bit?"

"His eyes *are* old! He *does* despise us all."

Lady Emily, who believed in personal comfort and as little thinking as possible, put her arm through her. friend's.

"Come along and give us some tea. He's a dear. Goodbye, you little darling. He *is* a pet. There, did you see him smiling? You *darling!* Tea I *must* have, Jane dear—at once."

"You go on. I'm coming. Ring for it. Tell Hunter. I'll be with you in two minutes, Mother."

Mrs. Tunster left her rattle in the nurse's hands. Then, with the two others, departed. Outside the nursery door she said in an American whisper: "Jane isn't quite right yet. Went about a bit too soon. She's headstrong. She always has been. Doesn't do for her to think too much."

Her Grace was alone now with her son and heir and the nurse. She bent over the cot and smiled upon Henry Fitzgeorge; he smiled back at her, and even gave an absent-minded crow; but his gaze almost instantly swung back again to the window, through which, deeply and with solemn absorption, he watched the clouds.

She gave him her hand, and he closed his fingers about one of hers; but even that grasp was abstracted, as though he were not thinking of her at all but was simply behaving like a gentleman.

"I don't believe he's realised me a bit, nurse," she said, turning away from the cot.

"Well, your Grace, they always take time. It's early days."

"But what's he thinking of all the time?"

"Oh, just nothing, your Grace."

"I don't believe it's nothing. He's trying to settle things. This— what it's all about—what he's got to do about it."

"It may be so, your Grace. All babies are like that at first."

"His eyes are so old, so grave."

"He's a jolly little fellow, your Grace."

"He's very little trouble, isn't he?"

"Less trouble than any baby I've ever had to do with. Got His Grace's happy temperament, if I may say so."

"Yes," the mother laughed. She crossed over to the window and looked down. "That poor woman singing down there. How awful! He'll be going down to Crole very shortly, Roberts. Splendid air for him there. But the Square's cheerful. He likes the garden, doesn't he?"

"Oh, yes, your Grace; all the children and the fountain. But he's a happy baby. I should say he'd like anything."

36

For a moment longer, she looked down into the Square. The discordant voice was giving "Annie Laurie" to the world.

"Goodbye, darling." She stepped forward, shook the silver and coral rattle. "See what Grannie's given you!" She left it lying near his hand, and, with a little sigh, was gone.

3

Now, as the sun was setting, the clouds had broken into little pink bubbles, lying idly here and there upon the sky. Higher, near the top of the window, they were large pink cushions, three fat ones, lying sedately against the blue.

During three months now, Henry Fitzgeorge Strether had been confronted with the new scene, the new urgency on his part to respond to it. At first, he had refused absolutely to make any response; behind him, around him, above him, below him were still the old conditions; but they were the old conditions viewed, for some reason unknown to him, at a distance, and at a distance that was ever increasing. With every day something here in this new and preposterous world struck his attention, and with every fresh lure was he drawn more certainly from his old consciousness. At first, he had simply rebelled; then, very slowly, his curiosity had begun to stir. It had stirred at first through food and touch; very pleasant this, very pleasant that.

Milk, sleep, light things that he could hold very tightly with his hands. Now, upon this March afternoon, he watched the pink clouds with a more intent gaze than he had given to them before. Their colour and shape bore some reference to the life that he had left. They were "like" a little to those other things. There, too, shadowed against the wall, was his Friend, now the last link with everything that he knew.

At first, during the first weeks, he had demanded again and again to be taken back, and always he had been told to wait, to wait and see what was going to happen. So long as his Friend was there, he knew that he was not completely abandoned, and that this was only a temporary business, with its strange limiting circumstances, the way that one was tied and bound, the embarrassment of finding that all one's old means of communication were here useless. How desperate, indeed, would it have been had his Friend not been there, reassuring, pervading him, surrounding him, always subduing those sudden inexplicable alarms.

He would demand: "When are we going to leave all this?"

"Wait. I know it seems absurd to you, but it's commanded you."

"Well, but—this is ridiculous. Where are all my old powers? Where are all the others?"

"You will understand everything one day. I'm afraid you're very uncomfortable. You will be less so as time passes. Indeed, very soon you will be very happy."

"Well, I'm doing my best to be cheerful. But you won't leave me?"

"Not so long as you want me."

"You'll stay until we go back again?"

"You'll never go back again."

"Never?"

"No."

Across the light the nurse advanced. She took him in her arms for a moment, turned his pillows, then laid him down again. As he settled down into comfort he saw his Friend, huge, a great shadow, mingling with the coloured lights of the flaming sky. All the world was lit, the white room glowed. A pleasant smell was in his nostrils.

"Where are all the others? They would like to share this pleasant moment, and I would warn them about the unpleasant ones."

"They are coming, some of them. I am with them as I am with you."

Swinging across the Square were the evening bells of St. Matthew's.

Henry Fitzgeorge smiled, then chuckled, then dozed into a pleasant sleep.

4

Asleep, awake, it had been for the most part the same to him. He swung easily, lazily upon the clouds; warmth and light surrounded him; a part of him, his toes, perhaps, would be suddenly cold, then he would cry, or he would strike his head against the side of his cot and it would hurt, and so then he would cry again. But these tears would not be tears of grief, but simply declarations of astonishment and wonder.

He did not, of course, realise that as, very slowly, very gradually, he began to understand the terms and conditions of his new life, so with the same gradation his Friend was expressed in those terms. Slowly the great shadow that filled the room took on human shape, until at last it would be only thus that He would appear.

But Henry would not realise the change, soon he would not know that it had ever been otherwise. Dimly, out of chaos, the world was being made for him. There a square of colour, here something round and hard that was cool to touch, now a gleaming rod that ran high into the air, now a shape very soft and warm against which it was pleasant to lean. The clouds, the sweep of dim colour, the vast horizons of that other world yielded, day by day, to little concrete things—a patch of carpet, the leg of a chair, the shadow of the fire, clouds beyond the window, buttons on someone's clothes, the rails of his cot. Then there were voices, the touch of hands, someone's soft hair, someone who sang little songs to him.

He woke early one morning and realised the rattle that his grandmother had given to him. He suddenly realised it. He grasped the handle of it with his hand and found this cool and pleasant to touch. He then, by accident, made it tinkle, and instantly the prettiest noise replied to him. He shook it more lustily, and the response was louder. He was, it seemed, master of this charming thing and could force it to do what he wished. He appealed to his Friend. Was not this a charming thing that he had found? He waved it and chuckled and crowed, and then his toes, sticking out beyond the bedclothes, were nipped by the cold so that he hallooed loudly. Perhaps the rattle had nipped his toes. He did not know, but he would cry because that eased his feelings.

That morning there came with his grandmother and mother a silly young woman who had, it was supposed, a great way with babies. "I adore babies," she said. "We understand one another in the most wonderful way."

Henry Fitzgeorge looked at her as she leaned over the cot and made faces at him. "Goo-goo-gum-goo," she cried.

"What is all this?" he asked his Friend. He laid down the rattle and felt suddenly lonely and unhappy.

"Little pet—ug—la—la—goo—losh!" Henry Fitzgeorge raised his eyes. His Friend was a long, long way away; his eyes grew cold with contempt. He hated this thing that made the noises and closed out the light. He opened his eyes, he was about to burst into one of his most abandoned roars when his stare encountered his mother. Her eyes were watching him, and they had in them a glow and radiance that gave him a warm feeling of companionship. "I know," they seemed to say, "what you are thinking of. I agree with all that you are feeling about her. Only don't cry, she really isn't worth it." His mouth slowly closed then to thank her for her assistance, he raised the rattle and shook it at her. His eyes never left her face.

"Little darling," said the lady friend, but nevertheless disappointed.

39

"Lift him up, Jane. I'd like to see him in your arms."

But she shook her head. She moved away from the cot. Something so precious had been in that smile of her son's that she would not risk any rebuff.

Henry Fitzgeorge gave the strange lady one last look of disgust.

"If that comes again I'll bite it," he said to his Friend.

When these visitors had departed, he lay there remembering those eyes that had looked into his. All that day he remembered them, and it may be that his Friend, as he watched, sighed because the time for launching him had now come, that one more soul had passed from His sheltering arms out into the high road of fine adventures. How easily they forget! How readily they forget! How eagerly they fling the pack of their old world from off their shoulders! He had seen, perhaps, so many go, thus lustily,' upon their way, and then how many, tired, worn, beaten to their very shadows, had He received at the end!

But it was so. This day was to see Henry Fitzgeorge's assertion of his independence. The hour when this life was to close, so definitely, so securely, the doors upon that other, had come. The shadow that had been so vast that it had filled the room, the Square, the world, was drawn now into small and human size.

Henry Fitzgeorge was never again to look so old.

5

As the fine, dim afternoon was closing, he was allowed, for half an hour before sleep, to sprawl upon the carpet in front of the fire. He had with him his rattle and a large bear which he stroked because it was comfortable; he had no personal feeling about it.

His mother came in.

"Let me have him for half an hour, nurse. Come back in half an hour's time."

The nurse left them.

Henry Fitzgeorge did not look at his mother. He had the bear in his arms and was feeling it, and in his mind the warmth from the flickering, jumping flame and the soft, friendly submission of the fur beneath his fingers were part of the same mystery.

His mother had been motoring; her cheeks were flushed, and her dark clothes heightened, by their contrast, her colour. She knelt down on the carpet and then, with her hands folded on her lap, watched her son. He rolled the bear over and over, he poked it, he banged its head upon the ground. Then he was tired with it and took up the rattle. Then he was tired of that, and he looked across at his mother and chuckled.

His mind, however, was not at all concentrated upon her. He felt on this afternoon a new, a fresh interest in things. The carpet before him was a vast country and he did not propose to explore it, but sucking his thumb, stroking the bear's coat, feeling the firelight upon his face, he felt that now something would occur. He had realised that there was much to explore and that, after all, perhaps there might be more in this strange condition of things than he had only a little time ago considered possible.

It was then that he looked up and saw hanging round his mother's neck a gold chain. This was a long chain hanging right down to her lap; as it hung there, very slowly it swayed from side to side, and as it swayed, the firelight caught it and it gleamed and was splashed with light. His eyes, as he watched, grew rounder and rounder; he had never seen anything so wonderful. He put down the rattle, crawled with great difficulty because of his clothes, on to his knees and sat staring, his thumb in his mouth. His mother stayed, watching him. He pointed his finger, crowing. "Come and fetch it," she said.

He tumbled forward on to his nose and then lay there, with his face raised a little, watching it. She did not move at all but knelt with her hands straight out upon her knees, and the chain with its large gold rings like flaming eyes swung from hand to hand. Then he tried to move forward, his whole soul in his gaze. He would raise a hand towards the treasure, and then because that upset his balance he would fall, but at once he would be up again. He moved a little and breathed little gasps of pleasure.

She bent forward to him, his hand was outstretched. His eyes went up and, meeting hers, instantly the chain was forgotten. That recognition that they had given him before was there now.

With a scramble and a lurch, desperate, heedless in its risks, he was in his mother's lap. Then he crowed. He crowed for all the world to hear because now, at last, he had become its citizen.

Was there not then, from someone, disregarded and forgotten at that moment, a sigh, lighter than the air itself, half ironic, half wistful regret?

The Silver Mask

Miss Sonia Herries, coming home from a dinner-party at the Westons', heard a voice at her elbow.

'If you please—only a moment—'

She had walked from the Westons' flat because it was only three streets away, and now she was only a few steps from her door, but it was late, there was no one about and the King's Road rattle was muffled and dim.

'I am afraid I can't—' she began. It was cold and the wind nipped her cheeks.

'If you would only—' he went on.

She turned and saw one of the handsomest young men possible. He was the handsome young man of all romantic stories, tall, dark, pale, slim, distinguished—oh! everything!—and he was wearing a shabby blue suit and shivering with the cold just as he should have been.

'I'm afraid I can't—' she repeated, beginning to move on.

'Oh, I know,' he interrupted quickly. 'Everyone says the same and quite naturally. I should if our positions were reversed. But I *must* go on with it. I *can't* go back to my wife and baby with simply nothing. We have no fire, no food, nothing except the ceiling we are under. It is my fault, all of it. I don't want your pity, but I *have* to attack your comfort.'

He trembled. He shivered as though he were going to fall. Involuntarily she put out her hand to steady him. She touched his arm and felt it quiver under the thin sleeve.

'It's all right . . .' he murmured. 'I'm hungry . . . I can't help it.'

She had had an excellent dinner. She had drunk perhaps just enough to lead to recklessness—in any case, before she realised it, she was ushering him in, through her dark-blue painted door. A crazy thing to do! Nor was it as though she were too young to know any better, for she was fifty if she was a day and, although sturdy of body and as strong as a horse (except for a little unsteadiness of the heart), intelligent enough to be thin, neurotic and abnormal; but she was none of these.

Although intelligent she suffered dreadfully from impulsive kindness. All her life she had done so. The mistakes that she had made—and there had been quite a few—had all arisen from the triumph of her heart over her brain. She knew it—how well she knew it!—and all her friends were for ever dinning it into her. When she reached her fiftieth birthday she said to herself—'Well, now at last I'm too old to be foolish anymore.' And here she was, helping an entirely unknown young man into her house at dead of night, and he in all probability the worst sort of criminal.

Very soon he was sitting on her rose-coloured sofa, eating sandwiches and drinking a whisky and soda. He seemed to be entirely overcome by the beauty of her possessions. 'If he's acting he's doing it very well,' she thought to herself. But he had taste and he had knowledge. He knew that the Utrillo was an early one, the only period of importance in that master's work, he knew that the two old men talking under a window belonged to Sickert's 'Middle Italian,' he recognised the Dobson head and the wonderful green bronze Elk of Carl Milles.

'You are an artist,' she said. 'You paint?'

'No, I am a pimp, a thief, a what you like—anything bad,' he answered fiercely. 'And now I must go,' he added, springing up from the sofa.

He seemed most certainly invigorated. She could scarcely believe that he was the same young man who only half an hour before had had to lean on her arm for support. And he was a gentleman. Of that there could be no sort of question. And he was astoundingly beautiful in the spirit of a hundred years ago, a young Byron, a young Shelley, not a young Ramon Novarro or a young Ronald Colman.

Well, it was better that he should go, and she did hope (for his own sake rather than hers) that he would not demand money and threaten a scene. After all, with her snow-white hair, firm broad chin, firm broad body, she did not look like someone who could be threatened. He had not apparently the slightest intention of threatening her. He moved towards the door.

'Oh!' he murmured with a little gasp of wonder. He had stopped before one of the loveliest things that she had—a mask in silver of a clown's face, the clown smiling, gay, joyful, not hinting at perpetual sadness as all clowns are traditionally supposed to do. It was one of the most successful efforts of the famous Sorat, greatest living master of Masks.

'Yes. Isn't that lovely?' she said. 'It was one of Sorat's earliest things, and still, I think, one of his best.'

'Silver is the right material for that clown,' he said.

'Yes, I think so too,' she agreed. She realised that she had asked him nothing about his troubles, about his poor wife and baby, about his past history. It was better perhaps like this.

'You have saved my life,' he said to her in the hall. She had in her hand a pound note.

'Well,' she answered cheerfully, 'I was a fool to risk a strange man in my house at this time of night—or so my friends would tell me. But such an old woman like me—where's the risk?'

'I could have cut your throat,' he said quite seriously.

'So, you could,' she admitted. 'But with horrid consequences to yourself.'

'Oh no,' he said. 'Not in these days. The police are never able to catch anybody.'

'Well, goodnight. Do take this. It can get you some warmth at least.'

He took the pound. 'Thanks,' he said carelessly. Then at the door he remarked: 'That mask. The loveliest thing I ever saw.'

When the door had closed and she went back into the sitting-room she sighed:

'What a good-looking young man!' Then she saw that her most beautiful white jade cigarette-case was gone. It had been lying on the little table by the sofa. She had seen it just before she went into the pantry to cut the sandwiches. He had stolen it. She looked every-where. No, undoubtedly, he had stolen it.

'What a good-looking young man!' she thought as she went up to bed.

Sonia Herries was a woman of her time in that outwardly she was cynical and destructive while inwardly she was a creature longing for affection and appreciation. For though she had white hair and was fifty she was outwardly active, young, could do with little sleep and less food, could dance and drink cocktails and play bridge to the end of all time. Inwardly she cared for neither cocktails nor bridge. She was above all things maternal and she had a weak heart, not only a spiritual weak heart but also a physical one. When she suffered, must take her drops, lie down and rest, she allowed no one to see her. Like all the other women of her period and manner of life she had a courage worthy of a better cause.

She was a heroine for no reason at all.

But, beyond everything else, she was maternal. Twice at least she would have married had she loved enough, but the man she had really loved had not loved her (that was twenty-five years ago), so she had pretended to despise matrimony. Had she had a child her nature would have been fulfilled; as she had not had that good fortune she had been maternal (with outward cynical indifference) to numbers of people who had made use of her, sometimes laughed at her, never deeply cared for her. She was named 'a jolly good sort,' and was always 'just outside' the real life of her friends. Her Herries relations, Rockages and Cards and Newmarks, used her to take odd places at table, to fill up spare rooms at house-parties, to make purchases for them in London, to talk to when things went wrong with them or people abused them. She was a very lonely woman.

She saw her young thief for the second time a fortnight later. She saw him because he came to her house one evening when she was dressing for dinner.

'A young man at the door,' said her maid Rose.

'A young man? Who?' But she knew.

'I don't know, Miss Sonia. He won't give his name.'

She came down and found him in the hall, the cigarette-case in his hand. He was wearing a decent suit of clothes, but he still looked hungry, haggard, desperate and incredibly handsome. She took him into the room where they had been before. He gave her the cigarette-case. 'I pawned it,' he said, his eyes on the silver mask.

'What a disgraceful thing to do!' she said. 'And what are you going to steal next?'

'My wife made some money last week,' he said. 'That will see us through for a while.'

'Do you never do any work?' she asked him.

'I paint,' he answered. 'But no one will touch my pictures. They are not modern enough.'

'You must show me some of your pictures,' she said, and realised how weak she was. It was not his good looks that gave him his power over her, but something both helpless and defiant, like a wicked child who hates his mother but is always coming to her for help.

'I have some here,' he said, went into the hall, and returned with

45

several canvases. He displayed them. They were very bad—sugary landscapes and sentimental figures.

'They are very bad,' she said.

'I know they are. You must understand that my aesthetic taste is very fine. I appreciate only the best things in art, like your cigarette-case, that mask there, the Utrillo. But I can paint nothing but these. It is very exasperating.' He smiled at her.

'Won't you buy one?' he asked her.

'Oh, but I don't want one,' she answered. 'I should have to hide it.' She was aware that in ten minutes her guests would be here.

'Oh, do buy one.'

'No, but of course not—'

'Yes, please.' He came nearer and looked up into her broad kindly face like a beseeching child.

'Well . . . how much are they?'

'This is twenty pounds. This twenty-five—'

'But how absurd! They are not worth anything at all.'

'They may be one day. You never know with modern pictures.'

'I am quite sure about these.'

'Please buy one. That one with the cows is not so bad.'

She sat down and wrote a cheque.

'I'm a perfect fool. Take this, and understand I never want to see you again. Never! You will never be admitted. It is no use speaking to me in the street. If you bother me I shall tell the police.'

He took the cheque with quiet satisfaction, held out his hand and pressed hers a little.

'Hang that in the right light and it will not be so bad—'

'You want new boots,' she said. 'Those are terrible.'

'I shall be able to get some now,' he said and went away.

All that evening while she listened to the hard and crackling iro-nies of her friends she thought of the young man. She did not know his name. The only thing that she knew about him was that by his own confession he was a scoundrel and had at his mercy a poor young wife and a starving child. The picture that she formed of these three haunted her. It had been, in a way, honest of him to return the cig-arette-case. Ah, but he knew, of course, that did he not return it he could never have seen her again. He had discovered at once that she was a splendid source of supply, and now that she had bought one of his wretched pictures—Nevertheless he could not be altogether bad. No one who cared so passionately for beautiful things could be quite worthless. The way that he had gone straight to the silver mask as soon as he entered the room and gazed at it as though with his very soul! And, sitting at her dinner-table, uttering the most cynical sentiments, she was all softness as she gazed across to the wall upon whose pale surface the silver mask was hanging. There was, she thought, a certain look of the young man in that jolly shining surface. But where? The clown's cheek was fat, his mouth broad, his lips thick—and yet, and yet—

For the next few days as she went about London she looked in spite of herself at the passers-by to see whether he might not be there. One thing she soon discovered, that he was very much more handsome than anyone else whom she saw. But it was not for his handsomeness that he haunted her. It was because he wanted her to be kind to him, and because she wanted—oh, so terribly—to be kind to someone!

The silver mask, she had the fancy, was gradually changing, the rotundity thinning, some new light coming into the empty eyes. It was most certainly a beautiful thing.

Then, as unexpectedly as on the other occasions, he appeared again. One night as she, back from a theatre, smoking one last cigarette, was preparing to climb the stairs to bed, there was a knock on the door. Everyone of course rang the bell—no one attempted the old-fashioned knocker shaped like an owl that she had bought, one idle day, in an old curiosity shop. The knock made her sure that it was he. Rose had gone to bed so she went herself to the door. There he was—and with him a young girl and a baby. They all came into the sitting-room and stood awkwardly by the fire. It was at that moment when she saw them in a group by the fire that she felt her first sharp pang of fear. She knew suddenly how weak she was—she seemed to be turned to water at sight of them, she, Sonia Herries, fifty years of age, independent and strong, save for that little flutter of the heart— yes, turned to water! She was afraid as though someone had whispered a warning in her ear.

The girl was striking, with red hair and a white face, a thin graceful little thing. The baby, wrapped in a shawl, was soaked in sleep. She gave them drinks and the remainder of the sandwiches that had been put there for herself. The young man looked at her with his charming smile.

'We haven't come to cadge anything this time,' he said. 'But I wanted you to see my wife and I wanted her to see some of your lovely things.'

'Well,' she said sharply. 'You can only stay a minute or two. It's late. I'm off to bed. Besides, I told you not to come here again.'

'Ada made me,' he said, nodding at the girl. 'She was so anxious to see you.'

The girl never said a word but only stared sulkily in front of her.

'All right. But you must go soon. By the way, you've never told me your name.'

'Henry Abbott, and that's Ada, and the baby's called Henry too.'

'All right. How have you been getting on since I saw you?'

'Oh, fine! Living on the fat of the land.' But he soon fell into silence and the girl never said a word. After an intolerable pause Sonia Herries suggested that they should go. They didn't move. Half an hour later she insisted. They got up. But, standing by the door, Henry Abbott jerked his head towards the writing-desk.

'Who writes your letters for you?'

'Nobody. I write them myself.'

'You ought to have somebody. Save a lot of trouble. I'll do them for you.'

'Oh no, thank you. That would never do. Well, goodnight, goodnight—'

'Of course, I'll do them for you. And you needn't pay me anything either. Fill up my time.'

'Nonsense . . . goodnight, goodnight.' She closed the door on them. She could not sleep. She lay there thinking of him. She was moved, partly by a maternal tenderness for them that warmed her body (the girl and the baby had looked so helpless sitting there), partly by a shiver of apprehension that chilled her veins. Well, she hoped that she would never see them again. Or did she? Would she not tomorrow, as she walked down Sloane Street, stare at everyone to see whether by chance that was he?

Three mornings later he arrived. It was a wet morning and she had decided to devote it to the settling of accounts. She was sitting there at her table when Rose showed him in.

'I've come to do your letters,' he said.

'I should think not,' she said sharply. 'Now, Henry Abbott, out you go. I've had enough—'

'Oh no, you haven't,' he said, and sat down at her desk.

She would be ashamed for ever, but half an hour later she was seated in the corner of the sofa telling him what to write. She hated to confess it to herself, but she liked to see him sitting there. He was company for her, and to whatever depths he might by now have sunk, he was most certainly a gentleman. He behaved very well that morning; he wrote an excellent hand. He seemed to know just what to say.

A week later she said, laughing, to Amy Weston: 'My dear, would you believe it? I've had to take on a secretary. A very good-looking young man—but you needn't look down your nose. You know that good-looking young men are nothing to *me*—and he does save me endless bother.'

For three weeks he behaved very well, arriving punctually, offering her no insults, doing as she suggested about everything. In the fourth week, about a quarter to one on a day, his wife arrived. On this occasion she looked astonishingly young, sixteen perhaps. She wore a simple grey cotton dress. Her red bobbed hair was strikingly vibrant about her pale face.

The young man already knew that Miss Herries was lunching alone. He had seen the table laid for one with its simple appurtenances. It seemed to be very difficult not to ask them to remain. She did, although she did not wish to. The meal was not a success. The two of them together were tiresome, for the man said little when his wife was there, and the woman said nothing at all. Also, the pair of them were in a way sinister.

She sent them away after luncheon. They departed without protest. But as she walked, engaged on her shopping that afternoon, she decided that she must rid herself of them, once and for all. It was true that it had been rather agreeable having him there; his smile, his wicked humorous remarks, the suggestion that he was a kind of malevolent gamin who preyed on the world in general but spared her because he liked her—all this had attracted her—but what really alarmed her was that during all these weeks he had made no request for money, made indeed no request for anything. He must be piling up a fine account, must have some plan in his head with which one morning he would balefully startle her! For a moment there in the bright sunlight, with the purr of the traffic, the rustle of the trees about her, she saw herself in surprising colour. She was behaving with a weakness that was astonishing. Her stout, thick-set, resolute body, her cheery rosy face, her strong white hair—all these disappeared, and in their place, there almost clinging for support to the Park railings, was a timorous little old woman with frightened eyes and trembling knees. What was there to be afraid of? She had done nothing wrong. There were the police at hand. She had never been a coward before. She went home, however, with an odd impulse to leave her comfortable little house in Walpole Street and hide herself somewhere, somewhere that no one could discover.

That evening they appeared again, husband, wife and baby. She had settled herself down for a cosy evening with a book and an 'early to bed.' There came the knock on the door.

On this occasion she was most certainly firm with them. When they were gathered in a little group she got up and addressed them.

'Here is five pounds,' she said, 'and this is the end. If one of you shows his or her face inside this door again I call the police. Now go.'

The girl gave a little gasp and fell in a dead faint at her feet. It was a perfectly genuine faint. Rose was summoned. Everything possible was done.

'She has simply not had enough to eat,' said Henry Abbott. In the end (so determined and resolved was the faint) Ada Abbott was put to bed in the spare room and a doctor was summoned. After examining her he said that she needed rest and nourishment. This was perhaps the critical moment of the whole affair. Had Sonia Herries been at this crisis properly resolute and bundled the Abbott family, faint and all, into the cold unsympathising street, she might at this moment be a hale and hearty old woman enjoying bridge with her friends. It was, however, just here that her maternal temperament was too strong for her. The poor young thing lay exhausted, her eyes closed, her cheeks almost the colour of her pillow. The baby (surely the quietest baby ever known) lay in a cot beside the bed. Henry Abbott wrote letters to dictation downstairs. Once Sonia Herries, glancing up at the silver mask, was struck by the grin on the clown's face. It seemed to her now a thin sharp grin—almost derisive.

Three days after Ada Abbott's collapse there arrived her aunt and her uncle, Mr. and Mrs. Edwards. Mr. Edwards was a large red-faced man with a hearty manner and a bright waistcoat. He looked like a publican. Mrs. Edwards was a thin sharp-nosed woman with a bass voice. She was very, very thin, and wore a large old-fashioned brooch on her flat but emotional chest. They sat side by side on the sofa and explained that they had come to enquire after Ada, their favourite niece. Mrs. Edwards cried, Mr. Edwards was friendly and familiar. Unfortunately, Mrs. Weston and a friend came and called just then. They did not stay very long. They were frankly amazed at the Edwards couple and deeply startled by Henry Abbott's familiarity. Sonia Herries could see that they drew the very worst conclusions.

A week later Ada Abbott was still in bed in the upstairs room. It seemed to be impossible to move her. The Edwardses were constant visitors. On one occasion they brought Mr. and Mrs. Harper and their girl Agnes. They were profusely apologetic, but Miss Herries would understand that 'with the interest they took in Ada it was impossible to stay passive.' They all crowded into the spare bedroom and gazed at the pale figure with the closed eyes sympathetically.

Then two things happened together. Rose gave notice and Mrs. Weston came and had a frank talk with her friend. She began with that most sinister opening: 'I think you ought to know, dear, what everyone is saying—' What everyone was saying was that Sonia Herries was living with a young ruffian from the streets, young enough to be her son.

'You must get rid of them all and at once,' said Mrs. Weston, 'or you won't have a friend left in London, darling.'

Left to herself, Sonia Herries did what she had not done for years, she burst into tears. What had happened to her? Not only had her will and determination gone but she felt most unwell. Her heart was bad again; she could not sleep; the house, too, was tumbling to pieces. There was dust over everything. How was she ever to replace Rose? She was living in some horrible nightmare. This dreadful handsome young man seemed to have some authority over her. Yet he did not threaten her. All he did was to smile. Nor was she in the very least in love with him. This must come to an end or she would be lost.

Two days later, at tea-time, her opportunity arrived. Mr. and Mrs. Edwards had called to see how Ada was; Ada was downstairs at last, very weak and pale. Henry Abbott was there, also the baby. Sonia Herries, although she was feeling dreadfully unwell, addressed them all with vigour. She especially addressed the sharp-nosed Mrs. Edwards.

'You must understand,' she said. 'I don't want to be unkind, but I have my own life to consider. I am a very busy woman, and this has all been forced on me. I don't want to seem brutal. I'm glad to have been of some assistance to you, but I think Mrs. Abbott is well enough to go home now—and I wish you all good night.'

'I am sure,' said Mrs. Edwards, looking up at her from the sofa, 'that you've been kindness itself, Miss Herries. Ada recognises it, I'm sure. But to move her now would be to kill her, that's all. Any movement and she'll drop at your feet.'

'We have nowhere to go,' said Henry Abbott.

'But Mrs. Edwards—' began Miss Herries, her anger rising.

'We have only two rooms,' said Mrs. Edwards quietly. 'I'm sorry, but just now, what with my husband coughing all night—'

'Oh, but this is monstrous!' Miss Herries cried. 'I have had enough of this. I have been generous to a degree—'

'What about my pay,' said Henry, 'for all these weeks?'

'Pay! Why, of course—' Miss Herries began. Then she stopped. She realised several things. She realised that she was alone in the house, the cook having departed that afternoon. She realised that none of them had moved. She realised that her 'things'—the Sickert, the Utrillo, the sofa—were alive with apprehension. She was fearfully frightened of their silence, their immobility. She moved towards her desk, and her heart turned, squeezed itself dry, shot through her body the most dreadful agony.

'Please,' she gasped. 'In the drawer—the little green bottle—oh, quick! Please, please!'

The last thing of which she was aware was the quiet handsome features of Henry Abbott bending over her.

When, a week later, Mrs. Weston called, the girl, Ada Abbott, opened the door to her.

'I came to enquire for Miss Herries,' she said. 'I haven't seen her about. I have telephoned several times and received no answer.'

'Miss Herries is very ill.'

'Oh, I'm so sorry. Can I not see her?'

Ada Abbott's quiet gentle tones were reassuring her. 'The doctor does not wish her to see anyone at present. May I have your address? I will let you know as soon as she is well enough.'

Mrs. Weston went away. She recounted the event. 'Poor Sonia, she's pretty bad. They seem to be looking after her. As soon as she's better we'll go and see her.'

The London life moves swiftly. Sonia Herries had never been of very great importance to anyone. Herries relations enquired. They received a very polite note assuring them that so soon as she was better—

Sonia Herries was in bed, but not in her own room. She was in the little attic bedroom but lately occupied by Rose the maid. She lay at first in a strange apathy. She was ill. She slept and woke and slept again. Ada Abbott, sometimes Mrs. Edwards, sometimes a woman she did not know, attended to her. They were all very kind. Did she need a doctor? No, of course she did not need a doctor, they assured her. They would see that she had everything that she wanted.

Then life began to flow back into her. Why was she in this room? Where were her friends? What was this horrible food that they were bringing her? What were they doing here, these women?

She had a terrible scene with Ada Abbott. She tried to get out of bed. The girl restrained her—and easily, for all the strength seemed to have gone from her bones. She protested, she was as furious as her weakness allowed her, then she cried. She cried most bitterly. Next day she was alone and she crawled out of bed; the door was locked; she beat on it. There was no sound but her beating. Her heart was beginning again that terrible strangled throb. She crept back into bed. She lay there, weakly, feebly crying. When Ada arrived with some bread, some soup, some water, she demanded that the door should be unlocked, that she should get up, have her bath, come downstairs to her own room.

'You are not well enough,' Ada said gently.

'Of course, I am well enough. When I get out I will have you put in prison for this—'

'Please don't get excited. It is so bad for your heart.'

Mrs. Edwards and Ada washed her. She had not enough to eat. She was always hungry.

Summer had come. Mrs. Weston went to Etretat. Everyone was out of town.

'What's happened to Sonia Herries?' Mabel Newmark wrote to Agatha Benson. 'I haven't seen her for ages. . . .'

But no one had time to enquire. There were so many things to do. Sonia was a good sort, but she had been nobody's business. . . .

Once Henry Abbott paid her a visit. 'I am so sorry that you are not better,' he said smiling. 'We are doing everything we can for you. It is lucky we were around when you were so ill. You had better sign these papers. Someone must look after your affairs until you are better. You will be downstairs in a week or two.'

Looking at him with wide-open terrified eyes, Sonia Herries signed the papers.

The first rains of autumn lashed the streets. In the sitting-room the gramophone was turned on. Ada and young Mr. Jackson, Maggie Trent and stout Harry Bennett were dancing. All the furniture was flung against the walls. Mr. Edwards drank his beer; Mrs. Edwards was toasting her toes before the fire.

Henry Abbott came in. He had just sold the Utrillo. His arrival was greeted with cheers.

He took the silver mask from the wall and went upstairs. He climbed to the top of the house, entered, switched on the naked light.

'Oh! Who—What—?' A voice of terror came from the bed.

'It's all right,' he said soothingly. 'Ada will be bringing your tea in a minute.'

He had a hammer and nail and hung the silver mask on the speckled, mottled wall-paper where Miss Herries could see it.

'I know you're fond of it,' he said. 'I thought you'd like it to look at.' She made no reply. She only stared.

'You'll want something to look at,' he went on. 'You're too ill, I'm afraid, ever to leave this room again. So, it'll be nice for you. Something to look at.'

He went out, gently closing the door behind him.

The Perfect Close

Old Paul Thomlinson was eighty-nine years of age, and everyone in his circle watched him eagerly to see whether he would capture ninety. Once, and not so long ago, it had been hoped that he would reach one hundred, and his sister, Ada Mailey, had very confidently promised it. She was supposed to have been so completely in control that she could surely manage his age as well as everything else. But maybe, in this particular respect, she was not altogether whole-hearted, for, although the old man was not at all a trouble, it would quite certainly be easier for her when her brother was gone. He would leave her the house, a tidy bit of money, and all the odds and ends. Her son, Morgan, would also benefit.

Paul Thomlinson was a very nice, clean old gentleman; a faint, pale shell, but a shell with fire burning inside it. Behind the delicate, almost intangible, age-washed mask you could see the glow and feel the heat. He was no trouble at all. He slept and passed the day in his library, a big, wide-windowed room on the second floor, with books, seventeenth and eighteenth century for the most part, reaching to the ceiling, a fine portrait of his grandfather in a red tortoiseshell frame, an atlas in old dark oak bound round with brass, a bright-green inkstand, and his dear old dog, Caesar. In his dark-red leather armchair he sat, a rug over his knees, and looked out to the garden, with the Cathedral towers, ancient, beneficent, and the colour of bird's-nest grey, looking over the old brick wall. He saw the swifts cutting the sky like messengers and, when the weather was warm and the windows open, he could smell the roses and the pinks.

He was very little trouble, but he did hold himself aloof. That was what his sister and her son Morgan felt. For, as Mrs. Mailey herself, a thin but friendly lady of seventy, said:

'It's as though he thought himself superior.'

But, then, his mother had thought *herself* superior. Paul and Ada's father had been twice married, Paul the child of one mother, Ada of another. Paul's mother had been remote, reserved, austere. Ada's had been everybody's friend, Ada herself was everybody's friend, and when, after Mailey's sudden death from heart-failure in a London restaurant, she had come with her baby boy to live in Polchester, she had known, in a lick of the thumb, everyone in Polchester worth knowing. Paul had been kind and generous. Ada had run the house and also, as it seemed to the world, her brother. But this last, as Ada had well known, was not the truth. She had never possessed, or even controlled, her brother. It had simply been that he had not wished to take the trouble to resist her about the unimportant things. So long as he had his books, his few friends, the Cathedral music and his summer trip abroad he had made no fuss. And, oh yes, his dog! There had always been a dog. Of his interest in women, Ada knew nothing—perfect discretion, at any rate in Polchester, whatever his annual trip abroad may have included.

He had been a handsome man, brown-haired, straight-backed, with rather gentle and easily amused eyes and a most distinguished mouth. He wore elegant clothes, liking them coloured, a bright-blue tie, a buff-coloured waistcoat. He had the shining cleanliness of Venetian glass. Well, here he was, a very old man indeed, and quite suddenly, on a late autumn afternoon in his library, he knew that he was going to die.

The knowledge came to him as though a bird from heaven had flown in through the closed and heavily curtained windows and whispered in his ear. In the light given by the sharp-flamed fire and the sheltered electric glow, he almost fancied that he saw the bird.

'Within an hour or two you're going to die. Within an hour or two you're going to die.'

He smiled to himself and laid on the little table at his side the volume of Dryden's prose that he had been reading. So, it had come at last! He had no pain—simply a quick access of weakness. It was as though he could see, through the glasslike shell of his body, the life force ebbing away. He knew that many old people had these alarms, and that, very often, they were false and meaningless scarings. But, this time, he had no doubt. He was in no way frightened. All his life, like every other human being, he had speculated on death. A child is immortal, for, during childhood, death is an incredibility. Maturity makes it the only certainty. Paul had loved life so intensely that death had seemed to him, for many years, an almost unbearable shame. Very simple things had always pleased him—light and dark, colours and scents, food and drink, friendship. His deeper experiences, hospital work in France during the war, love, once, twice, thrice—these had made death more understandable. They had gone to the roots of experience. But why should he not be permitted to watch the sunlight, keep company with his books, walk with his dog, enjoy the blessed indulgence of sleep, for ever and ever? Of these he would never tire and indulging in them did no one any harm.

For a long time, he had resented death. Then, as experience had gathered with the years, he had turned more to wonder as to how he would meet it when it came. He did not fear it. The only thing of which he was really afraid was long-continued physical pain. Once he had suffered acute arthritis in his left arm for a continuous six months and had realised, through that experience, how pain that never relaxes can do something to the spiritual side of man, something disgraceful and humiliating. If he knew that he was to die, would he be a coward? He often pictured to himself that familiar scene in the consulting-room, he seated, listening attentively to the surgeon's sentence of death. That sudden realisation of death! What a fearful thing! To know that, within a definite sum of months, you would be removed, extinct, forgotten!

Could he then summon a brave and philosophic serenity? He did hope so.

Then, as the years had passed and he had grown older and older, he had felt, without too much boastfulness, a sort of triumph. He was getting the better of that old devil, Death! Suppose he reached his century—what a snap of the fingers for that old humbug! He was proud of his birthdays and liked them solemnised. On his seventieth he had a great dinner party, with all his friends around him. On his ninetieth, he would have another! Now, this afternoon, he knew very certainly that he would never reach that ninetieth.

Of course, as age had advanced, his vitality had ebbed. This room had become his world, and a very agreeable world too. He slept a great deal, he had still a good appetite, his brain was as active as ever, and he was still able to feel his old energetic likes and dislikes of his fellow human beings. He liked his sister, for old times' sake, although he held the opinion that most men have about most women—that she had little sense of the important things in life. He detested his young nephew, Morgan. He had detested him from the first moment of seeing him, a baby, howling for something, screaming at sight of him.

Young Morgan had all the qualities that his uncle most abhorred—he was conceited without reason, cocksure without knowledge, noisy and extravagant. Morgan patronised his old uncle, without intending it of course, but that only made the patronage worse. He delivered his opinions on politics, the arts, love, religion, as though they were the only possible opinions. He had brains, and would make a good lawyer, but he was a horrible young man. Morgan and his uncle played chess together. Paul was an erratic player and Morgan usually defeated him. Paul hated the boy's supercilious pleasure at his victories, but Paul adored the game and, on every separate occasion, was certain that this time he would trounce the young devil.

And Morgan had a dog, a succession of dogs. Always the same kind of dog—barking, restless, selfish dogs, fox-terriers for the most part. He thought of Morgan's fox-terrier, Satan, the present one, and he motioned with his thin, blue-veined hand to his old Sealyham, Caesar, who, stretched near the fire, apparently sleeping, had nevertheless his eye closely fixed on his master. Caesar came slowly over to him and rested his head against his master's leg, sighing portentous satisfaction as he did so. Caesar, old as he was, could still put fear into the heart of young Satan. A grand fighter Caesar had always been!

So here then was Death, and it was neither terrifying nor humiliating. There was a strange agitation about his heart, as though all the forces there were engaged in a last battle together. His brain was extraordinarily lucid and clear. He seemed to possess a double vision, so that the dark plum-coloured curtains were almost transparent, and the black and white marble slabs of the fireplace nearly revealed to him the active world moving behind them. Soon he would know—ah, very soon!—the shapes, sounds, and vigours of that second world.

The door opened. It was young Morgan.

'Like a game of chess. Uncle, before tea?'

'Now,' the old man thought, 'I'm within an hour or less of death. I should be at charity with all the world. But I dislike that young man as much as ever. Why does he speak as though he owns the world? And,' he thought, 'if ever in all my life I wanted to beat him at chess. I want to beat him now.'

He was not a bad young man, Morgan. He thought himself irresistibly charming. He was thinking:

'Poor old boy—and aren't I a hero to play a game with him?'

He fetched, from a corner of the room, the chessmen. They were a beautiful set of dark-red agate and clear shining crystal. Very handsome they looked, set up there, with the firelight behind them.

'Red,' said Morgan.

'Red it is,' the old man answered.

Although he wished so eagerly to win, he found it difficult at first to concentrate—and chess demands absolute concentration. Why was it, he thought, that he disliked, almost bitterly, his nephew's appearance? For he was a handsome young man, hair the colour of ripe corn, blue eyes, a taut, trained, athletic body? The mouth was supercilious, the hands too grasping. . . . Yes, yes. That was the thing to do. Knight to Bishop Three and then, perhaps, if Morgan had not foreseen . . .

His thoughts were captured with the consciousness of the littleness of time that remained to him. Only an hour or two. . . . What did he wish to do? To win this game of chess. And Minna's dress . . . Before he moved his bishop, he said:

'There isn't a parcel for me downstairs, is there?'

'Didn't see anything. Your move. Uncle!'

Dear, *dear* Minna! Everyone thought her so plain, just a dry, ill-dressed, elderly virgin. But she had been always so very kind to him. There had been between them for so many years a most beautiful relationship. She and the dog Caesar were now everything to him. Yes, now that so many dear others were dead. His mind speculated yet further. Did death mean nothing? Would he, in another brief space of time, be aware of Nothing? Nothing! How appalling a word! But it seemed to him that God was more likely and, if God, why, then surely continuing experience.

'Your move, Uncle.'

With a mighty effort that seemed almost the most strenuous exercise he had ever commanded, he looked at the board. He saw with horror that he was in the greatest danger. Morgan's queen and bishop commanded a line threatening disastrously his king. Every piece of Morgan's—he had the red, sinister, dark, shadowed agate—seemed to be stirring with menace. His own crystal pieces were, he felt, appealing to him for succour. Oh, he must win this game, he *must* win this, the last game of his life! He glanced at young Morgan's cocky, supercilious smile, at the superior, confident fashion of his seat, his back taut, his thighs spread.

'Take your time, Uncle. . . . Take your time. You're in a bit of a hole.'

Never before had the old man wanted anything so badly as to win this game. No, not when he had gone on his knees to Maria Bock in the restaurant in Heidelberg and implored her mercy; nor when, at the Wagner Festival in Munich, he had hoped that David Warrinder would he his friend.

His long, long past life came together in the effort that now he summoned. His brain, as fine as ever it was, bit into the board. He could feel his heart leap and die, leap and die. He castled, a thing that he should have done before. Young Morgan's knight leapt sideways with a little toss of his sunset-coloured head.

'I must attack,' Paul thought. He brought out his queen.

'Check,' said Morgan with exultation and, his arrogance blinding him, had not seen that the checking knight had fallen into the path of his uncle's bishop. With how quiet a gesture, but with what inner triumph, did Paul remove that knight.

'Damn!' said Morgan, 'I never saw it!'

And then Paul discovered his opportunity. By moving that pawn, sending forward a bishop, offering that pawn as a sacrifice, he had a chance of a mate. Morgan's castled king was tied in—there was a chance . . . a chance. His brain reeled. If only Morgan were blind enough. He moved his pawn. Morgan threatened his king again. He sent his bishop forward. Morgan, intent on his own triumph, moved his knight. Paul offered his pawn. There was a pause and Morgan, almost sneeringly, took it.

'Checkmate,' said the old man.

Mate in a dozen moves! A really marvellous victory—and he would never play chess again!

'What about another?' said young Morgan, who simply hated to be beaten.

The old man looked at him maliciously.

'No. I'm going to rest on my victory. I was afraid you'd see through that move of mine.'

Morgan said: 'You won't work that on me a second time. Uncle Paul.'

'No. I don't believe I shall.'

'Come on, have another.'

'No. Allow me the satisfaction of telling everyone I've beaten you.'

'Well, you don't often. If it gives you any pleasure'

What a baby the boy was! The old man felt a sudden affection for him.

'It's very nice of you to come and play with an old man like me.'

Morgan smiled.

'I am *fearfully busy*. But I can always find time for a game.'

'What are you busy about?'

'Work. You know. Uncle, I'm going to be a damned fine lawyer. I feel it in my bones.'

'I expect you are. I hope you'll be a damned fine man too. There are so many lawyers.'

It seemed to him fantastically that the shadow of a man was outlined against the wall. A long-faced, thin shadow, Death no doubt. A friendly fellow.

'All right. Death. Make yourself comfortable. Give me another half-hour.'

He looked at his nephew and thought of his assured self-confidence. Not so had it been with him! Of all the things that he now regretted, the time wasted in placating his fellow human beings was the heaviest. Not that he wished that he had been bad-mannered. He rated courtesy very high. But, when younger, he had credited his companions with more wisdom, more knowledge of the world, than himself. He saw now that they had all been as stupid as he. He had been sensitive to their criticism, but now he realised that, when they criticised him, they were defending themselves. The distinguishing mark between people was kindness of heart, generosity of spirit, not wisdom. And so, he thought again of Minna Prinsep.

'Be a good boy, Morgan, and run down and see whether there isn't a parcel for me.'

'All right—if you really won't play another game.'

The boy went out and the old man grinned at Death against the wall.

'I beat him at chess. That's grand.'

He felt quite wonderfully cheerful. The room, and the house behind it, seemed filled with all the fun they'd had—and especially the Christmas parties. Ada had been good about those parties and, even into his very last year, the music and the dancing, the supper, the mistletoe, the holly, had all been rich with goodwill and friendliness. On this very last Christmas, Minna had thought only for him.

'I think you ought to know,' she had said, 'that I never can thank you enough for all your goodness to me.' She had spoken in her dry, rather sarcastic voice that frightened some people. She was terribly poor and terribly brave. He thought that sometimes she did not have enough to eat. And then, a month ago, he had found her looking at a catalogue. There was a dress that she coveted.

61

I'm no beauty, you know, but in *that* I might look quite attractive.'

She had sighed and put the dress catalogue away. And the other day he had written to London for it. If only it would arrive this afternoon!

'Do you think . . .?' he asked Death tentatively. But he knew that it was of no use to ask Death for anything. Death had his orders.

So, he settled himself comfortably in his chair and considered, without any fear or discomfort, this ebbing of his vitality. He had always considered the two possibilities—death under anaesthetic or dope of some sort—and death with himself fully conscious. The second of these would be surely most dreadful—the struggle not to die, *not* to surrender.

On the contrary, the approach, as he was now experiencing it, was one of the most pleasant he had ever known. It was not only easy and practicable, but it seemed like a real going forward to some agreeable experience. Friends, in earlier days, had fetched him to take him away for the weekend.

'Wait a minute,' he had called, 'I will be with you in a minute.' So now.

'Wait a minute. Death. I'm nearly ready.'

He noticed that Caesar had come very close to him and, once and again, shivered. Was he aware, as dogs are supposed to be aware, that Death was in the room? Never mind. The old dog would soon himself be gone. What a pleasant fancy that they might share together the Elysian fields!

The door opened.

'There *is* a parcel!' Morgan cried. 'Here it is!'

'Let's see it.' The old man raised his thin hand, almost like talc against the firelight. 'Give me those scissors. The large ones over by the window. . . . Here, you cut it. Open it for me.'

'Why, it's a dress!'

Morgan examined it.

'Nice stuff—but pretty severe. Mother likes bright colours.'

'I know she does. No, this is for someone else.'

'You dark horse! Giving dresses to the ladies!'

The boy was at his *most* irritating, for behind his sentences was plainly the conviction that he was the most enchanting of young men, tender with the aged, humorous about sex, wise about women. . . .

'Don't talk to me about ladies!' the old man snapped at him. 'Why, at your age, I knew already more than you'll ever know.' He winked at Death across the room, as much as to say:

'I know that in this last hour of mine I should be gentle, at peace with all men, unconscious of malice. . . . I'm afraid to the very last I shall be myself.'

It annoyed him to see Morgan fingering the dress.

'All right. . . . Leave it. There! on the table. . . .'

Then, as though to himself;

'I wonder if Minna Prinsep will look in!'

Morgan shouted with joy.

'Minna! Why, of course, how stupid! Old Minna! That's who the dress is for! Why didn't I think of it?'

'That's enough! That's enough! Leave me to myself now—that's a good boy—I'll have a nap before tea.'

He felt a tenderness to the boy again. After all, this child was at the beginning of life's experience, and he was at the end. How little, how very little he had to tell him! Be tolerant, realise yourself as a comic figure, expect no great things either of yourself or others, physical love does not last but spiritual love may, accept the inevitable egotism of all humans save the saints, take joy in little things, do not grieve over-much for sins of the body, but fight like the devil against meannesses of the spirit—oh, what use would any of this be to Morgan? An old man's platitudes, they would seem. No one ever learnt anything from the experience of others. He lay back, happy that he would never have to lay down the law about anything again.

He remembered his indignation once, when, at a party, someone had said:

'Constable! Milk-and-water English! Cows and mills and stormy skies! He might have been something of a painter if he hadn't been English!'

How Paul had exploded! How angry he had been, how his heart had hammered in his chest! Now, in retrospect, that scene was a little curl of grey smoke, a breath of air, a tolling beat of a vanishing drum! All angers, all tempestuous judgments, all dismays, betrayals, burning tears—all gone, all as though they had never been!

The door opened and Minna Prinsep stood there. He gazed at her. She seemed for a moment another shadow against the wall, like Death. And then, he was so rapturously delighted. Yes, although vitality was ebbing from him fast, he could still feel rapture of the spirit.

'Minna!'

Her ugly, rather twisted face, illuminated by the beautiful generous eyes, smiled.

'I looked in just to see how you were.'

'Oh, I'm all right.' He was growling weak. He motioned her rather feebly to his side. 'Come over here.'

She came across, moving in stiff awkward jerks her thin, angular body.

'Are you, all right? You look rather tired,'

'Of course, I am. I beat Morgan at chess this afternoon.'

'You didn't?'

'I did. And in a dozen moves too. Look here—I've got something for you.'

His hands, from which all strength seemed now to be departing, fingered about the tissue paper.

'You take it from the box.'

She lifted it out and held it up.

'Oh! . . . Oh!'

'It's for you. I sent for it from London. If it doesn't quite fit, you can have it altered here.'

'Oh, but it's lovely.' She held the stuff against her thin neck.

'Perfect. You—you darling.'

She let the dress drop, knelt down and kissed his forehead. He put his arm stiffly about her. They had forgotten the dress.

'Why do you do these things for me?'

Her voice broke. He thought she was going to cry.

'No one else in all my life has been good to me as you have. I've never loved anyone so much—'

'Nor have I. There *is* a love you know, Minna, deeper and deeper—not physical.'

'Yes—ours will last for ever. It has made me believe in immortality.'

His happiness was complete. As he lay there, his hand against her side, the house was suddenly filled with sound. The Christmas party. He was moving down the stairs. In his nostrils was the scent of burning candle-wax, sugar icing, the cold woody chill of mistletoe berries, the hot crackle of holly. Beyond the window were carol singers, and someone was taking the parcels from the tree. . . .

He was hand in hand with Death, and Death's grasp was warm and comforting.

'Now this is perfect!' he cried, and all the candles blazed and the coloured balls swung gallantly on the tree.

Minna looked up into his face and gave a cry.

Mrs. Lunt

1

'Do you believe in ghosts?' I asked Runciman. I had to ask him this very platitudinous question more because he was so difficult a man to spend an hour with than for any other reason. You know his books, perhaps, or more probably you don't know them—*The Running Man, The Elm Tree,* and *Crystal and Candlelight.* He is one of those little men who are constant enough in this age of immense over-production of books, men who publish every autumn their novel, who arouse by that publication in certain critics eager appreciation and praise, who have a small and faithful public, whose circulation is very small indeed, who when you meet them have little to say, are often shy and nervous, pessimistic and remote from daily life. Such men do fine work, are made but little of in their own day, and perhaps fifty years after their death are rediscovered by some digging critic and become a sort of cult with a new generation.

I asked Runciman that question because, for some unknown reason, I had invited him to dinner at my flat, and was now faced with a long evening filled with that most tiresome of all conversations, talk that dies every two minutes and has to be revived with terrific exertions. Being myself a critic, and having on many occasions praised Runciman's work, he was the more nervous and shy with me; had I abused it, he would perhaps have had plenty to say—he was that kind of man. But my question was a lucky one: it roused him instantly, his long, bony body became full of a new energy, his eyes stared into a rich and exciting reminiscence, he spoke without pause, and I took care not to interrupt him.

He certainly told me one of the most astounding stories I have ever heard. Whether it was true or not I cannot, of course, say: these ghost stories are nearly always at second or third hand. I had, at any rate, the good fortune to secure mine from the source. Moreover, Runciman was not a liar: he was too serious for that. He himself admitted that he was not sure, at this distance of time, as to whether the thing had gained as the years passed. However, here it is as he told it.

'It was some fifteen years ago,' he said. 'I went down to Cornwall to stay with Robert Lunt. Do you remember his name? No, I suppose you do not. He wrote several novels; some of those half-and-half things that are not quite novels, not quite poems, rather mystical and picturesque, and are the very devil to do well. De la Mare's *Return* is a good example of the kind of thing. I had reviewed somewhere his last book, and reviewed it favourably, and received from him a really touching letter showing that the man was thirsting for praise, and also, I fancied, for company. He lived in Cornwall somewhere on the sea-coast, and his wife had died a year ago; he said he was quite alone there, and would I come and spend Christmas with him; he hoped I would not think this impertinent; he expected that I would be engaged already, but he could not resist the chance.

'Well, I wasn't engaged; far from it. If Lunt was lonely, so was I; if Lunt was a failure, so was I; I was touched, as I have said, by his letter, and I accepted his invitation. As I went down in the train to Penzance I wondered what kind of a man he would be. I had never seen any photographs of him; he was not the sort of author whose picture the newspapers publish. He must be, I fancied, about my own age—perhaps rather older. I know when we're lonely how some of us are for ever imagining that a friend will somewhere turn up, that ideal friend who will understand all one's feelings, who will give one affection without being sentimental, who will take an interest in one's affairs without being impertinent—yes, the sort of friend one never finds.

'I fancy that I became quite romantic about Lunt before I reached Penzance. We would talk, he and I, about all those literary questions that seemed to me at that time so absorbing; we would perhaps often stay together and even travel abroad on those little journeys that are so swiftly melancholy when one is alone, so delightful when one has a perfect companion. I imagined him as sparse and delicate and refined, with a sort of wistfulness and rather childish play of fancy. We had both, so far, failed in our careers, but perhaps together we would do great things.

'When I arrived at Penzance it was almost dark, and the snow, threatened all day by an overhanging sky, had begun gently and timorously to fall. He had told me in his letter that a fly would be at the station to take me to his house; and there I found it—a funny old weather-beaten carriage with a funny old weather-beaten driver. At this distance of time my imagination may have created many things, but I fancy that from the moment I was shut into that carriage some dim suggestion of fear and apprehension attacked me. I fancy that I had some absurd impulse to get out of the thing and take the night train back to London again—an action that would have been very unlike me, as I had always a sort of obstinate determination to carry through anything that I had begun.

'In any case, I was uncomfortable in that carriage; it had, I remember, a nasty, musty smell of damp straw and stale eggs, and it seemed to confine me so closely as though it were determined that, once I was in, I should never get out again. Then, it was bitterly cold; I was colder during that drive than I have ever been before or since. It was that penetrating cold that seems to pierce your very brain, so that I could not think with any clearness, but only wish again and again that I hadn't come. Of course, I could see nothing—only feel the jolt over the uneven road—and once and again we seemed to fight our way through dark paths, because I could feel the overhanging branches of the trees knock against the cab with mysterious taps, as though they were trying to give me some urgent message.

'Well, I mustn't make more of it than the facts allow, and I mustn't see into it all the significance of the events that followed. I only know that as the drive proceeded I became more and more miserable: miserable with the cold of my body, the misgivings of my imagination, the general loneliness of my case.

'At last we stopped. The old scarecrow got slowly off his box, with many heavings and sighings, came to the cab door, and, with great difficulty and irritating slowness, opened it. I got out of it, and found that the snow was now falling very heavily indeed, and that the path was lighted with its soft, mysterious glow. Before me was a humped and ungainly shadow: the house that was to receive me. I could make nothing of it in that darkness, but only stood there shivering while the old man pulled at the door-bell with a sort of frantic energy as though he were anxious to be rid of the whole job as quickly as possible and return to his own place. At last, after what seemed an endless time, the door opened, and an old man, who might have been own brother to the driver, poked out his head. The two old men talked together, and at last my bag was shouldered and I was permitted to come in out of the piercing cold.

'Now this, I know, is not imagination. I have never at any period of my life hated at first sight so vigorously any dwelling-place into which I have ever entered as I did that house. There was nothing especially disagreeable about my first vision of the hall. It was a large, dark place, lit by two dim lamps, cold and cheerless; but I got no particular impression of it because at once I was conducted out of it, led along a passage, and then introduced into a room which was, I saw, as warm and comfortable as the hall had been dark and dismal.

'I was, in fact, so eagerly pleased at the large and leaping fire that I moved towards it at once, not noting, at the first moment, the presence of my host; and when I did see him I could not believe that it was he. I have told you the kind of man that I had expected; but, instead of the sparse, sensitive artist, I found facing me a large burly man, over six foot, I should fancy, as broad-shouldered as he was tall, giving evidence of great muscular strength, the lower part of his face hidden by a black, pointed beard.

'But if I was astonished at the sight of him, I was doubly amazed when he spoke. His voice was thin and piping, like that of some old woman, and the little nervous gestures that he made with his hands were even more feminine than his voice. But I had to allow, perhaps, for excitement, for excited he was; he came up to me, took my hand in both of his, and held it as though he would never let it go. In the evening he apologised for this. "I was so glad to see you," he said; "I couldn't believe that really you would come; you are the first visitor of my own kind that I have had here for ever so long. I was ashamed, indeed, of asking you, but I had to snatch at the chance—it means so much to me."

'His eagerness, in fact, had something disturbing about it; something pathetic, too. He simply couldn't do too much for me: he led me through funny crumbling old passages, the boards creaking under us at every step, up some dark stairs, the walls hung, so far as I could see in the dim light, with faded yellow photographs of places, and showed me into my room with a deprecating agitated gesture as though he expected me at the first sight of it to turn and run. I didn't like it any more than I liked the rest of the house; but that was not my host's fault. He had done everything he possibly could for me: there was a large fire flaming in the open fireplace, there was a hot bottle, as he explained to me, in the big four-poster bed, and the old man who had opened the door to me was already taking my clothes out of my bag and putting them away. Lunt's nervousness was almost sentimental. He put both his hands on my shoulders and said, looking at me plead-ingly: "If you only knew what it is for me to have you here, the talks we'll have. Well, well, I must leave you. You'll come down and join me, won't you, as soon as you can?"

'It was then, when I was left alone in my room, that I had my sec-ond impulse to flee. Four candles in tall old silver candlesticks were burning brightly, and these, with the blazing fire, gave plenty of light; and yet the room was in some way dim, as though a faint smoke per-vaded it, and I remember that I went to one of the old lattice windows and threw it open for a moment as though I felt stifled. Two things quickly made me close it. One was the intense cold which, with a flut-tering scamper of snow, blew into the room; the other was the quite deafening roar of the sea, which seemed to fling itself at my very face as though it wanted to knock me down. I quickly shut the window, turned round, and saw an old woman standing just inside the door.

'Now every story of this kind depends for its interest on its veri-similitude. Of course, to make my tale convincing I should be able to prove to you that I saw that old woman; but I can't. I can only urge upon you my rather dreary reputation of probity. You know that I'm a teetotaller, and always have been, and, most important evidence of all, I was not expecting to see an old woman; and yet I hadn't the least doubt in the world but that it was an old woman I saw. You may talk about shadows, clothes hanging on the back of the door, and the rest of it. I don't know. I've no theories about this story, I'm not a spir-itualist, I don't know that I believe in anything especially, except the beauty of beautiful things.

'We'll put it, if you like, that I fancied that I saw an old woman, and my fancy was so strong that I can give you to this day a pretty detailed account of her appearance. She wore a black silk dress and on her breast, was a large, ugly, gold brooch; she had black hair, brushed back from her forehead and parted down the middle; she wore a collar of some white stuff round her throat; her face was one of the wickedest, most malignant and furtive that I have ever seen—very white in col-our. She was shrivelled enough now, but might once have been rather beautiful. She stood there quietly, her hands at her side. I thought that she was some kind of housekeeper. "I have everything I want, thank you," I said. "What a splendid fire!"

'I turned for a moment towards it, and when I looked back she was gone. I thought nothing of this, of course, but drew up an old chair covered with green faded tapestry, and thought that I would read a little from some book that I had brought down with me before I went to join my host. The fact was that I was not very intent upon joining him before I must. I didn't like him. I had already made up my mind that I would find some excuse to return to London as soon as possible. I can't tell you why I didn't like him, except that I was myself very reserved and had, like many Englishmen, a great distrust of demonstrations, especially from another man. I hadn't cared for the way in which he had put his hands on my shoulders, and I felt perhaps that I wouldn't be able to live up to all his eager excitement about me.

'I sat in my chair and took up my book, but I had not been reading for more than two minutes before I was conscious of a most unpleasant smell. Now, there are all sorts of smells—healthy and otherwise—but I think the nastiest is that chilly kind of odour that comes from bad sanitation and stuffy rooms combined; you meet it sometimes at little country inns and decrepit town lodgings. This smell was so definite that I could almost locate it; it came from near the door. I got up, approached the door, and at once it was as though I were drawing near to somebody who, if you'll forgive the impoliteness, was not accustomed to taking too many baths. I drew back just as I might had an actual person been there. Then quite suddenly the smell was gone, the room was fresh, and I saw, to my surprise, that one of the windows had opened and that snow was again blowing in. I closed it and went downstairs.

'The evening that followed was odd enough. My host was not in himself an unlikeable man; he did his very utmost to please me. He had a fine culture and a wide knowledge of books and things. He became quite cheerful as the evening went on; gave me a good dinner in a funny little dining-room hung with some admirable mezzotints. The serving-man looked after us—a funny old man, with a long white beard like a goat—and, oddly enough, it was from him that I first re-caught my earlier apprehension. He had just put the dessert on the table, had arranged my plate in front of me, when I saw him give a start and look towards the door. My attention was attracted to this because his hand, as it touched the plate, suddenly trembled. My eyes followed, but I could see nothing. That he was frightened of something was perfectly clear, and then (it may, of course, very easily have been fancy) I thought that I detected once more that strange unwholesome smell.

'I forgot this again when we were both seated in front of a splendid fire in the library. Lunt had a very fine collection of books, and it was delightful to him, as it is to every book-collector, to have somebody with him who could really appreciate them. We stood looking at one book after another and talking eagerly about some of the minor early English novelists who were my especial hobby—Bage, Godwin, Henry Mackenzie, Mrs. Shelley, Mat Lewis and others—when once again he affected me most unpleasantly by putting his arm round my shoulders. I have all my life disliked intensely to be touched by certain people. I suppose we all feel like this. It is one of those inexplicable things; and I disliked this so much that I abruptly drew away.

'Instantly he was changed into a man of furious and ungovernable rage; I thought that he was going to strike me. He stood there quivering all over, the words pouring out of his mouth incoherently, as though he were mad and did not know what he was saying. He accused me of insulting him, of abusing his hospitality, of throwing his kindness back into his face, and of a thousand other ridiculous things; and I can't tell you how strange it was to hear all this coming out in that shrill piping voice as though it were from an agitated woman, and yet to see with one's eyes that big, muscular frame, those immense shoulders and that dark-bearded face.

'I said nothing. I am, physically, a coward. I dislike, above anything else in the world, any sort of quarrel. At last I brought out, "I am very sorry. I didn't mean anything. Please forgive me," and then hurriedly turned to leave the room. At once he changed again; now he was almost in tears. He implored me not to go; said it was his wretched temper, but that he was so miserable and unhappy, and had for so long now been alone and desolate that he hardly knew what he was doing. He begged me to give him another chance, and if I would only listen to his story I would perhaps be more patient with him.

'At once, so oddly is man constituted, I changed in my feelings towards him. I was very sorry for him. I saw that he was a man on the edge of his nerves, and that he really did need some help and sympathy, and would be quite distracted if he could not get it. I put my hand on his shoulder to quieten him and to show him that I bore no malice, and I felt that his great body was quivering from head to foot. We sat down again, and in an odd, rambling manner he told me his story.

'It amounted to very little, and the gist of it was that, rather to have some sort of companionship than from any impulse of passion, he had married some fifteen years before the daughter of a neighbouring clergyman. They had had no very happy life together, and at the last, he told me quite frankly, he had hated her. She had been mean, overbearing, and narrow-minded; it had been, he confessed, nothing but a relief to him when, just a year ago, she had suddenly died from heart failure.

'He had thought then that things would go better with him, but they had not; nothing had gone right with him since. He hadn't been able to work, many of his friends had ceased to come to see him, he had found it even difficult to get servants to stay with him, he was desperately lonely, he slept badly—that was why his temper was so terribly on edge. He had no one in the house with him save the old man, who was, fortunately, an excellent cook, and a boy—the old man's grandson. "Oh, I thought," I said, "that that excellent meal tonight was cooked by your housekeeper."

'"My housekeeper?" he answered. "There's no woman in the house."

'"Oh, but one came to my room," I replied, "this evening—an old lady-like-looking person in a black silk dress."

'"You were mistaken," he answered in the oddest voice, as though he were exerting all the strength that he possessed to keep himself quiet and controlled.

'"I am sure that I saw her," I answered. "There couldn't be any mistake." And I described her to him.

'"You were mistaken," he repeated again. "Don't you see that you must have been when I tell you there is no woman in the house?"

'I reassured him quickly lest there should be another outbreak of rage. Then there followed the strangest kind of appeal. Urgently, as though his very life depended upon it, he begged me to stay with him for a few days. He implied, although he said nothing definitely, that he was in great trouble, that if only I would stay for a few days all would be well, that if ever in all my life I had had a chance of doing a kind action I had one now, that he couldn't expect me to stop in so dreary a place, but that he would never forget it if I did. He spoke in a voice of such urgent distress that I comforted him as I might a child, promising that I would stay and shaking hands with him on it as though it were a kind of solemn oath between us.

2

'I am sure that you would wish me to give you this incident as it occurred, and if the final catastrophe seems to come, as it were, accidentally, I can only say to you that that was how it happened. It is since the event that I have tried to put two and two together, and that they don't altogether make four is the fault that mine shares, I suppose,

72

with every true ghost story.

'But the truth is that after that very strange episode between us I had a very good night. I slept the sleep of all justice, cosy and warm, in my four-poster, with the murmur of the sea beyond the windows to rock my slumbers. Next morning too was bright and cheerful, the sun sparkling down on the snow, and the snow sparkling back to the sun as though they were glad to see one another. I had a very pleasant morning looking at Lunt's books, talking to him, and writing one or two letters. I must say that, after all, I liked the man. His appeal to me on the night before had touched me. So few people, you see, had ever appealed to me about anything. His nervousness was there and the constant sense of apprehension, yet he seemed to be putting the best face on it, doing his utmost to set me at my ease in order to induce me to stay, I suppose, and to give him a little of that company that he so terribly needed.

'I dare say if I had not been so busy about the books I would not have been so happy. There was a strange eerie silence about that house if one ever stopped to listen; and once, I remember, sitting at the old bureau writing a letter, I raised my head and looked up, and caught Lunt watching as though he wondered whether I had heard or noticed anything. And so, I listened too, and it seemed to me as though someone were on the other side of the library door with their hand raised to knock; a quaint notion, with nothing to support it, but I could have sworn that if I had gone to the door and opened it suddenly someone would have been there.

'However, I was cheerful enough, and after lunch quite happy.

'Lunt asked me if I would like a walk, and I said I would; and we started out in the sunshine over the crunching snow towards the sea. I don't remember what we talked of; we seemed to be now quite at our ease with one another. We crossed the fields to a certain point, looked down at the sea—smooth now, like silk—and turned back. I remember that I was so cheerful that I seemed suddenly to take a happy view of all my prospects. I began to confide in Lunt, telling him of my little plans, of my hopes for the book that I was then writing, and even began rather timidly to suggest to him that perhaps we should do something together; that what we both needed was a friend of common taste with ourselves. I know that I was talking on, that we had crossed a little village street, and were turning up the path towards the dark avenue of trees that led to his house, when suddenly the change came.

'What I first noticed was that he was not listening to me; his gaze was fixed beyond me, into the very heart of the black clump of trees that fringed the silver landscape. I looked too, and my heart bounded. There was, standing just in front of the trees, as though she were waiting for us, the old woman whom I had seen in my room the night before. I stopped. "Why, there she is!" I said. "That's the old woman of whom I was speaking—the old woman who came to my room."

'He caught my shoulder with his hand. "There's nothing there," he said. "Don't you see that that's shadow? What's the matter with you? Can't you see that there's nothing?" I stepped forward, and there was nothing, and I wouldn't, to this day, be able to tell you whether it was hallucination or not. I can only say that, from that moment, the afternoon appeared to become dark. As we entered into the avenue of trees, silently and hurrying as though someone were behind us, the dusk seemed to have fallen so that I could scarcely see my way.

'We reached the house breathless. He hastened into his study as though I were not with him, but I followed and, closing the door behind me, said, with all the force that I had at command: "Now, what is this? What is it that's troubling you? You must tell me! How can I help you if you don't?"

'And he replied, in so strange a voice that it was as though he had gone out of his mind: "I tell you there's nothing! Can't you believe me when I tell you there's nothing at all? I'm quite all right. . . . Oh, my God!—my God! . . . don't leave me! . . . This is the very day—the very night she said. . . . But I did nothing, I tell you—I did nothing—it's only her beastly malice. . . ." He broke off. He still held my arm with his hand. He made strange movements, wiping his forehead as though it were damp with sweat, almost pleading with me; then suddenly angry again, then beseeching once more, as though I had refused him the one thing he wanted.

'I saw that he was truly not far from madness, and I began myself to have a sudden terror of this damp, dark house, this great, trembling man, and something more that was worse than they. But I pitied him. How could you or any man have helped it? I made him sit down in the armchair beside the fire, which had now dwindled to a few glimmering red coals. I let him hold me close to him with his arm and clutch my hand with his, and I repeated, as quietly as I might: "But tell me; don't be afraid, whatever it is you have done. Tell me what danger it is you fear, and then we can face it together."

'"Fear! fear!" he repeated; and then, with a mighty effort which I could not but admire, he summoned all his control. "I'm off my head," he said, "with loneliness and depression. My wife died a year ago on this very night. We hated one another. I couldn't be sorry when she died, and she knew it. When that last heart attack came on, between her gasps she told me that she would return, and I've always dreaded this night. That's partly why I asked you to come, to have someone here, anybody, and you've been very kind—more kind than I had any right to expect. You must think me insane going on like this, but see me through tonight and we'll have splendid times together. Don't desert me now—now, of all times!"

'I promised that I would not. I soothed him as best I could. We sat there, for I know not how long, through the gathering dark; we neither of us moved, the fire died out, and the room was lit with a strange dim glow that came from the snowy landscape beyond the uncurtained windows. Ridiculous, perhaps, as I look back at it. We sat there, I in a chair close to his, hand in hand, like a couple of lovers; but, in real truth, two men terrified, fearful of what was coming, and unable to do anything to meet it.

'I think that that was perhaps the queerest part of it; a sort of paralysis that crept over me. What would you or anyone else have done—summoned the old man, gone down to the village inn, fetched the local doctor? I could do nothing, but see the snow-shine move like trembling water about the furniture and hear, through the urgent silence, the faint hoot of an owl from the trees in the wood.

3

'Oddly enough, I can remember nothing, try as I may, between that strange vigil and the moment when I myself, wakened out of a brief sleep, sat up in bed to see Lunt standing inside my room hold-ing a candle. He was wearing a nightshirt, and looked huge in the candlelight, his black beard falling intensely dark on the white stuff of his shirt. He came very quietly towards my bed, the candle throwing flickering shadows about the room. When he spoke it was in a voice low and subdued, almost a whisper. "Would you come," he asked, "only for half an hour—just for half an hour?" he repeated, staring at me as though he didn't know me. "I'm unhappy without somebody—very unhappy." Then he looked over his shoulder, held the candle high above his head, and stared piercingly at every part of the room.

'I could see that something had happened to him, that he had taken another step into the country of Fear—a step that had withdrawn him from me and from every other human being. He whispered: "When you come, tread softly; I don't want anyone to hear us."

'I did what I could. I got out of bed, put on my dressing-gown and slippers, and tried to persuade him to stay with me. The fire was almost dead, but I told him that we would build it up again, and that we would sit there and wait for the morning; but no, he repeated again and again: "It's better in my own room; we're safer there." "Safe from what?" I asked him, making him look at me. "Lunt, wake up! You're as though you were asleep. There's nothing to fear. We've nobody but ourselves. Stay here and let us talk, and have done with this nonsense." But he wouldn't answer; only drew me forward down the dark passage, and then turned into his room, beckoning me to follow. He got into bed and sat hunched up there, his hands holding his knees, staring at the door, and every once and again shivering with a little tremor. The only light in the room was that from the candle, now burning low, and the only sound was the purring whisper of the sea.

'It seemed to make little difference to him that I was there. He did not look at me, but only at the door, and when I spoke to him he did not answer me nor seem to hear what I had said. I sat down beside the bed and, in order to break the silence, talked on about anything, about nothing, and was dropping off, I think, into a confused doze, when I heard his voice breaking across mine. Very clearly and distinctly he said: "If I killed her, she deserved it; she was never a good wife to me, not from the first; she shouldn't have irritated me as she did—she knew what my temper was. She had a worse one than mine, though. She can't touch me; I'm as strong as she is."

'And it was then, as clearly as I can now remember, that his voice suddenly sank into a sort of gentle whisper, as though he were almost glad that his fears had been confirmed. He whispered: "She's there!" I cannot possibly describe to you how that whisper seemed to let Fear loose like water through my body. I could see nothing—the candle was flaming high in the last moments of its life—I could see nothing; but Lunt suddenly screamed, with a shrill cry like a tortured animal in agony: "Keep her off me, keep her away from me, keep her off—keep her off!"

'He caught me, his hands digging into my shoulders; then, with an awful effect of constricted muscles, as though rigor had caught and held him, his arms slowly fell away, he slipped back on to the bed as though someone were pushing him, his hands fell against the sheet, his whole body jerked with a convulsive effort, and then he rolled over. I saw nothing; only, quite distinctly, in my nostrils was that same fœtid odour that I had known on the preceding evening. I rushed to the door, opened it, shouted down the long passage again and again, and soon the old man came running. I sent him for the doctor, and then could not return to the room, but stood there listening, hearing nothing save the whisper of the sea, the loud ticking of the hall clock. I flung open the window at the end of the passage; the sea rushed in with its precipitant roar; some bells chimed the hour. Then at last, beating into myself more courage, I turned back towards the room....'

'Well?' I asked as Runciman paused. 'He was dead, of course?'

'Dead, the doctor afterwards said, of heart failure.'

'Well?' I asked again.

'That's all.' Runciman paused. 'I don't know whether you can even call it a ghost story. My idea of the old woman may have been all hallucination. I don't even know whether his wife was like that when she was alive. She may have been large and fat. Lunt died of an evil conscience.'

'Yes,' I said.

'The only thing,' Runciman added at last, after a long pause, 'is that on Lunt's body there were marks—on his neck especially, some on his chest—as of fingers pressing in, scratches and dull blue marks. He may, in his terror, have caught at his own throat....'

'Yes,' I said again.

'Anyway'—Runciman shivered—'I don't like Cornwall—beastly county. Queer things happen there—something in the air....'

'So, I've heard,' I answered.

Barbara Flint

1

Barbara Flint was a little girl, aged seven, who lived with her parents at No. 36 March Square. Her brother and sister, Master Anthony and Miss Mirabel Flint, were years and years older, so you must understand that she led rather a solitary life. She was a child with very pale flaxen hair, very pale blue eyes, very pale cheeks—she looked like a china doll who had been left by a careless mistress out in the rain. She was a very sensitive child, cried at the least provocation, very affectionate, too, and ready to imagine that people didn't like her.

Mr. Flint was a stout, elderly gentleman, whose favourite pursuit was to read the newspapers in his club, and to inveigh against the Liberals. He was pale and pasty and suffered from indigestion. Mrs. Flint was tall, thin and severe, and a great helper at St. Matthew's, the church round the corner. She gave up all her time to Church work and the care of the poor, and it wasn't perhaps her fault that the poor hated her. Between the Scylla of politics and the Charybdis of religion there was very little left of poor Barbara; she faded away under the care of an elderly governess who suffered from a perfect cascade of ill-fated love affairs; it seemed that gentlemen were always "playing with her feelings." But in all probability a too vivid imagination led her astray in this matter; at any rate, she cried so often during Barbara's lessons, that the title of the lesson-book, *Reading without Tears,* was sadly belied. It might be expected that, under these unfavourable circumstances, Barbara was growing into a depressed and melancholy childhood.

Barbara, happily, was saved by her imagination. Surely nothing quite like Barbara's imagination had ever been seen before, because it came to her, outside inheritance, outside environment, outside observation. She had it altogether, in spite of Flints past and present. But, perhaps, not altogether in spite of March Square. It would be difficult to say how deeply the fountain, the almond tree, the green, flat shining grass had stung her intuition; but stung it only, not created it—the thing was there from the beginning of all time. She talked, at first to nurses, servants, her mother, about the things that she knew; about her Friend who often came to see her, who was there so many times—there in the room with her when they couldn't catch a glimpse of Him; about the days and nights when she was away anywhere, up in the sky, out on the air, deep in the sea; about all the other experiences that she remembered but was now rapidly losing consciousness of. She talked, at first easily, naturally, and inviting, as it were, return confidences. Then, quite suddenly, she realised that she simply wasn't believed, that she was considered a wicked little girl "for making things up so," that there was no hope at all for her unless she abandoned her "lying ways."

The shock of this discovery flung her straight back upon herself; if they refused to believe these things, then there was nothing to be done. But for herself, their incredulity should not stop her. She became a very quiet little girl—what her nurse called "brooding." This incredulity of theirs drove them all instantly into a hostile camp, and the affection that she had been longing to lavish upon them must now be reserved for other and, she could not help feeling, wiser persons. This division of herself from the immediate world hurt her very much. From a very early age, indeed, we need reassurance as to the necessity for our existence. Barbara simply did not seem to be wanted.

But still worse: now that her belief in certain things had been challenged, she herself began to question them. Was it true, possibly, when a flaming sunset struck a sword across the Square and caught the fountain, slashing it into a million glittering fragments, that that was all that occurred? Such a thing had been for Barbara simply a door into her earlier world. See the fountain—well, you have been tested; you are still simple enough to go back into the real world. But was Barbara simple enough? She was seven; it is just about then that we begin, under the guard of nurses carefully chosen for us by our parents, to drop our simplicity. It must, of course, be so, or the world would be all dreamers, and then there would be no commerce.

Barbara knew nothing of commerce, but she did know that she was unhappy, that her dolls gave her no happiness, and that her Friend did not come now so often to see her. She was, I am afraid, in character a "Flopper." She must be affectionate, she must demand affection of others, and will they not give it her, then must they simulate it. The tragedy of it all was, perhaps, that Barbara had not herself that coloured vitality in her that would prepare other people to be fond of her. The world is divided between those who place affection about, now here, now there, and those whose souls lie, like drawers, unawares, but ready for the affection to be laid there.

Barbara could not "place" it about; she had neither optimism nor a sense of humour sufficient. But she wanted it—wanted it terribly. If she were not to be allowed to indulge her imagination, then must she, all the more, love someone with fervour: the two things were inter-dependent. She surveyed her world with an eye to this possible lov-ing. There was her governess, who had been with her for a year now, tearful, bony, using Barbara as a means and never as an end. Barbara did not love her, how could she? Moreover, there were other physical things: the lean, shining marble of Miss Letts's long fingers, the dry thinness of her hair, the way that the tip of her nose would be sud-denly red, and then, like a blown-out candle, dull white again.

Fingers and noses are not the only agents in the human affections, but they have most certainly something to do with them. Moreover, Miss Letts was too busily engaged with the survey of her relations with now this gentleman, now that, to pay much attention to Barbara. She dismissed her as "a queer little thing." There were in Miss Letts's world "queer things" and "things not queer." The division was patent to anybody.

Barbara's father and mother were also surveyed. But here Barbara was baffled by the determination on the part of both of them that she should talk, should think, should dream about all the things con-cerning which she could not talk, think nor dream. "How to grow up into a nice little girl," "How to pray to God," "How never to tell lies," "How to keep one's clothes clean"—these things did not interest Barbara in the least; but had she been given love with them she might have paid some attention. But a too rigidly defined politics, a too rig-idly defined religion, find love a poor, loose, sentimental thing—very rightly so, perhaps. Mrs. Flint was afraid that Barbara was a "silly little girl."

"I hope, Miss Letts, that she no longer talks about her silly fancies."

"She has said nothing to me in that respect for a considerable pe-riod, Mrs. Flint."

"All very young children have fancies, but such things are danger-ous when they grow older."

"I agree with you."

Nevertheless, the fountain continued to flash in the sun, and births, deaths, weddings, love and hate continued to play their parts in March Square.

2

Barbara, groping about in the desolation of having no one to grope with her, discovered that her Friend came now less frequently to see her. She was even beginning to wonder whether He had ever really come at all. She had perhaps imagined Him just as on occasion she would imagine her doll, Jane, the Queen of England, or her afternoon tea the most wonderful meal, with sausages, blackberry jam and chocolates. Young though she was, she was able to realise that this imagination of hers was *capable de tout*, and that everyone older than herself said that it was wicked; therefore, was her Friend, perhaps, wicked also.

And yet, if the dark curtains that veiled the nursery windows at night, if the glimmering shape of the picture-frames, if the square black sides of the doll's house were real, real also was the figure of her Friend, real His arousal in her of all the memories of the old days before she was Barbara Flint at all—real, too, His love, His care, His protection; as real, yes, as Miss Letts's bony figure. It was all very puzzling. But He did not come now as in the old days.

Barbara played very often in the garden in the middle of the Square, but because she was a timid little girl she did not make many friends. She knew many of the other children who played there, and sometimes she shared in their games; but her sensitive feelings were so easily hurt, she frequently retired in tears. Every day on going into the garden she looked about her, hoping that she would find before she left it again someone whom it would be possible to worship. She tried on several occasions to erect altars, but our English temperament is against public display, and she was misunderstood.

Then, quite suddenly, as though she had sprung out of the fountain, Mary Adams was there. Mary Adams was aged nine, and her difference from Barbara Flint was that, whereas Barbara craved for affection, she craved for attention: the two demands can be easily confused. Mary Adams was the only child of an aged philosopher, Mr. Adams, who, contrary to all that philosophy teaches, had married a young wife. The young wife, pleased that Mary was so unlike her father, made much of her, and Mary was delighted to be made much of. She was a little girl with flaxen hair, blue eyes, and a fine pink-and-white colouring. In a few years' time she will be so sure of the attention that her appearance is winning for her that she will make no effort to secure adherents, but just now she is not sufficiently confident—she must take trouble. She took trouble with Barbara.

Sitting neatly upon a seat, Mary watched rude little boys throw sidelong glances in her direction. Her long black legs were quivering with the perception of their interest, even though her eyes were haughtily indifferent. It was then that Barbara, with Miss Letts, an absent-minded companion, came and sat by her side. Barbara and Mary had met at a party—not quite on equal terms, because nine to seven is as sixty to thirty—but they had played hide-and-seek together, and had, by chance, hidden in the same cupboard.

The little boys had moved away, and Mary Adams's legs dropped, suddenly, their tension.

"I'm going to a party tonight," Mary said, with a studied indifference.

Miss Letts knew of Mary's parents, and that, socially, they were "all right"—a little more "all right," were we to be honest, than Mr. and Mrs. Flint. She said, therefore:

"Are you, dear? That will be nice for you."

Instantly Barbara was trembling with excitement. She knew that the remark had been made to her and not at all to Miss Letts. Barbara entered once again, and instantly, upon the field of the passions. Here she was fated by her temperament to be in all cases a miserable victim, because panic, whether she were accepted or rejected by the object of her devotion, reduced her to incoherent foolishness. She could only be foolish now, and, although her heart beat like a leaping animal inside her, allowed Miss Letts to carry on the conversation.

But Miss Letts's wandering eye hurt Mary's pride. She was not really interested in her, and once Mary had come to that conclusion about anyone, complete, utter oblivion enveloped them. She perceived, however, Barbara's agitation, and at that, flattered and appeased, she was amiable again. There followed between the two a strangled and disconnected conversation.

Mary began:

"I've got four dolls at home."

"Have you?" breathlessly from Barbara. By such slow accuracies as these are we conveyed, all our poor mortal days, from realism to romance, and with a shocking precipitance are we afterwards flung back, out of romance into realism, our natural home, again.

"Yes—four dolls I have. My mother will give me another if I ask her. Would your mother?"

"Yes," said Barbara, untruthfully.

"That's my governess. Miss Marsh, there, with the green hat, that is. I've had her two months."

"Yes," said Barbara, gazing with adoring eyes.

"She's going away next week. There's another coming. I can do sums, can you?"

"Yes," again from Barbara.

"I can do up to twice sixty-three. I'm nine. Miss Marsh says I'm clever."

"I'm seven," said Barbara.

"I could read when I was seven—long, long words. Can you read?"

At this moment there arrived the green-hatted Miss Marsh, a plump, optimistic person, to whom Miss Letts was gloomily patronising. Miss Letts always distrusted stoutness in another; it looked like deliberate insult. Mary Adams was conveyed away; Barbara was bereft of her glory.

But, rather, on that instant that Mary Adams vanished did she become glorified. Barbara had been too absurdly agitated to transform on to the mirror of her brain Mary's appearance.

In all the dim-coloured splendour of flame and mist was Mary now enwrapped, with every step that Barbara took towards her home did the splendour grow.

3

Then followed an invitation to tea from Mary's mother. Barbara, preparing for the event, suffered her hair to be brushed, choked with strange half-sweet, half-terrible suffocation that comes from anticipated glories: half-sweet because things will, at their worst, be wonderful; half-terrible because we know that they will not be so good as we hope.

Barbara, washed paler than ever, in a white frock with pink bows, was conducted by Miss Letts. She choked with terror in the strange hall, where she was received with great splendour by Mary. The schoolroom was large and fine and bright, finer far than Barbara's room, swamped by the waters of religion and politics. Barbara could only gulp and gulp, and feel still at her throat that half-sweet, half-terrible suffocation. Within her little body her heart, so huge and violent, was pounding.

"A very nice room indeed," said Miss Letts, more friendly now to the optimist because she was leaving in a day or two, and could not, therefore, at the moment be considered a success. Her failure balanced her plumpness.

Here, at any rate, was the beginning of a great friendship between Barbara Flint and Mary Adams. The character of Mary Adams was admittedly a difficult one to explore; her mother, a cloud of nurses and a company of governesses had been baffled completely by its dark caverns and recesses. One clue, beyond question, was selfishness; but this quality, by the very obviousness of it, may tempt us to believe that that is all. It may account, when we are displeased, for so much. It accounted for a great deal with Mary—but not all. She had, I believe, a quite genuine affection for Barbara, nothing very disturbing, that could rival the question as to whether she would receive a second helping of pudding or no, or whether she looked better in blue or pink.

Nevertheless, the affection was there. During several months she considered Barbara more than she had ever considered anyone in her life before. At that first tea-party she was aware, perhaps, that Barbara's proffered devotion was for complete and absolute self-sacrifice, something that her vanity would not often find to feed it. There was, too, no question of comparison between them.

Even when Barbara grew to be nine she would be a poor thing beside the lusty self-confidence of Mary Adams—and this was quite as it should be. All that Barbara wanted was someone upon whom she might pour her devotion, and one of the things that Mary wanted was someone who would spend it upon her. But there stirred, nevertheless, some breath of emotion across that stagnant little pool, Mary's heart. She was moved, perhaps, by pity for Barbara's amazing simplicities, moved also by curiosity as to how far Barbara's devotion to her would go, moved even by some sense of distrust of her own self-satisfaction. She did, indeed, admire anyone who could realise, as completely as did Barbara, the greatness of Mary Adams.

It may seem strange to us, and almost terrible, that a small child of seven can feel anything as devastating as this passion of Barbara. But Barbara was made to be swept by storms stronger than she could control, and Mary Adams was the first storm of her life. They spent now a great deal of their time together. Mrs. Adams, who was beginning to find Mary more than she could control, hailed the gentle Barbara with joy; she welcomed also perhaps a certain note of rather haughty protection which Mary seemed to be developing.

During the hours when Barbara was alone she thought of the

many things that she would say to her friend when they met, and then at the meeting could say nothing. Mary talked or she did not talk according to her mood, but she soon made it very plain that there was only one way of looking at everything inside and outside the earth, and that was Mary's way. Barbara had no affection, but a certain blind terror for God. It was precisely as though someone were standing with a hammer behind a tree and were waiting to hit you on the back of your head at the first opportunity. But God was not, on the whole, of much importance; her Friend was the great problem, and before many days were passed Mary was told all about Him.

"He used to come often and often. He'd be there just where you wanted Him—when the light was out or anything. And He *was* nice." Barbara sighed.

Mary stared at her, seeming, in the first full sweep of confidence, to be almost alarmed.

"You don't mean—?" She stopped, then cried, "Why, you silly, you believe in ghosts!"

"No, I don't," said Barbara, not far from tears.

"Yes, you do."

"No, I don't."

"Of course, you do, you silly."

"No, I don't. He—He's real."

"Well," said Mary, with a final toss of the head, "if you go seeing ghosts like that you can't have me for your friend, Barbara Flint—you can choose, that's all."

Barbara was aghast. Such a catastrophe had never been contemplated. Lose Mary? Sooner life itself. She resolved, sorrowfully, to say no more about her Friend. But here occurred a strange thing. It was as though Mary felt that over this one matter Barbara had eluded her; she returned to it again and again, always with contemptuous but inquisitive allusion.

"Did He come last night, Barbara?"

"No."

"P'r'aps He did, only you were asleep."

"No, He didn't."

"You don't believe He'll come ever anymore, do you? Now that I've said He isn't there really?"

"Yes, I do."

"Very well, then, I won't see you tomorrow—not at all—not all day—I won't."

These crises tore Barbara's spirit. Seven is not an age that can reason with life's difficulties, and Barbara had, in this business, no reasoning powers at all. She would die for Mary; she could not deny her Friend. What was she to do? And yet——just at this moment when, of all others, it was important that He should come to her and confirm His reality—He made no sign. Not only did He make no sign, but He seemed to withdraw, silently and surely, all his supports. Barbara discovered that the company of Mary Adams did in very truth make everything that was not sure and certain absurd and impossible. There was visible no longer, as there had been before, that country wherein anything was possible, where wonderful things had occurred and where wonderful things would surely occur again.

"You're pretending," said Mary Adams sharply when Barbara ventured some possibly extravagant version of some ordinary occurrence, or suggested that events, rich and wonderful, had occurred during the night. "Nonsense! "said Mary sharply.

She said "nonsense" as though it were the very foundation of her creed of life—as, indeed, to the end of her days, it was. What, then, was Barbara to do? Her Friend would not come although passionately she begged and begged and begged that He would. Mary Adams was there every day, sharp, and shining, and resolved, demanding the whole of Barbara Flint, body and soul—nothing was to be kept from her, nothing. What was Barbara Flint to do?

She denied her Friend, denied that earlier world, denied her dreams and her hopes. She cried a good deal, was very lonely in the dark. Mary Adams, as was her way, having won her victory, passed on to win another.

4

Mary began, now, to find Barbara rather tiresome. Having forced her to renounce her gods, she now despised her for so easy a renunciation. Every day did she force Barbara through her act of denial, and the Inquisition of Spain held, in all its records, nothing more cruel.

"Did He come last night?"

"No."

"He'll never come again, will He?"

"No."

"Wasn't it silly of you to make up stories like that?"

"Oh, Mary—yes."

"There aren't ghosts, nor fairies, nor giants, nor wizards, nor Santa

Claus?"

"No; but, Mary, p'r'aps—"

"No; there aren't. Say there aren't."

"There isn't."

Poor Barbara, even as she concluded this ceremony, clutching her doll close to her to give her comfort, could not refrain from a hurried glance over her shoulder. He *might* be—— But upon Mary this all began soon enough to pall. She liked some opposition. She liked to defeat people and trample on them and then be gracious. Barbara was a poor little thing. Moreover, Barbara's standard of morality and righteousness annoyed her. Barbara seemed to have no idea that there was anything in this confused world of ours except wrong and right. No dialectician, argue he ever so stoutly, could have persuaded Barbara that there was such a colour in the world's paint-box as grey. "It's bad to tell lies. It's bad to steal. It's bad to put your tongue out. It's good to be kind to poor people. It's good to say 'No' when you want more pudding but mustn't have it."

Barbara was no prig. She did not care the least little thing about these matters, nor did she ever mention them, but let a question of conduct arise, then was Barbara's way plain and clear. She did not always take it, but there it was. With Mary, how very different! She had, I am afraid, no sense of right and wrong at all, but only a coolly ironical perception of the things that her elders disliked and permitted. Very foolish and absurd, these elders. We have always before our eyes some generation that provokes our irony, the one before us, the one behind us, our own perhaps; for Mary Adams it would always be any generation that was not her own. Her business in life was to avoid unpleasantness, to extract the honey from every flower, but above all to be admired, praised, preferred.

At first with her pleasure at Barbara's adoration she had found, within herself, a truly alarming desire to be "good." It might, after all, be rather amusing to be, in strict reality, all the fine things that Barbara considered her. She endeavoured for a week or two to adjust herself to this point of view, to consider, however slightly, whether it were right or wrong to do something that she particularly wished to do.

But she found it very tiresome. The effort spoilt her temper, and no one seemed to notice any change. She might as well be bad as good were there no one present to perceive the difference. She gave it up, and, from that moment found that she suffered Barbara less gladly than before. Meanwhile, in Barbara also strange forces had been at work. She discovered that her imagination (making up stories) simply refused to stop, in spite of all the Mary Adamses in the world. Still would the almond tree and the fountain, the gold dust on the roofs of the houses when the sun was setting, the racing hurry of raindrops down the window-pane, the funny old woman with the red shawl who brought plants round in a wheelbarrow, start her story-telling.

Still could she not hold herself from fancying, at times, that her doll Jane was a queen, and that Miss Letts could make "spells" by the mere crook of her bony fingers. Worst of all, still she must think of her Friend, tell herself with an ache that He would never come back again, feel, sometimes, that she would give up Mary and all the rest of the world if He would only be beside her bed, as He used to be, talking to her, holding her hand. During these days, had there been anyone to observe her, she was a pathetic little figure, with her thin legs like black sticks, her saucer eyes that so readily filled with tears, her eager, half-apprehensive expression, the passionate clutch of the doll to her heart, and it is, after all, a painful business, this adoration— no human soul can live up to the heights of it, and, what is more, no human soul ought to.

As Mary grew tired of Barbara she allowed to slip from her many of the virtuous graces that had hitherto, for Barbara's benefit, adorned her. She lost her temper, was cruel simply for the pleasure that Barbara's ill-restrained agitation yielded her, but, even beyond this, squandered recklessly her reputation for virtue. Twice, before Barbara's very eyes, she told lies, and told them, too, with a real mastery of the craft— long practice and a natural disposition had brought her very near perfection. Barbara, her heart beating wildly, refused to understand; Mary could not be so. She held Jane to her breast more tightly than before. And the denials continued; twice a day now they were extorted from her—with every denial the ghost of her Friend stole more deeply into the mist. He was gone; He was gone; and what was left?

Very soon, and with unexpected suddenness, the crisis came.

Upon a day Barbara accompanied her mother to tea with Mrs. Adams. The ladies remained downstairs in the dull splendour of the drawing-room; Mary and Barbara were delivered to Miss Fortescue, the most recent guardian of Mary's life and prospects.

"She's simply awful. You needn't mind a word she says," Mary instructed her friend, and prepared then to behave accordingly. They had tea, and Mary did as she pleased. Miss Fortescue protested, scolded, was weak when she should have been strong, and said often, "Now,

Mary, there's a dear."

Barbara, the faint colour coming and going in her cheeks, watched. She watched Mary now with quite a fresh intention. She had begun her voyage of discovery: what was in Mary's head, *what* would she do next? What Mary did next was to propose, after tea, that they should travel through other parts of the house.

"We'll be back in a moment," Mary flung over her head to Miss Fortescue. They proceeded then through passages, peering into dark rooms, looking behind curtains, Barbara following behind her friend, who seemed to be moved by a rather aimless intention of finding something to do that she shouldn't. They finally arrived at Mrs. Adams's private and particular sitting-room, a place that may be said, in the main, to stand as a protest against the rule of the ancient philosopher, being all pink and flimsy and fragile with precious vases and two postimpressionist pictures (a green apple tree one, the other a brown woman), and lace cushions and blue bowls with rose leaves in them. Barbara had never been into this room before, nor had she ever in all her seven years seen anything so lovely.

"Mother says I'm never to come in here," announced Mary. "But I do—lots. Isn't it pretty?"

"P'r'haps we oughtn't—" began Barbara.

"Oh, yes, we ought," answered Mary scornfully. "Always you and your 'oughtn't.'"

She turned, and her shoulders brushed a low bracket that was close to the door. A large vase was at her feet, shattered into a thousand pieces. Even Mary's proud indifference was stirred by this catastrophe, and she was down on her knees in an instant, trying to pick up the pieces. Barbara stared, her eyes wide with horror.

"Oh, Mary!" she gasped.

"You might help instead of just standing there!"

Then the door opened and, like the avenging gods from Olympus, in came the two ladies, eagerly, with smiles.

"Now I must just show you—" began Mrs. Adams. Then the catastrophe was discovered—a moment's silence, then a cry from the poor lady: "Oh, my vase! It was priceless!" (It was not, but no matter.)

About Barbara the air clung so thick with catastrophe that it was from a very long way indeed that she heard Mary's voice:

"Barbara didn't mean—"

"Did you do this, Barbara?" her mother turned round upon her.

"You know, Mary, I've told you a thousand times that you're not to come in here!" This from Mrs. Adams, who was obviously very angry indeed.

Mary was on her feet now and, as she looked across at Barbara, there was in her glance a strange look, ironical, amused, inquisitive, even affectionate. "Well, mother, I knew we mustn't. But Barbara wanted to *look*, so I said we'd just *peep*, but that we weren't to touch anything, and then Barbara couldn't help it really, her shoulder just brushed the shelf—" And still as she looked there was in her eyes that strange irony: "Well, now you see me as I am—I'm bored by all this pretending. It's gone on long enough. Are you going to give me away?"

But Barbara could do nothing. Her whole world was there, like the Nankin vase, smashed about her feet, as it never, never would be again.

"So, you did this, Barbara?" Mrs. Flint said.

"Yes," said Barbara. Then she began to cry.

5

At home she was sent to bed. Her mother read her a chapter of the Gospel according to St. Matthew, and then left her; she lay there, sick with crying, her eyes stiff and red, wondering how she would ever get through the weeks and weeks of life that remained to her. She thought: "I'll never love anyone again. Mary took my Friend away—and then she wasn't there herself. There isn't anybody."

Then it suddenly occurred to her that she need never be put through the agony of her denials again, that she could believe what she liked, make up stories.

Her Friend would, of course, never come to see her anymore, but at least now she would be able to think about Him. She would be allowed to remember. Her brain was drowsy her eyes half-closed. Through the humming air something was coming; the dark curtains were parted the light of the late afternoon sun was faint yellow upon the opposite wall—there was a little breeze. Drowsily, drowsily, her drooping eyes felt the light, the stir of the air, the sense that someone was in the room.

She looked up; she gave a cry! He had come back! He had come back after all!

Major Wilbraham

I am quite aware that in giving you this story, just as I was told it, I shall incur the charge of downright and deliberate lying.

Especially I shall be told this by anyone who knew Wilbraham personally. Wilbraham was not, of course, his real name, but I think that there are certain people who will recognise him from the description of him. I do not know that it matters very much if they do. Wilbraham himself would certainly not mind did he know. (Does he know?) It was the thing, above all, that he wanted those last hours before he died: that I should pass on my conviction of the truth of what he told me to others. What he did not know was that I was not convinced. How could I be? But when the whole comfort of his last hours hung on the simple fact that I was, of course I pretended to the best of my poor ability. I would have done more than that to make him happy.

Most men are conscious at some time in their lives of having felt for a member of their own sex an emotion that is something more than simple companionship. It is a queer feeling quite unlike any other in life, distinctly romantic, and the more so, perhaps, for having no sex feeling in it.

Wilbraham roused just that feeling in me I remember, with the utmost distinctness, at my first meeting with him. It was just after the Boer War, and old Johnny Beaminster gave a dinner-party to some men pals of his at the Phoenix.

There were about fifteen of us, and Wilbraham was the only man present I'd never seen before. He was only a captain then, and neither so red-faced nor so stout as he afterwards became. He was pretty bulky, though, even then, and, with his sandy hair cropped close, his staring blue eyes, his toothbrush moustache, and sharp, alert movements, looked the typical traditional British officer.

There was nothing at all to distinguish him from a thousand other officers of his kind, and yet, from the moment I saw him, I had some especial and personal feeling about him. He was not in type at all the man to whom at that time I should have felt drawn, but the fact remains that I wanted to know him more than any other man in the room, and, although I only exchanged a few words with him that night, I thought of him for quite a long time afterwards.

It did not follow from this, as it ought to have done, that we became great friends. That we never were, although it was myself whom he sent for, three days before his death, to tell me his queer little story. It was then, at the very last, that he confided to me that he, too, had felt something at our first meeting 'different' from what one generally feels, that he had always wanted to turn our acquaintance into friendship and had been too shy. I also was shy—and so we missed one another, as I suppose, in this funny, constrained-traditional country of ours, thousands of people miss one another every day.

But although I did not see him very often, and was in no way intimate with him, I kept my ears open for any account of his doings. From one point of view—the club window outlook—he was a very usual figure, one of those stout, rubicund, jolly men, a good polo player, a good man in a house-party, genial-natured, and none-too-brilliantly brained, whom everyone liked and no one thought about. All this he was on one side of the report, but, on the other, there were certain stories that were something more than ordinary.

Wilbraham was obviously a sentimentalist and an enthusiast; there was the extraordinary case shortly after I first met him of his championship of X., a man who had been caught card-sharping and received a year's imprisonment for it. On X. leaving prison, Wilbraham championed and defended him, put him up for months in his rooms in Duke Street, walked as often as possible in his company down Piccadilly, and took him over to Paris. It says a great deal for Wilbraham's accepted normality, and his general popularity, that this championship of X. did him no harm. Some men, it is true, did murmur something about 'birds of a feather,' and one or two kind friends warned Wilbraham in the way kind friends have, and to them he simply said:

'If a feller's a pal he's a pal.'

There followed a year or two later the much more celebrated business of Lady C. I need not go into all that now, but here again Wilbraham constituted himself her defender, although she robbed, cheated and maligned him as she robbed, cheated and maligned everyone who was good to her. It was quite obvious that he was not in love with her;

the obviousness of it was one of the things in him that annoyed her. He simply felt, apparently, that she had been badly treated—the very last thing she had been—gave her any money he had, put his rooms at the disposal of herself and her friends, and, as I have said, championed her everywhere.

This affair did very nearly finish him socially and in his regiment. It was not so much that they minded his caring for Lady C.—after all, any man can be fooled by any woman—but it was Lady C.'s friends who made the whole thing so impossible. Well, that affair luckily came to an end just in time. Lady C. disappeared to Berlin, and was no more seen.

There were other cases, into which I need not go, when Wilbraham was seen in strange company, always championing somebody who was not worth the championing. He had no 'social tact,' and for them, at any rate, no moral sense. In himself he was the ordinary normal man about town; no prude, but straight as a man can be in his debts, his love affairs, his friendships, and his sport. Then came the war. He did brilliantly at Mons, was wounded twice, went out to Gallipoli, had a touch of Palestine, and returned to France again to share in Foch's final triumph.

No man can possibly have had more of the war than he had, and it is my own belief that he had just a little too much of it.

He had been always perhaps a little 'queer,' as we are most of us 'queer' somewhere, and the horrors of that horrible war undoubtedly affected him. Finally, he lost, just a week before the Armistice, one of his best friends, Ross McLean, a loss from which he certainly never recovered.

I have now, I think, brought together all the incidents that can throw any kind of light upon the final scene.

★★★★★★

In the middle of 1919 he retired from the army, and it was from this time to his death that I saw something of him. He went back to his old rooms at Horton's in Duke Street, and as I was living at that time in Marlborough Chambers in Jermyn Street, we were within easy reach of one another. The early part of 1920 was a 'queer time.' People had become, I imagine, pretty well accustomed to realising that those two wonderful hours of Armistice Day had not ushered in the millennium, any more than those first marvellous moments of the Russian revolution produced it.

Everyone has always hoped for the millennium, but the trouble since the days of Adam and Eve has always been that people have such different ideas as to what exactly that millennium shall be. The plain facts of the matter simply were that during 1919 and 1920 the world changed from a war of nations to a war of classes, that inevitable change that history has always shown follows on great wars.

As no one ever reads history, it was natural enough that there should be a great deal of disappointment, and a great deal of astonishment. Wilbraham, being a sentimentalist and an idealist, suffered more from this general disappointment than most people. He had had wonderful relations with the men under him throughout the war. He was never tired of recounting how marvellously they had behaved, what heroes they were, and that it was they who would pull the country together.

At the same time, he had a *naïve* horror of Bolshevism and anything unconstitutional, and he watched the transformation of his 'brave lads' into discontented and idle workmen with dismay and deep distress. He used sometimes to come round to my rooms and talk to me; he had the bewildered air of a man walking in his sleep.

During these months I came to love the man. The attraction that I had felt for him from the very first deeply underlay all my relations to him, but as I saw more of him, I found many very positive reasons for my liking. He was the simplest, bravest, purest, most loyal and most unselfish soul alive. He seemed to me to have no faults at all, unless it were a certain softness towards the wishes of those whom he loved. He could not bear to hurt anybody, but he never hesitated if some principle in which he believed was called in question.

He was the best human being I have ever known, or am ever likely to know.

Well, the crisis arrived with astonishing suddenness. About August 2nd or 3rd I went down to stay with some friends at the little fishing village of Rafiel in Glebeshire.

I saw him just before I left London, and he told me that he was going to stay in town for the first half of August; that he liked London in August, even though his club would be closed and Horton's delivered over to the painters.

I heard nothing about him for a fortnight, and then I received a most extraordinary letter from Box Hamilton, a fellow clubman of mine and of Wilbraham's. Had I heard, he said, that poor old Wilbraham had gone right off his 'knocker'? Nobody knew exactly what had happened, but suddenly one day at lunch-time Wilbraham had turned up at Grey's—the club to which our own club was a visitor during its cleaning—had harangued everyone about religion in the most extraordinary way, had burst out from there and started shouting in Piccadilly; had, after collecting a crowd, disappeared and not been seen until the next morning, when he had been found nearly killed after a hand-to-hand fight with the market men in Covent Garden.

It may be imagined how deeply this disturbed me, especially as I felt I was myself to blame. I had noticed that Wilbraham was ill when I had seen him in London, and I should either have persuaded him to come with me to Glebeshire, or stayed with him in London. I was just about to pack up and go to town when I received a letter from a doctor in a nursing-home in South Audley Street, saying that a certain Major Wilbraham was in the home, dying, and asking persistently for myself. I took a motor to Drymouth, and was in London by five o'clock.

★★★★★★

I found the South Audley Street nursing-home, and was at once surrounded with the hush, the shaded rooms, the scents of medicine and flowers, and some undefinable cleanliness that belongs to those places.

I waited in a little room, the walls decorated with sporting prints, the green baize centre table laden with volumes of *Punch* and the *Tatler*. Wilbraham's doctor came in to see me, a dapper, smart little man, efficient and impersonal. He told me that Wilbraham had at most only twenty-four hours to live, that his brain was quite clear, and that he was suffering very little pain, that he had been brutally kicked in the stomach by some man in the Covent Garden crowd, and had there received the internal injuries from which he was now dying.

'His brain is quite clear,' the doctor said. 'Let him talk. It can do him no harm. Nothing can save him. His head is full of queer fancies; he wants everyone to listen to him. He's worrying because there's some message he wants to send—he wants to give it to you.'

When I saw Wilbraham, he was so little changed that I felt no shock. Indeed, the most striking change in him was the almost exultant happiness in his voice and eyes.

It is true that after talking to him a little I knew that he was dying. He had that strange peace and tranquillity of mind that one saw so often with dying men in the war.

I will try to give an exact account of Wilbraham's narrative; nothing else is of importance in this little story but that narrative. I can make no comment. I have no wish to do so. I only want to pass it on as he begged me to do.

'If you don't believe me,' he said, 'give other people the chance of doing so. I know that I am dying. I want as many men and women to have a chance of judging this as is humanly possible. I swear to you that I am telling the truth, and the exact truth in every detail.'

I began my account by saying that I was not convinced.

How could I be convinced?

At the same time, I have none of those explanations with which people are so generously forthcoming on these occasions. I can only say that I do not think Wilbraham was insane, nor drunk, nor asleep. Nor do I believe that someone played a practical joke.

Whether Wilbraham was insane between the hours when his visitor left him and his entrance into the nursing-home I must leave to my readers. I myself think he was not.

After all, everything depends upon the relative importance that we place upon ambitions, possessions, emotions—ideas.

Something then suddenly became of so desperate an importance to Wilbraham that nothing else at all mattered. He wanted everyone else to see the importance of it as he did. That is all.

★★★★★★

It had been a hot and oppressive day; London had seemed torrid and uncomfortable. The mere fact that Oxford Street was 'up' annoyed him. After a slight meal in his flat he went to the promenade concert at Queen's Hall. It was the second night of the season—Monday night—Wagner night.

He had heard no Wagner since August 1914, and was anxious to discover the effect that hearing it again would have upon him. The effect was disappointing.

The *Meistersinger* had always been a great opera for him. The third act music that the orchestra gave to him didn't touch him anywhere. He also discovered that six years' abstinence had not enraptured him any more deeply with the rushing fiddles in the *Tannhäuser* overture, nor with the spinning music in the *Flying Dutchman*. Then came suddenly the prelude to the third act of *Tristan*. That caught him, the peace and tranquillity that he needed lapped him round, he was fully satisfied and could have listened for another hour—a little strange, he told me, because the first half of the third act had always bored him with Tristan's eternal dying. He got up and went away, not caring to stay and listen to the efforts of an inadequate contralto to over-scream the orchestra in the last agonies of *Götterdämmerung*.

He walked home down Regent Street, the quiet melancholy of the pipe music accompanying him, pleasing him, and tranquillising him. As he reached his flat ten o'clock struck from St. James's Church. He asked the porter whether anyone had wanted him during his absence—whether anyone was waiting for him now. (Some friend has told him that he might come up and use his spare room one night that week.) No, no one had been. There was no one there waiting.

Great was his surprise, therefore, when opening the door of his flat he found someone standing there, one hand resting on the table. His face turned towards the open door. Stronger, however, than Wilbraham's surprise was his immediate conviction that he knew his visitor well, and this was curious, because the face was undoubtedly strange to him.

'I beg your pardon,' Wilbraham said, hesitating.

'I wanted to see you,' the stranger said, smiling.

When Wilbraham was telling me this part of his story he seemed to be enveloped—'enveloped' is the word that best conveys my own experience of him—by some quite radiant happiness; he smiled at me confidentially as though he were telling me something that I had experienced with him, and that must give me the same happiness that it gave him.

'Ought I to have expected—ought I to have known?' he stammered.

'No, you couldn't have known,' the stranger answered. 'You're not late. I knew when you would come.'

Wilbraham told me that during these moments he was surrendering himself to an emotion of intimacy and companionship that was the most wonderful thing that he had ever known. It was that intimacy and companionship, he told me, for which all his days he had been searching. It was the one thing that life never seemed to give; even in the greatest love, the deepest friendship, there was that seed of loneliness hidden. He had never found it in man or woman.

Now it was so wonderful that the first thing that he said was:

'And now you're going to stay, aren't you? You won't go away at once?'

'Of course, I'll stay,' he answered, 'if you want me.'

His guest was dressed in some dark suit; there was nothing about him in any way odd or unusual. His face thin and pale. His smile kindly.

His English was without accent. His voice was soft and very melodious.

But Wilbraham could notice nothing but his eyes; they were the most beautiful, tender, gentle eyes that he had ever seen in any human being.

They sat down. Wilbraham's overwhelming fear was lest his guest should leave him. They began to talk, and Wilbraham took it at once as accepted that his friend knew all about him—everything.

He found himself eagerly plunging into details of scenes, episodes that he had long put behind him—put behind him for shame, perhaps, or for regret or for sorrow. He knew at once that there was nothing that he need veil nor hide—nothing. He had no sense that he must consider susceptibilities or avoid self-confession that was humiliating.

But he did find, as he talked on, a sense of shame from another side creep towards him and begin to enclose him. Shame at the smallness, meanness, emptiness of the things that he declared.

He had had always behind his mistakes and sins a sense that he was a rather unusual, interesting person; if only his friends knew everything about him they would be surprised at the remarkable man that he really was. Now it was exactly the opposite sense that came over him. In the gold-rimmed mirror that was over his mantelpiece he saw himself diminishing, diminishing, diminishing. First himself, large, red-faced, smiling, rotund, lying back in his chair: then the face shrivelling, the limbs shortening, then the face small and peaked, the hands and legs little and mean, then the chair enormous about and around the little trembling animal cowering against the cushion.

He sprang up.

'No, no! I can't tell you any more—and you've known it all so long. I am mean, small, nothing. I have not even great ambition—nothing.'

His guest stood up and put his hand on his shoulder. They talked, standing side by side, and he said some things that belonged to Wilbraham alone, that he would not tell me.

Wilbraham asked him why he had come—and to him.

'I will come now to a few of my friends,' he said. 'First one and then another. Many people have forgotten me behind my words. They have built up such a mountain over me with the doctrines they have attributed to me, the things that they say that I did. I am not really,' he said, laughing, his hand on Wilbraham's shoulder, 'so dull and gloomy and melancholy as they have made me. I loved life; I loved men; I loved laughter and games and the open air. All things that they have forgotten. So, from now I shall come back to one or two. I am lonely when they see me so solemnly.'

Another thing he said: 'They are making life complicated now. To lead a good life, to be happy, to manage the world, only the simplest things are needed—love, unselfishness, tolerance.'

'Can I go with you and be with you always?' Wilbraham asked.

'Do you really want that?' he said.

'Yes,' said Wilbraham, bowing his head.

'Then you shall come and never leave me again. In three days from now.'

Then he kissed Wilbraham on the forehead and went away.

I think that Wilbraham himself became conscious as he told me this part of his story of the difference between the seen and remembered figure and the foolish, inadequate reported words. Even now, as I repeat a little of what Wilbraham said, I feel the virtue and power slipping away. But on that day when I sat beside Wilbraham's bed the conviction in his voice and eyes held me so that, although my reason kept me back, my heart told me that he had been in contact with some power that was a stronger force than anything that I myself had ever known.

But I have determined to make no personal comment on this story. I am here simply as a narrator of fact.

Wilbraham told me that after his guest left him he sat there for some time in a dream. Then he sat up, startled as though some voice, calling, had wakened him, with an impulse that was like a fire suddenly blazing up and lighting the dark places of his brain. I imagine that all Wilbraham's impulses in the past, chivalrous, idealistic, foolish, had been of that kind—sudden, of an almost ferocious energy and determination, blind to all consequences. He must go out at once and tell everyone of what had happened to him.

I once read a story somewhere about some town that was expecting a great visitor. Everything was ready, the banners hanging, the music prepared, the crowds waiting in the street.

A man who had once been for some years at the court of the expected visitor, saw him enter the city, sombrely clad, on foot. Meanwhile, his chamberlain entered the town in full panoply with the trumpets blowing and many riders in attendance. The man who knew the real king ran to everyone telling the truth, but they laughed at him and refused to listen. And the real king departed quietly as he had come.

It was, I suppose, an influence of this kind that drove Wilbraham now.

What followed might, I think, have been to some extent averted, had his appearance been different. London is a home of madmen, and casually permits any lunacy, so that public peace is not endangered. Had poor Wilbraham looked a fanatic, with pale face, long hair, ragged clothes, much would have been forgiven him, but for a staid, middle-aged gentleman, well-dressed, well-groomed, what could be supposed but insanity, and insanity of a very ludicrous kind?

He put on his coat and went out. From this moment his account was confused. His mind, as he spoke to me, kept returning to that visitor. What happened after his guest's departure was vague and un-certain to him, largely because it was unimportant. He does not know what time it was when he went out, but I gather it must have been about midnight. There were still people in Piccadilly.

Somewhere near the Berkeley Hotel he stopped a gentleman and a lady. He spoke, I am sure, so politely that the man he addressed must have supposed that he was asking for a match, or an address, or some-thing of the kind. Wilbraham told me that very quietly he asked the gentleman whether he might speak to him for a moment, that he had something very important to say; that he would not, as a rule, dream of interfering in any man's private affairs, but that the importance of his communication outweighed all ordinary conventions; that he expected that the gentleman had hitherto, as had been his own case, felt much doubt about religious questions, but that now all doubt was once and for ever over, that——

I expect that at that fatal word 'religious' the gentleman started as though he had been stung by a snake, felt that this mild-looking man was a dangerous lunatic and tried to move away. It was the lady with him, so far as I can discover, who cried out, 'Oh, poor man, he's ill!' and wanted at once to do something for him.

By this time a crowd was beginning to collect, and as the crowd closed around the central figures more people gathered upon the out-skirts and, peering through, wondered what had happened, whether there was an accident, whether it was a 'drunk,' whether there had been a quarrel, and so on.

Wilbraham, I fancy, began to address them all, telling them his great news, begging them with a desperate urgency to believe him. Some laughed, some stared in wide-eyed wonder, the crowd was in-creasing, and then, of course, the inevitable policeman, with his 'move on, please,' appeared.

How deeply I regret that Wilbraham was not there and then arrested. He would be alive and with us now if that had been done. But the policeman hesitated, I suppose, to arrest anyone as obviously a gentleman as Wilbraham, a man, too, as he soon perceived, who was perfectly sober, even though he was not in his right mind.

Wilbraham was surprised at the policeman's interference. He said that the last thing that he wished to do was to create any disturbance, but that he could not bear to let all these people go to their beds without giving them a chance of realising first that everything was now altered, that he had had the most wonderful news.

The crowd was dispersed, and Wilbraham found himself walking alone with the policeman beside the Green Park.

He must have been a very nice policeman, because, before Wilbraham's death, he called at the nursing-home and was very anxious to know how the poor gentleman was getting on.

He allowed Wilbraham to talk to him, and then did all he could to persuade him to walk home and go to bed. He offered to get him a taxi. Wilbraham thanked him, said he would do so himself, and bade him goodnight, and the policeman, seeing that Wilbraham was perfectly composed and sober, left him.

After that the narrative is more confused. Wilbraham apparently walked down Knightsbridge and arrived at last somewhere near the Albert Hall. He must have spoken to a number of different people. One man, a politician apparently, was with him for a considerable time, but only because he was so anxious to emphasise his own views about the government. Another was a journalist, who continued with him for a while because he scented a story for his newspaper. Some people may remember that there was a garbled paragraph about a 'Religious Army Officer' in the *Daily Record*.

He stayed at a cabman's shelter for a time and drank a cup of coffee and told the little gathering there his news. They took it very calmly. They had met so many queer things in their time that nothing seemed odd to them.

His account becomes clearer again when he found himself a little before dawn in the park and in the company of a woman of the town and a drunken, broken-down pugilist. I saw both these persons afterwards and had some talk with them. The pugilist had only the vaguest sense of what had happened. Wilbraham was a 'proper old bird,' and had given him half-a-crown to get his breakfast with. They had all slept together under a tree, and he had made some rather voluble protests because the other two would talk so continuously and prevented his sleeping. It was a warm night and the sun had come up behind the tree 'surprisin' quick.'

The woman was another story. She was quiet and reserved, dressed in black with a neat little black hat with a green feather in it. She had yellow, fluffy hair, and bright, childish, blue eyes, and a simple, innocent expression. She spoke very softly and almost in a whisper. She spoke of her life quite calmly as though she had been a governess or a waitress at a tea-shop. So far as I could discover, she could see nothing odd in Wilbraham, nor in anything that he had said. She was the one person in all the world who had understood him completely and found nothing out of the way in his talk. Strange when you come to think of it. The one person in the world.

She had liked him at once, she said. 'I could see that he was kind,' she added earnestly, as though to her that was the most important thing in all the world. No, his talk had not seemed odd to her. She had believed every word that he had said. Why not? You could not look at him and not believe what he said.

Of course, it was true. And why not? She had known lots of things funnier than that in her sordid life. What was there against it? She had always thought that there was something in what the parsons said, and now she knew it. It had been a great help to her, what the gentleman had told her. Yes, and he had gone to sleep with his head in her lap—and she had stayed awake all night thinking—and he had woken up just in time to see the sunrise. Some sunrise that was, too!

That was a curious little fact, that all three of them, even the battered pugilist, should have been so deeply struck by that sunrise. Wilbraham on the last day of his life, when he hovered between consciousness and unconsciousness, kept recalling it as though it had been a vision.

'The sun—and the trees suddenly green and bright like glittering swords—and the sky pale like ivory. See, now the sun is rushing up, faster than ever, to take us with him—up, up, leaving the trees like green clouds beneath us—far, far beneath us——'

The woman said it was the finest sunrise she had ever seen; and, at once, when she saw it, she began to think of a policeman. He'd be moving them on, naturally, and what would he say when he found her there with a gentleman of the highest class? Say that she had been robbing him, of course. She wanted to move away, but he insisted on going with her, and they woke up the pugilist, and the three of them moved down the park.

He talked to her all the time about his plans. He was looking dishevelled now, and unshaven and dirty. She suggested that he should go back to his flat. No, he wished to waste no time. Who knew how long he had got? It might be only a day or two. He would go to Covent Garden and talk to the men there.

★★★★★★

She was confused as to what happened after that. When they got to the market, the carts were coming in and the men were very busy.

She saw the gentleman speak to one of them very earnestly, but he was very busy and pushed him aside. He spoke to another, who told him to clear out.

Then he jumped on to a box, and almost the last sight she had of him was his standing there in his soiled clothes, a streak of mud on his face, his arms outstretched and crying: 'It's true! It's true! Stop just a moment! You must hear me!'

Someone pushed him off the box. The pugilist rushed in then, cursing them and saying that the man was a gentleman, and had given him half-a-crown, and then some hulking great fellow fought the pugilist and there was a regular *mêlée*. Wilbraham was in the middle of them, was knocked down and trampled upon. No one meant to hurt him, I think. They all seemed very sorry afterwards.

He died two days after being brought into the nursing-home. He was very happy just before he died, pressed my hand, and asked me to look after the girl.

'Isn't it wonderful,' were his last words to me, 'that it should be true after all?'

★★★★★★

As to Truth, who knows? Truth is a large order. This is true as far as Wilbraham goes, every word of it. Beyond that? Well, it must be jolly to be so happy as Wilbraham was.

Field with Five Trees

I was asked not long ago, at one of those dinner-parties where people ask such questions, to describe for my fellow-guests the oddest and queerest experience of my life. When one looks back, one discovers so many queer experiences, and then at the same time one realises that most of them refuse not only description but analysis—so I suppose with this one that I am about to relate.

I went to keep an appointment—five trees barred the way, and that was all there was to it. You can believe it or not, as you please.

It happened years and years ago before the war. I am now between sixty and seventy years of age, a widower with two grown-up children, on the whole content, although I have achieved so little—on the whole tranquil, even in this frantically disturbed world. It wasn't so disturbed then.

I had been married for five years. I had no children. I was a writer of sorts, and lived in a little stone cottage halfway up the hill from the village of Grange on Derwentwater in Cumberland, where I still live.

One of the important elements of this story, if it is to be true at all, is that I shall be frank about Mary Ellen, my wife. Poor Mary! She has been dead for fifteen years, but still keeps me company, as those one has truly loved always do, however long their bodies have been dust.

I think if Mary were to appear here now and give you an account of herself as she saw herself, she would agree very much with my estimate of her, except that she never knew as I did, how grandly unselfish, how sweetly forgiving, how beautifully maternal she was. She was above all things else, long before she had any children of her own, a mother. She mothered me, who badly needed it, with a goodness, a sense of humour, and a tolerance that I've never known any other human being to equal. I loved her and she loved me. But there came a time, as there comes in every marriage, when we were dissatisfied, fools that we were. Yet she loved me dearly—especially the companionship that we had. She was a wonderful companion. She had a grand, even a splendid, sense of enjoyment. She loved little things. She was perfectly content on our small income—perfectly happy to be there in the country alone with me from one end of the year to the other. The only thing that she wanted that she hadn't got was children.

It was just a year after this strange adventure that we had our first child. We had been married, as I've said, five years—and suddenly everything went wrong. That is the queerest thing about any relationship between two human beings, that for no reason at all everything suddenly moves out of perspective. Little personal tricks that have meant nothing for years are in a moment exasperating.

Mary had, I remember, a habit of leaving the room without shutting the door. And contrariwise, she would enter a room with a rush, banging the door behind her. Often, she would look untidy; her soft, brown hair, which I had once thought the most beautiful thing in the world, would tumble about her forehead. She was not very clever about her clothes. She was strong, robust, rosy-faced, bright-eyed, clean like an apple. Sometimes, when she was happy, she would talk very loudly and with great excitement.

I, on the other hand, in those days took myself rather grimly. I was determined to become a great writer, a thing, God forgive me, that I have never managed to be. I was earning a fair income at that time with my novels and stories, but I thought that I had real genius and that one day all the world would know it. Mary, I can now see on looking back, knew very well that genius I had not and would never have. Perhaps I detected, beneath her laughing praise and encouragement, this sense of disappointment. I was at that time meticulous in my habits. I liked everything to be very neat and careful about me. In fact, I took myself altogether with an absurd seriousness. I was immature for my years and she knew it. I was always a boy to her, to the very end. Perhaps that also, without my knowing it, irritated me.

We had, however, many things in common. We were, on the whole, amazingly happy. One joy that we deeply shared was our love for this especial country. I have no wish to employ pages of description in the manner of Mr. Fitz, the famous novelist, or Mrs. Grundy, the writer about gardens, but it is important to my little story that should make it clear why Mary and I were happier here on this exact spot of ground than anywhere else in the world.

It wasn't that I didn't know other places. I've experienced the long, purple nights of Arizona—the lovely, benignant glow of the Russian white night—the tawny, boastful pride of the Pyrenees—the lakes and blossoms of Japan—the flowered valleys of Cashmere.

I know that this small square of Cumbrian and Westmorland ground can seem like a mud patch on a wet day, like a garish coloured picture postcard on a sunny afternoon in August, can shrivel up and disappear and disappoint—do all the things that its detractors charge against it. But its beauty, when it chooses to be beautiful, no other place in the world can boast of.

This country was, in effect, the one thing that at this time Mary and I shared best with one another. Everything else began to have an edge—an edge of suspicion, mistrust and danger. But at no time from the first to last did we lose our companionship in this country—and I had almost forgotten to mention the sign and seal of the whole affair, namely, the field with the five trees.

I can see it now as I look from my library window, although it is closest and best visible from the windows of the bedroom Mary and I shared for so many years, and that I still inhabit. It is a field above Lodore on the way to Watendlath, formed like a half-moon. Its grass is, under sunlight, of the intensest green. The five trees that edge the ground are so alike that they resemble the brother Volsungs in Morris's *Sigurd*, except that they are not so tall as those splendid heroes were.

I remember saying to Mary when we first came to the cottage, that this field had eyes—or rather it was she, I think, who said that to me. 'We will never,' she said, 'be able to do anything that we are ashamed of, because that field will always know it. It is, I am sure, looking after us.'

In any case, it became one of the great joys of our daily life, to awaken in the morning and see first thing that field and those trees, so beautiful, quiet, permanent and strong. We, both of us, clung to it the more when our troubles began.

These troubles were at first all on my side. Which of us does not know the times when we are irritable without reason—when shame at ourselves makes us yet more irritable—and when we strike at the persons we love most because, I suppose, they will endure our tempers the most patiently? At first, I thought I was ill—that it was my liver or indigestion. Then I thought it was because my work was going badly, and here I began to complain bitterly of Mary. Whatever she said about it, my work was wrong.

Then examining myself and at heart bitterly ashamed of my unreason, I decided that I was still a young man—and was I, because I had married a good English woman, to spend the rest of my days as a kind of hermit? And one dreadful evening I broke out with all this, saying so much more than I really meant, reproaching her most unfairly for things that she had never done, accusing her of being what she was not. That evening I desperately hurt her pride. She was so seldom angry, never sulky, and very, very hard to offend. But that evening I offended her. She said very little—only at the end, quietly, 'I'm sorry. I see that you should have married someone quite different. But I can't change, however much you might wish it. I'm myself.' And she went out of the room.

It was after this that Mary made her great mistake. She invited her mother to stay with us. I don't know—I shall never know—whether she did this in a spirit of feminine revenge or whether it was simply that she thought the old lady would give her some companionship at a time when she must have been desperately lonely. Indeed, as I learned afterward, she was far more lonely and unhappy than I knew. I would say in passing that we never allow sufficiently for the loneliness of those near to us. We are aware often enough of our own loneliness and cry out bitterly against it, but we think that we are exceptional creatures in this.

Mary knew well enough that I detested her mother, Mrs. Millicent. She knew, too, that Mrs. Millicent cordially disliked me.

Physically she was unpleasant to me because she had bobbed her hair, painted her cheeks, wore dresses too young for her, and was altogether, I thought, a silly, tiresome, scandal-mongering old horror. And I did her a great injustice, as one always does when one dislikes people too much. She was courageous, had fine qualities of independence, adored Mary, and made a brave show of what life remained to her.

She thought me idle, lazy, spoiled, and altogether unworthy of her daughter. Her hatred of Cumberland was almost fanatical.

She was a sharp old lady and very soon discovered something was wrong between us.

When mothers discover that their beloved daughters are unhappy and that sons-in-law whom they greatly dislike are responsible, they have only one ambition in life—to punish the sons-in-law! And my mother-in-law wished not only to punish me, but also Cumberland, the English countryside, and everything rustic. She made, at once, my field with the five trees a symbol of her attack.

'I really believe, Walter,' she would say, 'that you could gladly sit all day and gaze at that silly field. Why don't you buy it if you are so fond of it?'

I have no doubt but that she also attacked Mary and tried to drag her secret from her. But there was no secret. We were moving in the dark—away, away, and knew no reason why.

One night I caught her to me and said to her, 'Mary, Mary, what is it?'

'I don't know—I don't know,' she sobbed. 'You don't love me anymore.'

'I do—I do,' I answered her. But as I said it I thought that I did not. I lay there, listening to the rain, and longed to escape, not only from Mary, perhaps, indeed not from Mary at all, but chiefly from myself. I think that this was the first time in my life when, poor defenceless egoist that I was, I began to wonder whether I was worth anyone's bother. But at least it was a step in the right direction! Love acts always independently of lovers. Sometimes it moves with them. Then, with a shrug of its beautiful shoulders, it moves away. 'Catch me if you can,' Love cries, and there is no way to recapture its company save to wait and be patient. But what lover ever was patient?

And then the country deserted us. After all, if you worship a place, it demands, I suppose, on your part, a certain fineness of conduct.

But we did not love the rain at that particular crisis in our lives, and oh! how old Mrs. Millicent hated it! I am sure that she thought it of my providing.

Then, as is always the way when the circumstances are ready for it, a quarrel emphasised the breach and made it appear intolerable.

Breakfast is a dangerous meal, as many writers before me have observed. It was especially dangerous for Mrs. Millicent, for she was an old lady who should never meet her fellows before midday. But there she was, as fresh as her paint and powder could make her, drinking her coffee, and thinking of her enforced, unhappy rusticity. For many a day, Mary and I each read our paper at breakfast and threw to one another little excitements from China or the latest gossip from London. Mrs. Millicent did not read a paper and, therefore, quite naturally hated that others should do so. On this especial morning I glanced at the pictures of my newspaper and then stared across at my beloved field, just now almost fraudulently green, with the five trees guarding it.

'Well,' said Mrs. Millicent, 'I've always hated that field—but at least I owe it something. It's made Walter polite at breakfast.'

And then I lost my temper. All the misery of the last weeks came out in that moment. I told the old lady all that I thought of her, all that I had ever thought of her. I blamed her for all the trouble between Mary and me. I said that I could not work while she was in the house. I said—oh, what matters now, after all these years, the things that I said!

Mrs. Millicent rose from her seat and said, 'Enough! Mary, I leave this house.'

And Mary, rising also, said, 'Mother, if you go I go too.'

And the field looked across at me and veiled its green with shadow and once again the rain began to fall. Of course, the trouble was for the moment calmed. Later in the day I apologised.

That night Mary said, 'Walter, what has come to you? What is it? Tell me and I will help. I must help or we're lost—both of us.' Which sounds melodramatic for Mary, but the word 'lost' was true. We were, indeed, close to some fatal and irreparable separation.

On the following day, so pat that it seemed as though fate were taking a maliciously personal interest in my small affairs, I met a lady. Here, even after all these years, I write with hesitation. Pearl Richardson is dead. I've not seen her for many, many years. I feel now that I never knew her, never had any real contact with her, that she was a shadow from a world filled with shadows, and yet at this moment as I sit here, she is more vivid and actual to me than men who have been my friends for a lifetime—more vivid to me than any woman I've ever known, except Mary.

★★★★★★

I was in Keswick, miserable, without plan or purpose. It had been a wet morning, but the sun had come out, and the hills, as they so often are after rain, were sharp and brilliant as though they had received an extra coat of paint. All the little town was gleaming and glittering. In the market square where I was standing, the light was almost blinding. Into this light stepped a young woman.

I'd been wondering what I would do. While I was hesitating, the girl passed me. She was wearing, as I so vividly remember, a dress of bright green which ill-suited her pale face with the light, fair eyebrows. Just after she passed me she turned and looked at me. It was a look of quiet and considering investigation. She stood there looking at me and then came toward me smiling.

'Could you tell me,' she asked, 'where I can find the Keswick Art Shop?'

'Oh, yes,' I answered. 'It's straight along in front of you—over the little bridge and you'll find it on the left.'

And as I spoke, it seemed to me that thereafter I would move like a man in a dream. I put it in that way, because I was still pausing on the border of that dangerous country. A moment's chance remained to me of turning around and walking away, and I knew with absolute certainty that if I did not walk away I would be a free agent no longer. I've never felt that with any other man or woman before or since. But I suppose on that particular day I was acutely unhappy, very lonely, with that kind of hurt pride and selfish resentment that comes from not getting one's own way.

She was, and it seems very odd to me now looking back, the exact opposite of Mary physically. She was pale, with rather weak grey eyes, with no cheerfulness, no sense of well-being about her at all. But my heart was thumping and I even stammered a little as I said, 'If you will allow me, I'm going that way and I'll show you where it is.'

'Thank you very much,' she said, and she spoke as though it were no new thing for her to be escorted by a stranger.

As we walked along we said very little to each other, but by the time that we had reached the bridge we had come to that sort of mutual agreement which strangers, who both want the same thing and want it badly, generally discover. We stood on the bridge before moving on, looking down at the little stream sparkling in the sunlight. She told me something about herself. She said that she was staying at the Station Hotel with a girl friend—that she'd never been in Cumberland before—that it had rained ever since their arrival, and that this was the first bit of sunshine that she had had—and as she said that, she looked at me.

'You are so bored, I suppose,' I said, 'that you'll be leaving early tomorrow.'

'Oh, no, I'm not,' she answered. 'Gracie, my friend, is. She can't stand the place, but I like it. It's grand when it rains.'

'Oh, then,' I said, 'this is the country for you.'

'Yes, it is,' she said. 'I don't know why I never came here before.' Then she looked at me and said abruptly, 'You live here? Are you married?'

I said that I did live here and that I was married.

'That's a pity,' she said, 'your being married, I mean.'

'Why?' I asked her.

'Oh, because we could have seen a bit of each other if you hadn't been,' she answered.

'We can, anyway,' I replied.

I remember that little conversation as though the words are being spoken now in this room in front of me by two complete strangers whom I am coldly observing. I remember that I thought that I didn't like her, and that I should like her less the more I saw of her. I remember, too, a funny fancy that I had that her green dress was like the green of my field in the sun. Yes, I remember that I didn't like her, and that I wanted there and then to take her in my arms and cover her face with kisses. She was so different from anything that I'd known for so long that she seemed to me exactly what I desperately needed.

And I suppose, too, in the low, dark cellars of my mind, there was the thought that I would teach Mary a lesson, and above all, show that nasty old woman, her mother, that there were other things in the world. I was certainly not the first man, nor the last, whom Miss Pearl Richardson tried to devour. In any case, whatever her purpose was, we succeeded in those few minutes in establishing a relationship. Before I left her, I had promised to give her dinner in Keswick the following evening.

I was no less unhappy when I went back that afternoon, but I was almost wildly excited. Why? I'm afraid I cannot say. I've always thought that love, in spite of modern cynicism, is the finest thing in the world. Besides, at this particular moment, although I did not then know it, I loved Mary more deeply than I had ever loved her.

Within a very few hours, Mary discovered that I had changed, and then, as she told me afterward, she began to be very frightened.

'It was that afternoon,' she said many months later, 'that I thought for the first time that I might really be going to lose you. Up to then I'd known something was very wrong, but I'd been sure that nothing could truly separate us. But as soon as you came in that day, and with a kind of forced geniality greeted us and talked with an empty friendliness about anything or nothing so that I knew that your mind was elsewhere, I was terrified. I knew that there was someone somewhere that I must fight, but I was fighting in the dark. I hadn't an idea what to do.'

I was to learn one more curious thing. Next morning, when I awoke and looked across at the field, I had a strange impression that it was nearer to me than it had ever been before. I could see every detail of it. It was almost as though I could count the blades of grass. I'd always had the absurd notion that the five trees were active—that they could move—and sometimes I would look expecting to find only three there, or two.

I lived, I suppose, although my memory of that is very faint, in a kind of armed truce with Mary during these weeks. Everything was unreal to me except Pearl. I remember that I hated her name. I thought it foolish and affected, and her first occasion for rapping me over the knuckles was my saying so. She was deeply offended. I was detached enough about her to realise that her vanity was excessive and that everything that belonged to her—the especial kind of rouge that she used, the flower that she wore on her dress, relations of hers (although she didn't like them), even places where she had been—were sanctified and important because she had had some connection with them. Even I took on a kind of importance because she thought that I was in love with her.

I'm quite sure that she was never in love with me—that she had from the very first a vindictiveness towards Mary, whom, of course, she had never seen—because if Mary had not been there she could have swallowed me up more quickly. She was irritated, too, and the more determined because I would not make love to her as other men had done. She said I behaved like a hero in one of the old story-books, by which she meant, I suppose, that I did nothing more than kiss her. The odd thing was that she represented to me, and this I find the hardest of all to understand, adventure and romance.

And yet I knew that she was common, with no interest in anything except herself and men, that she never would be different from this. I think for these very reasons she became pathetic to me—someone whom I wished to protect, educate as though she were a poor, strayed child come to me for help. Of all the sentimental nonsense! She was anything but a poor, strayed child.

Women, I venture to think, are of two kinds. Either they must look up to the man they love or they must protect him. Sometimes they must do both. With some women the worse a man is, the more they must protect him. But with many women, as with Mary, if they despise, they cannot love. If I did this she would despise me for ever. And how fantastic it is, upon looking back, that I could seriously contemplate this flight with someone whom I neither admired nor loved, throwing everything away for nothing at all. And yet this is what men so often do.

I was afraid lest people should talk, and Pearl therefore went to stay, of all places in the world, in the lonely hamlet of Watendlath. That, now I think of it, was her principal virtue. She really did love this country. She would meet me in a little valley between Watendlath and Lodore, or I would come up to the farm for tea, or she would be at the bottom of the hill in Rosthwaite.

The day came when I agreed to go with her for a fortnight to Scarborough. I went back to my home that night after it was settled, knowing quite well that I was, as Mary had said, a lost man. As I sat by myself that evening, looking across at my field which now to my excited fancy seemed to be so close that it was almost staring in at my window, I felt the same excitement that I'd known at the very first moment when I met the girl. It was a hot, feverish excitement, and when Mary came into the room and told me supper was ready it was as though she were removed from me by a whole life of experience.

I only wanted to sit beside the girl and look at her. When I was with her I felt a sort of weariness, as though I'd had no sleep for weeks. But when I was away from her, I ached to be with her again. I had no satisfaction, no calm, no peace, whether with her or away from her. We made our arrangements. There was to be a trap waiting at Rosthwaite. I was to walk over, meet her at the farm, take her down to the trap, and then we would drive away. A man from Keswick drove the trap with our bags out to Rosthwaite and left it there, and early on a dark afternoon I started to walk up from the lake road. Dusk came very early at that time of the year, and I knew that we should have a dark walk down to Rosthwaite, but the path was easy to follow and I wanted nobody to see us.

I left my house that morning to drive into Keswick. Mary and I had a few last words.

'You will be back for supper?' she asked me.

'Yes,' I said, 'about seven.' And that was really the first lie that I had ever told her. She said nothing, gave me one look, and then I left her.

Now this is the strange part of my little story. I can hardly expect you to believe me . . . I don't know that I even want you to . . . I only know that every word I say is true.

I walked up the path, across the bridge above the tumbling stream, and then stood looking back at what is one of the loveliest views in the world—across Lodore to the lake.

I passed the line of bungalows on my right and came to my beloved field. As I reached its edge darkness began to gather. It was too early for dusk and yet the field was obscure, as though curtained by some thin mist. I was really out of breath and I leaned against a little stone wall, wondering what was the matter with me. As I stayed there some thorn from a bush close by pricked my hand. I looked, but there was no bush near enough, I thought, to have touched me. The feeling of hostility greatly increased and I wondered what was the matter with my nerves.

I came away from the little wall and started to walk. The mist gathered more thickly and I found myself wondering, of all things in the world, whether I would find my way. Find my way—when I knew this field and the path that ran beside it utterly by heart. But I suddenly thought—no, I will cross the wall and go up the other side away from the field. But when I turned to find the wall, I found that I was slipping down a bank into the stream that ran under the wall. I caught at the turf with my hand, it broke away, and before I could stop myself, I was down in the stream. I stumbled about among the stones, the water soaking into my shoes, and clambered up again.

Then, as I reached the top, I felt exactly as though someone had struck me in the face. I had a momentary impulse to call out abusively, as though it had been a living person, and then I realised my folly. How strong the wind was, and yet it seemed nothing compared with so many other times I'd known. I couldn't find the stone wall again, so I turned and began to climb the field which runs on a gentle slope to the fell. The dusky light showed me quite clearly the separate forms of five trees. As I moved up the open ground they were well away from me. Yet, very soon it was as though the wind was beating me toward the left, and although I moved forward, I seemed to make no real progress. It is a very small field and can be crossed in two minutes.

But now, as the rain began to fall, striking my face, I felt as though I were blinded. I put my hand before my eyes and then stumbled and fell on to my knees, and now I began to feel quite unreasoning terror. The rain was falling fast and the mist was thick. But through the mist I seemed to see trees marching. I could see against the skyline the faint shape of the fell which seemed an infinite distance away. I began to draw my breath with difficulty. It came in gasps and my heart was hammering unsteadily. One knows that in nightmare dreams, and sometimes in actual fact, one moves round and round a very small space, losing altogether one's sense of direction.

Now when I moved forward, I could no longer see the line of the fell or the stone wall. But quite clearly outlined against the mist were five trees, forming, as it seemed to me (and this was, of course, a hallucination), a complete circle around me. So strong was this impression, however, (and after all what is reality except what one's fancy makes it?) that I saw what I thought was a gap between two of the trees and made desperately for it. And then the two trees seemed to close together and advance toward me. Panic seized me. I put my hands before my face and ran stumbling forward. Once again, this time more severely, I dashed against what seemed to be now a wall of rough and hostile bark. I even called out, 'Let me go! Let me go!'

Then I fell on my knees. The air about me seemed to grow suffocatingly close, just as though the walls of a room were closing in upon me. I could smell the wet bark, the thin timber essence of branches. I put up my hand, touched a branch, which broke, and then I felt tendrils about my legs. I began to beat with my hands, scraping the skin against the bark. The sense of suffocation grew more appalling with each instant, and the bitter scent of wet wood filled my nostrils.

I rose to my feet and looked. I could see with absolute distinctness the five trees close ringed about me. They seemed to be of great thickness and intolerable height. It was as though they whispered to me an order. I obeyed it and turned and climbed out with little frightened gasps. Down the hill toward Lodore I ran, as though dreadful destruction pursued me. I remember stumbling and falling—getting up again, going on past the bungalows, over the bridge, down the road to the lake, and then somehow, I found my way home.

Mary has told me since how I arrived at the house that night. My hat was gone; my face, covered with scratches, was bleeding; my clothes were torn, my knees soaked with mud. She was sitting reading. When I appeared at the door, she stood up. I cried, 'Mary! Mary!' and ran to her. Kneeling down before her and straining upward, I laid my bleeding face against her breast.

That is all. I did not see or hear of Miss Pearl Richardson again until five years later. There was a paragraph in the paper saying that in a lodging-house in Sheffield a woman named Pearl Richardson had killed herself by gas-poisoning.

This is the queerest experience of my life.

A year after this, as I have said, our first child was born, and until Mary's death there were not, I am sure, two happier married people anywhere in England. And the field with the five trees looks across at me now benevolently as I write. God allows us more protection from our follies than we know.

Mr Huffam a Christmas Story

1

Once upon a time (it doesn't matter when it was except that it was long after the Great War) young Tubby Winsloe was in the act of crossing Piccadilly just below Hatchard's bookshop. It was three days before Christmas and there had been a frost, a thaw, and then a frost again. The roads were treacherous, traffic nervous and irresponsible, while against the cliff-like indifference of brick and mortar a thin, faint snow was falling from a primrose-coloured sky. Soon it would be dusk and the lights would come out. Then things would be more cheerful.

It would, however, take more than light to restore Tubby's cheerfulness. Rubicund of face and alarmingly stout of body for a youth of twenty-three, he had just then the spirit of a damp face-towel, for only a week ago Diana Lane-Fox had refused to consider for a moment the possibility of marrying him.

'I like you, Tubby,' she had said. 'I think you have a kind heart. But marry you! You are useless, ignorant and greedy. You're disgracefully fat, and your mother worships you.'

He had not known, until Diana refused him, how bitterly alone he would find himself. He had money, friends, a fine roof above his head; he had seemed to himself popular wherever he went.

'Why, there's old Tubby!' everyone had cried.

It was true that he was fat, it was true that his mother adored him. He had not, until now, known that these were drawbacks. He had seemed to himself until a week ago the friend of all the world. Now he appeared a pariah.

Diana's refusal of him had been a dreadful shock. He had been quite sure that she would accept him. She had gone with him gladly to dances and the pictures. She had, it seemed, approved highly of his mother, Lady Winsloe, and his father, Sir Roderick Winsloe, Bart. She had partaken, again and again, of the Winsloe hospitality.

All, it seemed to him, that was needed was for him to say the word. He could choose his time. Well, he *had* chosen his time—at the Herries dance last Wednesday evening. This was the result.

He had expected to recover. His was naturally a buoyant nature. He told himself, again and again, that there were many other fish in the matrimonial sea. But it appeared that there were not. He wanted Diana and only Diana.

He halted at the resting-place halfway across the street, and sighed so deeply that a lady with a little girl and a fierce-looking Chow dog looked at him severely, as though she would say:

'Now this is Christmas time—a gloomy period for all concerned. It is an unwarranted impertinence for anyone to make it yet more gloomy.'

There was someone else clinging to this small fragment of security. A strange-looking man. His appearance was so unusual that Tubby forgot his own troubles in his instant curiosity. The first unusual thing about this man was that he had a beard, beards were very seldom worn today. Then his clothes, although they were clean and neat, were most certainly old-fashioned. He was wearing a high sharp-pointed collar, a black stock with a jewelled tie-pin, and a most remarkable waistcoat, purple in colour, and covered with little red flowers. He was carrying a large, heavy looking brown bag. His face was bronzed and he made Tubby think of a retired sea captain.

But the most remarkable thing of all about him was the impression that he gave of restless, driving energy. It was all that he could do to keep quiet. His strong, wiry figure seemed to burn with some secret fire. The traffic rushed madly past, but, at every moment when there appeared a brief interval between the cars and the omnibuses, this bearded gentleman with the bag made a little dance and once he struck the Chow with his bag and once nearly thrust the small child into the road.

The moment came when, most unwisely, he darted forth. He was almost caught by an imperious, disdainful Rolls-Royce. The lady gave a little scream and Tubby caught his arm, held him, drew him back.

'That nearly had you, sir!' Tubby murmured, his hand still on his arm. The stranger smiled—a most charming smile that shone from his eyes, his beard, his very hands.

'I must thank you,' he said, bowing with old-fashioned courtesy.

'But damn it, as the little boy said to the grocer, "there's no end to the dog," as he saw the sausages coming from the sausage machine.'

At this he laughed very heartily and Tubby had to laugh, too, although the remark did not seem to him very amusing.

'The traffic's very thick at Christmas-time,' Tubby said. 'Everyone doing their shopping, you know.'

The stranger nodded

'Splendid time, Christmas!' he said 'Best of the year!'

'Oh, do you think so?' said Tubby 'I doubt if you'll find people to agree with you. It isn't the thing to admire Christmas these days.'

'Not the thing!' said the stranger, amazed. 'Why, what's the matter?'

This was a poser because so many things were the matter, from Unemployment to Diana. Tubby was saved for the moment from answering.

'Now there's a break,' he said. 'We can cross now.' Cross they did, the stranger swinging his body as though at any instant he might spring right off the ground.

'Which way are you going?' Tubby asked. It astonished him afterwards when he looked back and remembered this question. It was not his way to make friends of strangers, his theory being that everyone was out to 'do' everyone, and in these days especially.

'To tell you the truth I don't quite know,' the stranger said. 'I've only just arrived.'

'Where have you come from?' asked Tubby.

'The stranger laughed.

'I've been moving about for a long time. I'm always on the move. I'm considered a very restless man by my friends.'

They were walking along very swiftly, for it was cold and the snow was falling fast now.

'Tell me,' said the stranger, '—about its being a bad time. What's the matter?'

What was the matter? What a question!

Tubby murmured:

'Why, everything's the matter—unemployment—no trade—*you* know.'

'No, I don't. I've been away. I think everyone looks very jolly.'

'I say, don't you feel cold without an overcoat?' Tubby asked.

'Oh, that's nothing,' the stranger answered. 'I'll tell you when I *did* feel cold though. When I was a small boy I worked in a factory putting labels on to blacking-bottles. It was cold *then*. Never known such cold.

Icicles would hang on the end of your nose!'

'No!' said Tubby.

'They did, I assure you, and the blacking-bottles would be coated with ice!'

By this time, they had reached Berkeley Street. The Winsloe mansion was in Hill Street.

'I turn up here,' said Tubby.

'Oh, do you?'

The stranger looked disappointed. He smiled and held out his hand.

Then Tubby did another extraordinary thing. He said:

'Come in and have a cup of tea. Our place is only five yards up the street.'

'Certainly,' the stranger said. 'Delighted.'

As they walked up Berkeley Street, he went on confidentially.

'I haven't been in London for a long time. All these vehicles are very confusing. But I like It—I like it immensely. It's so lively, and then the town's so quiet compared with what it was when I lived here.'

'Quiet!' said Tubby.

'Certainly. There were cobbles, and the carts and drays screamed and rattled like the damned.'

'But that's years ago!'

'Yes. I'm older than I look.'

Then, pointing, he added:

'But that's where Dorchester House was. So, they've pulled it down. What a pity!'

'Oh, everything's pulled down now,' said Tubby.

'I acted there once—a grand night we had. Fond of acting?'

'Oh, I'd be no good,' said Tubby modestly, 'too self-conscious.'

'Ah, you mustn't be self-conscious,' said the stranger. 'Thinking of yourself only breeds trouble, as the man said to the hangman just before they dropped him.'

'Isn't that bag a terrible weight?' Tubby asked.

'I've carried worse things than this,' said the stranger. 'I carried a four-poster once, all the way from one end of the Marshalsea to the other.'

They were outside the house now and Tubby realised for the first time his embarrassment. It was not his way bring anyone into the house unannounced, and his mother could be very haughty with strangers. However, here they were and it was snowing hard and the poor man was without a coat. So, in they went. The Winsloe mansion was magnificent, belonging in all its features to an age that was gone, there was a marble staircase and up the stranger almost ran, carrying his bag like a feather. Tubby toiled behind him but was, unhappily, not in time to prevent the stranger from entering through the open doors of the drawing-room.

Here, seated in magnificent state, was Lady Winsloe, a roaring fire encased with marble on one side of her, a beautiful tea-table in front of her, and walls hung with magnificent imitations of the great Masters.

Lady Winsloe was a massive woman with snow-white hair, a bosom like a small skating-rink, and a little face that wore a look of perpetual astonishment. Her dress of black-and-white silk fitted her so tightly that one anticipated with pleasure the moment when she would be compelled to rise. She moved as little as possible, she said as little as possible, she thought as little as possible. She had a very kind heart and was sure that the world was going straight to the devil.

The stranger put his bag on the floor and went over to her with his hand outstretched.

'How are you?' he said. 'I'm delighted to meet you!'

By good fortune, Tubby arrived in the room at this moment.

'Mother,' he began, 'this is a gentleman—'

'Oh, of course,' said the stranger, 'you don't know my name. My name's Huffam,' and he caught the small white podgy hand and shook it. At this moment, two Pekinese dogs, one brown and one white, advanced from somewhere violently barking. Lady Winsloe found the whole situation so astonishing that she could only whisper:

'Now, Bobo—now, Coco!'

'You see, Mother,' Tubby went on, 'Mr. Huffam was nearly killed by a motorcar and I rescued him and it began to snow heavily.'

'Yes, dear,' Lady Winsloe said,' in her queer husky little voice that was always a surprise coming from so vast a bosom. Then she pulled herself together. For some reason Tubby had done this amazing thing, and whatever Tubby did was right.

'I do hope you'll have some tea, Mr—?'

She hesitated.

'Huffam, ma'am. Yes, thank you. I *will* have some tea!'

'Milk *and* sugar?'

'All of it!' Mr. Huffam laughed and slapped his knee. 'Yes, milk *and* sugar. Very kind of you indeed. A perfect stranger as I am. You have a beautiful place here, ma'am. You are to be envied.'

'Oh, do you think so?' said Lady Winsloe, in her husky whisper. 'Not in these days—not in these terrible days. Why, the taxes alone! You've no idea, Mr—?'

'Huffam.'

'Yes. How stupid of me! Now, Bobo! Now, Coco!'

Then a little silence followed and Lady Winsloe gazed at her strange visitor. Her manners were beautiful. She never looked *directly* at her guests. But there was something about Mr. Huffam that *forced* you to look at him. It was his energy. It was his obvious happiness (for happy people were so very rare). It was his extraordinary waistcoat.

Mr. Huffam did not mind in the least being looked at. He smiled back at Lady Winsloe, as though he had known her all his life.

'I'm so very fortunate,' he said, 'to find myself in London at Christmas-time. And snow, too! The very thing. Snowballs, Punch and Judy, mistletoe, holly, the pantomime—nothing so good in life as the pantomime!'

'Oh, do you think so?' said Lady Winsloe faintly. 'I can't, I'm afraid, altogether agree with you. It lasts such a *very* long time and is often so exceedingly vulgar!'

'Ah, it's the sausages!' said Mr. Huffam, laughing. 'You don't like the sausages! For my part I dote on 'em. I know it's silly at my age. but there it is—Joey and the Sausages. I wouldn't miss them for anything.'

At that moment a tall and exceedingly thin gentleman entered. This was Sir Roderick Winsloe, Sir Roderick had been once an Undersecretary, once a Chairman of a Company, once famous for his smart and rather vicious repartees. All these were now glories of the past. He was now nothing but the husband of Lady Winsloe, the father of Tubby, and the victim of an uncertain and often truculent digestion. It was natural that he should be melancholy, although perhaps not so melancholy as he found it necessary to be. Life for him was altogether without savour. He now regarded Mr. Huffam, his bag and his waistcoat, with unconcealed astonishment.

'This is my father,' said Tubby.

Mr. Huffam rose at once and grasped his hand.

'Delighted to meet you, sir,' he said.

Sir Roderick said nothing but 'Ah'—then he sat down. Tubby was suffering now from a very serious embarrassment. The odd visitor had drunk his tea and it was time that he should go. Yet it seemed that he had no intention of going. With his legs spread apart, his head thrown back, his friendly eyes taking everyone in as though they were all his dearest friends, he was asking for his second cup.

Tubby waited for his mother. She was a mistress of the art of making a guest disappear. No one knew quite how she did it. There was nothing so vulgarly direct as a glance at the clock or a suggestion as to the imminence of dressing for dinner. A cough, a turn of the wrist, a word about the dogs, and the thing was done. But *this* guest, Tubby knew, was a little more difficult than the ordinary. There was something old-fashioned about him. He took people naively at their word. Having been asked to tea, he considered that he *was* asked to tea. None of your five minutes' gossip and then hastening on to a cocktail-party. However, Tubby reflected, the combination of father, mother *and* the drawing-room, with its marble fireplace and row of copied Old Masters, was, as a rule, enough to ensure brief visitors. On this occasion also, it would have its effect.

And then—an amazing thing occurred! Tubby perceived that his mother *liked* Mr. Huffam, that she was smiling and even giggling, that her little eyes shone, her tiny mouth was parted in expectation as she listened to her visitor.

Mr. Huffam was telling a story—an anecdote of his youth. About a boy whom he had known in his own childhood, a gay, enterprising, and adventurous boy who had gone as page-boy to a rich family. Mr. Huffam described his adventures in a marvellous manner, his *rencontre* with the second footman, who was a snob and Evangelical, of how he had handed biscuits through the pantry window to his little sister, of the friendship that he had made with the cook. And, as Mr. Huffam told these things, all these people lived before your eyes, the pompous mistress with her ear-trumpet, the cook's husband who had a wooden leg, the second footman who was in love with a pastry-cook's daughter.

The house of this young page-boy took on life, and all the furniture in it, the tables and chairs, the beds and looking-glasses, everything down to the very red woollen muffler that the footman wore in bed, because he was subject to colds in the neck. Then Lady Winsloe began to laugh and Sir Roderick Winsloe even laughed, and the butler, a big, red-faced man, coming in to remove the tea, could not believe his parboiled eyes, but stood there, looking first of all at his mistress, then at his master, then at Mr. Huffam's bag, then at Mr. Huffam himself, until he remembered his manners and, with a sudden apologetic cough, set sternly (for himself this disgraceful behaviour of his employers was no laughing matter) about his proper duties.

But best of all perhaps was the pathos at the end of Mr. Huffam's story. Pathos is a dangerous thing in these days. We so easily call it sentimentality. Mr. Huffam was a master of it. Quite easily and with no exaggeration he described how the sister of the little page-boy lost some money entrusted to her by her only too bibulous father, of her terror, her temptation to steal from her aged aunt's purse, her final triumphant discovery of the money in a band-box!

How they all held their breaths! How vividly they saw the scene! How real was the sister of the little page-boy! At last the story was ended. Mr. Huffam rose.

'Well, ma'am, I must thank you for a very happy hour,' he said.

Then the most remarkable thing of all occurred, for Lady Winsloe said:

'If you have not made any other arrangements, why not stay here for a night or two—while you are looking about you, you know? I'm sure we should be delighted—would we not, Roderick?'

And Sir Roderick said:

'Ah—ah—certainly.'

2

On looking back, as he so often did afterwards, into the details of this extraordinary adventure. Tubby was never able to arrange the various incidents in their proper order. The whole affair had the inconsequence, the coloured fantasy, of a dream—one of those rare and delightful dreams that are so much more true and reasonable than anything in one's waking life.

After that astounding invitation of Lady Winsloe's, in what order did the events follow—the cynical luncheon-party, the affair of Mallow's young woman (Mallow was the butler), the extraordinary metamorphosis of Miss Allington? All of these were certainly in the first twenty-four hours after Mr. Huffam's arrival. The grand sequence of the Christmas Tree, the Mad Party, the London Vision, were all parts of the tremendous climax.

At once Tubby realised, the house itself changed. It had never been a satisfactory house; always one of those places rebelliously determined not to live. Even the rooms most often inhabited—the drawing-room, the long, dusky dining-room, Sir Roderick's study. Tubby's own bedroom—sulkily refused to play the game. The house was too large, the furniture too heavy, the ceilings too high. Nevertheless, on the first evening of Mr. Huffam's visit, the furniture began to move about. After dinner on that evening there was only the family present. (Miss Agatha Allington, an old maid, a relation with money to be left, an unhappy old woman, suffering from constant neuralgia, had not yet arrived.) There they were in the drawing-room and, almost at once, Mr. Huffam had moved some of the chairs away from the wall, had turned the sofa with the gilt, spiky back more cosily towards the fire. He was not impertinent nor officious. Indeed, on this first evening, he was very quiet, asking them some questions about present-day London, making some rather odd social enquiries about prisons and asylums and the protection of children.

He was interested, too, in the literature of the moment and wrote down in a little note-book an odd collection of names, for Lady Winsloe told him that Ethel M. Dell, Warwick Deeping, and a lady called Wilhelmina Stitch who wrote poetry, were her favourite writers, while Tubby suggested that he should look into the work of Virginia Woolf, D. H. Lawrence and Aldous Huxley. They had, in fact, a quiet evening which ended with Mr. Huffam having his first lesson in Bridge. (He had been, he told them, when he had last 'tried' cards, an enthusiastic whist player.)

It was a quiet evening, but, as Tubby went up the long, dark staircase to his room, he felt that, in some undefined way, there was excitement in the air. Before undressing he opened his window and looked out on to the roofs and chimney-pots of London. Snow glittered and sparkled under a sky that quivered with stars. Dimly he heard the recurrent waves of traffic, as though the sea gently beat at the feet of the black, snow-covered houses.

'*What* an extraordinary man!' was his last thought before he slept. Before he had known that he would have Mr. Huffam as his guest. Tubby had invited a few of his clever young friends to luncheon—Diana, Gordon Wolley, Ferris Band, Mary Polkinghorne. Gathered round the Winsloe luncheon-table, Tubby regarded them with new eyes. Was it because of the presence of Mr. Huffam? He, gaily flaunting his tremendous waistcoat, was in high spirits. He had, all morning, been revisiting some of his old haunts, he was amazed. He could not conceal, he did not attempt to conceal, his amazement.

He gave them, as they sat there, languidly picking at their food, a slight notion of what East London had once been—the filth, the degradation, the flocks of wild, haggard-eyed, homeless children—Mary Polkinghorne, who had a figure like an umbrella-handle, an Etot. crop and an eye-glass, gazed at him with bemused amazement.

'But they say our slums are awful. I haven't been down there my-self, but Bunny Carlisle runs a Boys' Club and *he* says . . .'

Mr. Huffam admitted that he had seen some slums that morning, but they were nothing, nothing at all, to the things he had seen in his youth.

'Who is this man?' Ferris Band whispered to Diana.

I don't know,' she answered. 'Someone Tubby picked up. But I like him.'

And then this Christmas!

'Oh dear,' young Wolley sighed, 'here's Christmas again! Isn't it aw-ful! I'm going to bed. I shall sleep, and I hope dream, until this dreadful time is over.'

Mr. Huffam looked at him with wonder.

'Hang up your stocking and see what happens,' he said.

Everyone screamed with laughter at the idea of young Wolley hanging up his stocking. Afterwards, in the drawing-room, they dis-cussed literature.

'I've just seen,' Ferris Band explained, 'the proofs of Hunter's new novel. It's called *Pigs in Fever*. It's quite marvellous. The idea is, a man has scarlet fever and it's an account of his ravings. Sheer poetry.'

There was a book on a little table. He picked it up. It was a first edition of *Martin Chuzzlewit* bound in purple leather.

'Poor old Dickens,' he said. 'Hunter has a marvellous idea. He's go-ing to rewrite one or two of the Dickens books.'

Mr. Huffam was interested.

'Rewrite them?' he asked.

'Yes. Cut them down to about half. There's some quite good stuff in them hidden away, he says. He'll cut out all the sentimental bits, bring the humour up to date, and put in some stuff of his own. He says it's only fair to Dickens to show people that there's something there.'

Mr. Huffam was delighted.

'I'd like to see it,' he said. 'It will make quite a new thing of it.'

'That's what Hunter says,' Band remarked 'People will be surprised.'

'I should think they will be,' Mr. Huffam remarked.

The guests stayed a long time. Mr. Huffman was something quite new in their experience. Before she went, Diana said to Tubby:

'What a delightful man! Where did you find him?'

Tubby was modest. She was nicer to him than she had ever been before.

'What's happened to you, Tubby?' she asked. 'You've woken up suddenly.'

During the afternoon, Miss Agatha Allington arrived with a number of bags and one of her worst colds.

'How are you. Tubby? It's kind of you to ask me. What horrible weather! What a vile thing Christmas is! You won't expect me to give you a present, I hope?'

Before the evening, Mr. Huffam made friends with Mallow the butler. No one knew quite how he did it. No one had ever made friends with Mallow before. But Mr. Huffam went down to the lower domestic regions and invaded the world of Mallow, Mrs. Spence, the housekeeper, Thomas the footman, Jane and Rose the housemaids, Maggie the scullery-maid.

Mrs. Spence, who was a little round woman like a football, was a Fascist in politics, said that she was descended from Mary Queen of Scots, and permitted no one, except Lady Winsloe, in her sitting-room. But she showed Mr. Huffam the photographs of the late Mr. Spence and her son, Darnley, who was a steward on the Cunard Line. She laughed immeasurably at the story of the organ-grinder and the lame monkey. But Mallow was Mr. Huffam's great conquest. It seemed (no one had had the least idea of it) that Mallow was hopelessly in love with a young lady who assisted in a flower shop in Dover Street. This young lady, apparently, admired Mallow very much and he had once taken her to the pictures. But Mallow was shy. (No one had conceived it!) He wanted to write her a letter, but simply hadn't the courage. Mr. Huffam dictated a letter for him. It was a marvellous letter, full of humour, poetry and tenderness.

'But I can't live up to this, sir,' said Mallow. 'She'll find me out in no time.'

'That's all right,' said Mr. Huffam. 'Take her out to tea tomorrow, be a little tender. She won't worry about letters after that!'

He went out after tea and returned powdered with snow, in a taxi-cab filled with holly and mistletoe.

'Oh dear,' whispered Lady Winsloe, 'we haven't decorated the house for years. I don't know what Roderick will say. He thinks holly so messy.'

'I'll talk to him,' said Mr. Huffam. He did, with the result that Sir Roderick came himself and assisted. Through all this, Mr. Huffam was in no way dictatorial. Tubby observed that he had even a kind of shyness—not in his opinions, for here he was very clear-minded indeed, seeing exactly what he wanted, but he seemed to be aware, by a sort of ghostly guidance, of the idiosyncrasies of his neighbours. How did he know, for instance, that Sir Roderick was afraid of a ladder? When he. Mallow, Tubby and Sir Roderick were festooning the hall with holly, he saw Sir Roderick begin timidly, with trembling shanks, to climb some steps. He went to him, put his hand on his arm, and led him safely to ground again.

'I know you don't like ladders,' he said. 'Some people can't stand 'em. I knew an old gentleman once terrified of ladders, and his eldest son, a bright, promising lad, *must* become a steeple-jack. Only profession he had a liking for.'

'Good heavens!' cried Sir Roderick, paling. 'What a horrible pursuit! Whatever did his father do.?'

'Persuaded him to be a diver instead,' said Mr. Huffam. 'The lad took to it like a duck to water. Up or down, it was all the same to him, he said.'

In fact, Mr. Huffam looked after Sir Roderick as a father his child, and, before the day was out, the noble Baronet was asking Mr. Huffam's opinion on everything—the right way to grow carnations, the Gold Standard, how to breed dachshunds, and the wisdom of Lord Beaverbrook. The Gold Standard and Lord Beaverbrook were new to Mr. Huffam, but he had his opinions all the same. Tubby, as he listened, could not help wondering where Mr. Huffam had been all these years. In some very remote South Sea island surely! So many things were new to him. But his kindness and energy carried him forward through everything. There was much of the child about him, much of the wise man of the world also, and behind these a heart of melancholy, of loneliness.

'He has, it seems,' thought Tubby, 'no home, no people, nowhere especially to go.' And he had visions of attaching him to the family as a sort of secretarial family friend. Tubby was no sentimentalist about his own sex, but he had to confess that he was growing very fond of Mr. Huffam. It was almost as though he had known him before. There were, in fact, certain phrases, certain tunes in the voice that were curiously familiar and reminded Tubby in some dim way of his innocent, departed childhood.

And then, after dinner, there was the conquest of Agatha Allington. Agatha had taken an instant dislike to Mr. Huffam. She prided herself on her plain speech.

'My dear,' she said to Lady Winsloe, 'what a ruffian! He'll steal the spoons.'

'I don't think so,' said Lady Winsloe with dignity. 'We like him very much.'

He seemed to perceive that Agatha disliked him. He sat beside her at dinner—he wore a tail-coat of strange, old-fashioned cut, and carried a large gold fob. He was, as Tubby perceived, quite different with Agatha. He was almost, you might say, an old maid himself—or, rather, a confirmed old bachelor. He discovered that she hid a passion for Italy—she visited Rome and Florence every year—and he described to her some of his own Italian journeys, taken many years ago: confessed to her that he didn't care for *frescoes*, which he described as 'dim virgins with mildewed glories'. But Venice! Ah! Venice! with its prisoners and dungeons and lovely iridescent waters! All the same, he was always homesick when he was out of London, and he described the old London to her, the fogs and the muffin-bells and the 'growlers,' and enchanted her with a story about a shy little bachelor, and how he went out one evening to dine with a vulgar cousin and be kind to a horrible godchild. Indeed, they all listened, spellbound: even Mallow stood, with a plate in his hand and his mouth open, forgetting his duties. Then, after dinner, he insisted that they should dance. They made a space in the drawing-room, brought up a gramophone, and set about it. Then how Mr. Huffam laughed when Tubby showed him a one-step.

'Call that dancing!' he cried. Then, humming a polka, he caught Agatha by the waist and away they polkaed! Then Lady Winsloe, who had adored the polka once, joined in. Then the Barn Dance. Then, few though they were. Sir Roger.

'I know!' Mr. Huffam cried. 'We must have a party!'

'A party!' almost screamed Lady Winsloe. 'What kind of a party?'

'Why, a children's party, of course. On Christmas night.'

'But we don't know any children! And children are bored with parties. And they'll all be engaged anyway.'

'Not the children *I'll* ask!' cried Mr. Huffam. 'Not the party *I'll* have! It shall be the best party London has seen for years!'

3

It is well known that good-humoured, cheerful, and perpetually well-intentioned people are among the most tiresome of their race. They are avoided by all wise and comfort-loving persons. Tubby often wondered afterwards why Mr. Huffam was *not* tiresome. It was perhaps because of his childlikeness; it was also, most certainly, because of his intelligence. Most of all it was because of the special circumstances of the case. In ordinary daily life, Mr. Huffam *might* be a bore—most people are at one time or another. But on this occasion, no one was a bore, not even Agatha.

It was as though the front wall of the Hill Street house had been taken away and all the detail and incidents of these two days, Christmas Eve and Christmas Day, became part of it. It seemed that Berkeley Square was festooned with crystal trees, that candles—red and green and blue—blazed from every window, that small boys, instead of chanting 'Good King Wenceslas' in the usual excruciating fashion, carolled with divine voices, that processions of Father Christmases, with snowy beards and red gowns, marched from Selfridges and Harrods and Fortnum's, carrying in their hands small Christmas trees, and even attended by reindeer, as though brown-paper parcels tied with silver bands and decorated with robins fell in torrents through the chimney, and gigantic Christmas puddings rolled on their own stout bellies down Piccadilly, attended by showers of almonds and raisins. And upon all this, first a red-faced sun, then a moon, cherry-coloured and as large as an orange, smiled down, upon a world of crusted, glittering snow, while the bells pealed and once again the Kings of the East came to the stable with gifts in their hands. . . .

Of course, it was not like that—but most certainly the Winsloe house was transformed. For one thing, there was not the usual present-giving. At breakfast on Christmas Day, everyone gave everyone else presents that must not by order cost more than sixpence apiece. Mr. Huffam had discovered some marvellous things—toy dogs that barked, Father Christmases glistening with snow, a small chime of silver bells, shining pieces of sealing-wax.

Then they all went to church at St. James's, Piccadilly. At the midday meal Sir Roderick had turkey and Christmas pudding, which he hadn't touched for many a day.

In the evening came the Party. Tubby had been allowed to invite Diana—for the rest the guests were to be altogether Mr. Huffam's. No one knew what was in his mind. At 7.15 exactly came the first ring of the door-bell. When Mallow opened the portals, there on the steps were three very small children, two girls and a boy.

'Please, sir, this was the number the gentleman said?' whispered the little girl, who was very frightened. Then up Hill Street the children came, big children, little children, children who could scarcely walk, boys as bold as brass, girls mothering their small relations, some of them shabby, some of them smart, some with shawls, some with mufflers, some with collars, some brave, some frightened, some chattering like monkeys, some silent and anxious—all coming up Hill Street, crowding up the stairs, passing into the great hall.

It was not until they had all been ushered up the stairs by Mallow, were all in their places, that Sir Roderick Winsloe, Bart., Lady Winsloe, his wife. Tubby Winsloe, their son, were permitted to see their own drawing-room. When they did they gasped with wonder. Under the soft and shining light the great floor had been cleared, and at one end of the room all the children were gathered.

At the other end was the largest, the strongest, the proudest Christmas Tree ever beheld, and this tree shone and gleamed with candles, with silver tissue, with blue and gold and crimson balls, and so heavily weighted was it with dolls and horses and trains and parcels that it was a miracle that, tree as it was, it could support its burden. So, there it was, the great room shining with golden light, the children massed together, the gleaming floor like a sea, and only the crackle of the fire, the tick of the marble clock, the wondering whispers of the children for sound.

A pause, and from somewhere or other (but no one knew whence) Father Christmas appeared. He stood there, looking across the floor at his guests.

'Good evening, children' he said, and the voice was the voice of Mr. Huffam.

'Good evening, Father Christmas' the children cried in chorus.

'It's all his own money,' Lady Winsloe whispered to Agatha. 'He wouldn't let me spend a penny.'

He summoned them then to help with the presents. The children (who behaved with the manners of the highest of the aristocracy— even *better* than that, to be truthful) advanced across the shining Moor. They were told to take turn according to size, the smallest first. There was no pushing, no cries of 'I *want* that,' as so often happens at parties, no greed and satiety. At last the biggest girl (who was almost a giantess), and the biggest boy (who might have been a heavyweight boxing champion) received their gifts. The tree gave a little quiver of relief at its freedom from its burden, and the candles, the silver tissue, the red and blue and golden balls shook with a shimmer of pleasure because the present-giving had been so successful.

Games followed. Tubby could never afterwards remember what

the games had been. They were no doubt Hunt the Slipper, Kiss in the Ring, Cross-your-Toes, Last Man Out, Blind Man's Buff, Chase the Cherry, Here Comes the Elephant, Count Your Blessings, and all the other games. But Tubby never knew. The room was alive with movement, with cries of joy and shouts of triumph, with songs and kisses and forfeits. Tubby never knew. He only knew that he saw his mother with a paper cap on her head, his father with a false nose, Agatha beating a child's drum—and on every side of him children and children and children, children dancing and singing and running and sitting and laughing.

There came a moment when Diana, her hair dishevelled, her eyes shining, caught his arm and whispered:

'Tubby, you are a dear. Perhaps—one day—if you keep this up—who knows?'

And there was a sudden quiet, Mr. Huffam, no longer Father Christmas, arranged all the children round him. He told them a story, a story about a circus and a small child who, with her old grandfather, wandered into the company of those strange people—of the fat lady and the Living Skeleton, the jugglers and the beautiful creatures who jumped through the hoops, and the clown with the broken heart and how his heart was mended.

'And so, they all lived happily ever after,' he ended. Everyone said goodnight. Everyone went away.

'Oh dear, I *am* tired!' said Mr. Huffam. 'But it has been a jolly evening!'

Next morning when Rose the housemaid woke Lady Winsloe with her morning cup of tea she had startling news.

'Oh dear, my lady, the gentleman's gone!'

'What gentleman.?'

'Mr. Huffam, my lady. His bed's not been slept in and his bag's gone. There isn't a sign of him anywhere.'

Alas, it was only too true. Not a sign of him anywhere. At least one sign only.

The drawing-room was as it had always been, every chair in its proper place, the copied Old Masters looking down solemnly from the dignified walls.

One thing alone was different. The first edition of *Martin Chuzzlewit* in its handsome purple binding was propped up against the marble clock.

'How very strange!' said Lady Winsloe. But, opening it, she found that on the fly-leaf these words were freshly written:

For Lady Winsloe
with gratitude
from her Friend
the Author

And, under this, the signature, above a scrawl of thick black lines, 'Charles Dickens'.

Tarnhelm or, the Death of
My Uncle Robert

1

I was, I suppose, at that time a peculiar child, peculiar a little by nature, but also because I had spent so much of my young life in the company of people very much older than myself.

After the events that I am now going to relate, some quite indelible mark was set on me. I became then, and have always been since, one of those persons, otherwise insignificant, who have decided, without possibility of change, about certain questions.

Some things, doubted by most of the world, are for these people true and beyond argument; this certainty of theirs gives them a kind of stamp, as though they lived so much in their imagination as to have very little assurance as to what is fact and what fiction. This 'oddness' of theirs puts them apart. If now, at the age of fifty, I am a man with very few friends, very much alone, it is because, if you like, my Uncle Robert died in a strange manner forty years ago and I was a witness of his death.

I have never until now given any account of the strange proceedings that occurred at Faildyke Hall on the evening of Christmas Eve in the year 1890. The incidents of that evening are still remembered very clearly by one or two people, and a kind of legend of my Uncle Robert's death has been carried on into the younger generation. But no one still alive was a witness of them as I was, and I feel it is time that I set them down upon paper.

I write them down without comment. I extenuate nothing; I disguise nothing. I am not, I hope, in any way a vindictive man, but my brief meeting with my Uncle Robert and the circumstances of his death gave my life, even at that early age, a twist difficult for me very readily to forgive.

As to the so-called supernatural element in my story, everyone must judge for himself about that. We deride or we accept according to our natures. If we are built of a certain solid practical material the probability is that no evidence, however definite, however first-hand, will convince us. If dreams are our daily portion, one dream more or less will scarcely shake our sense of reality.

However, to my story.

My father and mother were in India from my eighth to my thirteenth years. I did not see them, except on two occasions when they visited England. I was an only child, loved dearly by both my parents, who, however, loved one another yet more. They were an exceedingly sentimental couple of the old-fashioned kind. My father was in the Indian Civil Service, and wrote poetry. He even had his epic, *Tantalus: A Poem in Four Cantos,* published at his own expense.

This, added to the fact that my mother had been considered an invalid before he married her, made my parents feel that they bore a very close resemblance to the Brownings, and my father even had a pet name for my mother that sounded curiously like the famous and hideous 'Ba.'

I was a delicate child, was sent to Mr. Ferguson's Private Academy at the tender age of eight, and spent my holidays as the rather unwanted guest of various relations.

'Unwanted' because I was, I imagine, a difficult child to understand. I had an old grandmother who lived at Folkestone, two aunts who shared a little house in Kensington, an aunt, uncle and a brood of cousins inhabiting Cheltenham, and two uncles who lived in Cumberland. All these relations, except the two uncles, had their proper share of me and for none of them had I any great affection.

Children were not studied in those days as they are now. I was thin, pale and bespectacled, aching for affection but not knowing at all how to obtain it; outwardly undemonstrative but inwardly emotional and sensitive, playing games, because of my poor sight, very badly, reading a great deal more than was good for me, and telling myself stories all day and part of every night.

All of my relations tired of me, I fancy, in turn, and at last it was decided that my uncles in Cumberland must do their share. These two were my father's brothers, the eldest of a long family of which he was the youngest. My Uncle Robert, I understood, was nearly seventy, my Uncle Constance some five years younger. I remember always thinking that Constance was a funny name for a man.

My Uncle Robert was the owner of Faildyke Hall, a country house between the lake of Wastwater and the little town of Seascale on the sea coast. Uncle Constance had lived with Uncle Robert for many years. It was decided, after some family correspondence, that the Christmas of this year, 1890, should be spent by me at Faildyke Hall.

I was at this time just eleven years old, thin and skinny, with a bulging forehead, large spectacles and a nervous, shy manner. I always set out, I remember, on any new adventures with mingled emotions of terror and anticipation. Maybe this time the miracle would occur: I should discover a friend or a fortune, should cover myself with glory in some unexpected way; be at last what I always longed to be, a hero.

I was glad that I was not going to any of my other relations for Christmas, and especially not to my cousins at Cheltenham, who teased and persecuted me and were never free of ear-splitting noises. What I wanted most in life was to be allowed to read in peace. I understood that at Faildyke there was a glorious library.

My aunt saw me into the train. I had been presented by my uncle with one of the most gory of Harrison Ainsworth's romances, *The Lancashire Witches,* and I had five bars of chocolate cream, so that that journey was as blissfully happy as any experience could be to me at that time. I was permitted to read in peace, and I had just then little more to ask of life.

Nevertheless, as the train puffed its way north, this new country began to force itself on my attention. I had never before been in the North of England, and I was not prepared for the sudden sense of space and freshness that I received.

The naked, unsystematic hills, the freshness of the wind on which the birds seemed to be carried with especial glee, the stone walls that ran like grey ribbons about the moors, and, above all, the vast expanse of sky upon whose surface clouds swam, raced, eddied and extended as I had never anywhere witnessed. . . .

I sat, lost and absorbed, at my carriage window, and when at last, long after dark had fallen, I heard 'Seascale' called by the porter, I was still staring in a sort of romantic dream. When I stepped out on to the little narrow platform and was greeted by the salt tang of the sea wind my first real introduction to the North Country may be said to have been completed. I am writing now in another part of that same Cumberland country, and beyond my window the line of the fell runs strong and bare against the sky, while below it the Lake lies, a fragment of silver glass at the feet of Skiddaw.

It may be that my sense of the deep mystery of this country had its origin in this same strange story that I am now relating. But again, perhaps not, for I believe that that first evening arrival at Seascale worked some change in me, so that since then none of the world's beauties—from the crimson waters of Kashmir to the rough glories of our own Cornish coast—can rival for me the sharp, peaty winds and strong, resilient turf of the Cumberland hills.

That was a magical drive in the pony-trap to Faildyke that evening. It was bitterly cold, but I did not seem to mind it. Everything was magical to me.

From the first I could see the great slow hump of Black Combe jet against the frothy clouds of the winter night, and I could hear the sea breaking and the soft rustle of the bare twigs in the hedgerows.

I made, too, the friend of my life that night, for it was Bob Armstrong who was driving the trap. He has often told me since (for although he is a slow man of few words he likes to repeat the things that seem to him worthwhile) that I struck him as 'pitifully lost' that evening on the Seascale platform. I looked, I don't doubt, pinched and cold enough. In any case it was a lucky appearance for me, for I won Armstrong's heart there and then, and he, once he gave it, could never bear to take it back again.

He, on his side, seemed to me gigantic that night. He had, I believe, one of the broadest chests in the world: it was a curse to him, he said, because no ready-made shirts would ever suit him. I sat in close to him because of the cold; he was very warm, and I could feel his heart beating like a steady clock inside his rough coat. It beat for me that night, and it has beaten for me, I'm glad to say, ever since.

In truth, as things turned out, I needed a friend. I was nearly asleep and stiff all over my little body when I was handed down from the trap and at once led into what seemed to me an immense hall crowded with the staring heads of slaughtered animals and smelling of straw.

I was so sadly weary that my uncles, when I met them in a vast billiard-room in which a great fire roared in a stone fireplace like a demon, seemed to me to be double.

In any case, what an odd pair they were! My Uncle Robert was a little man with grey untidy hair and little sharp eyes hooded by two of the bushiest eyebrows known to humanity. He wore (I remember as though it were yesterday) shabby country clothes of a faded green colour, and he had on one finger a ring with a thick red stone.

Another thing that I noticed at once when he kissed me (I detested to be kissed by anybody) was a faint scent that he had, connected at once in my mind with the caraway-seeds that there are in seed-cake. I noticed, too, that his teeth were discoloured and yellow.

My Uncle Constance I liked at once. He was fat, round, friendly and clean. Rather a dandy was Uncle Constance. He wore a flower in his buttonhole and his linen was snowy white in contrast with his brother's.

I noticed one thing, though, at that very first meeting, and that was that before he spoke to me and put his fat arm around my shoulder he seemed to look towards his brother as though for permission. You may say that it was unusual for a boy of my age to notice so much, but in fact I noticed everything at that time. Years and laziness, alas! have slackened my observation.

2

I had a horrible dream that night; it woke me screaming, and brought Bob Armstrong in to quiet me.

My room was large, like all the other rooms that I had seen, and empty, with a great expanse of floor and a stone fireplace like the one in the billiard-room. It was, I afterwards found, next to the servants' quarters. Armstrong's room was next to mine, and Mrs. Spender's, the housekeeper's, beyond his.

Armstrong was then, and is yet, a bachelor. He used to tell me that he loved so many women that he never could bring his mind to choose any one of them. And now he has been too long my personal bodyguard and is too lazily used to my ways to change his condition. He is, moreover, seventy years of age.

Well, what I saw in my dream was this. They had lit a fire for me (and it was necessary; the room was of an icy coldness) and I dreamt that I awoke to see the flames rise to a last vigour before they died away. In the brilliance of that illumination I was conscious that something was moving in the room. I heard the movement for some little while before I saw anything.

I sat up, my heart hammering, and then to my horror discerned, slinking against the farther wall, the evillest-looking yellow mongrel of a dog that you can fancy.

I find it difficult, I have always found it difficult, to describe exactly the horror of that yellow dog. It lay partly in its colour, which was vile, partly in its mean and bony body, but for the most part in its evil head—flat, with sharp little eyes and jagged yellow teeth.

As I looked at it, it bared those teeth at me and then began to creep, with an indescribably loathsome action, in the direction of my bed. I was at first stiffened with terror. Then, as it neared the bed, its little eyes fixed upon me and its teeth bared, I screamed again and again.

The next I knew was that Armstrong was sitting on my bed, his strong arm about my trembling little body. All I could say over and over was, 'The Dog! the Dog! the Dog!'

He soothed me as though he had been my mother.

'See, there's no dog there! There's no one but me! There's no one but me!'

I continued to tremble, so he got into bed with me, held me close to him, and it was in his comforting arms that I fell asleep.

3

In the morning I woke to a fresh breeze and a shining sun and the chrysanthemums, orange, crimson and dun, blowing against the grey stone wall beyond the sloping lawns. So, I forgot about my dream. I only knew that I loved Bob Armstrong better than anyone else on earth.

Everyone during the next days was very kind to me. I was so deeply excited by this country, so new to me, that at first, I could think of nothing else. Bob Armstrong was Cumbrian from the top of his flaxen head to the thick nails under his boots, and, in grunts and monosyllables, as was his way, he gave me the colour of the ground.

There was romance everywhere: smugglers stealing in and out of Drigg and Seascale, the ancient Cross in Gosforth churchyard, Ravenglass, with all its seabirds, once a port of splendour.

Muncaster Castle and Broughton and black Wastwater with the grim Screes, Black Combe, upon whose broad back the shadows were always dancing—even the little station at Seascale, naked to the seawinds, at whose bookstalls I bought a publication entitled the *Weekly Telegraph* that contained, week by week, instalments of the most thrilling story in the world.

Everywhere romance—the cows moving along the sandy lanes, the sea thundering along the Drigg beach, Gable and Scafell pulling their cloud-caps about their heads, the slow voices of the Cumbrian farmers calling their animals, the little tinkling bell of the Gosforth church—everywhere romance and beauty.

Soon, though, as I became better accustomed to the country, the people immediately around me began to occupy my attention, stimulate my restless curiosity, and especially my two uncles. They were, in fact, queer enough.

Faildyke Hall itself was not queer, only very ugly. It had been built about 1830, I should imagine, a square white building, like a thick-set, rather conceited woman with a very plain face. The rooms were large, the passages innumerable, and everything covered with a very hideous whitewash. Against this whitewash hung old photographs yellowed with age, and faded, bad water-colours. The furniture was strong and ugly.

One romantic feature, though, there was—and that was the little Grey Tower where my Uncle Robert lived. This Tower was at the end of the garden and looked out over a sloping field to the Scafell group beyond Wastwater. It had been built hundreds of years ago as a defence against the Scots. Robert had had his study and bedroom there for many years and it was his domain; no one was allowed to enter it save his old servant Hucking, a bent, wizened, grubby little man who spoke to no one and, so they said in the kitchen, managed to go through life without sleeping. He looked after my Uncle Robert, cleaned his rooms, and was supposed to clean his clothes.

I, being both an inquisitive and romantic-minded boy, was soon as eagerly excited about this Tower as was Bluebeard's wife about the forbidden room. Bob told me that whatever I did I was never to set foot inside.

And then I discovered another thing—that Bob Armstrong hated, feared and was proud of my Uncle Robert. He was proud of him because he was head of the family, and because, so he said, he was the cleverest old man in the world.

'Nothing he can't seemingly do,' said Bob, 'but he don't like you to watch him at it.'

All this only increased my longing to see the inside of the Tower, although I couldn't be said to be fond of my Uncle Robert either.

It would be hard to say that I disliked him during those first days. He was quite kindly to me when he met me, and at meal-times, when I sat with my two uncles at the long table in the big, bare, whitewashed dining-room, he was always anxious to see that I had plenty to eat. But I never liked him; it was perhaps because he wasn't clean. Children are sensitive to those things. Perhaps I didn't like the fusty, seed-caky smell that he carried about with him.

Then there came the day when he invited me into the Grey Tower and told me about Tarnhelm.

Pale slanting shadows of sunlight fell across the chrysanthemums and the grey stone walls, the long fields and the dusky hills. I was playing by myself by the little stream that ran beyond the rose garden, when Uncle Robert came up behind me in the soundless way he had, and, tweaking me by the ear, asked me whether I would like to come with him inside his Tower. I was, of course, eager enough; but I was frightened too, especially when I saw Hucking's moth-eaten old countenance peering at us from one of the narrow slits that pretended to be windows.

However, in we went, my hand in Uncle Robert's hot dry one. There wasn't, in reality, so very much to see when you were inside— all untidy and musty, with cobwebs over the doorways and old pieces of rusty iron and empty boxes in the corners, and the long table in Uncle Robert's study covered with a thousand things—books with the covers hanging on them, sticky green bottles, a looking-glass, a pair of scales, a globe, a cage with mice in it, a statue of a naked woman, an hour-glass—everything old and stained and dusty.

However, Uncle Robert made me sit down close to him, and told me many interesting stories. Among others the story about Tarnhelm.

Tarnhelm was something that you put over your head, and its magic turned you into any animal that you wished to be. Uncle Robert told me the story of a god called Wotan, and how he teased the dwarf who possessed Tarnhelm by saying that he couldn't turn himself into a mouse or some such animal; and the dwarf, his pride wounded, turned himself into a mouse, which the god easily captured and so stole Tarnhelm.

On the table, among all the litter, was a grey skull-cap.

'That's my Tarnhelm,' said Uncle Robert, laughing. 'Like to see me put it on?'

But I was suddenly frightened, terribly frightened. The sight of Uncle Robert made me feel quite ill. The room began to run round and round. The white mice in the cage twittered. It was stuffy in that room, enough to turn any boy sick.

4

That was the moment, I think, when Uncle Robert stretched out his hand towards his grey skull-cap—after that I was never happy again in Faildyke Hall. That action of his, simple and apparently friendly though it was, seemed to open my eyes to a number of things.

We were now within ten days of Christmas. The thought of Christmas had then—and, to tell the truth, still has—a most happy effect on me. There is the beautiful story, the geniality and kindliness, still, in spite of modern pessimists, much happiness and goodwill. Even now I yet enjoy giving presents and receiving them—then it was an ecstasy to me, the look of the parcel, the paper, the string, the exquisite surprise.

Therefore, I had been anticipating Christmas eagerly. I had been promised a trip into Whitehaven for present-buying, and there was to be a tree and a dance for the Gosforth villagers. Then after my visit to Uncle Robert's Tower, all my happiness of anticipation vanished. As the days went on and my observation of one thing and another developed, I would, I think, have run away back to my aunts in Kensington, had it not been for Bob Armstrong.

It was, in fact, Armstrong who started me on that voyage of observation that ended so horribly, for when he had heard that Uncle Robert had taken me inside his Tower his anger was fearful. I had never before seen him angry; now his great body shook, and he caught me and held me until I cried out.

He wanted me to promise that I would never go inside there again. What? Not even with Uncle Robert? No, most especially not with Uncle Robert; and then, dropping his voice and looking around him to be sure that there was no one listening, he began to curse Uncle Robert. This amazed me, because loyalty to his masters was one of Bob's great laws. I can see us now, standing on the stable cobbles in the falling white dusk while the horses stamped in their stalls, and the little sharp stars appeared one after another glittering between the driving clouds.

'I'll not stay,' I heard him say to himself. 'I'll be like the rest. I'll not be staying. To bring a child into it. . . .'

From that moment he seemed to have me very specially in his charge. Even when I could not see him I felt that his kindly eye was upon me, and this sense of the necessity that I should be guarded made me yet more uneasy and distressed.

The next thing that I observed was that the servants were all fresh, had been there not more than a month or two. Then, only a week before Christmas, the housekeeper departed. Uncle Constance seemed greatly upset at these occurrences; Uncle Robert did not seem in the least affected by them.

I come now to my Uncle Constance. At this distance of time it is strange with what clarity I still can see him—his stoutness, his shining cleanliness, his dandyism, the flower in his buttonhole, his little brilliantly shod feet, his thin, rather feminine voice. He would have been kind to me, I think, had he dared, but something kept him back. And what that something was I soon discovered; it was fear of my Uncle Robert.

It did not take me a day to discover that he was utterly subject to his brother. He said nothing without looking to see how Uncle Robert took it; suggested no plan until he first had assurance from his brother; was terrified beyond anything that I had before witnessed in a human being at any sign of irritation in my uncle.

I discovered after this that Uncle Robert enjoyed greatly to play on his brother's fears. I did not understand enough of their life to realise what were the weapons that Robert used, but that they were sharp and piercing I was neither too young nor too ignorant to perceive.

Such was our situation, then, a week before Christmas. The weather had become very wild, with a great wind. All nature seemed in an uproar. I could fancy when I lay in my bed at night and heard the shouting in my chimney that I could catch the crash of the waves upon the beach, see the black waters of Wastwater cream and curdle under the Screes. I would lie awake and long for Bob Armstrong—the strength of his arm and the warmth of his breast—but I considered myself too grown a boy to make any appeal.

I remember that now almost minute by minute my fears increased. What gave them force and power who can say? I was much alone, I had now a great terror of my uncle, the weather was wild, the rooms of the house large and desolate, the servants mysterious, the walls of the passages lit always with an unnatural glimmer because of their white colour, and although Armstrong had watch over me he was busy in his affairs and could not always be with me.

I grew to fear and dislike my Uncle Robert more and more. Hatred and fear of him seemed to be everywhere and yet he was always soft-voiced and kindly. Then, a few days before Christmas, occurred the event that was to turn my terror into panic.

I had been reading in the library Mrs. Radcliffe's *Romance of the Forest,* an old book long forgotten, worthy of revival. The library was a fine room run to seed, bookcases from floor to ceiling, the windows small and dark, holes in the old faded carpet. A lamp burnt at a distant table. One stood on a little shelf at my side.

Something, I know not what, made me look up. What I saw then can even now stamp my heart in its recollection. By the library door, not moving, staring across the room's length at me, was a yellow dog.

I will not attempt to describe all the pitiful fear and mad freezing terror that caught and held me. My main thought, I fancy, was that that other vision on my first night in the place had not been a dream. I was not asleep now; the book in which I had been reading had fallen to the floor, the lamps shed their glow, I could hear the ivy tapping on the pane. No, this was reality.

The dog lifted a long, horrible leg and scratched itself. Then very slowly and silently across the carpet it came towards me.

I could not scream; I could not move; I waited. The animal was even more evil than it had seemed before, with its flat head, its narrow eyes, its yellow fangs. It came steadily in my direction, stopped once to scratch itself again, then was almost at my chair.

It looked at me, bared its fangs, but now as though it grinned at me, then passed on. After it was gone there was a thick foetid scent in the air—the scent of caraway-seed.

5

I think now on looking back that it was remarkable enough that I, a pale, nervous child who trembled at every sound, should have met the situation as I did. I said nothing about the dog to any living soul, not even to Bob Armstrong. I hid my fears—and fears of a beastly and sickening kind they were, too—within my breast. I had the intelligence to perceive—and *how* I caught in the air the awareness of this I can't, at this distance, understand—that I was playing my little part in the climax to something that had been piling up, for many a month, like the clouds over Gable.

Understand that I offer from first to last in this no kind of explanation. There is possibly—and to this day I cannot quite be sure—nothing to explain. My Uncle Robert died simply—but you shall hear.

What was beyond any doubt or question was that it was after my seeing the dog in the library that Uncle Robert changed so strangely in his behaviour to me. That may have been the merest coincidence. I only know that as one grows older one calls things coincidence more and more seldom. In any case, that same night at dinner Uncle Robert seemed twenty years older. He was bent, shrivelled, would not eat, snarled at anyone who spoke to him and especially avoided even looking at me. It was a painful meal, and it was after it, when Uncle Constance and I were sitting alone in the old yellow-papered

143

drawing-room—a room with two ticking clocks for ever racing one another—that the most extraordinary thing occurred. Uncle Constance and I were playing draughts. The only sounds were the roaring of the wind down the chimney, the hiss and splutter of the fire, the silly ticking of the clocks. Suddenly Uncle Constance put down the piece that he was about to move and began to cry.

To a child it is always a terrible thing to see a grown-up person cry, and even to this day to hear a man cry is very distressing to me. I was moved desperately by poor Uncle Constance, who sat there, his head in his white plump hands, all his stout body shaking. I ran over to him and he clutched me and held me as though he would never let me go. He sobbed incoherent words about protecting me, caring for me . . . seeing that that monster. . . .

At the word I remember that I too began to tremble. I asked my uncle what monster, but he could only continue to murmur incoherently about hate and not having the pluck, and if only he had the courage. . . .

Then, recovering a little, he began to ask me questions. Where had I been? Had I been into his brother's Tower? Had I seen anything that frightened me? If I did would I at once tell him? And then he muttered that he would never have allowed me to come had he known that it would go as far as this, that it would be better if I went away that night, and that if he were not afraid. . . . Then he began to tremble again and to look at the door, and I trembled too. He held me in his arms; then we thought that there was a sound and we listened, our heads up, our two hearts hammering. But it was only the clocks ticking and the wind shrieking as though it would tear the house to pieces.

That night, however, when Bob Armstrong came up to bed he found me sheltering there. I whispered to him that I was frightened; I put my arms around his neck and begged him not to send me away; he promised me that I should not leave him and I slept all night in the protection of his strength.

How, though, can I give any true picture of the fear that pursued me now? For I knew from what both Armstrong and Uncle Constance had said that there was real danger, that it was no hysterical fancy of mine or ill-digested dream. It made it worse that Uncle Robert was now no more seen. He was sick; he kept within his Tower, cared for by his old wizened manservant. And so, being nowhere, he was everywhere. I stayed with Armstrong when I could, but a kind of pride prevented me from clinging like a girl to his coat.

A deathly silence seemed to fall about the place. No one laughed or sang, no dog barked, no bird sang. Two days before Christmas an iron frost came to grip the land. The fields were rigid, the sky itself seemed to be frozen grey, and under the olive cloud Scafell and Gable were black.

Christmas Eve came.

On that morning, I remember, I was trying to draw—some childish picture of one of Mrs. Radcliffe's scenes—when the double doors unfolded and Uncle Robert stood there. He stood there, bent, shrivelled, his long, grey locks falling over his collar, his bushy eyebrows thrust forward. He wore his old green suit and on his finger gleamed his heavy red ring. I was frightened, of course, but also, I was touched with pity. He looked so old, so frail, so small in this large empty house.

I sprang up. 'Uncle Robert,' I asked timidly, 'are you better?'

He bent still lower until he was almost on his hands and feet; then he looked up at me, and his yellow teeth were bared, almost as an animal snarls. Then the doors closed again.

The slow, stealthy, grey afternoon came at last. I walked with Armstrong to Gosforth village on some business that he had. We said no word of any matter at the Hall. I told him, he has reminded me, of how fond I was of him and that I wanted to be with him always, and he answered that perhaps it might be so, little knowing how true that prophecy was to stand. Like all children I had a great capacity for forgetting the atmosphere that I was not at that moment in, and I walked beside Bob along the frozen roads, with some of my fears surrendered.

But not for long. It was dark when I came into the long, yellow drawing-room. I could hear the bells of Gosforth church pealing as I passed from the ante-room.

A moment later there came a shrill, terrified cry: 'Who's that? Who is it?'

It was Uncle Constance, who was standing in front of the yellow silk window curtains, staring at the dusk. I went over to him and he held me close to him.

'Listen!' he whispered. 'What can you hear?'

The double doors through which I had come were half open. At first, I could hear nothing but the clocks, the very faint rumble of a cart on the frozen road. There was no wind.

My uncle's fingers gripped my shoulder. 'Listen!' he said again. And now I heard. On the stone passage beyond the drawing-room was the patter of an animal's feet. Uncle Constance and I looked at one another. In that exchanged glance we confessed that our secret was the same. We knew what we should see.

A moment later it was there, standing in the double doorway, crouching a little and staring at us with a hatred that was mad and sick—the hatred of a sick animal crazy with unhappiness, but loathing us more than its own misery.

Slowly it came towards us, and to my reeling fancy all the room seemed to stink of caraway-seed.

'Keep back! Keep away!' my uncle screamed.

I became oddly in my turn the protector.

'It shan't touch you! It shan't touch you, uncle!' I called.

But the animal came on.

It stayed for a moment near a little round table that contained a composition of dead waxen fruit under a glass dome. It stayed here, its nose down, smelling the ground. Then, looking up at us, it came on again.

Oh God!—even now as I write after all these years it is with me again, the flat skull, the cringing body in its evil colour and that loathsome smell. It slobbered a little at its jaw. It bared its fangs.

Then I screamed, hid my face in my uncle's breast and saw that he held, in his trembling hand, a thick, heavy, old-fashioned revolver.

Then he cried out:

'Go back, Robert. . . . Go back!'

The animal came on. He fired. The detonation shook the room. The dog turned and, blood dripping from its throat, crawled across the floor.

By the door it halted, turned and looked at us. Then it disappeared into the other room.

My uncle had flung down his revolver; he was crying, sniffling; he kept stroking my forehead, murmuring words.

At last, clinging to one another, we followed the splotches of blood, across the carpet, beside the door, through the doorway.

Huddled against a chair in the outer sitting-room, one leg twisted under him, was my Uncle Robert, shot through the throat.

On the floor, by his side, was a grey skull-cap.

The Tarn

1

As Foster moved unconsciously across the room, bent towards the bookcase, and stood leaning forward a little, choosing now one book, now another with his eye, his host, seeing the muscles of the back of his thin, scraggy neck stand out above his low flannel collar, thought of the ease with which he could squeeze that throat and the pleasure, the triumphant, lustful pleasure, that such an action would give him.

The low white-walled, white-ceilinged room was flooded with the mellow, kindly Lakeland sun. October is a wonderful month in the English Lakes, golden, rich, and perfumed, slow suns moving through apricot-tinted skies to ruby evening glories; the shadows lie then thick about that beautiful country, in dark purple patches, in long web-like patterns of silver gauze, in thick splotches of amber and grey. The clouds pass in galleons across the mountains, now veiling, now revealing, now descending with ghost-like armies to the very breast of the plains, suddenly rising to the softest of blue skies and lying thin in lazy languorous colour.

Fenwick's cottage looked across to Low Fells; on his right, seen through side windows, sprawled the hills above Ullswater.

Fenwick looked at Foster's back and felt suddenly sick, so that he sat down, veiling his eyes for a moment with his hand. Foster had come up there, come all the way from London, to explain, to want to put things right. For how many years had he known Foster? Why, for twenty at least, and during all those years Foster had been for ever determined to put things right with everybody. He could not bear to be disliked; he hated that anyone should think ill of him; he wanted everyone to be his friend. That was one reason, perhaps, why Foster had got on so well, had prospered so in his career; one reason, too, why Fenwick had not.

For Fenwick was the opposite of Foster in this. He did not want friends; he certainly did not care that people should like him—that is, people for whom, for one reason or another, he had contempt—and he had contempt for quite a number of people.

Fenwick looked at that long, thin, bending back and felt his knees tremble. Soon Foster would turn round and that high reedy voice would pipe out something about the books. 'What jolly books you have, Fenwick!' How many, many times in the long watches of the night when Fenwick could not sleep had he heard that pipe sounding close there—yes, in the very shadows of his bed! And how many times had Fenwick replied to it: 'I hate you! You are the cause of my failure in life! You have been in my way always. Always, always, always! Patronising and pretending, and in truth showing others what a poor thing you thought me, how great a failure, how conceited a fool! I know. You can hide nothing from me! I can hear you!'

For twenty years now, Foster had been persistently in Fenwick's way. There had been that affair, so long ago now, when Robins had wanted a sub-editor for his wonderful review, the *Parthenon*, and Fenwick had gone to see him and they had had a splendid talk. How magnificently Fenwick had talked that day, with what enthusiasm he had shown Robins (who was blinded by his own conceit, anyway) the kind of paper the *Parthenon* might be, how Robins had caught his own enthusiasm, how he had pushed his fat body about the room, crying, 'Yes, yes, Fenwick—that's fine! That's fine indeed!'—and then how, after all, Foster had got that job.

The paper had only lived for a year or so, it is true, but the connection with it had brought Foster into prominence just as it might have brought Fenwick!

★★★★★★

Then five years later there was Fenwick's novel, *The Bitter Aloe*—the novel upon which he had spent three years of blood-and-tears endeavour—and then, in the very same week of publication, Foster brings out *The Circus*, the novel that made his name, although, Heaven knows, the thing was poor sentimental trash. You may say that one novel cannot kill another—but can it not? Had not *The Circus* appeared would not that group of London know-alls—that conceited, limited, ignorant, self-satisfied crowd, who nevertheless can do, by their talk, so much to affect a book's good or evil fortunes—have talked about *The Bitter Aloe*, and so forced it into prominence? As it was, the book was still-born, and *The Circus* went on its prancing, triumphant way.

After that there had been many occasions—some small, some big—and always in one way or another that thin, scraggy body of Foster's was interfering with Fenwick's happiness.

The thing had become, of course, an obsession with Fenwick. Hiding up there in the heart of the Lakes, with no friends, almost no company, and very little money, he was given too much to brooding over his failure. He *was* a failure, and it was not his own fault. How could it be his own fault with his talents and his brilliance? It was the fault of modern life and its lack of culture, the fault of the stupid material mess that made up the intelligence of human beings—and the fault of Foster.

Always Fenwick hoped that Foster would keep away from him. He did not know what he would not do did he see the man. And then one day to his amazement he received a telegram: 'Passing through this way. May I stop with you Monday and Tuesday? Giles Foster.'

Fenwick could scarcely believe his eyes, and then—from curiosity, from cynical contempt, from some deeper, more mysterious motive that he dared not analyse—he had telegraphed 'Come.'

And here the man was. And he had come—would you believe it?—to 'put things right.' He had heard from Hamlin Eddis that 'Fenwick was hurt with him, had some kind of a grievance.'

'I didn't like to feel that, old man, and so I thought I'd just stop by and have it out with you, see what the matter was, and put it right.'

Last night after supper Foster had tried to put it right. Eagerly, his eyes like a good dog's who is asking for a bone that he knows that he thoroughly deserves, he had held out his hand and asked Fenwick to 'say what was up.'

Fenwick simply had said that nothing was up; Hamlin Eddis was a damned fool.

'Oh, I'm glad to hear that!' Foster had cried, springing up out of his chair and putting his hand on Fenwick's shoulder. 'I'm glad of that, old man. I couldn't bear for us not to be friends. We've been friends so long.'

Lord! how Fenwick hated him at that moment!

2

'What a jolly lot of books you have!' Foster turned round and looked at Fenwick with eager, gratified eyes. 'Every book here is interesting! I like your arrangement of them too, and those open bookshelves—it always seems to me a shame to shut up books behind glass!'

Foster came forward and sat down quite close to his host. He even reached forward and laid his hand on his host's knee. 'Look here! I'm mentioning it for the last time—positively! But I do want to make quite certain. There *is* nothing wrong between us, is there, old man? I know you assured me last night, but I just want——'

Fenwick looked at him and, surveying him, felt suddenly an exquisite pleasure of hatred. He liked the touch of the man's hand on his knee; he himself bent forward a little and, thinking how agreeable it would be to push Foster's eyes in, deep, deep into his head, crunching them, smashing them to purple, leaving the empty, staring, bloody sockets, said:

'Why, no. Of course not. I told you last night. What could there be?'

The hand gripped the knee a little more tightly.

'I *am* so glad! That's splendid! Splendid! I hope you won't think me ridiculous, but I've always had an affection for you ever since I can remember. I've always wanted to know you better. I've admired your talents so greatly. That novel of yours—the—the—the one about the Aloe——'

'*The Bitter Aloe?*'

'Ah, yes, that was it. That was a splendid book. Pessimistic, of course, but still fine. It ought to have done better. I remember thinking so at the time.'

'Yes, it ought to have done better.'

'Your time will come, though. What I say is that good work always tells in the end.'

'Yes, my time will come.'

The thin, piping voice went on:

'Now, I've had more success than I deserved. Oh, yes, I have. You can't deny it. I'm not being falsely modest. I mean it. I've got some talent, of course, but not so much as people say. And you! Why, you've got so much *more* than they acknowledge. You have, old man. You have indeed. Only—I do hope you'll forgive my saying this—perhaps you haven't advanced quite as you might have done. Living up here, shut away here, closed in by all these mountains, in this wet climate—always raining—why, you're out of things! You don't see people, don't talk and discover what's really going on. Why, look at me!'

Fenwick turned round and looked at him.

'Now, I have half the year in London, where one gets the best of everything, best talk, best music, best plays, and then I'm three months abroad, Italy or Greece or somewhere, and then three months in the country. Now that's an ideal arrangement. You have everything that way.'

'Italy or Greece or somewhere!'

Something turned in Fenwick's breast, grinding, grinding, grinding. How he had longed, oh, how passionately, for just one week in Greece, two days in Sicily! Sometimes he had thought that he might run to it, but when it had come to the actual counting of the pennies—and now this fool, this fathead, this self-satisfied, conceited, patronising——

He got up, looking out at the golden sun.

'What do you say to a walk?' he suggested. 'The sun will last for a good hour yet.'

3

As soon as the words were out of his lips he felt as though someone else had said them for him. He even turned half-round to see whether anyone else were there. Ever since Foster's arrival on the evening before he had been conscious of this sensation. A walk? Why should he take Foster for a walk, show him his beloved country, point out those curves and lines and hollows, the long silver shield of Ullswater, the cloudy purple hills hunched like blankets about the knees of some recumbent giant? Why? It was as though he had turned round to someone behind him and had said, 'You have some further design in this.'

They started out. The road sank abruptly to the lake, then the path ran between trees at the water's edge. Across the lake, tones of bright yellow light, crocus-hued, rode upon the blue. The hills were dark.

The very way that Foster walked bespoke the man. He was always a little ahead of you, pushing his long, thin body along with little eager jerks as though did he not hurry he would miss something that would be immensely to his advantage. He talked, throwing words over his shoulder to Fenwick as you throw crumbs of bread to a robin.

'Of course, I was pleased. Who would not be? After all it's a new prize. They've only been awarding it for a year or two, but it's gratifying—really gratifying—to secure it. When I opened the envelope, and found the cheque there—well, you could have knocked me down with a feather. You could, indeed. Of course, a hundred pounds isn't much. But it's the honour——'

Whither were they going? Their destiny was as certain as though they had no free-will. Free-will? There is no free-will. All is Fate. Fenwick suddenly laughed aloud.

Foster stopped.

'Why, what is it?'

'What's what?'

'You laughed.'

'Something amused me.'

Foster slipped his arm through Fenwick's.

'It *is* jolly to be walking alone together like this, arm-in-arm, friends. I'm a sentimental man, I won't deny it. What I say is that life is short and one must love one's fellow-beings or where is one? You live too much alone, old man.' He squeezed Fenwick's arm. 'That's the truth of it.'

It was torture, exquisite, heavenly torture. It was wonderful to feel that thin, bony arm pressing against his. Almost you could hear the beating of that other heart. Wonderful to feel that arm and the temptation to take it in your two hands and to bend it and twist it and then to hear the bones *crack* . . . . . *crack* . . . . *crack*. . . . . Wonderful to feel that temptation rise through one's body like boiling water and yet not to yield to it. For a moment Fenwick's hand touched Foster's. Then he drew himself apart.

'We're at the village. This is the hotel where they all come in the summer. We turn off at the right here. I'll show you my tarn.'

4

'Your tarn?' asked Foster. 'Forgive my ignorance, but what *is* a tarn exactly?'

'A tarn is a miniature lake, a pool of water lying in the lap of the hill. Very quiet, lovely, silent. Some of them are immensely deep.'

'I should like to see that.'

'It is some little distance—up a rough road. Do you mind?'

'Not a bit. I have long legs.'

'Some of them are immensely deep—unfathomable—nobody touched the bottom—but quiet, like glass, with shadows only——'

'Do you know, Fenwick, but I have always been afraid of water—I've never learnt to swim. I'm afraid to go out of my depth. Isn't that ridiculous? But it is all because at my private school, years ago, when I was a small boy, some big fellows took me and held me with my head under the water and nearly drowned me. They did indeed. They went further than they meant to. I can see their faces.'

Fenwick considered this. The picture leapt to his mind. He could see the boys—large, strong fellows, probably—and this little skinny thing like a frog, their thick hands about his throat, his legs like grey sticks kicking out of the water, their laughter, their sudden sense that something was wrong, the skinny body all flaccid and still——

He drew a deep breath.

Foster was walking beside him now, not ahead of him, as though he were a little afraid, and needed reassurance. Indeed, the scene had changed. Before and behind them stretched the uphill path, loose with shale and stones. On their right, on a ridge at the foot of the hill, were some quarries, almost deserted, but the more melancholy in the fading afternoon because a little work still continued there, faint sounds came from the gaunt listening chimneys, a stream of water ran and tumbled angrily into a pool below, once and again a black silhouette, like a question mark, appeared against the darkening hill.

It was a little steep here and Foster puffed and blew.

Fenwick hated him the more for that. So thin and spare, and still he could not keep in condition! They stumbled, keeping below the quarry, on the edge of the running water, now green, now a dirty white-grey, pushing their way along the side of the hill.

Their faces were set now towards Helvellyn. It rounded the cup of hills closing in the base and then sprawling to the right.

'There's the tarn!' Fenwick exclaimed—and then added, 'The sun's not lasting as long as I had expected. It's growing dark already.'

Foster stumbled and caught Fenwick's arm.

'This twilight makes the hills look strange—like living men. I can scarcely see my way.'

'We're alone here,' Fenwick answered. 'Don't you feel the stillness? The men will have left the quarry now and gone home. There is no one in all this place but ourselves. If you watch you will see a strange green light steal down over the hills. It lasts but for a moment, and then it is dark.

'Ah, here is my tarn. Do you know how I love this place, Foster? It seems to belong especially to me, just as much as all your work and your glory and fame and success seem to belong to you. I have this and you have that. Perhaps in the end we are even after all. Yes. . . . .

'But I feel as though that piece of water belonged to me and I to it, and as though we should never be separated—yes. . . . . Isn't it black?

'It is one of the deep ones. No one has ever sounded it. Only Helvellyn knows, and one day I fancy that it will take me, too, into its confidence—will whisper its secrets———'

Foster sneezed.

'Very nice. Very beautiful, Fenwick. I like your tarn. Charming. And now let's turn back. That is a difficult walk beneath the quarry. It's chilly, too.'

'Do you see that little jetty there?' Fenwick led Foster by the arm. 'Someone built that out into the water. He had a boat there, I suppose. Come and look down. From the end of the little jetty it looks so deep and the mountains seem to close round.'

Fenwick took Foster's arm and led him to the end of the jetty. Indeed, the water looked deep here. Deep and very black. Foster peered down, then he looked up at the hills that did indeed seem to have gathered close around him. He sneezed again.

'I've caught a cold, I am afraid. Let's turn homewards, Fenwick, or we shall never find our way.'

'Home then,' said Fenwick, and his hands closed about the thin, scraggy neck. For the instant the head half turned and two startled, strangely childish eyes stared; then, with a push that was ludicrously simple, the body was impelled forward, there was a sharp cry, a splash, a stir of something white against the swiftly gathering dusk, again and then again, then far-spreading ripples, then silence.

5

The silence extended. Having enwrapped the tarn, it spread as though with finger on lip to the already quiescent hills. Fenwick shared in the silence. He luxuriated in it. He did not move at all. He stood there looking upon the inky water of the tarn, his arms folded, a man lost in intensest thought. But he was not thinking. He was only conscious of a warm luxurious relief, a sensuous feeling that was not thought at all.

Foster was gone—that tiresome, prating, conceited, self-satisfied fool! Gone, never to return. The tarn assured him of that. It stared back into Fenwick's face approvingly as though it said: 'You have done well—a clean and necessary job. We have done it together, you and I. I am proud of you.'

He was proud of himself. At last he had done something definite with his life. Thought, eager, active thought, was beginning now to flood his brain. For all these years, he had hung around in this place doing nothing but cherish grievances, weak, backboneless—now at last there was action. He drew himself up and looked at the hills. He was proud—and he was cold. He was shivering. He turned up the collar of his coat. Yes, there was the faint green light that always lingered in the shadows of the hills for a brief moment before darkness came. It was growing late. He had better return.

Shivering now so that his teeth chattered, he started off down the path, and then was aware that he did not wish to leave the tarn. The tarn was friendly; the only friend he had in all the world. As he stumbled along in the dark, this sense of loneliness grew. He was going home to an empty house. There had been a guest in it last night. Who was it? Why, Foster, of course—Foster with his silly laugh and amiable, mediocre eyes. Well, Foster would not be there now. No, he never would be there again. And suddenly Fenwick started to run. He did not know why, except that, now that he had left the tarn, he was lonely. He wished that he could have stayed there all night, but because he was cold he could not, and now he was running so that he might be at home with the lights and the familiar furniture—and all the things that he knew to reassure him.

As he ran the shale and stones scattered beneath his feet. They made a tit-tattering noise under him, and someone else seemed to be running too. He stopped, and the other runner also stopped. He breathed in the silence. He was hot now. The perspiration was trickling down his cheeks. He could feel a dribble of it down his back inside his shirt. His knees were pounding. His heart was thumping. And all around him, the hills were so amazingly silent, now like india-rubber clouds that you could push in or pull out as you do those india-rubber faces, grey against the night sky of a crystal purple upon whose surface, like the twinkling eyes of boats at sea, stars were now appearing.

His knees steadied, his heart beat less fiercely, and he began to run again. Suddenly he had turned the corner and was out at the hotel. Its lamps were kindly and reassuring. He walked then quietly along the lake-side path, and had it not been for the certainty that someone was treading behind him he would have been comfortable and at his ease. He stopped once or twice and looked back, and once he stopped and called out 'Who's there?' Only the rustling trees answered.

He had the strangest fancy, but his brain was throbbing so fiercely that he could not think, that it was the tarn that was following him, the tarn slipping, sliding along the road, being with him so that he should not be lonely. He could almost hear the tarn whisper in his ear: 'We did that together, and so I do not wish you to bear all the responsibility yourself. I will stay with you, so that you are not lonely.'

He climbed the road towards home, and there were the lights of his house. He heard the gate click behind him as though it were shutting him in. He went into the sitting-room, lighted and ready. There were the books that Foster had admired.

The old woman who looked after him appeared.

'Will you be having some tea, sir?'

'No, thank you, Annie.'

'Will the other gentleman be wanting any?'

'No; the other gentleman is away for the night.'

'Then there will be only one for supper?'

'Yes, only one for supper.'

He sat in the corner of the sofa and fell instantly into a deep slumber.

6

He woke when the old woman tapped him on the shoulder and told him that supper was served. The room was dark save for the jumping light of two uncertain candles. Those two red candlesticks—how he hated them up there on the mantelpiece! He had always hated them, and now they seemed to him to have something of the quality of Foster's voice—that thin, reedy, piping tone.

He was expecting at every moment that Foster would enter, and yet he knew that he would not. He continued to turn his head towards the door, but it was so dark there that you could not see. The whole room was dark except just there by the fireplace, where the two candlesticks went whining with their miserable twinkling plaint.

He went into the dining-room and sat down to his meal. But he could not eat anything. It was odd—that place by the table where Foster's chair should be. Odd, naked, and made a man feel lonely.

He got up once from the table and went to the window, opened it and looked out. He listened for something. A trickle as of running water, a stir, through the silence, as though some deep pool were filling to the brim. A rustle in the trees, perhaps. An owl hooted. Sharply, as though someone had spoken to him unexpectedly behind his shoulder, he closed the window and looked back, peering under his dark eyebrows into the room.

Later on, he went up to bed.

7

Had he been sleeping, or had he been lying lazily as one does, half-dozing, half-luxuriously not-thinking? He was wide awake now, utterly awake, and his heart was beating with apprehension. It was as though someone had called him by name. He slept always with his window a little open and the blind up. Tonight the moonlight shadowed in sickly fashion the objects in his room. It was not a flood of light nor yet a sharp splash, silvering a square, a circle, throwing the rest into ebony blackness. The light was dim, a little green, perhaps, like the shadow that comes over the hills just before dark.

He stared at the window, and it seemed to him that something moved there. Within, or rather against the green-grey light, something silver-tinted glistened. Fenwick stared. It had the look, exactly, of slipping water.

Slipping water! He listened, his head up, and it seemed to him that from beyond the window he caught the stir of water, not running, but rather welling up and up, gurgling with satisfaction as it filled and filled.

He sat up higher in bed, and then saw that down the wallpaper beneath the window water was undoubtedly trickling. He could see it lurch to the projecting wood of the sill, pause, and then slip, slither down the incline. The odd thing was that it fell so silently.

Beyond the window there was that odd gurgle, but in the room, itself, absolute silence. Whence could it come? He saw the line of silver rise and fall as the stream on the window-ledge ebbed and flowed.

He must get up and close the window. He drew his legs above the sheets and blankets and looked down.

He shrieked. The floor was covered with a shining film of water. It was rising. As he looked it had covered half the short stumpy legs of the bed. It rose without a wink, a bubble, a break! Over the sill it poured now in a steady flow, but soundless. Fenwick sat back in the bed, the clothes gathered to his chin, his eyes blinking, the Adam's apple throbbing like a throttle in his throat.

But he must do something, he must stop this. The water was now level with the seats of the chairs, but still was soundless. Could he but reach the door!

He put down his naked foot, then cried again. The water was icy cold. Suddenly, leaning, staring at its dark unbroken sheen, something seemed to push him forward. He fell. His head, his face was under the icy liquid; it seemed adhesive and in the heart of its ice hot like melting wax. He struggled to his feet. The water was breast-high. He screamed again and again. He could see the looking-glass, the row of books, the picture of Dürer's 'Horse,' aloof, impervious. He beat at the water and flakes of it seemed to cling to him like scales of fish, clammy to his touch. He struggled, ploughing his way, towards the door.

The water now was at his neck. Then something had caught him by the ankle. Something held him. He struggled, crying, 'Let me go! Let me go! I tell you to let me go! I hate you! I hate you! I will not come down to you! I will not——'

The water covered his mouth. He felt that someone pushed in his eyeballs with bare knuckles. A cold hand reached up and caught his naked thigh.

8

In the morning the little maid knocked and, receiving no answer, came in, as was her wont, with his shaving water. What she saw made her scream. She ran for the gardener.

They took the body with its staring, protruding eyes, its tongue sticking out between the clenched teeth, and laid it on the bed.

The only sign of disorder was an overturned water-jug. A small pool of water stained the carpet.

It was a lovely morning. A twig of ivy idly, in the little breeze, tapped the pane.

Nancy Ross

1

Mr. Munty Ross's house was certainly the smartest in March Square; No. 14, where the Duchess of Crole lived, was shabby in comparison. Very often you may see a line of motorcars and carriages stretching down the Square, then round the corner into Lent Street, and you may know then—as, indeed, all the Square did know and most carefully observed—that Mrs. Munty Ross was giving another of her smart little parties. That dark green door, that neat overhanging balcony, those rows—in the summer months—of scarlet geraniums, that roll of carpet that ran, many times a week, from the door over the pavement to the very foot of the waiting vehicle—these things were Mrs. Munty Ross's.

Munty Ross—a silent, ugly, black little man—had made his money in potted shrimps, or something equally compact and indigestible, and it really was very nice to think that shrimps in time could blossom out into beauty as striking as Mrs. Munty's lovely dresses, or melody as wonderful as the voice of M. Radiziwill, the famous tenor, whom she often "turned on" at her little evening parties. Upon Mr. Munty alone the shrimps seemed to have made no effect. He was as black, as insignificant, as ugly as ever he had been in the days before he knew of a shrimp's possibilities. He was very silent at his wife's parties, and sometimes dropped his h's.

What Mrs. Munty had been before her marriage no one quite knew, but now she was flaxen and slim and beautifully clothed, with a voice like an insincere canary; she had "a passion for the Opera," a "passion for motoring," "a passion for the latest religion," and "a passion for the simple life." All these things did the shrimps enable her to gratify, and "the simple life" cost her more than all the others put together.

159

Heaven had blessed them with one child, and that child was called Nancy. Nancy, her mother always said with pride, was old for her age, and, as her age was only just five, that remark was quite true. Nancy Ross was old for any age. Had she herself, one is compelled when considering her to wonder, any conception during those first months of the things that were going to be made out of her, and had she, perhaps at the very commencement of it all, some instinct of protest and rebellion? Poor Nancy! The tragedy of her whole case was now none other than that she hadn't, here at five years old in March Square, the slightest picture of what she had become, nor could she, I suppose, have imagined it possible for her to become anything different.

Nancy, in her own real and naked person, was a small child with a good flow of flaxen hair and light blue eyes. All her features were small and delicate, and she gave you the impression that if you only pulled a string or pushed a button somewhere in the middle of her back you could evoke any cry, smile or exclamation that you cared to arouse. Her eyes were old and weary, her attitude always that of one who had learnt the ways of this world, had found them sawdust, but had nevertheless consented still to play the game. Just as the house was filled with little gilt chairs and china cockatoos, so was Nancy arrayed in ribbons and bows and lace. Mrs. Munty had, one must suppose, surveyed during certain periods in her life certain real emotions rather as the gaping villagers survey the tiger behind his bars in the travelling circus.

The time had then come when she put these emotions away from her as childish things and determined never to be faced with any of them again. It was not likely, then, that she would introduce Nancy to any of them. She introduced Nancy to clothes and deportment and left it at that. She wanted her child to "look nice." She was able, now that Nancy was five years old, to say that she "looked very nice indeed."

2

From the very beginning nurses were chosen who would take care of Nancy Ross's appearance. There was plenty of money to spend, and Nancy was a child who, with her flaxen hair and blue eyes, would repay trouble. She *did* repay it, because she had no desires towards grubbiness or rebellion, or any wildnesses whatever. She just sat there with her doll balanced neatly in her arms and allowed herself to be pulled and twisted and squeezed and stretched. "There's a pretty little lady," said nurse, and a pretty little lady Nancy was sure that she was.

The order for her day was that in the morning she went out for a walk in the garden in the Square, and in the afternoon, she went out for another. During these walks she moved slowly, her doll delicately carried, her beautiful clothes shining with approval of the way that they were worn, her head high, "like a little queen," said her nurse. She was conscious of the other children in the garden, who often stopped in the middle of their play and watched her. She thought them hot and dirty and very noisy. She was sorry for their mothers.

It happened sometimes that she came downstairs, towards the end of a luncheon party, and was introduced to the guests. "You pretty little thing," women in very large hats said to her. "Lovely hair," or "She's the very image of *you*, Clarice," to her mother. She liked to hear that, because she greatly admired her mother. She knew that she, Nancy Ross, was beautiful; she knew that clothes were of an immense importance; she knew that other children were unpleasant. For the rest, she was neither extravagantly glad nor extravagantly sorry. She preserved a fine indifference. . . . And yet, although here my story may seem to matter-of-fact persons to take a turn towards the fantastic, this was not quite all. Nancy herself, dimly and yet uneasily, was aware that there was something else.

She was not a little girl who believed in fairies or witches or the "bogey man," or anything indeed that she could not see. She inherited from her mother a splendid confidence in the reality, the solid, unquestioned reality, of all concrete and tangible things. She had been presented once with a fine edition of *Grimm's Fairy Tales*, an edition with coloured pictures and every allure. She had turned its pages with a look of incredulous amazement. "What," she seemed to say—she was then aged three and a half—"are these absurd things that you are telling me? People aren't like that. Mother isn't in the least like that. I don't understand this, and it's tedious!"

"I'm afraid the child has no imagination," said her nurse.

"What a lucky thing!" said her mother.

Nor could Mrs. Ross's house be said to be a place that encouraged fairies. They would have found the gilt chairs hard to sit upon, and there were no mysterious corners. There was nothing mysterious at all. And yet Nancy Ross, sitting in her magnificent clothes, was conscious as she advanced towards her sixth year that she was not perfectly comfortable. To say that she felt lonely would be, perhaps, to emphasize too strongly her discomfort. It was perhaps rather that she felt inquisitive—only a little, a very little—but she did begin to wish that she could ask a few questions.

There came a day—an astonishing day—when she felt irritated with her mother. She had during her walk through the garden seen a little boy and a little girl, who were grubbing about in a little pile of earth and sand there in the corner under the trees and grubbing very happily. They had dirt upon their faces, but their nurse was sitting, apparently quite easy in her mind, and the sun had not stopped in its course nor had the birds upon the trees ceased to sing. Nancy stayed for a moment her progress and looked at them, and something not very far from envy struck, in some far-distant hiding-place, her soul. She moved on, but when she came indoors and was met by her mamma and a handsome lady, her mamma's friend, who said: "Isn't she a pretty dear?" and her mother said: "That's right, Nancy darling, been for your walk?" she was, for an amazing moment, irritated with her beautiful mother.

3

Once she was conscious of this desire to ask questions she had no more peace. Although she was only five years of age she had all the determination not "to give herself away" of a woman of forty. She was not going to show that she wanted anything in the world, and yet she would have liked—— A little wistfully she looked at her nurse. But that good woman, carefully chosen by Mrs. Ross, was not the one to encourage questions. She was as shining as a new brass nail, and a great deal harder.

The nursery was as neat as a pin, with a lovely bright rocking-horse upon which Nancy had never ridden; a pink doll's house with every modern contrivance, whose doors had never been opened; a number of expensive dolls, which had never been disrobed. Nancy approached these joys—diffidently and with caution. She rode upon the horse, opened the doll's house, embraced the dolls, but she had no natural imagination to bestow upon them, and the horse and the dolls, hurt, perhaps, at their long neglect, received her with frigidity. Those grubby little children in the Square would, she knew, have been "there" in a moment. She began then to be frightened. The nursery, her bedroom, the dark little passage outside, were suddenly alarming. Sometimes, when she was sitting quietly in her nursery, the house was so silent that she could have screamed.

"I don't think Miss Nancy's quite well, ma'am," said the nurse.

"Oh, dear! What a nuisance," said Mrs. Ross, who liked her little girl to be always well and beautiful. "I do hope she's not going to catch something."

"She doesn't take that pleasure in her clothes she did," said the nurse.

"Perhaps she wants some new ones," said her mother. "Take her to Florice, nurse."

Nancy went to Florice, and beautiful new garments were invented, and once again she was squeezed, and tightened, and stretched, and pulled. But Nancy was indifferent. As they tried these clothes, and stood back, and stepped forward, and admired and criticised, she was thinking, "I wish the nursery clock didn't make such a noise."

Her little bedroom next to nurse's large one was a beautiful affair, with red roses up and down the wallpaper and in and out of the crockery and round and round the carpet. Her bed was magnificent, with lace and more roses, and there was a fine photograph of her beautiful mother in a silver frame on the mantelpiece. But all these things were of little avail when the dark came. She began to be frightened of the dark.

There came a night when, waking with a suddenness that did of itself contribute to her alarm, she was conscious that the room was intensely dark, and that everyone was very far away. The house, as she listened, seemed to be holding its breath, the clock in the nursery was ticking in a frightened, startled terror, and hesitating, whimsical noises broke, now close, now distant, upon the silence. She lay there, her heart beating as it had surely never been allowed to beat before. She was simply a very small, very frightened little girl. Then, before she could cry out, she was aware that someone was standing beside her bed. She was aware of this before she looked, and then, strangely (even now she had taken no peep), she was frightened no longer.

The room, the house, were suddenly comfortable and safe places; as water slips from a pool and leaves it dry, so had terror glided from her side. She looked up then, and, although the place had been so dark that she had been unable to distinguish the furniture, she could figure to herself quite clearly her visitor's form. She not only figured it, but also quite easily and readily recognised it. All these years she had forgotten Him, but now at the vision of His large comfortable presence she was back again amongst experiences and recognitions that evoked for her once more all those odd first days when, with how much discomfort and puzzled dismay, she had been dropped, so suddenly, into this distressing world. He put His arms round her and held her; He bent down and kissed her, and her small hand went up to His face in exactly the way that it used to do. She nestled up against Him.

"It's a very long time, isn't it," He said, "since I paid you a visit?"

"Yes, a long, long time."

"That's because you didn't want me. You got on so well without me."

"I didn't forget about you," she said. "But I asked mummy about you once, and she said you were all nonsense, and I wasn't to think things like that."

"Ah! your mother's forgotten altogether. She knew me once, but she hasn't wanted me for a very, very long time. She'll see me again though, one day."

"I'm so glad you've come. You won't go away again now, will you?"

"I never go away," He said. "I'm always here. I've seen everything you've been doing, and a very dull time you've been making of it."

He talked to her and told her about some of the things the other children in the Square were doing. She was interested a little, but not very much; she still thought a great deal more about herself than about anything or anybody else.

"Do they all love you?" she said.

"Oh, no, not at all. Some of them think I'm horrid. Some of them forget me altogether, and then I never come back, until just at the end. Some of them only want me when they're in trouble. Some very soon think it silly to believe in me at all, and the older they grow the less they believe, generally. And when I do come they won't see me; they make up their minds not to. But I'm always there just the same; it makes no difference what they do. They can't help themselves. Only it's better for them just to remember me a little, because then it's much safer for them. You've been feeling rather lonely lately, haven't you?"

"Yes," she said. "It's stupid now all by myself. There's nobody to ask questions of."

"Well, there's somebody else in your house who's lonely."

"Is there?" She couldn't think of anyone.

"Yes. Your father."

"Oh! Father—" She was uninterested.

"Yes. You see, if he isn't—" and then, at that, He was gone; she was alone and fast asleep.

In the morning when she awoke she remembered it all quite clearly, but, of course, it had all been a dream. "Such a funny dream," she told her nurse, but she would give out no details.

"Some food she's been eating," said her nurse.

Nevertheless, when, on that afternoon, coming in from her walk, she met her dark, grubby little father in the hall, she did stay for a moment on the bottom step of the stairs to consider him.

"I've been for a walk, Daddy," she said, and then, rather frightened at her boldness, tumbled up on the next step. He went forward to catch her.

"Hold up," he said, held her for a moment, and then hurried, confused and rather agitated, into his dark sanctum. These were very nearly the first words that they had ever, in the course of their lives together, interchanged. Munty Ross was uneasy with grown-up persons (unless he were discussing business with them), but that discomfort was nothing to the uneasiness that he felt with children. Little girls (who certainly looked at him as though he were an ogre) frightened him quite horribly; moreover, Mrs. Munty had, for a great number of years, pursued a policy with regard to her husband that was not calculated to make him bright and easy in any society. "Poor old Munty," she would say to her friends, "it's not all his fault—" It was, as a fact, very largely hers. He had never been an eloquent man, but her playful derision of his uncouthness slew any little seeds of polite conversation that might, under happier conditions, have grown into brilliant blossom. It had been understood from the very beginning that Nancy was not of her father's world. He would have been scarcely aware that he had a daughter had he not, at certain periods, paid bills for her clothes.

"What's a child want with all this?" he had ventured once to say.

"Hardly your business, my dear," his wife had told him. "The child's clothes are marvellously cheap considering. I don't know how Florice does it for the money."

He resented nothing—it was not his way—but he did feel, deep down in his heart, that the child was overdressed, that it must be bad for any little girl to be praised in the way that his daughter was praised, that "the kid will grow up with the most tremendous ideas."

He resented it, perhaps a little, that his young daughter had so easily accustomed herself to the thought that she had no father. "She might just want to see me occasionally. But I'd only frighten her, I suppose, if she did."

Munty Ross had very little of the sentimentalist about him; he was completely cynical about the value of the human heart and believed in the worth and goodness of no one at all. He had, for a brief wild moment, been in love with his wife, but she had taken care to kill that, "the earlier the better." "My dear," she would say to a chosen friend, "what Munty's like when he's romantic!" She never, after the first month of their married life together, caught another glimpse of that side of him.

Now, however, he did permit his mind to linger over that vision of his little daughter tumbling on the stairs. He wondered what had made her do it. He was astonished at the difference that it made to him.

To Nancy also, it had made a great difference. She wished that she had stayed there on the stairs a little longer to hold a more important conversation. She had thought of her father as "all horrid"—now his very contrast to her little world pleased and interested her. It may also be that, although she was young, she had even now a picture in her mind of her father's loneliness. She may have seen into her mother's attitude with an acuteness much older than her actual years.

She thought now continually about her father. She made little plans to meet him, but these meetings were not, as a rule, successful, because so often he was down in the City. She would wait at the end of her afternoon walk on the stairs.

"Come along. Miss Nancy, do. What are you hanging about there for?"

"Nothing."

"You'll be disturbing your mother."

"Just a minute."

She peered anxiously, her little head almost held by the railings of the banisters; she gazed down into black, mysterious depths wherein her father might be hidden. She was driven to all this partly by some real affection that had hitherto found no outlet, partly by a desire for adventure, but partly, also, by some force that was behind her and quite recognized by her. It was as though she said: "If I'm nice to my father and make friends with him, then you must promise that I shan't be frightened in the middle of the night, that the clock won't tick too loudly, that the blind won't flap, that it won't all be too dark and dreadful." She knew that she had made this compact.

Then she had several little encounters with her father. She met him one day on the doorstep. He had come up whilst she was standing there.

"Had a good walk?" he said nervously. She looked at him and laughed. Then he went hurriedly indoors.

On the second occasion she had come down to be shown off at

166

a luncheon party. She had been praised and petted, and then, in the hall, had run into her father's arms. He was in his top-hat, going down to his old City, looking, the nurse thought, "just like a monkey." But Nancy stayed, holding on to the leg of his trousers. Suddenly he bent down and whispered:

"Were they nice to you in there?"

"Yes. Why weren't you there?"

"I was. I left. Got to go and work."

"What sort of work?"

"Making money for your clothes."

"Take me too."

"Would you like to come?"

"Yes. Take me."

He bent down and kissed her, but suddenly hearing the voices of the luncheon-party, they separated like conspirators. He crept out of the house.

After that there was no question of their alliance. The sort of affection that most children feel for old, ugly, and battered dolls, Nancy now felt for her father, and the warmth of this affection melted her dried, stubborn little soul, caught her up into visions, wonders, sympathies that had seemed surely denied to her for ever.

"Now sit still, Miss Nancy, while I do up the back."

"Oh, silly old clothes!" said Nancy.

Then one day she declared, "I want to be dirty like those children in the garden."

"And a nice state your mother would be in!" cried the amazed nurse.

"Father wouldn't," Nancy thought. "Father wouldn't mind."

There came at last the wonderful day when her father penetrated into the nursery. He arrived furtively, very much, it appeared, ashamed of himself and exceedingly shy of the nurse. He did not remain very long. He said very little; a funny picture he had made with his blue face, his black shiny hair, his fat little legs, and his anxious, rather stupid eyes. He sat rather awkwardly in a chair, with Nancy on his knee; he wrung his hair for things to say.

The nurse left them for a moment alone together, and then Nancy whispered:

"Daddy, let's go into the garden together, you and me; just us—no silly old nurse—one mornin'." (She found the little "g" still a difficulty.)

"Would you like that?" he whispered back. "I don't know I'd be much good in a garden."

"Oh, you'll be all right," she asserted with confidence. "I want to dig."

She'd made up her mind then to that. As Hannibal determined to cross the Alps, as Napoleon set his feet towards Moscow, so did Nancy Ross resolve that she would, in the company of her father, dig in the garden. She stroked her father's hand, rubbed her head upon his sleeve; exactly as she would have caressed, had she been another little girl, the damaged features of her old rag doll. She was beginning, however, for the first time in her life, to love someone other than herself.

He came, then, quite often to the nursery. He would slip in, stay a moment or two, and slip out again. He brought her presents and sweets which made her ill. And always in the presence of Mrs. Munty they appeared as strangers.

The day came when Nancy achieved her desire—they had their great adventure.

4

A fine summer morning came, and with it, in a bowler hat, at the nursery door, the hour being about eleven, Mr. Munty Ross.

"I'll take Nancy this morning, nurse," he said, with a strange, choking little "cluck" in his throat. Now, the nurse, although, as I've said, of a shining and superficial appearance, was no fool. She had watched the development of the intrigue; her attitude to the master of the house was composed of pity, patronage, and a rather motherly interest. She did not see how her mistress could avoid her attitude: it was precisely the attitude that she would herself have adopted in that position, but, nevertheless, she was sorry for the man. "So out of it as he is!" Her maternal feelings were uppermost now. "It's nice of the child," she thought, "and him so ugly."

"Of course, sir," she said.

"We shall be back in about an hour." He attempted an easy indifference, was conscious that he failed, and blushed.

He was aware that his wife was out.

He carried off his prize.

The garden was very full on this lovely summer morning, but Nancy, without any embarrassment or confusion, took charge of the proceedings.

"Where are we going?" he said, gazing rather helplessly about him, feeling extremely shy. There were so many bold children—so many bolder nurses; even the birds on the trees seemed to deride him, and a stumpy fox-terrier puppy stood with its four legs planted wide barking at him.

"Over here," she said without a moment's hesitation, and she dragged him along. She halted at last in a corner of the garden where was a large, overhanging chestnut and a wooden seat. Here the shouts and cries of the children came more dimly, the splashing of the fountain could be heard like a melodious refrain with a fascinating note of hesitation in it, and the deep green leaves of the tree made a cool, thick covering. "Very nice," he said, and sat down on the seat, tilting his hat back and feeling very happy indeed.

Nancy also was very happy. There, in front of her, was the delightful pile of earth and sand untouched, it seemed. In an instant, regardless of her frock, she was down upon her knees.

"I ought to have a spade," she said.

"You'll make yourself dreadfully dirty, Nancy. Your beautiful frock—" But he had nevertheless the feeling that, after all, he had paid for it, and if he hadn't the right to see it ruined, who had?

"Oh!" she murmured with the ecstasy of one who has abandoned herself, freely and with a glad heart, to all the vices. She dug her hands into the mire, she scattered it about her, she scooped and delved and excavated. It was her intention to build something in the nature of a high, high hill. She patted the surface of the sand and behold! it was instantly a beautiful shape, very smooth and shining.

It was hot, her hat fell back, her knees were thick with the good brown earth—that once lovely creation of Florice was stained and black.

She then began softly, partly to herself, partly to her father, and partly to that other Friend who had helped her to these splendours, a song of joy and happiness. To the ordinary observer, it might have seemed merely a discordant noise proceeding from a little girl engaged in the making of mud pies. It was, in reality, as the chestnut tree, the birds, the fountain, the flowers, the various small children, even the very earth she played with, understood, a fine offering—thanksgiving and triumphal *paen* to the God of Heaven, of the earth, and of the waters that were under the earth.

Munty himself caught the refrain. He was recalled to a day when mud pies had been to him also things of surpassing joy. There was a day when, a naked and very ugly little boy, he had danced beside a mountain burn.

He looked upon his daughter and his daughter looked upon him; they were friends forever and ever. She rose; her fingers were so sticky with mud that they stood apart; down her right cheek ran a fine black smear; her knees were caked.

"Good heavens!" he exclaimed. She flung herself upon him and kissed him; down his cheek also now a fine smear marked its way.

He looked at his watch—one o'clock. "Good heavens!" he said again. "I say, old girl, we'll have to be going. Mother's got a party." He tried ineffectually to cleanse his daughter's face.

"We'll come back," she cried, looking down triumphantly upon her handiwork.

"We'll have to smuggle you up into the nursery somehow." But he added, "Yes, we'll come again."

5

They hurried home. Very furtively Munty Ross fitted his key into the Yale lock of his fine door. They slipped into the hall. There before them were Mrs. Ross and two of her most splendid friends. Very fine was Munty's wife in a tight-clinging frock of light blue and wearing upon her head a hat like a waste-paper basket with a blue handle at the back of it; very fine were her two lady friends, clothed also in the tightest of garments, shining and lovely and precious.

"Good God! Munty—and the child!"

It was a terrible moment. Quite unconscious was Munty of the mud that stained his cheek, perfectly tranquil his daughter as she gazed with glowing happiness about her. A terrible moment for Mrs. Ross, an unforgettable one for her friends; nor were they likely to keep the humour of it entirely to themselves.

"Down in a minute. Going up to clean." Smiling, he passed his wife. On the bottom step Nancy chanted:

"We've had the most lovely mornin'. Daddy and I. We've been diggin'. We're goin' to dig again. Aren't I dirty, Mummy?"

Round the corner of the stairs in the shadow Nancy kissed her father again.

"I'm never goin' to be clean anymore," she announced.

And you may fancy, if you please, that somewhere in the shadows of the house someone heard those words and chuckled with delighted pleasure.

The Ruby Glass

Poor Cousin Jane (as she was for ever afterwards known) arrived on a visit to the Cole family in Polchester in the spring of Jeremy's eighth year. He remembered the day exactly, because on that afternoon he had bought a bunch of daffodils as a peace-offering for his mother. A peace-offering was badly needed, both on his own part and that of his dog, Hamlet, for they had both of late been repeatedly in disgrace.

On Tuesday of that week Jeremy in a temper had thrown ink at Mary, his sister; on Wednesday he broke the window of the bathroom with a cricket-ball; on Thursday he insulted Miss Jones, their governess, so brutally that she gave notice, and was only with the greatest difficulty persuaded to remain.

It was perhaps the spring—it was certainly the hard truth that it was time that he went to school.

Hamlet also was unfortunate. On Tuesday he brought two filthy bones into the drawing-room at the very moment when the Dean's wife was paying a call. On Wednesday he frightened Mrs. Cole by running out on her from a dark passage, and on Thursday he was horribly sick on the dining-room carpet.

They were both in disgrace; they were both punished. In fact, matters were in a very ticklish state indeed. So, Jeremy bought some daffodils and prayed most fervently that Fate would leave him alone for a while.

He disliked to be in disgrace; he disliked to make his incomprehensible elders unhappy; most of all did he dislike it when people muttered concerning Hamlet, 'That dog must go. We really cannot *endure* him any longer.'

So, he was walking on egg-shells when Poor Cousin Jane arrived.

They christened her that immediately. In the first place she was a miserable scrap of a thing. When she stood in the hall, covered with innumerable wraps, she did not appear to be there at all.

Only her very red (for it was April weather) sharply peaked little nose and strange pepper-and-salt eyes, with their sandy eyebrows, were visible.

Unwrapped she was revealed as a thin, little girl, with an untidy bow in her hair and wrinkled black stockings on her spindly legs.

But what struck Jeremy, Mary and Helen immediately on sight of her was her terror. She was shaking with fright; her eyes roamed the room as though she were a wild animal for the first time caged, and when her aunt who had brought her from her home in Drymouth left her she burst into floods of tears.

Now the Coles were not an unkind family. The Rev. Mr. Cole, Jeremy's father, could certainly be severe on occasion when he felt it his duty to be so, but Mrs. Cole was the soul of maternal comfort—a nicer woman didn't exist anywhere.

Her three children also were kindly intentioned, only, like all normal children, they were healthy savages in process of being civilised.

Mary in especial was sentimental and emotional, wanted a girl friend, and would willingly have romanticised Cousin Jane had she been given the opportunity.

However, the odd thing about this story is that the only person who from the first did romanticise Jane was Hamlet, and that was queer indeed, because he hated little girls and liked to snap at their legs when nobody in authority was near.

Jeremy disliked Cousin Jane from the start. He could not help it. He was easily touched by females in distress, he was at times both courteous and chivalrous, and he had a good heart—but Jane he could not abide.

There was something about her terror that revolted him. He was not touched by it because it was so complete. He was not old enough to understand how anyone *could* be such a coward and *could* be such a fool.

His sister Mary was often both a coward *and* a fool, but she made brave attempts to conquer her weak points. He understood that. He had weak points himself.

But Jane made no attempt to conquer anything. She was frightened of Mr. Cole, Mrs. Cole, Jeremy, Mary, Helen, Miss Jones, the cook, the housemaid, and terrified of Hamlet.

She started at the slightest sound, blinked with alarm if anyone addressed her, and sat in a corner, straight on a chair, waiting for some-one to attack her.

But—strangest of all strange things—Hamlet adored her. When on her arrival she stood among them all, bitterly weeping, he smelt her black stockings, then lay down, his pointed beard flat on his paws, and waited for her to ask him to do something for her. She did, of course, nothing of the kind. No matter. He devoted himself to her service.

Now, from the very moment of her arrival, Jeremy felt that some-thing awful would occur in connection with her. He felt also perhaps ashamed of himself for disliking her, although it is difficult to say what small boys of eight feel and what they do not.

On the first afternoon of her stay it poured with rain and the children sat in the schoolroom trying to play games. Cousin Jane, however, was a blight on all the proceedings.

'I know!' said Jeremy. 'We'll play buffaloes. I'll be the buffalo. Jane shall be captured by the Indians, and Mary and Hamlet shall rescue her.'

Jane's eyes nearly split with terror. 'Wouldn't you like that, Jane dear?' asked Mary in her propitiatory, mother-visiting-the-sick-and-ailing voice.

'Oh no, no, no!' cried Jane.

'There's halma,' said Jeremy disgustedly.

But Jane could understand nothing. She sat at the schoolroom ta-ble staring in front of her.

'Mary shall play with you and show you how to move.'

But it was of no use. She had an awful way of whispering under her breath. She was probably saying that she wanted to go home, but nobody could be sure.

'Mary shall tell us a story,' said Jeremy, trying hard to be a perfect gentleman. They sat round the fire and Mary began (very quickly lest someone should stop her, for she loved telling stories). 'Once upon a time there was a king who had three lovely daughters. One had black hair, one yellow, and one was between the two, and one day when the king—'

But Jane interrupted by slipping off her chair and creeping away to the window-seat, where she sat desolately looking out on to the rain. This was as bad an insult as any author ever received! This sense of misfortune that Jeremy had in connection with his weeping cousin grew in the following days. He was in no way a morbid child, his im-aginings were healthy, he very rarely saw visions, but just now he had

173

the sense of the world that it was waiting round the corner to catch him.

He had had nightmares after stolen cheese or too much toffee, and in these to move a step was to lose your life!

So, it was now. Something would happen to plunge him into disgrace, and Cousin Jane would be the agent. He knew it. He felt it in all his bones.

On a certain morning he woke and at once knew that this was an Evil Day. There were Evil Days, there were Ordinary Days and Days of Delight, and the kind of Day it intended to be it began from the very first moment by being!

This day began badly because Hamlet was not there. Always at a quarter to eight Hamlet, released by the cook from his basket in the kitchen, his hair brushed, his beard in shape, rushed upstairs and scratched on Jeremy's door. He was admitted and games followed.

Today there was no scratching at the door. Jeremy knew at once what had occurred. He was scratching at Cousin Jane's door. What did he see in the girl? What was it that had softened his ironic heart?

She had, Jeremy would have supposed, no charms for dogs at all. She did not like dogs. She screamed whenever they came near her.

Jeremy, his heart torn by a jealousy that he was far too proud to admit, went down to breakfast. Here for a moment things took a better turn.

'What do you think, my dears?' cried Mrs. Cole (who, loving her children, had never realised how intensely Mary and Jeremy hated to be 'my deared'). 'Miss Willink has asked us all to tea on Friday.'

Now, Miss Willink was one of life's joys. She was an elderly lady living five miles out of Polchester in the middle of one of the loveliest gardens in the world. Her house was large and grand, but Jeremy never gave it a thought.

The point was the garden with its lawns, rockeries, ponds, terraces, shrubberies, conservatories and gigantic trees. Moreover, Miss Willink understood what children wanted—namely, food, freedom and fraternity. She was a jolly old lady.

'Oh, hurray!' cried Jeremy, wondering whether he had been wrong about the day's omens. But he had not.

'Now mind, Jeremy,' said his father, who had neuralgia that morning. 'I don't know what's been the matter with you this week. One thing after another. Take care or Miss Willink's is not for *you*.'

He *would* take care, and it occurred to him that he would propitiate

174

the fates by being nice to Cousin Jane. They were to go for a walk that morning, it being a lovely spring morning, with clouds like galleons, sunny and shining, stretches of sky like violet-fields, and excited birds in flight.

He would take Cousin Jane to his secret place in Conmer Wood, where the daffodils were so thick that they were like shadowed plates of gold.

Smiling, he suggested it to her. But she shook her head. They were standing together alone in the schoolroom and Hamlet was watching the girl, his eyes soft with sentiment. Every once and again he snapped dramatically at an imaginary fly, but plainly his thoughts were only for his adored one.

Jeremy was so deeply irritated that it was all he could do not to pull her long and lanky hair, but, remembering the fates, he held himself in.

'Don't you want to go *anywhere?*' he cried disgustedly. 'Don't you want to do *anything?*'

Her under-lip trembled.

'I don't like daffodils,' was her amazing statement.

'Don't like daffodils? But you don't like *anything!* All the time you've been here you haven't liked a *thing!* We're all being as nice as nice. Don't you like being here?'

Upon which Cousin Jane burst into tears, and at the same moment Mrs. Cole came into the room.

'Now, Jeremy, what *have* you been doing to Jane? What *is* it, dear? ... Never mind. Come with me and I'll show you some pretty things. Jeremy, I don't know *what* has come over you lately. You're always doing something wrong. Your father is very vexed. Remember what he said about Miss Willink. Now, come along, dear. Dry your eyes. We'll see what we've got downstairs to show you.'

Hamlet attempted to follow his heroine, but that at least Jeremy prevented.

'What *has* come over you?' he asked him. 'You can't *like* her. You don't like girls and this is one of the worst. Besides, she *hates you!*'

These remarks had no effect whatever on Hamlet, who had the art of sulking when he *wanted* to sulk beyond any dog ever known. He would half close his eyes, bury his mouth in his beard, turn his head away and yawn lazily, impertinently.

'Now come on,' said Jeremy. 'We'll go out and enjoy ourselves.'

But Hamlet refused. He would *not* go out. He would not *budge.* He sat there, his feet firmly planted, his head obstinately screwed away from his master. Jeremy dragged at his collar; his paws seemed to stick to the carpet. Jeremy pulled him, however, as far as the passage, then bumped, breathless and exasperated, into his father.

'Really, Jeremy,' Mr. Cole, whose neuralgia was worse, cried, 'you must look where you are going, my boy. And what are you doing to the poor dog?'

'Oh, nothing.' And Jeremy, running downstairs, left dog, father and all to their proper destinies.

'Sulky,' thought Mr. Cole sadly. 'Sulky and ill-tempered. The boy will have to go to school.'

At luncheon another misfortune befell.

It happened that it was cold-beef day—cold beef and potatoes in their jackets. Now, Jeremy hated cold fat. So, apparently, did Cousin Jane. Her eyes filled with tears and she looked beseechingly at Mrs. Cole.

'Mother says I needn't eat fat when I feel sick,' she remarked. 'I feel sick now.'

'Very well, dear,' said Mrs. Cole, benevolently smiling.

A short while later Mr. Cole said cheerfully: 'Eat it up, Jeremy, my boy. You know what I've always told you. One day perhaps you will be glad—'

The injustice was more than he could bear.

'Jane didn't have to!' he said.

'Jeremy!'

'Well, father, Jane didn't—'

'Jeremy!'

'Well, but, father—'

He ate it, and most disgusting it was. He swallowed with splutterings a full glass of water. His eye rested on the splendid, tall, ruby glass that stood in the middle of a small table opposite him. This was the family pride.

It was, the children understood, Bohemian. There were little patterns of gold traced delicately over its crimson glories. Jeremy thought that it was laughing at him.

After luncheon he brooded miserably. Hamlet was nowhere to be seen. Even his sisters seemed to hold aloof from him. A hatred of his Cousin Jane stronger than any hatred that he had ever known for anyone possessed him.

He would like to torture her, to stick pins into her legs, to twist her arms, to pull her hair till she screamed.

Meanwhile, as the afternoon drew on, he felt catastrophe drawing nearer.

At tea-time he could have burst into tears, although he was not given to crying. The intensity of those moments in childhood when one is deserted, helpless, under a curse that is eternal, is unknown to maturity.

It would be a miracle if he reached bedtime without disaster. Even the clocks seemed to say to him: 'Now—You—Are—Done—For—Little—Man. Now—You—Are—Done—For—Little—Man.' And indeed, there is nothing more complacent and patronising than a moonfaced, stubborn clock. The blow fell.

It was the pleasant Cole custom that one or two nights a week Mrs. Cole should read to the children for half an hour before bedtime. Tonight, the reading was to be in the dining-room, because a good fire was burning there. The book was *The Chaplet of Pearls* by Charlotte Mary Yonge.

The children—Hamlet, Mary, Helen, Jeremy and Jane—assembled and stood by the fire waiting. Hamlet sat, licking a tangled foot and sniffing between licks. Jane showed a little animation. She began in her thin voice that was like a violin-string struck just out of tune:

'We've got nicer things in our house than you have, Mary.'

'Oh no, you haven't,' said Mary, who was loyal if she was anything.

'Oh yes, we have.'

'Oh no, you haven't.'

'Oh yes, we have. We've got a clock with a Chinaman that nods his head, and a picture as big as this room almost, and a rug with a tiger's head, and—'

'You haven't,' said Mary slowly, pushing her spectacles straight, 'anything as lovely as the ruby glass.'

'Oh yes, we have,' said Jane. But she was attracted nevertheless. The firelight danced on the deep colours, the thin tracery of gold. She went to the table and picked it up.

'Oh, you mustn't!' cried Mary.

Jane heard the door opening, and, in alarm, dropped the glass. It lay at her feet, 'smashed,' as the story-books have it, 'into a thousand fragments.'

Mrs. Cole had entered. Her cry was an agonised one.

'Oh! My glass! My glass!'

Jeremy saw then terror as he was never in all his life again to see it. Nothing, years later, in the Great War equalled it.

To say that Jane was 'frozen' with it says little; her face paled to ash, her whole body was seized with a fearful trembling. It was as though she saw the devil.

Something in that agony moved Jeremy to a revulsion of disgust. It was horrible, indecent. Eight years of age though he was, he understood that there was something dreadful here that had nothing to do with his own world—something from beyond boundaries.

Mrs. Cole looked up from her knees.

'Oh, who—?' she began.

'I broke it,' said Jeremy.

'You were told never to touch it.'

He stared defiantly. None of the children spoke a word. Mary and Helen knew, as Jeremy knew, that Jane, dislike her as they did, must be protected. The door opened on the scene, and Mr. Cole entered:

'Well, children—' he began, and then saw what had happened.

'The glass! . . . Who touched it?'

'I did,' said Jeremy.

For the first time in his life Jeremy was locked in his bedroom. He was to have no supper. Miss Willink's garden would not, on this occasion, offer him a greeting.

He moved up and down, hot tears in his eyes, feeling sick, feeling utterly alone, deserted by all the world. Why had he done it? He did not know. He hated Cousin Jane. It would have given him joy to have seen her disgraced. Yet if it occurred again he would do as he had done.

He was a pariah (although he did not know what a pariah was). He would never be back any more in a world of sunshine, friendliness, good-will.

It was too much. He sat down by the dressing-table and burst into a passion of angry, desolated tears. Worst of all—oh, far, far worst of all—was Hamlet's desertion. That Hamlet should leave him for an ugly, stupid, miserable, little . . .

He heard a sound. He choked down his sobs, raised his head and listened. There was a scratching at his door. Was he mistaken? He moved across the room. No, there was no mistake. The scratching continued. He went to the door and, pressing against it, whispered:

'Hamlet! Hamlet! Are you there?'

The scratching was eager, demonstrative, and then, quite beyond question, between the scratches, that sniff! That sniff of comradeship, of loyalty, of understanding.

'Hamlet, I can't get out. They've locked me in!'

He heard a soft thud. Hamlet had laid himself down, and nothing, no power, no authority, was going to move him.

Jeremy, smiling, himself again, all the curses and forebodings suddenly removed, turned to the table by the bed, found a pencil and a piece of paper, and, with wrinkled brow and lickings of the stubborn lead, began to draw pictures of Cousin Jane as a witch.

Portrait of a Man with Red Hair

1
You're my friend:
I was the man the Duke spoke to:
I helped the Duchess to cast off his yoke too:
So, here's the tale from beginning to end,
My friend!
2
Ours is a great wild country;
If you climb to our castle's top,
I don't see where your eye can stop;
For when you've passed the cornfield country,
Where vineyards leave off, flocks are packed,
And sheep-range leads to cattle-tract,
And cattle-tract to open-chase,
And open-chase to the very base
Of the mountain where, at a funeral pace,
Round about, solemn and slow,
One by one, row after row,
Up and up the pine trees go,
Go, like black priests up, and so
Down the other side again
To another greater, wilder country. . . . . .
'To another greater, wilder country. . . . . .
'To another greater. . . . . .'

1

The soul of Charles Percy Harkness slipped, like a neat white pocket-handkerchief, out through the carriage window into the silver-blue

180

air, hung there changing into a tiny white fleck against the immensity, struggling for escape above the purple-pointed trees of the dark wood, then, realising that escape was not yet, fluttered back into the carriage again, was caught by Charles Percy, neatly folded up, and put away.

The Browning lines—old-fashioned surely?—had yielded it a moment's hope. Those and some other lines from another outmoded book:

'But the place reasserted its spell, marshalling once again its army, its silver-belted knights, its castles of perilous frowning darkness, its meadows of gold and silver streams.

'The old spell working the same purpose. For how many times and for what intent? That we may be reminded yet once again that there is the step behind the door, the light beyond the window, the rustle on the stair, and that it is for these things only that we must watch and wait?'

For Harkness had committed the folly of having two books open on his knee—a peck at one, a peck at another, a long, eager glance through the window at the summer scene, but above all a sensuous state of slumber hovering in the hot scented afternoon air just above him, waiting to pounce . . . . . . .to pounce . . . . .

First Browning, then this other, the old book in a faded red-brown cover, 'To Paradise: Frederick Lester.' At the bottom of the title-page, 1892—how long ago! How faded and pathetic the old book was! He alone in all the British Isles at that moment reading it—certainly no other living soul—and he had crossed to Browning after Lester's third page.

He swung in mid-air. The open fields came swimming up to him like vast green waves, gently to splash upon his face, hanging over him, laced about the telegraph poles, rising and falling with them. . . . . .

The voice of the old man with the long white beard, the only occupant of the carriage with him, broke sharply in like a steel knife cutting through blotting-paper.

'Pardon me, but there is a spider on your neck!'

Harkness started up. The two books slipped to the floor. He passed his hand, damp with the afternoon warmth, over his cool neck. He hated spiders. He shivered. His fingers were on the thing. With a shudder he flung it out of the window.

'Thank you,' he said, blushing very slightly.

'Not at all,' the old man said severely, 'you were almost asleep, and in another moment, it would have been down your back.'

He was not the old man you would have expected to see in an English first-class carriage, save that now in these democratic days you may see anyone anywhere. But first-class fares are so expensive. Perhaps that is why it is only the really poor who can afford them. The old man, who was thin and wiry, had large shabby boots, loose and ancient trousers, a flopping garden straw hat. His hands were gnarled like the knots of trees. He was terribly clean. He had blue eyes. On his knees was a large basket and from this he ate his massive luncheon—here an immense sandwich with pieces of ham like fragments of banners, there a colossal apple, a monstrous pear—

'Going far?' munched the old man.

'No,' said Harkness, blushing again. 'To Treliss. I change at Trewth, I believe. We should be there at 4.30.'

'*Should be*,' said the old man, dribbling through his pear. 'The train's late........Another tourist,' he added suddenly.

'I beg your pardon?' said Harkness.

'Another of these damned tourists. You are, I mean. *I* lived at Treliss. Such as you drove me away.'

'I am sorry,' said Harkness, smiling faintly. 'I suppose I *am* that if by tourist you mean somebody who is travelling to a place to see what it is like and enjoy its beauty. A friend has told me of it. He says it is the most beautiful place in England.'

'Beauty,' said the old man, licking his fingers—'a lot you tourists think about beauty—with your char-a-bangs and oranges and babies and Americans. If I had my way I'd make the Americans pay a tax, spoiling our country as they do.'

'*I* am an American,' said Harkness faintly.

The old man licked his thumb, looked at it, and licked it again. 'I wouldn't have thought it,' he said. 'Where's your accent?'

'I have lived in this country a great many years off and on,' he explained, 'and we don't all say "I guess" every moment as novelists make us do,' he added, smiling.

Smiling, yes. But how deeply he detested this unfortunate conversation! How happy he had been, and now this old man with his rudeness and violence had smashed the peace into a thousand fragments. But the old man spoke little more. He only stared at Harkness out of his blue eyes, said:

'Treliss is too beautiful a place for you. It will do you harm,' and fell instantly asleep.

2

Yes, Harkness thought, looking at the rise and fall of the old man's beard, it is strange and indeed lamentable how deeply I detest a cross word! That is why I am always creeping away from things, why, too, I never make friends—not *real* friends—why at thirty-five I am a complete failure—that is, from the point of view of anything real.

I am filled too with self-pity, he added as he opened *To Paradise* again and groped for page four, and self-pity is the most despicable of all the vices.

He was not unpleasing to the eye as he sat there thinking. He was dressed with exceeding neatness, but his clothes had something of the effect of chain armour. Was that partly because his figure was so slight that he could never fill any suit of clothes adequately? That might be so. His soft white collar, his pale blue tie, his mild blue eyes, his long tranquil fingers, these things were all gentle. His chin protruded. He was called 'gaunt' by undiscerning friends, but that was a poor word for him. He was too slight for that, too gentle, too unobtrusive. His hair was already retreating deprecatingly from his forehead. No gaunt man would smile so timidly. His neatness and immaculate spotless purity of dress showed a fastidiousness that granted his cowardice an excuse.

For I am a coward, he thought. This is yet another holiday that I am taking alone. Alone after all these years. And Pritchard or Mason, Major Stock or Henry Trenchard, Carstairs Willing or Falk Brandon—any one of these might have wished to go if I had had courage . . . . . . or even Maradick himself might have come.

The only companions, he reflected, that he had taken with him on this journey were his etchings, kinder to him, more intimate with him, rewarding him with more affection than any human being. His seven etchings—the seven of his forty—Lepère's '*Route de St. Gilles*,' Legros' '*Cabane dans les Marais*,' Rembrandt's 'Flight into Egypt,' Muirhead Bone's 'Orvieto,' Whistler's 'Drury Lane,' Strang's 'Portrait of himself Etching,' and Meryon's '*Rue des Chantres*.' His seven etchings—his greatest friends in the world, save of course Hetty and Jane his sisters. Yes, he reflected, you can judge a man by his friends, and in my cowardice I have given all my heart to these things because they can't answer me back, cannot fail me when I most eagerly expect something of them, are always there when I call them, do not change nor betray me. And yet it is not only cowardice. They are intimate and individual as is no other form of graphic art. They are so personal that every separate impression has a fresh character. They are so lovely in soul that they never age nor have their moods. My Aldegrevers and Penczs, he was reflecting........He was a little happier now.......The Browning and *To Paradise* fell once more to the ground. I hope the old man does not waken, he thought, and yet perhaps he will pass his station. What a temper he will be in if he does that, and then I too shall suffer!

He read a line or two of the Browning:

Ours is a great wild country;
If you climb to our castle's top,
I don't see where your eye can stop . . . . .

How strange that the book should have opened again at that same place as though it were there that it wished him to read!

And then *To Paradise* a line or two, now page 376, '*And the Silver Button? Would his answer defy that too? Had he some secret magic? Was he stronger than God Himself? . . . . .*'

And then, Harkness reflected, this business about being an American. He had felt pride when he had told the old man that that was his citizenship. He was proud, yes, and yet he spent most of his life in Europe. And now as always when he fell to thinking of America his eye travelled to his own home there—Baker at the portals of Oregon. All the big trains pass it on their way to the coast—three hundred and forty miles from Portland, fifty from Huntington. He saw himself on that eager arrival coming out by the 11.30 train from Salt Lake City steaming in at 4.30 in the afternoon, an early May afternoon perhaps with the colours violet in the sky and the mountains elephant-dusk—so quiet and so gentle.

And when the train has gone on and you are left on the platform and you look about you and find everything as it was when you departed a year ago—the Columbia Café. The Antlers Hotel. The mountains still with their snow caps. The Lumber Offices. The notice on the wall of the *café*: 'You can eat here if you have no money.' The Crabill Hotel. The fresh sweet air, three thousand five hundred feet up. The soft pause of the place. Baker did not grow very fast as did other places. It is true that there had been but four houses when his father had first landed there, but even now as towns went it was small and quiet and unprogressive.

Strange that his father with that old-cultured New England stock should have gone there, but he had fled from mankind after the death of his wife, Harkness' mother, fled with his three little children, shut himself away, there under the mountains with his books, a sad, severe man in that long, rambling, ramshackle house.

Still long, still rambling, still ramshackle, although Hetty and Jane, who never moved away from it, had made it as charming as they could. They were darlings, and lived for the month every year when their brother came to visit them. But he could not live there! No, he could not! It was exile for him, exile from everything for which he most deeply cared. But Europe was exile too. That was the tragedy of it! Every morning that he waked he thought that perhaps today he would find that he was a true European! But no, it was not so. Away from America, how deeply he loved his country! How clearly, he saw its idealism, its vitality, its marvellous promise for the future, its loving contact with his own youthful dreams. But back in America again it seemed crude and noisy and materialistic. He longed for the Past. Exile in both with his New England culture that was not enough, his half-cocked vitality that was not enough.

Never enough to permit his half-gods to go! But he loved America always; he saw how little these Europeans truly knew or cared about her, how hasty their visits to her, how patronising their attitude, how weary their stale conventions against her full, bursting energy. And yet——! And yet——! He could not live there. After two weeks of Baker, even though he had with him his etchings, his diary in its dark blue cover, Frazer's *Golden Bough*, and some of the Loeb Classics, life was not enough.

Hetty and Jane bored him with their goodness and little Culture Club. It was not enough for him that Hetty had read a very good paper on 'Archibald Marshall—the modern Trollope' to the inhabitants of Baker and Haines. Nevertheless they seemed to him finer women than the women of any other country, with their cheery independence, their admirable common sense, their warm hearts, their unselfishness, but—it was not enough—no, it was not enough. . . . . . . What he wanted . . . . .

3

The old man awoke with a start.

'And when you come to this Prohibition question,' he said, 'the Americans have simply become a laughing stock. . . . . .'

Harkness picked up the Browning firmly. 'If you don't mind,' he remarked, 'I have a piece of work here of some importance and I have but little time. Pray excuse me. . . . . .'

How had he dared? Never in all his life had he spoken to a stranger so. How often had he envied and admired those who could be rude and indifferent to people's feelings. It seemed to him that this was a crisis with him, something that he would never forget, something that might alter all his life. Perhaps already the charm of which Maradick had spoken was working. He looked out of his window and always, afterwards, he was to remember a stream that, now bright silver, now ebony dark, ran straight to him from the heart of an emerald green field like a greeting spirit. It laughed up to his window and was gone.

He had asserted himself. The old man with the beard was reading the *Hibbert Journal*. Strange old man—but defeated! Harkness felt a triumph. Could he but henceforward assert himself in this fashion, all might be easy for him. Instead of retreating he might advance, stretch out his hand and take the things and the people that he wanted as he had seen others do. He almost wished that the old man might speak to him again, that he might once more be rude.

He had had, ever since he could remember, the belief that one day, suddenly, some magic door would open, some one step before him, some magic carpet unroll at his feet, and all life would be changed. For many years he had had no doubt of this. He would call it, perhaps, the coming of romance, but as he had grown older he had come to distrust both himself and life. He had always been interested in contemporary literature. Every new book that he opened now seemed to tell him that he was extremely foolish to expect anything of life at all. He was swallowed by the modern realistic movement as a fly is swallowed by an indifferent spider. These men, he said to himself, are very clever. They know so much more about everything than I do that they must be right. They are telling the truth at last about life as no one has ever done it before.

But when he had read a great many of these books (and every word of Mr. Joyce's *Ulysses*), he found that he cared much less about truth than he had supposed. He even doubted whether these writers were telling the truth any more than the *naïve* and sentimental Victorians; and when at last he read a story all about an American manufacturer of washing machines whose habit it was to strip himself naked on every possible occasion before his nearest and dearest relations and friends, and when the author told him that this was a typical American citizen, he, knowing his own country people very well, frankly disbelieved it.

These realists, he exclaimed, are telling fairy stories quite as thoroughly as Grimm, Fouqué, and De la Mare; the difference is that the realistic fairy stories are depressing and discouraging, the others are not. He determined to desert the realists and wait until something pleasanter came along. Since it was impossible to have the truth about life anyway let us have only the pleasant hallucinations. They are quite as likely to be as true as the others.

But he was lonely and desolate. The women whom he loved never loved him, and indeed he never came sufficiently close to them to give them any encouragement. He dreamt about them and painted them as they certainly were not. He had his passions and his desires, but his Puritan descent kept him always at one remove from experience. He never, in fact, seemed to have contact with anything at all—except Baker in Oregon, his two sisters, and his forty etchings. He was so shy that he was thought to be conceited, so idealistic that he was considered cynical, so chaste that he was considered a most immoral fellow with a secret double life.

Like the hero of *Flegeljahre*, he '*loved every dog and wanted every dog to love him*,' but the dogs did not know enough about him to be interested; he was so like so many other immaculately dressed, pleasant-mannered, and wandering American cosmopolitans that nobody had any permanent feeling for him—fathered by Henry James, uncled by Howells, aunted (severely) by Edith Wharton—one of a million cultured, kindly, impersonal Americans seen as shadows by the matter-of-fact, unimaginative British. Who knew or cared that he was lonely, longing for love, for home, for someone to whom he might give his romantic devotion? He was all these things, but no one minded.

And then he met James Maradick.

5

The meeting was of the simplest. At the Reform Club one day he was lunching with two men, one a novelist, Westcott, whom he knew very slightly, the other a fellow-American. Westcott, a dark, thick-set man of about forty, with a reputation that without being sensational was solid and well merited, said very little. Harkness liked him and recognised in him a kindly shyness rather like his own. After luncheon they moved into the big smoking-room upstairs to drink their coffee.

A large, handsome man of between fifty and sixty came up and spoke to Westcott. He was obviously pleased to see him, putting his hand on his shoulder, looking at him with kindly, smiling eyes. Westcott also flushed with pleasure. The big man sat down with them and Harkness was introduced to him. His name was Maradick—Sir James Maradick. A strange, unreal kind of name for so real and solid a man. As he sat forward on the sofa with his heavy shoulders, his deep chest, his thick neck, red-brown colour, and clear open gaze, he seemed to Harkness to be the typical, rather naïve, friendly, but cautious British man of business.

That impression soon passed. There was something in Maradick that almost instantly warmed his heart. He responded—as do all American men—immediately, even emotionally, to any friendly contact. The reserves that were in his nature were from his superficial cosmopolitanism; the native warm-hearted, eager, and trusting American was as real and active as it ever had been. It was, in five minutes, as though he had known this large kindly man always. His shyness dropped from him. He was talking eagerly and with great happiness.

Maradick did not patronise, did not check that American spontaneity with traditional caution as so many Englishmen do; he seemed to like Harkness as truly as Harkness liked him.

Westcott had to go. The other American also departed, but Maradick and Harkness sat on there, amused, and even absorbed.

'If I am keeping you——' Harkness said suddenly, some of his shyness for a moment returning.

'Not at all,' Maradick answered. 'I have nothing urgent this afternoon. I've got the very place for you, I believe.'

They had been speaking of places. Maradick had travelled, and together they found some of the smaller places that they both knew and loved—Dragör on the sea beyond Copenhagen, the woods north of Helsingfors, the beaches of Ischia, the enchantment of Girgente with the white goats moving over carpets of flowers through the ruined temples, the silence and mystery of Mull. He knew America too—the places that foreigners never knew; the teeth-shaped mountains at Las Cruces, the lovely curve of Tacoma, the little humped-up hills of Syracuse, the purple horizons beyond Nashville, the lone lake shore of Marquette——

'And then in this country there is Treliss,' he said softly, staring in front of him.

'Treliss?' Harkness repeated after him, liking the name.

'Yes. In North Cornwall. A beautiful place.'

He paused—sighed.

'I was there more than ten years ago. I shall never go back.'

'Why not?'

'I liked it too well. I daresay they've spoiled it now as they have many others. Thanks to wretched novelists, the railway company and char-a-bancs, Cornwall and Glebeshire are ruined. No, I dare not go back.'

'Was it very beautiful?' Harkness asked.

'Yes. Beautiful? Oh yes. Wonderful. But it wasn't that. Something happened to me there.' (See *Maradick at Forty*.)

'So that you dare not go back?'

'Yes. Dare is the word. I believe that the same thing would happen again. And I'm too old to stand it. In my case now it would be ludicrous. It was nearly ludicrous then.' Harkness said nothing. 'How old are you? If it isn't an impertinence——'

'Thirty-five? You're young enough. I was forty. Have you ever noticed about places——?' He broke off. 'I mean——Well, you know with people. Suppose that you have been very intimate with someone and then you don't see him or her for years, and then you meet again—don't you find yourself suddenly producing the same set of thoughts, emotions, moods that have, perhaps, lain dormant for years, and that only this one person can call from you? And it is the same with places. Sometimes of course in the interval something has died in you or in them, and the second meeting produces nothing. Hands cross over a grave. But if those things haven't died, how wonderful to find them all alive again after all those years, how you had forgotten the way they breathed and spoke and had their being; how interesting to find yourself drawn back again into that old current, perilous perhaps, but deep, real after all the shams——'

He broke off. 'Places do the same, I think,' he said. 'If you have the sort of things in you that stir them they produce in their turn *their* things . . . . . . .and always will for your kind . . . . . . .a sort of secret society; I believe,' he added, suddenly turning on Harkness and looking him in the face, 'that Treliss might give you something of the same adventure that it gave me—if you want it to, that is—if you need it. Do you *want* adventure, romance, something that will pull you right out of yourself and test you, show you whether you *are* real or no, give you a crisis that will change you for ever? Do you want it?'

Then he added quietly, reflectively: 'It changed *me* more than the war ever did.'

'Do I *want* it?' Harkness was breathing deeply, driven by some excitement that he could not stop to analyse. 'I should say so. I want nothing so much. It's just what I need, what I've been looking for——'

'Then go down there. I believe you're just the kind—but go at the right time. There's a night in August when they have a dance, when they dance all round the town. That's the time for you to go. That will liberate you if you throw yourself into it. It's in August. August the——I'm not quite sure of the date. I'll write to you if you'll give me your address.'

Soon afterwards, with a warm clasp of the hand, they parted.

6

Two days later Harkness received a small parcel. Opening it he discovered an old brown-covered book and a letter.

The letter was as follows:

Dear Mr. Harkness—In all probability in the cold light of reason, and removed from the fumes of the Reform Club, our conversation of yesterday will seem to you nothing but foolishness. Perhaps it was. The merest chance led me to think of something that belongs, for me, to a life quite dead and gone; not perhaps as dead, though, as I had fancied it. In any case, I had not, until yesterday, thought directly of Treliss for years.
Let us put it on the simplest ground. If you want a beautiful place, near at hand, for a holiday, that you have not yet seen, here it is—Treliss, North Cornwall—take the morning train from Paddington and change at Trewth.
If you will be advised by me you really should go down for August 6th, when they have their dance. I could see that you are interested in local customs, and here is a most entertaining one surviving from Druid times, I believe. Go down on the day itself and let that be your first impression of the place. The train gets you in between five and six. Take your room at the 'Man-at-Arms Hotel,' ten years ago the most picturesque inn in Great Britain. I cannot, of course, vouch for what it may have become. I should get out at Trewth, which you will reach soon after four, and walk the three miles to the town. Well worth doing.
One word more. I am sending you a book. A completely forgotten novel by a completely forgotten novelist. Had he lived he would, I think, have done work that would have lasted, but he was killed in the first year of the war and his earlier books are uncertain. He hadn't found himself. This book, as you will

see from the inscription, he gave me. I was with him down there. Some things in it seem to me to belong especially to the place. Pages 102 and 236 will show you especially what I mean. When you are at the 'Man-at-Arms' go and look at the Minstrels' Gallery, if it isn't pulled down or turned into a jazz dancing-hall. That too will show you what I mean.

Or go, as perhaps after all is wiser, simply to a beautiful place for a week's holiday, forgetting me and anything I have said.

Or, as is perhaps wiser still, don't go at all. In any case I am your debtor for our delightful conversation of yesterday.—

Sincerely yours,

James Maradick.

What Maradick had said occurred. As the days passed the impression faded. Harkness hoped that he would meet Maradick again. He did not do so. During the first days he watched for him in the streets and in the clubs. He devised plans that would give him an excuse to meet him once more; the simplest of all would have been to invite him to luncheon. He knew that Maradick would come. But his own distrust of himself now as always forbade him. Why should Maradick wish to see him again? He had been pleasant to him, yes, but he was of the type that would be agreeable to any one, kindly, genial, and forgetting you immediately.

But Maradick had not forgotten him. He had taken the trouble to write to him and send him a book. It had been a friendly letter too. Why not ask Westcott and Maradick to dinner? But Westcott was married. Harkness had met his wife, a charming and pretty English girl, younger a good deal than her husband. Yes, all right about Mrs. Westcott, but then Harkness must ask another woman. Maradick, he understood, was a widower. The thing was becoming a party. They would have to go somewhere, to a theatre or something. The thing was becoming elaborate, complicated, and he shrank from it. So, he always shrank from everything were he given time to think.

He paid all the gentle American's courtesy and attention to fine details of conduct. Englishmen often shocked him by their casual inattention, especially to ladies. He must do social things elaborately did he do them at all. He was gathering around him already some of the fussy observances of the confirmed bachelor. And therefore, as Maradick became to him something of a problem, he put him out of his mind just as he had put so many other things and persons out of his

191

mind because he was frightened of them.

Treliss too, as the days passed, lost some of the first magic of its name. He had felt a strange excitement when Maradick had first mentioned it, but soon it was the name of a beautiful but distant place, then a seaside resort, then nowhere at all. He did not read Lester's book.

Then an odd thing occurred. It was the last day in July and he was still in London. Nearly everyone had gone away—every one whom he knew. There were still many millions of human beings on every side of him, but London was empty for himself and his kind. His club was closed for cleaning purposes, and the Reform Club was offering him and his fellow-clubmen temporary hospitality.

He had lunched alone, then had gone upstairs, sunk into an arm-chair and read a newspaper. Read it or seemed to read it. It was time that he went away. Where should he go? There was an uncle who had taken a shooting-box in Scotland. He did not like that uncle. He had an invitation from a kind lady who had a large house in Wiltshire. But the kind lady had asked him because she pitied him, not because she liked him. He knew that very well.

There were several men who would, if he had caught them sooner, have gone with him somewhere, but he had allowed things to drift and now they had made their own plans.

He felt terribly lonely, soused suddenly with that despicable self-pity to which he was rather too easily prone. He thought of Baker— Lord! how hot it must be there just now! He was half asleep. It was hot enough here. Only one other occupant of the room, and he was fast asleep in another arm-chair. Snoring. The room rocked with his snores. The papers laid neatly one upon another wilted under the heat. The subdued London roar came from behind the windows in rolling waves of heat. A faint iridescence hovered above the enormous chairs and sofas that lay like animals panting.

He looked across the long room. Almost opposite him was a square of wall that caught the subdued light like a pool of water. He stared at it as though it had demanded his attention. The water seemed to move, to shift. Something was stirring there. He looked more intently. Colours came, shapes shifted. It was a scene, some place. Yes, a place. Houses, sand, water. A bay. A curving bay. A long sea-line dark like the stroke of a pencil against faint egg-shell blue. Water. A bay bordered by a ring of saffron sand, and behind the sand, rising above it, a town. Tier on tier of houses, and behind them again in the farthest distance a fringe of dark wood.

He could even see now little figures, black spots, dotted upon the sand. The sea now was very clear, shimmering mother-of-pearl. A scattering of white upon the shore as the long wave-line broke and retreated. And the houses tier upon tier. He gazed, filled with an overwhelming breathless excitement. He was leaning forward, his hands pressing in upon the arms of the chair. It stayed, trembling with a kind of personal invitation before him. Then, as though it had nodded and smiled farewell to him, it vanished. Only the wall was there.

But the excitement remained, excitement quite unaccountable.

He got up, his knees trembling. He looked at the stout bellying occupant of the other chair, his mouth open, his snores reverberant.

He went out. Six days later he was in the train for Treliss.

7

Now too, of course, he had his reactions just as he always had. He could explain the thing easily enough; for a moment or two he had slept, or, if he had not, a trick of light on that warm afternoon and his own thoughts about possible places had persuaded him.

Nevertheless, the picture remained strangely vivid—the sea, the shore, the rising town, the little line of darkening wood. He would go down there, and on the day that Maradick had suggested to him. Something might occur. You never could tell. He packed his etchings—his St. Gilles, Marais, his Flight into Egypt and Orvieto, his Whistler and Strang and Meryon. They would protect him and see that he did nothing foolish.

He had special confidence in his St. Gilles.

He had intended to read the Lester book all the way, but as we have seen, managed only a bare line or two; the Browning he had not intended even to have with him, but in some fashion, with the determined resolve that books so often show, it had crept into his bag and then was on his knee, he knew not whence, and soon out of self-defence against the old man he was reading *The Flight of the Duchess*, carried away on the wings of its freedom, strength, and colour.

Nevertheless, that is the kind of man I am, he thought, even the books force me to read them when I have no wish. And soon he had forgotten the old man, the carriage, the warm weather. How many years since he had read it? No matter. Wasn't it fine and touching and true? When he came to the place:

> .... *the door opened and more than mortal*
> *Stood, with a face where to my mind centred*

193

All beauties I ever saw or shall see,
The Duchess—I stopped as if struck by palsy.
She was so different, happy and beautiful,
I felt at once that all was best,
And that I had nothing to do, for the rest
But wait her commands, obey and be dutiful.
Not that, in fact, there was any commanding,
—I saw the glory of her eye
And the brow's height and the breast's expanding,
And I was hers to live or to die.

'Hurrah!' Harkness cried.

'I beg your pardon?' the old man said, looking up.

Harkness blushed. 'I was reading something rather fine,' he said, smiling.

'You'd better look out for what you're reading, to whom you're speaking, where you're walking, what you're eating, everything, when you're in Treliss,' he remarked.

'Why? Is it so dangerous a place?' asked Harkness.

'It doesn't like tourists. I've seen it do funny things to tourists in my time.'

'I think you're hard on tourists,' Harkness said. 'They don't mean any harm. They admire places the best way they can.'

'Yes, and how long do they stay?' the old man replied. 'Do you think you can know a place in a week or a month? Do you think a real place likes the dirt and the noise and the silly talk they bring with them?'

'What do you mean by a real place?' Harkness asked.

'Places have souls just like people. Some have more soul and some have less. And some have none at all. Sometimes a place will creep away altogether, it is so disgusted with the things people are trying to do to it, and will leave a dummy instead, and only a few know the difference. Why, up in the Welsh hills there are several places that have gone up there in sheer disgust the way they've been treated, and left substitutes behind them. Parts of London, for instance. Do you think that's the real Chelsea you see in London? Not a bit of it. The real Chelsea is living—well, I mustn't tell you where it is living—but you'll never find it. However, Americans are the last to understand these things. I am wasting my breath talking.'

The train had drawn now into Drymouth. The old man was silent, looking out at the hurrying crowds on the platform. He was certainly a pessimist and a hater of his kind. He was looking out at the innocent people with a lowering brow as though he would slaughter the lot of them had he the power. 'Old Testament Moses' Harkness named him. After a while the train slowly moved on. They passed above the mean streets, the hoardings with the cheap theatres, the lines with the clothes hanging in the wind, the grimy windows. But even these things the lovely sky, shining, transmuted.

They came to the river. It lay on either side of the track, a broad sheet of lovely water spreading, on the left, to the open sea. The warships clustered in dark ebony shadows against the gold; the hills rose softly, bending in kindly peace and happy watchfulness.

'Silence! We're crossing!' the old man cried. He was sitting forward, his gnarled hands on his broad knees, staring in front of him.

The train drew in to a small wayside station, gay with flowers. The trees blew about it in whispering clusters. The old man got up, gathered his basket and lumbered out, neither looking at nor speaking to Harkness.

He was alone. He felt an overwhelming relief. He had not liked the old man, and very obviously the old man had not liked him. But it was not only that he was alone that pleased him. There was something more than that.

It was indeed as though he were in a new country. The train seemed to be going now more slowly, with a more casual air, as though it too felt a relief and did not care what happened—time, engagements, schedules, all these were now forgotten as they went comfortably lumbering, the curving fields embracing them, the streams singing to them, the little houses perched on the clear-lit skyline smiling down upon them.

It would not be long now before they were in Trewth, where he must change. He took his two books and put them away in his bag. Should he send the bag on and walk as Maradick had advised him? Three miles. Not far, and it was a most lovely day. He could smell the sea now through the windows. It must be only over that ridge of hill. He was strangely, oddly happy. London seemed far, far away. America too. Any country that had a name, a date, a history. This country was timeless and without a record. How beautifully the hills dipped into valleys! Streams seemed to be everywhere, little secret coloured streams with happy thoughts. Everything and everyone surely here was happy. Then suddenly he saw a deserted mine tower like a gaunt and ruined temple. Haggard and fierce it stood against the skyline, and, as Harkness looked back to it, it seemed to raise an arm to heaven in desperate protest.

The train drew into Trewth.

8

Trewth was nothing more than a long wooden platform open to all the winds of heaven, and behind it a sort of shed with a ticket collector's box in one side of it.

Harkness was annoyed to see that others beside himself climbed out and scattered about the platform waiting for the Treliss train to come in.

He resented these especially because they were grand and elegant, two men, long, thin, in baggy knickerbockers, carrying themselves as though all the world belonged to them with that indifferent assurance that only Englishmen have; a large, stout woman, quietly but admirably dressed, with a Pekinese and a maid to whom she spoke as Cleopatra to Charmian. Five boxes, gun-cases, magnificent golf-bags, these things were scattered about the naked bare platform. The wind came in from the sea and sported everywhere, flipping at the stout lady's skirts, laughing at the elegant sportsmen's thin calves, mocking at the pouting Pekinese. It was fresh and lovely: all the cornfields were waving invitation.

It was characteristic of Harkness that a fancied haughty glance from the sportsman's eye decided him. He's laughing at my clothes, Harkness thought. How was it that Englishmen wore old things so carelessly and yet were never wrong? Harkness bought his clothes from the best London tailors, but they were always finally a little hostile. They never surrendered to his personality, keeping their own proud reserve.

I'll walk, he thought suddenly. He found a young porter who, in anxious fashion, so unlike American porters who were always so superior to the luggage that they conveyed, was wheeling magnificent trunks on a very insecure barrow.

'These two boxes of mine,' Harkness said, stopping him. 'I want to walk over to Treliss. Can they be sent over?'

'Happen they can,' said the young porter doubtfully.

'They are labelled to the "Man-at-Arms Hotel,"' Harkness said.

'They'll be there as soon as you will,' said the young porter, cheered at the sight of an American tip which he put in his pocket, thinking in his heart that these foreigners were 'dam fools' to throw their money around as they did. He advanced towards the stout lady hopefully. She might also prove to be American.

Harkness plunged out of the station into the broad white road. A sign pointed 'Treliss—Three Miles.' So Maradick had been exactly right.

As he left the village behind him and strode on between the corn-fields he felt a marvellous freedom. He was heading now directly for the sea. The salt tang of it struck him in the face. Larks were circling in the blue air above him, poppies scattered the corn with plashes of crimson. Here and there gaunt rocks rose from the heart of the gold. No human being was in sight.

His love of etching had given him something of an etcher's eye, and he saw here a spreading tree and a pool of dark shadow, there a distant spire on the curving hill that he thought would have caught the fancy of his beloved Lepère, or Legros. Here a wayside pool like brittle glass that would have enchanted Appian, there a cottage with a sweeping field that might have made Rembrandt happy.

He seemed to be in unison with the whole of nature, and when the road left the fields and dived into the heart of a common his happiness was complete. He stood there, his feet pressing in upon the rough springing turf. A lark, singing above him, came down as though welcoming him, then circled up and up and up. He raised his head, staring into the pale faint blue until he seemed himself to circle with the bird, the turf pressing him upwards, his hands lifting him, he swinging into spaceless ecstasy. Then his gaze fell again and swung out beyond, and—there was the sea.

The Down ran in a green wave to the blue line of the sky, but in front of him it split, breaking into brown rocky patches, and between the brown curves a pool of purple sea lay like water in a cup.

He walked forward, deserting for a moment the road. He stood at the edge of the cliff and looked down. The tide was high and the line of the sea slipped up to the feet of the cliff, splashed there its white fringe of spray, then very gently fell back. Sea-pinks starred the cliffs with colour. Seagulls whirled, fragments of white foam, against the blue. Just below him one bird sat, its head cocked, waiting. With a shrill cry of vigour and assurance it flashed away, curving, circling, bending, dipping, as though it were showing to Harkness what it could do.

He walked along the cliff path happier than he had been for many, many months. This was enough were there no more than this. For this at least he must thank Maradick—this peace, this air, this silence. . . . . .

Turning a bend of the cliff he saw the town.

9

It was absolutely the town of his vision. He saw, with a strange tightening of his heart as though he were being warned of something, that that was so. There was the curving bay with the faint fringe of white pencilling the yellow sand, there the houses rising tier on tier above the beach, there the fringe of dusky wood. What did it mean? Why had he a clutch of terror as though some one was whispering to him that he must turn tail and run? Nothing could be more lovely than that town basking in the mellow afternoon light, and yet he was afraid at the sight of it—afraid so that his content and happiness of a moment ago were all gone and of a sudden he longed for company.

He was so well accustomed to his own reactions and so deeply despised them that he shrugged his shoulders and walked forward. Never, it seemed, was it possible for him to enjoy anything for more than a moment. Trouble and regret always came. But this was not regret, it was rather a kind of forewarning. He did not know that he had ever before looked on a place for the first time with so odd a mingling of conviction that he had already seen it, of admiration for its beauty, and of some sort of alarmed dismay. Beautiful it was, more Italian than English, with its white walls, its purple sea, and warm scented air.

So peaceful and of so happy a tranquillity. He tried to drive his fear from him, but it hung on so that he was often turning back and looking behind him over his shoulder.

He struck the road again. It curved now, white and broad, down the hill toward the town. At the very peak of the hill before the descent began a man was standing watching something.

Harkness walked forward, then also stood still. The man was so deeply absorbed that his absorption held you. He was standing at the edge of the road and Harkness must pass him. At the crunch of Harkness's step on the gravel of the road the man turned and looked at him with startled surprise. Harkness had come across the soft turf of the Down, and his sudden step must have been an alarm. The fellow was broad-shouldered, medium height, clean-shaven, tanned, young, under thirty at least, dressed in a suit of dark blue. He had something of a naval air.

Harkness was passing, when the man said:

'Have you the right time on you, sir?' His voice was fresh, pleasant, well-educated.

Harkness looked at his watch. 'Quarter past five,' he said. He was moving forward when the man, hesitating, spoke again:

'You don't see anyone coming up the road?'

Harkness stared down the white, sun-bleached expanse.

'No,' he said after a moment, 'I don't.'

They looked for a while standing side by side silently.

After all he wasn't more than a boy—not a day more than twenty-five—but with that grave reserved look that so many British boys who were old enough to have been in the war had.

'Sure, you don't see anybody?' he asked again, 'coming up that farther bend?'

'No,' said Harkness, shading his eyes with his hand against the sun; 'can't say as I do.'

'Damn nuisance,' the boy said. 'He's half an hour late now.'

The boy stood as though to attention, his figure set, his hands at his side.

'Ah, there's someone,' said Harkness. But it was only an old man with his cart. He slowly pressed up the hill past them, urging his horses with a thick guttural cry, an old man brown as a berry.

'I beg your pardon,' the boy turned to Harkness. 'You'll think it an awful impertinence—but—are you in a terrible hurry?'

'No,' said Harkness, 'not terrible. I want to be at the "Man-at-Arms" by dinner time. That's all.'

'Oh, you've got lots of time,' the boy said eagerly. 'Look here. This is desperately important for me. The man ought to have been here half an hour ago. If he doesn't come in another twenty minutes I don't know what I shall do. It's just occurred to me. There's another way up this hill—a short cut. He may have chosen that. He may not have understood where it was that I wanted him to meet me. Would you mind—would you do me the favour of just standing here while I go over the hill there to see whether he's waiting on the other side? I won't be away more than five minutes; I'd be so awfully grateful.'

'Why, of course,' said Harkness.

'He's a fisherman with a black beard. You can't mistake him. And if he comes, if you'd just ask him to wait for a moment until I'm back.'

'Certainly,' said Harkness.

'Thanks most awfully. Very decent of you, sir.'

The boy touched his cap, climbed the hill, and vanished.

Harkness was alone again—not a sound anywhere. The town

shimmered below him in the heat. He waited, absorbed by the picture spread in front of him, then apprehensive again and conscious that he was alone. The alarm that he had originally felt at sight of the town had not left him. Suppose the boy did not return? Was playing some joke on him perhaps? No, whatever else it was, it was not that. The boy had been deeply serious, plunged into some crisis that was of tremendous importance to him.

Harkness decided that he would wait until the shadow of a solitary tree to his right reached him, and then go. The shadow crept slowly to his feet. At the same moment a figure turned the bend, a man with a black beard. He was walking quickly up the hill as though he knew that he were late.

Harkness went forward to meet him. The man stopped as though surprised. 'I beg your pardon,' said Harkness; 'were you expecting to meet someone here?'

'I was—yes,' said the man.

'He will be back in a moment. He was afraid that you might have come up the other way. He went over the hill to see.'

'Aye,' said the man, standing, his legs apart, quite unconcerned. He was a handsome fellow, broad-shouldered, wearing dark blue trousers and a knitted jersey. 'You'll be a friend of Mr. Dunbar's, maybe?'

'No, I'm not,' Harkness explained. 'I was passing, and he asked me to wait for a moment and catch you if you came while he was away.'

'Aye,' said the fisherman, taking out a large wedge of tobacco and filling his pipe, 'I'm a bit later than I said I'd be. Wife kept me.'

'Fine evening,' said Harkness.

'Aye,' said the man.

At that moment the boy came over the hill and joined them. 'Very good of you, sir,' he said. 'You're late, Jabez!'

'Goodnight,' said Harkness, and moved down the hill. He could see the two in urgent conversation as he moved forward. The incident occupied his mind. Why had the matter seemed of such importance to the boy? Why a meeting so elaborately appointed out there on the hillside? The fisherman too had seemed surprised that he, a stranger, should be concerned in the matter.

Had he been in America the affair would have been at once explained—boot-legging, of course. But here in England. . . . . .

10

When he reached the bottom of the hill he found that he was in the environs of the town. He was walking now along a road shaded by thick trees and close to the sea-shore.

The cottages, white-washed, crooked and, many of them, thatched, ran down to the road, their gardens like little coloured carpets spreading in front of them. The evening air was thick with the scent of flowers, above all of roses. He had never smelt such roses, no, not in California.

There was a breeze from the sea, and it seemed to blow the roses into his very heart, so that they seemed to be all about him, dark crimson, burning white, scattering their petals over his head. He could hear the tune of the sea upon the sand beyond the trees.

He stood for a moment inhaling the scent—delicious, wonderful. He seemed to be crushing multitudes of the petals between his hands.

After a while the road broke away and he saw a path that led directly through the trees to the sea.

So soon as he had taken some steps across the soft sand he seemed to be alone in a world that was watching every movement that he made. It was as though he were committing some intrusion. He stopped and looked behind him: the thin line of trees had retreated, the cottages vanished. Before him was a waste of yellow sand, the deep purple of the sea rose like a wall to his right, hiding, as it were, some farther scene, the sky stretching over it a pale blue curtain tightly held.

A mist was rising, veiling the town. No living person was in sight. He reached a stretch of hard firm sand, thin rivulets of water lacing it. The air was wonderfully mild and sweet.

Never before in his life had he known such a feeling of anticipation. It was as though he knew the stretch of sand to be the last brook to cross before he would come into some mysterious country.

How commonplace this will all seem to me tomorrow, he said to himself, when, over my eggs and bacon at a prosperous modern hotel, I shall be reading my *Daily Mail* and hearing of the trippers at Eastbourne and who has taken 'shooting' in Scotland and whether Yorkshire has beaten Surrey at cricket. He wanted to keep this moment, not to enter the town; even he had a mad impulse to walk on the sand for an hour, to see the colour fade from the sky and the sea change to a ghostly grey, then to return up the hill to Trewth and catch the night train back to London.

It would be wonderful like that; to have only the impression of the walk from the station, the talk with the boy on the hill, the scent of the roses and the afternoon sky. Everything is destroyed if you go into it too closely, or it is so for me. I should have a memory that would last me all my life.

But now the town was advancing towards him. His steps made no sound so that it seemed that he himself stood still, waiting to be seized. He took one last look at the sea. Then he was caught up and the houses closed about him.

11

Six was striking from some distant clock as he started up the street. At the bottom of the hill there were fishermen's cottages, nets spread out on the stones to dry, some boats drawn up above a wooden jetty. Then, as the street spread out before him, some little shops began. Figures were passing hither and thither all transmuted in the afternoon light. Maradick need not have feared, he thought, this town has not been touched at all.

As he advanced yet further the houses delighted him with their broad doorways, their overhanging eaves, crooked roof and worn flights of steps. He came to a place where wooden stairs led to an upper path that ran before a higher row of houses and under the steps there were shops.

He could feel a stir and bustle in the place as though this were a night of festivity. Groups were gathered at corners, women stood in doorways laughing and whispering, a group of children was marching, wearing cocked hats of paper, beating on a wooden box and blowing on penny trumpets.

Then on coming into the Square he paused in sheer delighted wonder. This stands on a raised plateau above the sea, and the town hall, solid and virtuous above its flight of wide grey steps, is its great glory. Streets seemed to tumble in and out of the Square on every side. On a far corner there was a merry-go-round and there were booths and wooden trestles, some tents and flags waving above them. But just now it was almost deserted, only a man or two, some children playing in and out of the tents, a dog hunting among the scraps of paper that littered the cobbles.

A church of Norman architecture filled the right side of the Square, and squeezed between its grey walls and the modern town hall was a tall old tower of infinite age, with thin slits of windows and iron bars that pushed out against the pale blue sky like pointing fingers.

There were houses in the Square that were charming, houses with queer bow-windows and protruding doors like pepper-pots, little balconies, and here and there old carved figures on the walls, houses that Whistler would have loved to etch. Harkness stopped a man.

'Can you tell me where I shall find "The Man-at-Arms Hotel"?' he asked.

'Why, yes,' the man answered as though he were surprised that Harkness should not know. 'Straight up that street in front of you. You'll find it at the top.'

And he did find it at the top, after what seemed to him an endless climb. The houses fell away. An iron gate was in front of him as though he were entering some private residence. Going up a long drive he passed beautiful lawns that shone like silk, to the right the grass fell away to a pond fringed with trees. Flowers were around him on every side, and again in his nostrils was the heavy scent of innumerable roses.

The drive swept a wide circle before the great eighteenth-century house that now confronted him. But it is not a hotel at all, he thought, and he would have turned back had not, at that moment, a large hotel omnibus swept up to the door and discharged a chattering heap of men and women, who scattered over the steps screaming about their luggage, collecting children. The spell was broken. He had not realised how alone he had been during the last hour and with what domination his imagination had been working, creating for him a world of his own, encouraging in him what hopes, fears, and anticipations!

He slipped in after the rest, and stood shyly in the hall while the others made their wants triumphantly felt. A man of about forty, stout and round like an egg, but very shinily dressed, came forward and, bending and bowing, smiled at the women and spoke deferentially to the men.

This must be Mr. Bannister—'the King of the Castle' Maradick had told him in the Club. Not the original Mr. Bannister who has made the place what it is. He is, alas, dead and gone. Had he been still there and you had mentioned my name he would have done wonders for you. I don't know this fellow, and for all I know he may have ruined the place.

However, the original Bannister could not have been politer. Harkness was always afraid of hotel officials, and it was only when the invasion had broken up and begun to scatter that he came forward. But Mr. Bannister knew all about him—indeed was expecting him. His luggage had already arrived. He should be shown his room, and Mr. Bannister did hope that it would be........If anything in the least wasn't . . . . .

203

Harkness started upstairs. There is a lift here, but if the gentleman doesn't mind. . . . . . . .His room is only on the second floor and instead of waiting. . . . . . . .Of course the gentleman doesn't mind. And still less does he mind when he sees his room.

This is mine absolutely, Harkness said, as though it had been waiting for me for years and years with its curved bow-window, its view over that enchanting garden and the line of sea beyond, its white wall unbroken by those coloured prints that hotel managers in my own country find it so necessary always to provide. Those chintz curtains with the roses are delicious. Just enough furniture. There is no private bath, of course?

'The bathroom is just across the passage. Very convenient,' said the man.

'Yes, in England we haven't reached the private bathroom yet, although we are supposed to be so fond of bathing.'

'No, sir,' said the man. 'Anything else I can do for you?'

'No, thank you,' said Harkness, smiling, as he looked on the white sunlit walls, and checking the tip that, American fashion, he was about to give. 'How strong the smell of the roses. It is very late for them, isn't it?'

'They are just about over, sir.'

'So I should have thought.'

Left alone he slowly unpacked. He liked unpacking and putting things away. It was packing that he detested. He had a few things with him that he always carried when he travelled—a red leather writing-case, a little Japanese fisherman in coloured ivory, two figures in red amber, photographs of his sisters in a silver frame. He put out these little things on a table of white wood near his bed, not from any affectation, but because when they were there the room seemed to understand him, to settle about him with a little sigh as though it granted him citizenship—for so long as he wished to stay.

Then there were his prints. He took out four, the Lepère 'St. Gilles,' Strang's 'Etcher,' the Rembrandt 'Flight into Egypt,' and the Whistler 'Drury Lane.' The Strang he had on one side of the looking-glass, the 'Drury Lane' on the other, the 'Flight into Egypt' at the back of the writing-table, whither he might glance across the room at it as he lay in bed, the 'St. Gilles' close to him near to the red writing-case and the ivory fisherman.

He sighed with satisfaction as, sitting down on his bed, he looked at them. He felt that he needed them tonight as he had never needed them before. The sense of excited anticipation that had increased with him all day was now surely approaching its climax. That excitement had in it the strangest mixture of delight, sensuous thrill, and something that was nothing but panicky terror. Yes, he was frightened. Of what? Of whom? He could not tell. But only as he looked across the room at those familiar scenes, at the massive dark tree of the 'St. Gilles' with the hot road, the high comfortable hedge, the happy figures, at the adorable face of the donkey in the Rembrandt, at the little beings so marvellously placed under the dancing butterfly in the Whistler, at the strong, homely, friendly countenance of Strang himself, he felt as he had so often felt before, that those beautiful things were trying themselves to reassure him, to tell him that they did not change nor alter, and that where he would be there they would be too.

He took Maradick's letter from his pocket and read it again. Here he was—now what must happen next? He would dress now at once for dinner, and then walk in the garden before the light began to fail. Or no. Wasn't he to go down into the town after dinner and to see this dance, to share in it even? Hadn't Maradick said that that was what, above all else, he must do?

And then what was this about a Minstrels' Gallery somewhere? He would have a bath, change his linen, and then begin his explorations. He undressed, found the bathroom, enjoyed himself for twenty minutes or more, then slipped back across the passage into his room again. It was now nearly seven o'clock. As he was dressing, the sun was getting low in the sky. A beam of sunshine caught the intent gaze of Strang, who seemed to lean across his etching board as though to tell him, to reassure him, to warn him. . . . . .

He slipped out of his room and began his explorations.

12

For a while he wandered, lost in a maze of passages. He understood that the Minstrels' Gallery was at the top of the house. He did not use the lift, but climbed the stairs, meeting no one; then he was on a floor that must, he thought, be servants' quarters. It had another air, something less arranged, less handsome, old-fashioned, as though it were even now as it had been two hundred years ago—a survival, as the old grey tower in the market-place was a survival.

For a little while he stood hesitating. The passage was dark and he did not wish to plunge into a servant's room. Strange that up here there was no sound at all—an absolute deathly stillness!

He walked down to the end of the passage, then, turning, came to a door that was larger than the others. He could see as he looked at it more closely that there was some faint carving on the woodwork above it. He turned the handle, entered the room, then stopped with a little cry of surprise and pleasure.

Truly Maradick had been right. Here was a room that, if there was nothing more to come, made the journey sufficiently of value. An enchanting room! On the left side of it were broad bright windows, and at the farther end, under the Minstrels' Gallery, windows again. There were no curtains to the windows—the whole room had an empty, deserted air—but the more for that reason the place was illuminated with the glow of the evening light. The first thing that he realised was the view—and what a view!

The windows were deep set and hung forward, it seemed, over the hill, so that town, gardens, trees, were all lost and you saw only the sea.

At this hour you seemed to swing in space; the division lost between sea and sky in the now nearly horizontal rays of the sun—only a golden glow covering the blue with a dazzling blaze of colour. He stood there drinking it in, then sat in one of the window-seats, his hands clasped, lost in happiness.

After a while he turned back to the room. Flecks of dust, changed into gold by the evening light, floated in mid-air. The room was disregarded indeed. The walls were panelled. The little Minstrels' Gallery was supported on two heavy pillars. The floor was bare of carpet and had even a faint waxen sheen, as though, in spite of the room's general neglect, it was used, once and again, for dances.

But what pathos the room had! He did not know that, almost fifteen years before, Maradick had felt that same thing. How vastly now that pathos was increased, how greatly since Maradick's day the world's history had relentlessly cut away those earlier years. He saw that round the platform of the gallery was intricate carving, and, going forward more closely to examine, saw that in every square was set the head of a grinning lion. Some high-backed, quaintly-shaped chairs, that looked as though they might be of great age, were ranged against the wall.

Being now right under the gallery he saw some little wooden steps. He climbed up them, and then from the gallery's shadow looked down across the room. How clearly, he could picture that old scene, something straight from Jane Austen with Miss Bates and Mrs. Norris, stiff-backed, against the wall, and Anne Elliot and Elizabeth Bennet,

Mr. Collins and the rest. The fiddlers scraping, the negus for refreshment, the night darkening, the carriages with their lights gathering...
...The door at the far end of the room closed with a gentle click. He started, not imagining that anyone would choose that room at such an hour.

Two figures were there in the shadow beyond the end room. The light fell on the man's face—Harkness could see it very clearly. The other was a woman wearing a white dress. He could not see her face.

For an instant they were silent, then the man said something that Harkness could not hear.

The girl at once broke out: 'No, no. Oh, please, Herrick.'

She must be a very young girl. The voice was that of a child. It had in it a desperate note that held Harkness's attention instantly.

The man said something again, very low.

'But if you don't care,' the girl's voice pleaded, 'then let me go back. Oh, Herrick, let me go! Let me go!'

'My father does not wish it.'

'But I am not married to your father. It is to you.'

'My father and I are the same. What he says I must do, I do.'

'But you can't be the same.' Her voice now was trembling in its urgency. 'No one could love their father more than I do and yet we are not the same.'

'Nevertheless, you did what your father asked you to do. So, must I.'

'But I didn't know. I didn't know. And he didn't know. He has never seen me frightened of anything, and now I am frightened.....
... I've never said I was to anyone before, but now ....now .....'

She was crying, softly, terribly, with the terrified crying of real and desperate fear.

Harkness had been about to move. He did not, unseen and his presence unrealised, wish to overhear, but her tears checked him. Although he could not see her he had detected in her voice a note of pride. He fancied that she would wish anything rather than to be thus seen by a stranger. He stayed where he was. He could see the man's face, thin, white, the nose long pointed, a dark, almost grotesque shadow.

'Why are you frightened?'

'I don't know. I can't tell. I have never been frightened before.'

'Have I been unkind to you?'

'No, but you don't love me.'

207

'Did I ever pretend to love you? Didn't you know from the very first that no one in the world matters to me except my father?'

'It is of your father that I am afraid. . . . . . . .These last three days in that terrible house. . . . . . . .I'm so frightened, Herrick. I want to go home only for a little while. Just for a week before we go abroad.'

'All our plans are made now. You know that we are sailing to-morrow evening.'

'Yes, but I could come afterwards. Forgive me, Herrick. You may do anything to me if I can only go home for just some days. . . . . . .You may do anything. . . . . .'

'I don't want to do anything, Hesther. No one wishes to do you any harm. But whatever my father wishes, that everyone must do. It has always been so.'

She seemed to be seized by an absolute frenzy of fear; Harkness could see her white shadow quivering. It appeared to him as though she caught the man by the arm. Her voice came in little breathless stifled cries, infinitely pitiful to hear.

'Please, please, Herrick. I dare not speak to your father. I don't dare. I don't dare. But you—let me go—Oh! let me go—just this once, Herrick. Only this once. I'll only be home for a few days and then I'll come back. Truly I'll come back. I'll just see father and Bobby and then I'll come back. They'll be missing me. I know they will. And I'll be going to a foreign country—such a long way. And they'll be wanting me. Bobby's so young, Herrick, only a baby. He's never had any one do anything for him but me. . . . . .'

'You should have thought of that before you married me, you cannot leave me now.'

'I won't leave you. I've never broken my word to anyone. I won't break it now. It's only for a few days.'

'How can you be so selfish, Hesther, as to want to upset every one's plans just for a whim of your own? For myself I don't care. You could go home for ever, for all I care. I didn't want to marry anyone. But what my father wished had to be.'

She clung to him then, crying again and again between her sobs:

'Oh, let me go home! Let me go home! Let me go home!'

Harkness fancied that the man put his hands on her shoulders. His voice, cold, lifeless, impersonal, crossed the room.

'That is enough. He is waiting for us downstairs. He will be wondering where we are.'

The little white shadow seemed to turn to the window, towards the limitless expanse of sunlit sea. Then a voice, small, proud, empty of emotion, said:

'Father wished me——'

Harkness was once more alone in the room.

13

They had gone but the girl's fear remained. It was there as truly as the two figures had been and its reality was stronger than their reality.

Harkness had the sense of having been caught, and it was exactly as though now, as he stood alone there in the gallery staring down into the room, some Imp had touched him on the shoulder, crying, 'Now you're in for it! Now you're in for it! The situation has got you now!'

He was, of course, not 'in for it' at all. How many such conversations between human beings there were; it simply was that he had happened against his will to overhear a fragment of one of them. Yes, 'against his will.' How desperately he wished that he hadn't been there. What induced them to choose that room and that time for their secret confidences? He felt still in the echo of their voices the effect of their urgency.

They had chosen that room because there was some one watching their every movement and they had had only a few moments. The child—for surely, she could not be more—had almost driven her companion into that two minutes' conversation, and Harkness could realise how desperate she must have been to have taken such a course.

But after all it *was* no business of his! Girls married every day men whom they did not love, and although apparently in this case the man also did not love her and they were both of them in evil plight, still that too had happened before and nothing very terrible had come of it.

It *was* no business of his, and yet he did wish, all the same, that he could get the ring of the girl's voice out of his ears. He had never been able to bear the sight, sound, or even inference of any sort of cruelty to helpless humans or to animals. Perhaps because he was so frantic a coward himself about physical pain! And yet not altogether that. He had on several occasions taken risks of pretty savage pain to himself in order to save a horse a beating or a dog a kicking. Nevertheless, those had been spontaneous emotions roused at the instant; there was something lingering, a sad and tragic echo, in the voice that was still with him.

The very pathos of the room that he was in—the lingering of so

many old notes that had been rung and rung again, notes of anticipation, triumph, disappointment, resignation, made this fresh, living
sound the harder to escape.

By Jupiter, the child *was* frightened—that was the final ringing of
it upon Harkness's heart and soul. But he was going to have his life
sufficiently full were he to step in and rescue every girl frightened by
matrimony! Rescue! No, there was no question of rescue. It wasn't,
once again, his affair. But he did wish that he could just take her hand
and tell her not to worry, that it would all come right in the end. But
would it? He hadn't at all cared for the fragment of countenance that
fellow had shown to him, and he had liked still less the tone of his
voice, cold, unfeeling, hard. Poor child! And suddenly the thought of
his Browning's *Duchess* came to him:

> I was the man the Duke spoke to:
> I helped the Duchess to cast off his yoke too;
> So, here's the tale from beginning to end,
> My friend!

Well, here was a tale with which he had definitely nothing to do.
Let him remember that. He was here in a most beautiful place for a
holiday—that was his purpose, that his intention—what were these
people to him or he to them?

Nevertheless, the voice lingered in his ear, and to be rid of it he left
the room. He stepped carefully down the wooden steps, and then at
the bottom of them, under the dark lee of the gallery, he paused. He
was so foolishly frightened that he could not move a step.

He waited. At last he whispered 'Is anyone there?'

There was no answer. He pushed his way then out of the shadow, his heart drumming against his shirt. There was no one there. Of
course, there was not.

In his room once more with his friend Strang and the Rembrandt
Donkey to take him home he sat on his bed holding his hands between his knees.

He was positively afraid of going down to dinner. Afraid of what?
Afraid of being drawn in. Drawn into what? That was precisely what
he did not know, but something that ever since his first glimpse of
Maradick at the Reform Club had been preparing. It was that he saw,
as he sat there thinking of it, that he feared—this Something that was
piling up outside him and with which he had nothing to do at all.

Why should he mind because he had heard a girl say that she was frightened and wanted to go home? And yet he did mind—minded terribly and with increasing violence from every moment that passed. The thought of that child without a friend and on the very edge of an experience that might indeed be fatal for her, the thought of it was more than he could endure.

He was clever at escaping things did they only give him a moment's pause, but in this case the longer he thought about it the harder it was to escape from. It was as though the girl had made her personal appeal to himself. But what an old scamp her father must be, Harkness thought, to give her up like this to a man for whom she has no love, who doesn't love her. Why did she do it? And what kind of a man is the father-in-law of whom she is so afraid and who dominates his son so absolutely? In any case I must go down to dinner. I must just take what comes. . . . . .

Yes, but his prudence whispered, don't meddle in this affair actively. It isn't the kind of thing in which you are likely to distinguish yourself.

'No, by Jove, it isn't.'

'Well, then, be careful.'

'I mean to be.' Then suddenly the girl's voice came sharp and clear. 'Damn it, I'll do anything I can,' he cried aloud, jumped from the bed and went downstairs.

14

As he went downstairs he felt a tremendous sense of liberation. It was as though he had, after many hesitations and fears, passed through the first room successfully and closed the door behind him. Now there was the second room to be confronted.

What he immediately confronted was the garden of the hotel. The sun was slowly setting in the west, and great amber clouds, spreading out in swathes of colour, ate up the blue.

The amber flung out arms as though it would embrace the whole world. The deep blue ebbed from the sea, was pale crystal, then from length to length a vast bronze shield. The amber receded as though it had done its work, and myriads of little flecks of gold ran up into the pale blue-white, thousands of scattered fragments like coins flung in some God-like largesse.

The bronze sea was held rigid as though it were truly of metal. The town caught the gold and all the windows flashed. In the fresh evening light, the grass of the lawn seemed to shine with a fresh iridescence—the farther hills were coldly dark.

Several people were walking up and down the gravel paths, pausing, before going in to dinner. In the golden haze only those things stood out that were more important for the scene, nature, as always, being more theatrical than any man-contrived theatre. The stage being set, the principal actor made his entrance.

A window running to the gravel path caught the level rays of the setting sun. A man stepped before this, stopping to light a cigarette, and then, being there, stayed like an oriental image staring out into the garden.

Harkness looked casually, then looked again, then, fascinated, remained watching. He had never before seen such red hair nor so white a face, nor so large a stone as the green one that shone in a ring on the finger of his raised hand. He was lighting his cigarette—it was after this that he fell into rigid immobility—and the fire of the match caught the ring until, like a great eye, it seemed to open, wink at Harkness, and then regard him with a contemptuous stare.

The man's hair was *en brosse*, standing straight on end as Loge's used to do in the old pre-war Bayreuth 'Ring.' It was, like Loge's, a flaming red, short, harsh, instantly arresting. Evening dress. One small black pearl in his shirt. Very small feet in shining shoes.

There had stuck in Harkness's mind a phrase that he had encountered once in George Moore's description of Verlaine in *Memories and Opinions*—'I shall not forget the glare of the bald prominent forehead (*une tête glabre*). . . . .' That was the phrase now, *une tête glabre*—the forehead glaring like a challenge, the red hair springing from it like something alive of its own independence. For the rest, this interesting figure had a body round, short, and fat like a ball. Over his protruding stomach stretched a white waistcoat with three little plain black buttons.

The colour of his face had an unnatural pallor, something theatrical like the clown in *Pagliacci*, or again, like one of Benda's masks. Yes, this was the truer comparison, because through the mask the eyes were alive and beautiful, dark, tender, eloquent, but spoilt because above them the eyebrows were so faint as to be scarcely visible. The mouth in the white of the face was a thin, hard, red scratch. The eyes stared into the garden. The body soon became painted into the window behind it, the round short limbs, the shining shoes, the little black pearl in the gleaming shirt.

Harkness, from the shadow where he stood, looked and looked again. Then, fearing that he might be perceived and his stare be held offensive, he moved forward. The man saw him and, to Harkness's surprise, stepped forward and spoke to him.

'I beg your pardon,' he said; 'but do you happen to have a light? My cigarette did not catch properly and I have used my last match.'

Here was another surprise for Harkness. The voice was the most beautiful that he had ever heard from man. Soft, exquisitely melodious, with an inflection in it of friendliness, courtesy, and culture that was enchanting. Absolutely without affectation.

'Why, yes. Certainly,' said Harkness.

He felt for his little gold matchbox, found it, produced a match and, guarding it with his hand, struck it. In the light the other's forehead suddenly sprang up again like a live thing. For an instant two of his fingers rested on Harkness's hand. They seemed to be so soft as to be quite boneless.

'Thank you. What an exquisite evening!'

'Yes,' said Harkness. 'This is a very beautiful place.'

'Yes,' said the other, 'is it not? And this is incidentally the best hotel in England.'

The voice was so beautiful to Harkness, who was exceedingly sensitive to sound, that his only desire was that by some means he should prolong the conversation so that he might indulge himself in the luxury of it.

'I have only just arrived,' he said; 'I came only an hour ago, and it is my first visit.'

'Is that so? Then you have a great treat in store for you. This is splendid country round here, and although everyone has been doing their best to spoil it, there are still some lovely places. Treliss is the only town in Southern England where the place is still triumphant over modern improvements.'

There was a pause, then the man said:

'Will you be here for long?'

'I have made no plans,' Harkness replied.

'I wish I could show you around a little. I know this country very well. There is nothing I enjoy more than showing off some of our beauties. But, unfortunately, I leave for abroad early tomorrow morning.'

Harkness thanked him. They were soon talking very freely, walking up and down the gravel path. The exquisite modulation of the man's voice, its rhythm, gentleness, gave Harkness such delight that he could listen for ever. They spoke of foreign countries. Harkness had travelled much and remembered what he had seen. This man had been apparently everywhere.

Suddenly a gong sounded. 'Ah, there's dinner.' They paused. The stranger said: 'I beg your pardon. You tell me that you are American, and I know therefore that you are not hampered by ridiculous conventionalities. Are you alone?'

'I am,' said Harkness.

'Well, then—why not dine with us? There is myself, my son and a charming girl to whom he has lately been married. Do me that pleasure. Or, if people are a bore to you, be quite frank and say so.'

'I shall be delighted,' said Harkness.

'Good. My name is Crispin.'

'Harkness is mine.'

They walked in together.

15

He had, as he walked into the hall, an overwhelming sense that everything that was occurring to him had happened to him before, and it was only part of this dream-conviction that Crispin should pause and say: 'Here they are, waiting for us,' and lead him up to the girl who, half an hour before, had been with him in the little gallery. He had even a moment of protesting panic crying to the little imp whose voice he had already heard that evening: 'Let me out of this. I am not so passive as you fancy. It is a holiday I am here for. There is no knight-errantry in me—you have caught the wrong man for that.'

But the girl's face stopped him. She was beautiful. He had from the first instant of seeing her no doubt of that, and it was as though her voice had already built her up for him in that dim room.

Straight and dark, her face had child-like purity in its rounded cheeks, its large brow and wondering eyes, its mouth set now in proud determination, but trembling a little behind that pride, its cheeks very soft and faintly coloured. Her hair was piled up as though it were only recently that it had come to that distinction. She was wearing a very simple white frock that looked as though it had been made by some little local dressmaker of her own place. She had been proud of it, delighted with it, Harkness could be sure, perhaps only a week or two ago. Now experiences were coming to her thick and fast. She was clutching them all to her, determined to face them whatever they might be, finding them, as Harkness knew from what he had overheard, more terrible than she had ever conceived.

She had been crying, as he knew, only half an hour ago, but now there were no traces of tears, only a faint shell-like flush on her cheeks.

The man standing beside her was not much more than a boy, but Harkness thought that he had seldom perceived an uglier countenance. A large broad nose, a long thin face like a hatchet, grey colourless eyes and a bony body upon which the evening clothes sat awkwardly, here was ugliness itself, but the true unpleasantness came from the cold aloofness that lay in the unblinking eyes, the hard straight mouth.

'He might be walking in his sleep,' Harkness thought, 'for all the life he's showing. What a pair for the girl to be in the hands of!' Harkness was introduced.

'Hesther, my dear, this is Mr. Harkness, who is going to give us the pleasure of dining with us. Mr. Harkness, this is my boy Herrick.'

The little man led the way, and it was interesting to perceive the authoritative dignity with which he moved. He had a walk that admirably surmounted the indignities that the short legs and stumpy body would, in a less clever performer, have inevitably entailed. He did not strut, nor trot, nor push out his stomach and follow it with proud resolve.

His dignity was real, almost regal, and yet not absurd. He walked slowly, looking about him as he went. He stopped at the entrance of the dining-hall, now crowded with people, spoke to the head waiter, a stout pompous-looking fellow, who was at once obsequious, and started down the room to a reserved table.

The diners looked up and watched their progress, but Harkness noticed that no one smiled. When they came to their table in the middle of the room Mr. Crispin objected to it, and they were at once shown to another one beside the window and looking out to the sea.

'It will amuse you to see the room, Hesther. You sit there. You can look out of the window too when you are bored with people. Will you sit here, Mr. Harkness, on my right?'

Harkness was now opposite the girl and looking out to the sea that was lit with a bronze flame that played on the air like a searchlight. The window was slightly open, and he could hear the sounds from the town, the merry-go-round, a harsh trumpet, and once and again a bell.

'Do you mind that window?' Crispin asked him. 'I think it is rather pleasant. You don't mind it, Hesther dear? They are having festivities down there this evening. The night of their annual ceremony when they dance round the town—something as old as the hill on which the town is built, I fancy. You ought to go down and look at them, Mr.

215

Harkness.'

'I think I shall,' Harkness replied, smiling.

He noticed that now that the man was seated he did not look small. His neck was thick, his shoulders broad, that forehead in the brilliantly-lit room absolutely gleamed, the red hair springing up from it like a challenge. The mention of the dance led Crispin to talk of other strange customs that he had known in many parts of the world, especially in the East. Yes, he had been in the East very often and especially in China. The old China was going. You would have to hurry up if you were to see it with any colour left. It was too bad that the West could not leave the East alone.

'The matter with the West, Mr. Harkness, is that it always must be improving everything and everybody. It can't leave well alone. It must be thrusting its morals and customs on people who have very nice ones of their own—only they are not Western, that's all. We have too many conventional ideas over here. Superstitious observances that are just as foolish as any in the South Seas—more foolish indeed. Now I'm shocking you, Hesther, I'm afraid. Hesther,' he explained to Harkness, 'is the daughter of an English country doctor—a very fine fellow. But she hasn't travelled much yet. She only married my son a month ago. This is their honeymoon, and it is very nice of them to take their old father along with them. He appreciates it, my dear.'

He raised his glass and bowed to her. She smiled very faintly, staring at him for an instant with her large brown eyes, then looking down at her plate.

'I have been driven,' Crispin explained, 'into the East by my collector's passions as much as anything. You know, perhaps, what it is to be a collector, not of anything especial, but a collector. Something in the blood worse than drugs or drink. Something that only death can cure. I don't know whether you care for pretty things, Mr. Harkness, but I have some pieces of jade and amber that would please you, I think. I have, I think, one of the best collections of jade in Europe.'

Harkness said something polite.

'The trouble with the collector is that he is always so much more deeply interested in his collection than anyone else is, and he is not so interested in a thing when he owns it as he was when he was wondering whether he could afford it.

'However, women like my jade. Their fingers itch. It is pleasant to see them. Have you ever felt the collector's passion yourself?'

'In a tiny way only,' said Harkness. 'I have always loved prints very dearly, etchings especially. But I have so small and unimportant a collection that I never dream of showing it to anybody. I have not the means to make a real collection, but if I were a millionaire it is in that direction that I think I would go. Etchings are so marvellously human, unaccountably personal.'

'Why, Herrick, listen to that! Mr. Harkness cares about etchings! We must show him some of ours. I have a "Hundred Guilders" and a "De Jonghe" that are truly superb. Do you know my favourite etcher in the world? I am sure that you will never guess.'

'There is a large field to choose from,' said Harkness, smiling.

'There is indeed. But Samuel Palmer is the man for me. You will say that he goes oddly enough with my jade, but whenever I travel abroad "The Bellman" and "The Ruined Tower" go with me. And then Lepère—what a glorious artist! and Legros' woolly trees, and our old friend Callot—yes, we have an enthusiasm in common there.'

For the first time Harkness addressed the girl directly:

'Do you also care about etchings, Mrs. Crispin?'

She flushed as she answered him: 'I am afraid that I know nothing about them. Our things at home were not very valuable, I am afraid—except to us,' she added.

She spoke so softly that Harkness scarcely caught her words. 'Ah, but Hesther will learn,' Crispin said. 'She has a fine taste already. It needs only some more experience. You are learning already, are you not, Hesther?'

'Yes,' she answered almost in a whisper, then looked up directly at Harkness. He could not mistake her glance. It was an appeal absolutely for help. He could see that she was at the end of her control. Her hand was trembling against the cloth. She had been drinking some of her Burgundy, and he guessed that this was a desperate measure. He divined that she was urging herself to some act from which, during all these weeks, she had been shuddering.

His own heart was beating furiously. The food, the wine, the lights, Crispin's strange and beautiful voice were accompaniments to some act that he saw now hanging in front of him, or rather waiting, as a carriage waits, into which now of his own free-will he is about to step to be whirled to some terrific destination.

He tried to put purpose into his glance back to her, as though he would say 'Let me be of some use to you. I am here for that. You can trust me.'

He felt that she knew that she could. She might, such was her case,

217

trust anyone at this crisis, but she had been watching him, he felt sure, throughout the meal, listening to his voice, studying his movements, wondering, perhaps, whether he too were in this conspiracy against her.

He had the sudden conviction that on an instant she had resolved that she could trust him, and had he had time to do as was usual with him, to step back and regard himself, he would have been amazed at his own happiness.

They had come to the dessert. Crispin, as though he had no purpose in life but to make everyone happy, was cracking walnuts for his daughter-in-law and talking about a thousand things. There was nothing apparently that he did not know and nothing that he did not wish to hand over to his dear friends.

'It is too bad that I can't show you my "Hundred *Guilders.*"' He cracked a walnut, and his soft boneless fingers seemed suddenly to be endued with an amazing strength. 'But why shouldn't I? What are you doing this evening?'

'I have no plans,' said Harkness; 'I thought I would go perhaps down to the market and look at the fun.'

'Yes—well. . . . . . . Let me see. But that will fit splendidly. We have an engagement for an hour or two—to say goodbye to an old friend. Why not join us here at—say—half-past ten? I have my car here. It is only half an hour's drive. Come out for an hour or two and see my things. It will give me so much pleasure to show you what I have. I can offer you a good cigar too and some brandy that should please you. What do you say?'

Harkness looked across at the girl. 'Thank you,' he said gravely, 'I shall be delighted.'

'That's splendid. Very good of you. The house also should interest you. Very old and curious. It has a history too. I have rented it for the last year. I shall be quite sorry to leave it.'

Then, smiling, he leant across—'What do you say, Hesther? Shall we have our coffee outside?'

'Yes, thank you,' she answered, with a curious childish inflection as though she were repeating some lesson that was only half remembered.

She rose and started down the room. Harkness followed her. Half-way to the door Crispin was stopped for a moment by the head waiter and stayed with his son.

Harkness spoke rapidly. 'There is no time at all, but I want you to know that I was in the room at the top of the house just now when you were there. I heard everything. I apologise for overhearing. I could not escape, but I want you to know that if there's anything I can do—anything in the world—I will do it. Tell me if there is. We have only a moment.'

On looking back afterwards he thought it marvellous of her that, realising who was behind them, she scarcely turned her head, showed no emotion, but speaking swiftly, answered:

'Yes, I am in great trouble—desperate trouble. I am sure you are kind. There is a thing you can do.'

'Tell me,' he urged. They were now nearly by the door and the two men were coming up.

'I have a friend. I told him that if I would agree to his plan I would send a message to him tonight. I did not mean to agree, but now— I'm not brave enough to go on. He is to be at half-past nine at a little hotel—"The Feathered Duck"—on the sea-front. Any one will tell you where it is. His name is Dunbar. He is young, short, you can't mistake him. He will be waiting there. Go to him. Tell him I agree. I'll never forget . . . . .'

Crispin's forehead confronted them. 'What do you say to this? Here is a sheltered corner.'

Dunbar? Dunbar? Where had he heard the name before?

They all sat down.

PART 2: THE DANCE ROUND THE TOWN

1

Quarter of an hour later he left them, making his excuses, promising to return at half-past ten. He could not have stayed another moment, sitting there quietly in his wicker armchair looking out on the darkening garden, listening to Crispin's pleasure in Peter Breughel, without giving some kind of vent to his excitement.

He must get away and be by himself. Because—yes, he knew it, and nothing could alter the vehement pulsating truth of it—he was in love for the first time in his life.

As he threaded his way along the garden paths that was at first all that he could see—that he was in love with that child in the shabby frock who was married to that odious creature, that bag-of-bones, who had not opened his mouth the whole evening long—that child terrified out of her life and appealing to him, a stranger, in her despair, to help her.

In love with a married woman, he, Charles Percy Harkness? What would his two sisters, nay, what would the whole of Baker, Oregon, say, did they know?

But, bless you, he was not in love with her like that—no hero of a modern realistic novel he! He had no thought in that first ecstatic glow, of any thought for himself at all—only his eyes were upon her, of how he could help her, how serve her, now—at once—before it was too late.

He was deeply touched that she should trust him, but he also realised that at that particular moment she would have trusted anybody. And yet she had waited, watching him through all the first part of that meal, making up her mind—there was some tribute to him at least in that!

It was a considerable time before he could fight his way behind his own singing happiness into any detailed consideration of the facts.

He was in touch with real life at last, had it in both hands like a magic ball of crystal, after which for so long he had been searching.

Where had he been all his life, fancying that this was love and that? That ridiculous touching of hands over a tea-cup, that fancied glance at a crowded party, that half-uttered suggested exchange of gimcrack phrases? And this! Why, he could not have stopped himself had he wished! None of the old considered caution to which he had now grown so accustomed that it had seemed like part of his very soul, could have any say in this. He was committed up to his very boots in the thing, and he was glad, glad, glad!

Meanwhile he had lost his way. He pulled himself up short. He had been walking just in any direction. He was in a far part of the garden. A lawn in the twilight, like dark glass beneath whose surface green water played, stretched between scattered trees and beds of flowers now grey and shadowy. Sparks of fire were already scattered across a sky that was smoky with coils of mist as though some giant train had but now thundered through on its journey to Paradise. Little whistles of wind stole about the garden making secret appointments among the trees. Somewhere near to him a fountain was splashing, and behind the lingering liquid sound of it he could hear the merry-go-round and the drum. He cared little about the dance now, but in some fashion, he must pass the time until nine-thirty, when he would see her friend and learn what he might do.

Her friend? A sudden agitation held him. Her friend? Had she a lover? Was that all that there was behind this—that she had married in haste, for money, luxury, to see the world, perhaps, and now that she had had a month of it with that miserable bag-of-bones and his painted, talkative father, discovered that she could not endure it and called to her aid some earlier lover? Was that all that his fine knight-errantry came to, that he should assist in some vulgar ordinary intrigue? He stopped, standing beside a small white gate that led out from the garden into the road. It was as though the gate held him from the outer world and he would never pass through it until this was decided for him. Her face came before him as she had sat there on the other side of the table, as it had been when their glances met. No, he did not doubt her for an instant.

Whatever her experiences of the last month she was pure in heart and soul as some child at her mother's knee. She had her pride, her pluck, her resolve, but also, above all else, her innocent simplicity, her ignorance of all the evil in the world. And as though the most urgent problem of all his life had been solved, he gave the little white gate a push and stepped through it into the open road.

2

He was now in the country to the left of, and above, the town. He could see its lights clustered, like gold coins thrown into some capacious lap, there below him in the valley.

He struck off along a path that led between deeply scented fields and that led straight down the hill. He began now more soberly to consider the facts of the case, and a certain depression stole about him. He didn't after all see very well what he would be able to do. They were going, on the following morning, the three of them, abroad, and once there how was he to effect any sort of rescue?

The girl was apparently quite legally married, and, although the horrible young Crispin had been silent and sinister, there were no signs that he was positively cruel. The deeper Harkness looked into it the more he was certain that the secret of the whole mystery lay in the older Crispin—it was of him that the girl was terrified rather than the son. Harkness did not know how he was sure of this, he could trace no actual words or looks, but there—yes, there the centre of the plot lay.

The man was strange and queer enough to look at, but a more charming companion you could not find. He had been nothing but amiable, friendly, and courteous. His attitude to his daughter-in-law had been everything that anyone could wish. He had seemed to consider her in every possible way.

Harkness, with his American *naïveté* of conduct, was fond of the word 'wholesome,' or rather, had he not spent so much of his life in Europe, would have found it his highest term of praise to call his fellow-man 'a regular feller!' Crispin Senior was *not* 'a regular feller' whatever else he might be. There had, too, been one moment towards the end of dinner when a waiter, passing, had jolted the little man's chair. There had been for an instant a glance that Harkness now, in his general survey of the situation, was glad to have caught—a glance that seemed to tear the pale powdered mask away for the moment and to show a living moving visage, something quite other, something the more alive in contrast with its earlier immobility.

Once, years before, Harkness had seen in the Naples Aquarium two octopi. They lay like grey slimy stones at the bottom of the shining sun-lit tank. An attendant had let down through the water a small frog at the end of a string. The frog had nearly reached the bottom of the tank when in one flashing instant the pile of shiny stone had been a whirling sickening monster, tentacles, thousands of them it seemed, curving, two loathsome eyes glowing. In one moment of time the frog was gone and in another moment the muddy pile was immobile once again. An unpleasant sight. Were the etchings of Samuel Palmer Crispin's only appetite? Harkness fancied not.

3

Plunging almost recklessly down the hill he was soon in the town, and, pushing his way through two or three narrow little streets, found himself in the market-place.

He caught his breath at the strange transformation of the place since his last view of it more than three hours before. He learnt later that this dance was held always as the Grand Finale of the Three Days' Annual Fair, and on the last of the days there is an old custom that, from four-thirty to six-thirty no trading shall be done, but that everyone shall entertain or be entertained within their homes. This pause had its origin, I should fancy, in some kind of religious ceremony, to ask the Good God's blessing on the trading of the three days, but it had become by now a most convenient interval for the purpose of drinking healths, so that when, at seven o'clock, all the citizens of the town poured out of their doors once again, they were truly and happily primed for the fun of the evening.

Harkness found, therefore, what at first seemed to be naked pandemonium, and, stepping into it, crossed into the third room of his house of delivery.

The old buildings—the town hall, the church, the old grey tower—were lit up as though by some supernatural splendour, all the lights of the booths, the hanging clusters of fairy lamps, and, in the very middle of the place, a huge bonfire flinging arms of flame to heaven.

In one corner there was the merry-go-round, a twisting, heaving, gesticulating monster screaming out 'Coal Black Mammy of Mine,' and suddenly whooping with its own excitement, showing so much emotion that it would not have been surprising to find it, at any moment, leap its bearings and come hurtling down into the middle of the crowd.

The booths were thick with buyers and sellers, and every one, to Harkness's excited fancy, seemed to be screaming at the highest pitch of his or her strident voice.

Here was everything for sale—hats, feathers, coats, skirts, dolls, wooden dolls, rag dolls, china dolls, monkeys on sticks, ribbons, gloves, shoes, umbrellas, pies, puddings, cakes, jams, oranges, apples, melons, cucumbers, potatoes, cabbages, cauliflowers, brooches, diamonds (glass), rubies (glass), emeralds (glass), prayer books, bibles, pictures (King George, Queen Mary), cups, plates, tea-pots, coffee-pots, rabbits, white mice, dogs, sheep, pigs, one grey horse, tables, chairs, beds, and one wooden house on wheels. More than these, much more. And around them, about them, in and out of them, before them and beside them and behind them men, women, children, singing, crying, shouting, sneezing, laughing, hiccupping, quarrelling, kissing, arguing, denying, confirming, whistling, and snoring.

Men of the sea bronzed with dark hair, flashing eyes, rings on their fingers and bells on their toes; men of the fields, the soil interpenetrated with the very soul of their being, bearded to the eyes, broad-shouldered, broad-buttocked, their Sunday coats flapping over their corduroy thighs, their rough thick necks moving restlessly in their unaccustomed collars; women of the fair with eyes like black coals; gipsy women straight from the tents with crimson kerchiefs and black hair piled high under feathered hats; women of the town with soft voices, sidling eyes, and creeping hands; women of the farm with gaze wondering and adrift, hands like leather, children at their skirts; women householders with their purses carefully clutched, their hands feeling the cabbages, pinching the cauliflowers, estimating the chairs and tables, stroking the china; young boys and girls, confidence in their gaze, timidity in their hearts, suddenly catching hands, suddenly embracing, suddenly triumphant on their merry-go-round, suddenly everything, conscious of the last penny burning deep down in the pocket, conscious of love, conscious of appetite, conscious of possible remorse, conscious of blood pounding in their veins.

And the magicians, the wonder workers, the steal-a-pennies, the old men with white beards and trays of coloured treasures, the bold bad men with their thimble and their penny, the little stumpy fellow with his cards, the long thin melancholy fellow with his medicines, the thick jolly drunken fellow with his tales of the sea, the twisty turn-his-head-both-ways fellow with his gold watches and silver chains, the red wizard with his fortunes in envelopes, his magic on strings of coloured paper, his mysterious signs and countersigns whispered into blushing ears. And then the children that should have been in bed hours ago—little children, large children, young children, old children, fat children, thin children, children clinging to mother's skirts, children running in and out, like mice, between legs and trousers, children riding on father's shoulder, children sticky with sweets and sucking their thumbs, children screaming with pleasure, shrieking with terror, howling with weariness—and one child all by itself on the steps of the town hall, curled up and fast asleep.

Away, to one side of the place, just as he had been there fifteen years ago when Maradick had been present, was a preacher, aloft on an overturned box, singing with hand raised, his thin earnest face illumined with the lights, his scant hair blowing in the breeze. Around him a thin scattering of people singing just as fifteen years ago they had sung:

So, like little candles
We shall shine,
You in your small corner
And I in mine.

The same recipe, the same cure, the same key offered to the unlocking of the same mysterious door—and so it will be to the end of created life—Amen!

The hymn was over. The preacher's voice was raised. Children step to the edge of the circle, looking up with wondering eyes, their fingers in their mouths.

'And so, dear friends, we have offered to us here the Blood of the Lamb for our salvation. Can we refuse it? What right have we to disregard our salvation? I tell you, my dear friends, that Judgement is upon

224

us even now. There cometh the night when no man may work. How shall we be found? Sleeping? With our sins heavy upon us? There is yet time. The hour is not yet. Let us remember that God is merciful— there is still time given us for repentance——'

The Town Hall clock stridently, with clanging verberation, heard clearly above all the din, struck nine.

4

Even as the strokes sounded in the air the wide doors of the Town Hall unfolded and a tall stout man, dressed in the cocked hat and the cape and cloak of a Dickensian beadle, appeared. Flaming red they were, and very fine and important he looked as he stood there on the steps, his legs spread, holding his gold staff in his hands. He was attended by several other gentlemen who looked down with benignant approval upon the crowd, and by a drum, a trumpet, and a flute, these last being instruments rather than men.

A crowd began to gather at the foot of the steps and the beadle to address them at the top of his voice, but unlike his rival, the preacher, his voice did not carry very far.

And now the Fair, having only five minutes more of life before it, lifted itself into a final screaming manifestation. Now was the time for which the wise and the cautious had been waiting throughout the three days of the Fair—the moment when all the prices would tumble down with a rush because it was now or never. The merry-go-round shrieked; the animals bellowed, lowed, mooed, and grunted; the purchasers argued, quarrelled, shouted, and triumphed; the preacher and his followers sang and sang again; the bells clanged, the gas-jets flared, the bonfire rose furiously to heaven. But meanwhile the crowd was growing larger and larger around the Town Hall steps; they came with penny whistles and horns and hand-bells and even tea-trays. Then suddenly, strong above the babel, carried by men's stout voices, the song began:

Now, gentles all, attend this song,
  Tra-la, la-la, Tra-la,
It is but short, it can't be long,
  Tra-la-la-la, Tra-la,
How Farmer Brown one summer day
Was in his field a-gathering hay,
When by there came a pretty maid
Who smiling sweetly to him said,

Tra-la-la-la-Tra-la.

Then Farmer Brown, though forty year,
  Tra-la, la-la, Tra-la,
When he that pretty voice did hear,
  Tra-la-la-la, Tra-la,
He threw his fork the nearest ditch
And caught the maiden tightly, which
Was what she wanted him to do,
And so, the same would all of you,
  Tra-la-la-la-Tra-la.
But she withdrew from his embrace,
  Tra-la, la-la, Tra-la,
And mocked poor Farmer to his face,
  Tra-la-la-la, Tra-la,
And danced away along the lane,
And cried, 'Before I'm here again,
Poor Farmer Brown, you'll dance with Pain,'
  Tra-la-la-la-Tra-la.

And that was true, as you shall hear,
  Tra-la-la-la, Tra-la;
Poor Farmer Brown danced many a year,
  Tra-la-la-la, Tra-la,
But never once that maid did see,
He grew as aged as aged could be,
And danced into Eterni-tee,
  Tra-la-la-la-Tra-la.

The red-flaming beadle moved down the steps, and behind him came the drum, the trumpet, and the flute. The drum, a stout fellow with wide-spreading legs, had from the practice of many a year, and his father and grandfather having been drummers before him, caught the exact measure of the tune. Along the market-place went the beadle, the drum, the trumpet, and the flute.

For a moment a marvellous silence fell.

To Harkness this silence was exquisite. The myriad stars, the high buildings, their façades ruby-coloured with the leaping light, the dark piled background, the crowd humming now with quiet, like water on the boil, the glow of rich suffused colour sheltering everything with its beautiful cloak, the rich voices tossing into the air the jolly song, the sense of well-being and the tradition of the lasting old time and the spirit of England eternally fresh and sturdy and strong; all this sank into his very soul and seemed to give him some hint of the deliverance that was, very soon, to come to him.

Then the procession definitely formed. All the voices—men's, women's, and children's alike—caught it up. One—two—three, one—two—three. The drum, the trumpet, and the flute came to them through the air:

> *How Farmer Brown one summer day*
> *Was in his field a-gathering hay,*
> *When by there came a pretty maid*
> *Who smiling sweetly to him said,*
> *Tra-la-la-la-Tra-la.*

He was never to be sure whether or no he had intended to join in the dance. He was not aware of more than the colour, the lights, the rhythm of the tune, when a man like a mountain caught him by the arm, shouting, 'Now we're off, brother—now we're off,' and he was carried along.

There had always been a superstition about the dance that to join in it, to be in it from the beginning to the end, meant the best of good luck, and to miss it was misfortune. There was, therefore, now a flinging from all sides of eager bodies into the fray. No one must be left out, and as the path between the line of bodies and houses was a narrow one, everyone was pressed close together, and as there had been much friendly swilling of beer and ale, everyone was in the highest humour, shouting, laughing, singing, ringing their bells, and blowing their whistles.

Harkness was crushed in upon his enormous friend so completely that he had no other impression for the moment but of a vast expanse of heaving, leaping, corduroy waistcoat, of a hard brass button in his eye, and of himself clutching with both hands to a shiny trouser that must hold himself from falling. But they were off indeed! Four of them now in a row and the song was swinging fine and strong. One—two—three, one—two—three. Forward bend, one leg in air, backward bend, t'other leg in air, forward bend again, down the market-place and round the corner, voices raised in one tremendous song.

He was easier now and able more clearly to realise his position. One arm was tightly wedged in that of his companion, and he could feel the thick welling muscles taut through the stuff of the shirt. On the other side of him was a girl, and he could feel her hand pressing on his sleeve. On her side, again, was a young man—her lover. He said so, and shouted it to the world.

He leaned across her and cried out her beauties as they moved, and she threw her head back and sang.

The giant on the hither side seemed to have taken Harkness into his especial protection. He had been drinking well, but it had done him no order of harm. Only he loved the world and especially Harkness. He felt, he knew, that Harkness was a stranger from 'up-along.' On an average day he would have resented him, been suspicious of him, and tried 'to do him out of some of his blasted money.' But tonight, he would be his friend and protect him from the world.

He would rather have had a girl crooked there under his arm, but the girl he had intended to have had somehow missed him when the fun began—but it didn't matter—the beer made everything glorious for him—and after all he had two daughters 'nigh grown up,' and his old missus was around somewhere, and it was just as good he didn't slip into any sort of mischief, which it was easy to do on a night like this—and his name was Gideon. All this he confided to Harkness while the procession halted, for a minute or two, at the corner of the market-place to pull itself straight before it started down the hill.

He had his arm around Harkness's neck and words poured from him. Gideon what or something Gideon? It didn't matter. Gideon, it was and Gideon it would be so long as Harkness's memory remained.

All the soil of the English country, all the deep lanes with their high dark hedges, the russet cornfields with their sudden dips to the sea, the high ridges with the white cottages perched like birds resting against the sky, the smell of the earth, the savour of the leaves wet after rain, the thick smoke and damp of the closed-in rooms, the mud, the clay, the running streams, the wind through the thick-sheltering trees—all these were in Gideon's speech as he stood, close pressed, thigh to thigh with Harkness.

He was happy although he knew not why, and Harkness was happy because he was in love for the first time in his life and tingled from head to foot with that knowledge. And up and down and all around it was the same. This was the night of all the nights of the year when enmities were forgotten and new friendships made. As Maradick once had felt the current of love running strong and true through a thousand souls, so Harkness felt it now, and, as with Maradick once, so with Harkness now, it seemed strange that life might not be simply run, that the lion might not lie down with the lamb, that nations might not be for ever at peace the one with another, and that the Grand Millennium might not immediately be at hand.

All beer you say? Maybe, and yet not altogether so. Something anxious and longing in the human heart was rising, free and strong, that night, and would never again entirely leave some of the hearts that knew it.

Harkness for one. There were to be many years in the future when he was to feel again the beating of Gideon's heart under his arm. Something of Gideon's was his, and something of his was Gideon's for evermore, though they would never meet again.

5

And now the procession was arranged. Harkness, looking back, could see how it stretched, a winding serpent black in the shadows of the leaping bonfire, through the square. They were off again. The drum had started. Down the hill they went, all packed together, all swinging with the tune. A kind of divine frenzy united them all. Young and old, men and women, married and single, good and evil, vicious and virtuous, all were together bound in one chain. Harkness was with them. For the first time in all his life, restraint was flung aside. He did not smell the beer, nor did the sweat of the perspiring bodies offend his sensitive nostrils, nor the dung from the fields, nor the fishy odours of the sea. With Gideon on one side and a young man's girl on the other, he swung through the town.

Details for a time eluded him. He was singing the song at the top of his voice, but what words he was singing he could not have told you; he was dancing to the measure, but for the life of him he could not have afterwards repeated the rhythm.

They swung down into the heart of the town. The doors of all the houses were crowded with the very aged and the very young, who stood laughing and crying out, pointing to their friends and acquaintances, laughing at this and cheering at that.

And always more were joining in, pushing their way, dancing the more energetically because they had missed the first five minutes. Now they were down on the fish-market all sprinkled with silver under the little moon and the cloth of stars. Here the wind from the sea came to meet them, and through the music and the singing and the laughter and the press-press of the dancing crowd could be heard the faint breath of the tide on the shore 'seep-seep-sough-sough,' wistful and powerful, remaining for ever when they all were gone. The sheds of the fish-market were gaunt and dark and deserted. For one moment all the naked place was filled with colour and movement. Then up the hill they all pressed.

It was difficult up the hill. There were breaths and pants and 'Eh, sirs,' and 'Oh, the poor worm,' and 'But my heart's beating,' and 'I cannot! I cannot!' One woman fell, was picked up and planted by the side of the road, a young man staying with melancholy kindness beside her. The rest passed on.

Soon they were at the top of the hill before they turned to the left again back into the town. And this was Harkness's greatest moment. For an instant the dance paused, and just then it happened that Harkness was at the highest point of the climb.

Catching his breath, his hand to his heart, for he was out of training and the going had been hard, he looked about him. Below him to the right and to the left and to the farthest horizon the sea, a grey silk shadow, hung, so soft, so gentle, that the stars that crackled above it seemed to be taunting it with its lethargy. On the other side of the hill was all the clustered town, and before him and behind him the dark multitudes of human beings.

He was happy, ecstatically happy. Pressed close to Gideon, who was drinking something out of a bottle, he was unconscious of any personality—only that time had found for him, it seemed, a solution to the whole problem of life. The sea-wind fanning his temples, the salt snap of the sea, the pounding of his own heart in union with that other heart of his companion who was with him—all these things together made of him, who had been always afraid and timorous and edged with caution, a triumphant soul.

And it was good that it was so, because of all that he would be called upon to do that night.

Gideon put his arm around him, pressing him close to him, and pushed the bottle up to his lips. 'Drink, brother,' he said. 'Drink, then, my dear.' And Harkness drank.

Now they were starting down the hill into the town once more, and the dance reached the height of its madness.

He threw his fork the nearest ditch
And caught the maiden tightly, which
Was what she wanted him to do,
And so, the same would all of you,
* Tra-la-la-la-Tra-la.*

They screamed, they shrieked, they tumbled on to one another, they held on where they could, they swung from side to side. The red beadle himself caught the frenzy, flinging his fat body now here, now there. The very houses and the cobbles of the streets seemed to swing and sway as the lights flashed and flared. All the bells of the town were pealing. In the market-place they were setting off the fireworks, and the rockets, green and red and gold, streaked the purple sky and fought for rivalry with the stars. All the sky now was scattered with sparks of gold. From the highest heaven to the lowest of man's ditches the world crackled and split and sang.

Now was the moment when all enmities were truly forgotten, when love was declared without fear, when lips sought lips and hands clasped hands, and heaven opened and all the human souls marched in.

Tra-la-la-la-Tra-la
Tra-la-la-la-Tra-la.

Back into the market-place they all tumbled; then, standing in a serried mass as the beadle and his followers mounted the Town Hall steps, they shouted:

'*All together: One—two—three.*
One—Two—Three.
One. Two. Three.
Hurray! Hurray! Hurray!'

The dance of all the hearts was, for one more year, at an end.

6

Everyone was splitting up into little groups, some to look at the fireworks, some to have a last drink together, some to creep off into the dark shadows and there confirm their vows, some to drive home on their carts and waggons to their distant farms, some to sit in their homes for a last chatting about all the news, some to go straight to their beds—the common impulse was over although it would not be forgotten.

Harkness looked around to find Gideon, but that giant was gone nor was he ever to see him again. He paused there panting, happy, forgetting for an instant everything but the fun and freedom that he had just passed through. Then, as though it would forcibly remind him, the Town Hall clock struck half-past nine.

He spoke to a man standing near him:

'Can you kindly tell me where a hotel called "The Feathered

Duck" is?' he asked.

'Certainly,' said the man, wiping the sweat from the hair matted on his forehead. 'It's out on the sea-front. Go down High Street—that'll take you to the sea front. Then walk to your right and it's about five houses down.'

Harkness thanked him and hurried away. He had no difficulty in finding the High Street, but there how strange to walk so quietly down it, hearing your own foot tread, watched by all the silent houses, when only five minutes ago you had been whirling in Dionysian frenzy! He was on the sea front and two steps afterwards was looking up at the quiet and modest exterior of 'The Feathered Duck.'

The long road stretched shining and sleek. Not a living soul about. The little hotel offered a discreet welcome with plants in large green pots, one on either side of the door, a light warm enough to greet you and not too startling to frighten you, and the knob gleaming like an inviting eye.

Harkness pushed open the door and entered. The hall was anaemic and dark, with the trap to catch visitors some way down on the right. There seemed to be no one about. Harkness pushed open a door and at once found himself in one of those little hotel drawing-rooms that are so peculiarly British, compounded as they are of ferns and discretion, convention and an untuned piano. In this little room a young man was sitting alone. Harkness knew at once that his search was over. He knew where it was that he had heard the name Dunbar before— this was his young man of the high road, the wandering seaman and the serious appointment, the young man of his expectant charge.

There was yet, however, room for mistake, and so he waited standing in the doorway. The young man was bending forward in a red plush armchair, eagerly watching. He recognised Harkness at once as his friend of the afternoon.

'Hullo!' he said, and then hurriedly, 'why, what *has* been happening to you?'

Harkness stepped forward into the room. 'To me?' he said.

'Why, yes. You're sweating. Your collar's undone. You look as though you had run a mile.'

'Oh that!' Harkness blushed, fingering his collar, that had broken from its stud. 'I've been dancing.'

'Dancing?'

'Yes. All round the town. Like the lion and the unicorn.'

'Oh, I heard you. On any other night——' He broke off. During this time, he had been watching Harkness with a curious expression, something between eagerness, distrust, and an impatience which he was finding very difficult to conceal. He said nothing more. Harkness also was silent. They stared the one at the other, and could hear beyond the door the noises of the little hotel, a shrill female voice, the rattle of plates, some man's laughter.

At last Harkness said: 'Your name is Dunbar, isn't it?'

The young man, instead of answering, asked his own question. 'Look here, what the devil are you after? I don't say that it is or it isn't, but anyway why do *you* want to know?'

'It's only this,' said Harkness slowly, 'that if your name *is* Dunbar, then I have a message for you.'

'You *have?*'

He started out of his chair, standing up in front of Harkness as though challenging him.

'Yes, a friend of yours asked me to come here, to meet you at half-past nine and tell you that she agrees to your proposal——'

'She does? . . . . . . .At last!'

Then his voice changed to suspicion. 'You seem to be a lot in this. Forgive my curiosity. I don't want to seem rude, but meeting me on the hill this afternoon and now this. . . . . . . .I've got to be so *damn* careful——'

'My name is Harkness. It was quite by chance that I was walking down the hill this afternoon and met you. As I told you then, I was on my way to "The Man-at-Arms." This evening I offered my help to a lady there who seemed to be in distress, and asked her whether there was anything that I could do. She asked me to bring you that message. There was no one else for her to ask.'

Dunbar stared at Harkness, then suddenly held out his hand. 'Jolly decent of you. I won't forget it. My name is Dunbar, as you know, David Dunbar.'

'And mine Harkness, Charles Harkness.'

'I can't tell you what you've done for me by bringing me that message. Here, don't go for a minute. Have something, won't you?'

'Yes, I think I will,' said Harkness, conscious of a sudden weariness.

'What shall it be? Whisky? Small soda?'

They sat down. Dunbar touched a bell and then, in silence, they waited. Harkness was humorously conscious that he seemed to be the younger of the two. The boy had taken complete command of the situation.

The older man was also aware that there was some very actual and positive situation here that was developing under his eyes. As he sat there, sticking to the plush of his chair, listening to the ridiculous chatter of the marble clock, staring into the Wardour Street Puritans of 'When did you see father last?' he felt urgency beating in upon them both. A shabby waiter looked in upon them, received his order, and departed.

Dunbar suddenly plunged. 'Look here, I know I can trust you, I'm sure of it. And *she* trusted you, so that should be enough for me. But—would you mind—telling me exactly how it happened that you got this message?'

'Certainly,' Harkness said. 'I——'

'Wait,' Dunbar interrupted; 'forgive me, but drop your voice, will you? One doesn't know who's hanging round here.'

They drew their chairs closer together, and Harkness, sitting forward, continued. 'I had dressed for dinner early. A friend of mine in London had told me that there was a little old room at the top of the hotel that was well worth seeing. I guess, like most Americans, I care for old-fashioned things, so I got to the top of the house and found the room. I was up in a little gallery at the back when two people came in, a man and a girl. They began to talk before I could move or let them know I was there. It was all too quick for me to do anything. The girl begged the man, to whom she was apparently married, to let her go home for a week before they went abroad, and the man refused. That was all there was, but the girl's terror struck me as extreme——'

'My God!' Dunbar broke in, 'if you only knew!'

'Well, I was touched by that, and I didn't like the man's face either. They went out. I came down to dinner. While I was waiting in the garden an extraordinary man spoke to me—extraordinary to look at, I mean—short, fat, red hair——'

'You needn't describe him,' Dunbar interrupted, 'I know him.'

'He came and asked me for a match. He was very polite, and finally invited me to dine with him, his son, and daughter-in-law. I accepted. Of course, the son and daughter-in-law were the two that I had overheard upstairs. I saw that throughout dinner she was in great distress, and at the end as we were leaving the room I let her know that I had overheard her inadvertently before dinner, and that I was eager to help her if there was any way in which I could do so. We had only a moment, Crispin and his son were close upon us. She was, I suppose, at the end of her endurance and snatched at any chance, so she told me to do this—to find you here and give you that message—that's all—absolutely all.'

The door opened, making both men turn apprehensively. It was only the shabby little waiter with his tray and the whiskies. He set down the glasses, split the soda, and stared at them both as Dunbar paid him.

'Will that be all, gentlemen?' he asked, scratching his ear.

'Everything,' said Dunbar abruptly.

'Gentlemen sleeping here?'

'No, we're not. Goodnight.'

'Goodnight, sir.' With a little sigh the waiter withdrew. The door closed, and instantly the ferns in the pots, the plush chairs and sofa closed round as though they also wanted to hear.

'It's an extraordinary piece of luck,' Dunbar began. Then he hesitated. 'But I don't want to bother you with any more of this. It isn't your affair. You've come into it, after all, only by accident——'

He hesitated as though he were making an invitation to Harkness. And Harkness hesitated. He saw that this was his last opportunity of withdrawal. Once again, he could hear the voice of the imp behind his shoulder: 'Well, clear out if you want to. You have still plenty of time. And this is positively the last chance I give you——'

He drank his whisky and, drinking, crossed his Rubicon.

'No, no, I am interested, tremendously interested. Tell me anything you care to, and if I can be of any help——'

'No, no,' Dunbar assured him, 'I'm not going to drag you into it. You needn't be afraid of that.'

'But I *am* in it!' Harkness answered, smiling; 'I'm going back with Crispin to his house this evening!'

7

The effect of that upon Dunbar was fantastic. The young man jumped from his chair crying:

'You're going back?'

'Yes.'

'To the house?'

'Why, yes!'

'And tonight!'

He stared down at him as though he could not believe the evidence of his ears nor of his eyes nor of anything that was his. Then he finished his whisky with a desperate gulp.

'But what's pushing you into this anyway?' he cried at last. 'You don't look like the kind of man——And yet there you were on the hill this afternoon, and then at the hotel and overhearing what Hesther said, and then dining with the man and his asking you——He did ask you, didn't he?'

'Of course, he asked me,' Harkness answered. 'You don't suppose I'd have gone if he didn't.'

'No, I don't suppose you would,' agreed Dunbar. 'I bet he offered to show you his jewels and his pictures, his collections.'

'Yes,' said Harkness, 'he did.'

'Well, that's just a miracle of good luck for me, that's all. You can help me tonight, help me marvellously. But I don't like to ask you. Things might turn out all wrong and then we'd all be in for a bad time and that wouldn't be fair to you.' He paused, thinking, then he went on. 'I'll tell you what I'll do. You saw that girl tonight and talked to her, didn't you?'

Harkness nodded his head.

'You saw that she was a damned fine girl?'

Harkness nodded again.

'Worth doing a lot for. Well, I'll put the whole story to you—let you have it all. We've got nearly three-quarters of an hour. I can tell you most of it in that time, and then you can make up your mind. If, when I've told you everything, you decide to have nothing whatever to do with it, that's all right. There's no obligation on you at all, of course. But if you *did* help me, being in the house at that very time, it would make the whole difference. My God, yes!' he ended with a sigh of eagerness, staring at Harkness.

Harkness sat there, thinking only of the girl. His own personal history, the town, the dance, Crispin and his son, all these things had faded away from his mind; he saw only her—as she had been when turning her head for a moment she had spoken to him with such marvellous self-control.

He loved her just as she stood there granting him permission to help her. His own prayer was that it might not be long before he was allowed to help her again. He was recalled to the immediate moment by Dunbar's voice:

'You'll forgive me if I go back to the beginning of things—it's the only way really to explain. Have you ever heard of Polchester, a town in Glebeshire, north of this? There's a rather famous cathedral there.'

'Yes,' said Harkness, 'I thought I might go there from here.'

236

'Well,' Dunbar went on, 'out of Polchester about ten miles there's a village—Milton Haxt. I was born there and so was Hesther. Her name was Hesther Tobin, and she was the only daughter of the doctor of the place—she had two brothers younger than herself. We've known one another all our lives.'

'Wait a moment,' Harkness interrupted; 'are you and she the same age?'

'No. I'm thirty, she's only twenty.'

'You look younger than that, or you did this afternoon, I'm not so sure now.' Indeed, the boy seemed to have acquired some new weight and responsibility as he sat there.

'No,' he went on. 'When I said that we'd known one another always I mean that she's always known about me. I used to take her on my knee and toss her up and down. That was where all the trouble began. If she hadn't been always used to me and fancied that I was years older than she—a kind of grandfather—she'd have married me.'

'Married you!' Harkness brought out.

'Yes. I can't remember a time when I wasn't in love with her. I always was, and she never was with me. She liked me—she likes me now—but she's always been so used to the idea of me. I've always been David Dunbar—and that's all,—a friend who was always there, but nothing more. There was just a moment when I was missing for six months in the middle of the war, I think she really cared then—but soon they heard that I was safe in Germany and it was all as it had been before.'

'Were her father and mother living?' Harkness asked.

'Her father. Her mother died when her youngest brother was born, when she was only six years old. The mother's death upset the father and he took to drink. He'd always been inclined that way I expect. He was too brilliant a doctor to have landed in that small village without there being some reason. Well, after Mrs. Tobin's death there was simply one trouble after another. Tobin's patients deserted him. The big house on the hill had to be sold and they moved into a small one in the village. He had been a big, jolly, laughing, generous man before; now he was always quarrelling with everybody, insulting the few patients left to him, and so on. Hesther was wonderful. How she kept the house together all those years nobody knew. There was very little she didn't know about life by the time she was ten years old—ordinary life, I mean, not this damned Crispin monstrosity. She always had the pluck and courage of the devil, and you can fancy what

I felt just now when you told me about her asking young Crispin to let her off. That *swine*!'

He paused for a moment, then went on hurriedly:

'But we haven't much time. I must buck ahead. I was quite an ordinary sort of fellow, of course, but there was nothing I wouldn't do for her if I got a chance. I helped her sometimes, but not so much as I'd have liked. She was always terribly proud. All the things that happened at home made her hold up her head in a kind of defiance.

'The odd thing was that she loved her father, and the worse he got the more she loved him. But she loved her young brothers still more. She was mother, sister, nurse, everything to them, and would be still if she'd been let alone. They were nice little chaps too, only a lot younger, of course—one three years, one six. One's in the navy—very decent fellow—and if he'd been home he'd never have allowed any of this to happen.

'Well, the war came when she was quite a kid. I was away most of that time. Then in 1918 my father died and left me a bit of property there in Milton. I came home and asked her to marry me. She thought I was pitying her, and anyway she didn't love me. And I hadn't enough of this world's goods to make the old man keen about me.

'Then this devil came along.' Dunbar stopped for a moment. They both listened. There was not a sound in the whole house.

'What brought him to a village like yours?' asked Harkness, lowering his voice. 'I shouldn't have thought that a man like that——'

'No, you wouldn't,' said Dunbar. 'But that's one of his passions apparently, suddenly landing on some small village where there's a big house and bossing everyone around him........I shall never forget the day I first saw him. It was just about a year ago.

'I had heard that some foreigner had taken Haxt, that was the big house in Milton that the Dombeys, the owners, were too poor to keep up. Soon all the village was talking. Furniture arrived, then lots of servants, Japs and all sorts. Then one evening going up the hill I saw him leaning over one of the Haxt gates looking into the road.

'It was a lovely July evening and he was without a hat. You've spoken of his hair. I tell you that evening it was just flaming in the sun. It looked for a moment like some strange sort of red flower growing on the top of the gate. He stopped me as I was passing and asked me for a match.'

'That's what he asked me for,' murmured Harkness.

'Yes, his opening gambits are all the same. He offered me a cigarette and I took one. We talked for a little. I didn't like him at first, of course, with his hair, white face, painted lips; but—did you notice what a beautiful voice he has?'

'I should think I did,' said Harkness.

'And then he can make himself perfectly charming. The beginning of your acquaintance with him is exactly like your introduction to the villain of any melodrama—painted face, charming voice, cosmopolitan, delightful information. The change comes afterwards. But I must hurry on, I'll never be done. I'm as bad as Conrad's Marlowe. Have another whisky, won't you?'

'No thanks,' said Harkness.

'Well, it wasn't long before he was the talk of the whole place. At first everyone liked him. Odd though he looked, you can just fancy how a man with his wealth and knowledge of the world would fascinate a countryside if he chose to make himself agreeable, and he *did* choose. He gave parties, he went round to people's houses, sent his motors to give old ladies a ride, allowed people to pick flowers in his garden, adored showing people his collections. I happened to be in Milton during the rest of that year looking after my little property, and he seemed to take to me. I was up at Haxt a good deal.

'Looking back now I can see that I never really liked him. I was aware of my caution and laughed at myself for it. I like pretty things, you know, and I loved his jade and emeralds, and still more his prints. And he knew so much and was never tired of telling me and never seemed to laugh at one's ignorance.

'He was, as I have said, all the talk that summer. It was "Mr. Crispin" this and "Mr. Crispin" that—Mr. Crispin everything. The men didn't take to him much, but of course they wouldn't! They had always thought *me* a bit queer because I liked reading and played the piano. The first thing that people didn't like about him was his son. That beauty arrived at Haxt somewhere in September, and everybody hated him. I ask you, could you help it? And he was the exact opposite of his father. *He* didn't try to make himself agreeable to anybody—simply went about scowling and frowning. But it wasn't that that people disliked—it was his relation to his father. He was absolutely in his father's power—that is the only way to put it—and there was something despicable, something almost obscene, you know, almost as though he were hypnotised, the way he obeyed him, listened to his voice, slaved away for him.'

'I noticed something of that myself this evening,' said Harkness.

'You couldn't help it if you saw them together. Somehow the son turning up beside the father made the *father* look queer—as though the son showed him up. People round Milton are not very perceptive, you know, but they soon smelt a rat, several rats in fact. For one thing the people in the village didn't like the Jap servants, then one or two maids that Crispin had hired abruptly left. They wouldn't say anything except that they didn't like the place, that old Crispin walked in his sleep or something of the kind.

'It was just about this time, early in October or so, that Crispin became friendly with the Tobins. Young Crispin had a cold or something and Tobin came up and doctored him. Crispin gave him the best liquor he'd ever had in his life, so he came again, and then again. That was the beginning of my dislike of Crispin. It seemed to me rotten of him, when Tobin was already going as fast downhill as he could, to give him an extra push. And Crispin liked doing that. One could see it at a glance. I hated him from the moment when I caught him watching with an amused smile Tobin fuddled in his chair. You can imagine that Tobin's drunkenness, having cared for Hesther as I had for so long, was a matter of some importance for me. I had tried to pull him up, without any sort of success, of course, and it simply maddened me to see what Crispin was doing. So, I lost my temper and spoke out. I told him what I thought of him. He listened to me very quietly, then he suddenly threw his head up at me like a snake hissing. He said a lot of things. That was the first time I heard all his nonsensical stuff about sensations. We haven't time now, and anyway it wasn't very new—the philosophy that as this was our only existence we had better make the most of it, that we had been given our senses to use, not to stifle, and the rest of it. Omar put it better than Crispin.

'He had also a lot of talk about Power, that if he liked he could have any one in his power, and so could I if I liked. You had only to know other people's weaknesses enough. And more than that. Some stuff about its being good for people to suffer. That the thing that made life interesting and worthwhile was its intensity, and that life was never so intense as when we were suffering. That, after all, God liked us to suffer. Why shouldn't *we* be gods? We might be if we only had courage enough.

'It was then, that morning, that it first entered my head that there was something wrong with him—something wrong with his brain. It had never occurred to me during all those months because he had always been so logical, but now—he seemed to step across the little bridge that separates the sane from the insane. You know how small that bridge is?' Harkness nodded his head.

'Then all in a moment he took my arm and twisted it. I can't give you any sort of idea how queer and nasty that was. As he did it he peered into my face as though he didn't want to miss the slightest shadow of an expression. Then—I don't know if you noticed when he shook hands with you—his fingers haven't any bones in them, and yet they are beastly powerful. He ought to be soft all over and he *isn't*. He twisted my arm once and smiled. It was all I could do to keep from knocking him down. But I broke away, told him to go to hell and left the house. From that moment I hated him.

'It was directly after this that I noticed for the first time that he had his eye on Hesther, and he had his eye upon her exactly because she hated him and wouldn't go near him if she could possibly help it. I must stop for a moment and tell you something about her. You've seen her, but you cannot have any kind of idea how wonderful she really is.

'She has the most honourable loyal character you've ever seen in woman. And she's never been in love—she doesn't know what love is. Those are the two most important things about her. That doesn't mean that she's ignorant of life. There's nothing mean or sordid or disgusting that hasn't come into her experience through her beauty of a father, but she's stood up to it all—until this, this Crispin marriage. The first thing in her life she's funked.

'She's been saved all along by her devotion to one thing, her family—her father and two brothers. She must have given her father up pretty completely by now, seen that it was hopeless; but her small brothers—why, they are the key to the whole thing! If it weren't for them she wouldn't be where she is tonight, and, as I have said, if the elder one had known anything about it he wouldn't have allowed it, but he's away on a foreign station and Bobby's too young to understand.

'She was always very independent in the village, keeping to herself. Not being rude to people, you understand, but making no real friends. She simply lived for those two boys, and she had to work so hard that she had no time for friends. She knew that I loved her—I had told her often enough. She saw more of me than of anyone else, and she would allow me to do things for her sometimes, but even with me she kept her independence. Tonight, is the very first time in both our lives that she has begged me to do anything!'

He stopped for a moment. 'By God!' he cried, 'if I can't help her tonight I'll finish myself; there'll be nothing left in life for me!'

241

'We *will* help her,' Harkness said. 'Both of us. But go on. Time's advancing. I mustn't miss my appointment.'

'No, by Jove, you mustn't,' said Dunbar. 'Everything hangs on that. Well, to get on. It didn't take me very long to see what Crispin was doing to her father, and one day she went up to see him alone and begged him to be merciful. She says that he was charming to her and that she hated him worse than ever.

'He promised her that he would stop her father's drinking, and, of course, he didn't keep his promise, but made Tobin drink more than ever.

'It was round about Christmas that these things happened, and just about this time all sorts of stories began to circulate about him. He suddenly left, came over to Treliss, and took the White Tower where you're going tonight. After he had gone the stories grew in volume— the most ridiculous things you ever heard, about his catching rabbits and skinning them alive and holding witches' Sabbaths with his Japs— every kind of fantastic thing. And all the women who had gone to see his pretty things and raved about him when he first came said they didn't know how they "ever could have seen anything in him," and that he deserved imprisonment and worse.

'It was now that I discovered that Hesther was desperately worried. I had known her all my life and had never seen her worried like this before. She lost her colour, was always thinking about other things when one spoke to her, and, several times, had been crying when I came upon her. Naturally I couldn't stand this, and I bullied her until I got the truth out of her. And what do you think that was? Why, of all the horrible things, that the younger Crispin had asked her to marry him, and that all the time her blackguard of a father was pressing her to do it.

'You can imagine what I felt like when I heard this! I cursed and swore and blasphemed, and still couldn't believe that she was in any way taking it seriously until, when I pressed her, I found that she was!

'She was always as obstinate as sin, had her own way of looking at things, made up her own mind and stuck to it. She didn't hate the son as she hated the father, although she disliked the little she'd seen of him well enough; but, remember, she knew very little about marriage. All her thoughts were on those two boys, her brothers.

'I found out that old Crispin had offered Tobin any amount of money if he'd give his daughter up, and that Tobin had put this to Hesther, telling her that he was desperately in debt, that he'd be put in prison if the money didn't turn up from somewhere, and, above all, that the boys would be ruined if she didn't agree, that he'd have to take the younger boy away from school and so on.

'I did everything I could. I went and saw Tobin and told him what I thought of him, and he was drunk as usual and we had a scuffle, in the course of which I unfortunately tumbled him over. Hesther came in and saw him on the floor, turned on me, and then said she'd marry young Crispin.

'I begged, I implored her. I said that if she would marry me I'd give her everything that I had in the world, that we'd manage so that Bobby shouldn't have to be taken away from school, and the rest of it. Then Father Tobin got up from the floor and asked me with a sneer how much I'd got, and I tried to bluster it out, but of course they both of them knew that I hadn't got very much.

'Anyway, Hesther was angry with me—ashamed, I think, that I'd seen her father in such a state, and her pride hurt that I should know how badly they were placed. She accepted young Crispin by the next mail. If the Crispins had actually been there in the flesh I don't think she would have done it, but some weeks' absence had softened her horror of them, and she could only think how wonderful it was going to be to do all the marvellous things for the boys that she was planning.

'I'm sure that when young Crispin did turn up with his long body and cadaverous face she repented and was frightened, but her pride wouldn't let her then back out of it.

'I had one last talk with her before her marriage. I begged her to forgive me for anything that I had done that might seem casual or insulting, that she must put me out of her mind altogether, but just consider in a general way whether this wasn't a horrible thing that she was doing, marrying a man that she didn't love, taking on a father-in-law whom she hated. She was very sweet to me, sweeter than she had ever been before. She just shook her head and let me kiss her. And I knew that this was a final goodbye.'

8

'She married Crispin and came to Treliss. I wasn't at the wedding. I heard nothing from her. And then a story came to my ears that, after I had once heard it, gave me no peace.

'It was an old woman—a Mrs. Martin. She had, months before, been up at Haxt doing some kind of extra help. She was an old mottled woman like a strawberry—I'd known her all my life—and a grandmother. She suddenly left, and it was only weeks after Crispin went that I found out why. She was very shy about it, and to this day I've never discovered exactly what happened. Something one evening when she was alone in the kitchen preparing to go home. The elder Crispin came in followed by one of his Japs. He made her sit down in one of the kitchen chairs, sat down beside her, and began to talk to her in his soft beautiful voice. What it was all about to this day she doesn't know—some of his fine stuff about Sensation, I daresay, and the benefit of suffering so that you could touch life at its fullest! I shouldn't wonder—anyway an old woman like Mrs. Martin, who had borne eight or nine children of her husband who beat her, knew plenty about suffering without Crispin trying to teach her. Anyway, he went on in his soft beautiful voice, and she sat there bewildered, fascinated a bit by his red hair which she told me "she never could get out of her mind like," and the Jap standing silent beside her.

'Suddenly Crispin took hold of her old wrinkled neck and began stroking it, putting his face close to hers, talking, talking, talking all the time. Then the Jap stepped behind her, caught the back of her head and pulled it.

'What would have happened next, I don't know had not the younger Crispin come in, and at the sight of him the older man instantly got up, the Jap disappeared—it was as though nothing had been. Old Mrs. Martin got out of the house, then tumbled to pieces in the shrubbery. She was ill for days afterwards, but she kept the whole thing quiet with a kind of villager's pride, you know—"she wasn't going to have other folks talking as they did anyway when they saw how quickly she had left."

'But she told one of her daughters and the daughter told me. There was almost nothing in the actual incident, but it told me two things, one, that the older Crispin really is mad—definitely, positively insane, the other that the son, in spite of his seeming so submissive, has some sort of hold over him. There is something between the two that I don't understand.

'Well, that decided me. I went to Treliss to find out what I could. I had to hang about for quite a time before I could learn anything at all. Crispin was going on at Treliss just as he had done at Milton. He's taken this strange house outside the town which you'll see tonight. Quite a famous place in a way, built on the sea-cliff with a tangled overgrown wood behind it and a high white tower that you can see for miles over the countryside. At first the people liked him just as they had done at Milton and were interested in him. Then there were stories and more stories. Suddenly, only a week ago he said he was going abroad, and tomorrow he's going.

'Now the point I want to make clear to you is that the man's mad. I'm not a clever chap. I don't know any of your medical theories. I've never had any leaning that way, but I take it that the moment that any one crosses the division between sanity and insanity it means that they can control their brain no longer, that they are dominated by some desire or ambition or lust or terror that nothing can stop, no fear of the law, of public shame, of losing social caste. Crispin is mad, and Hesther, whom I love more than anything in this world and the next, is in his hands completely and absolutely. They go abroad tomorrow morning where no one can touch them.

'The time's been so short, and I've not been sufficiently clever to give you any clear idea of the man himself. I've got practically no facts. You can't say that his stroking an old woman's neck is a fact that proves anything. All the same I believe you've seen enough yourself to know that it isn't all imagination, and that the girl is in terrible peril. My God, sir,' the boy's voice was shaking, 'before the war there were all sorts of things that didn't seem possible, we knew that they couldn't exist outside the books of the story-tellers. But the war's changed all that. There's nothing too horrible, nothing too beastly, nothing too bad to be true—yes, and nothing too fine, nothing too sporting.

'And this thing is quite simple. There are those two madmen and my girl in their hands, and only tonight to get her out of them.

'I must tell you something more,' he went on more quietly. 'I've been making desperate attempts to see her, and at the same time to prevent either of those devils from seeing *me*. I saw her twice, once in the grounds of the White Tower, once on the beach below the house. Neither time would she listen to me. I could see that she was miserable, altogether changed, but all that she would say was that she was married and that she must go through with what she had begun.

'She begged me to go away and leave Treliss. Her one fear seemed to be lest Crispin should find out I was there and do something to me. 'Her terror of him was dreadful to witness—but she would tell me nothing. I hung about the place and made a friend of a fisherman he had up there working on the place—Jabez Marriot—you saw him on the hill today.

'He's a fine fellow. He's only been working on the grounds, had nothing to do with inside the house, but he didn't love the Crispins any better than I did, and he had lost his heart to Hesther. She spoke to him once or twice, and he would do anything for her. I sent letters to her through him: she replied to me in the same way, but they were all to the same effect, that I was to go away quickly lest Crispin should do something to me, that she wasn't being badly treated and that there was nothing to be done.

'Then, about a week ago, Crispin saw me. It was in one of the Treliss lanes, and we met face to face. He just gave me one look and passed on, but since then I've had to be terribly careful. All the same I've made my plans. All that was needed was her consent to them, and that, until tonight, she has steadily refused to give. However, something worse than usual has broken her down. What he has been doing to her I don't know, I dare not think—but tonight I've got to get her out. I've *got* to, or never show my face anywhere again. Now I've told you this as quickly as I could. Will you help me?'

Harkness stood up holding out his hand: 'Yes,' he said, 'I will.'

'It can be beastly, you know.'

'That's all right.'

'You don't mind what happens?'

'I don't mind what happens.'

'Sportsman.'

The two men shook hands. They sat down again. Dunbar spread out a paper on the little green-topped table.

'This is a rough plan of the house,' he said. 'I can't draw, but I think you can make this out.'

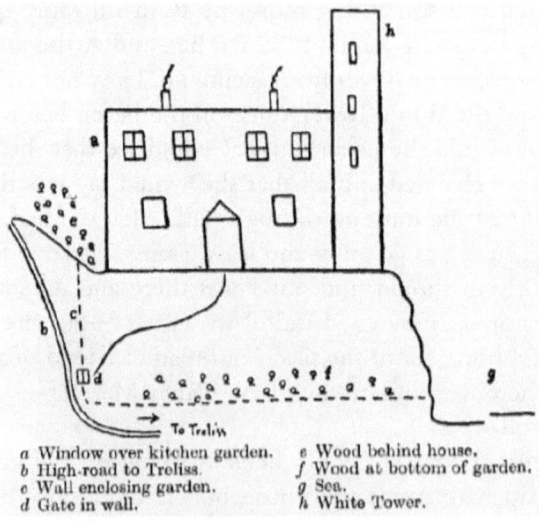

a Window over kitchen garden.   e Wood behind house.
b High-road to Treliss.   f Wood at bottom of garden.
c Wall enclosing garden.   g Sea.
d Gate in wall.   h White Tower.

'Please forgive this childish drawing,' he said again. 'It's the best I can do. I think it makes the main things plain. Here's the house, the tower over the sea, the wood, the garden, the high road. Now look at this other plan of the second floor.

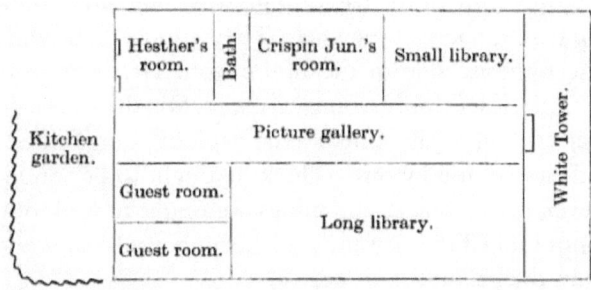

'You'll see from this that Hesther's room is at the very end of the house and her husband's room next to hers. The two guest rooms are empty, and there are no other bedrooms on that floor. The picture gallery runs right along the whole floor. The small library is a rather cheerful bright room. Crispin has put his prints in there, some on the walls, the rest in solander boxes. The large library is a gaunt, dusty, deserted place hung with heads of many animals that one of the Pontifexes (the real owners of the place) shot at some time or other. No one ever goes there. In fact, this second floor is generally deserted. Crispin spends his time either in the tower or on the ground floor. He is in the small library playing about with his prints some of the time though.

'Now, my plan is this. I have told Hesther everything to the very tiniest detail, and all that she had to do was to send word at any moment that she agreed to it. That she has now done.

'Tonight at one o'clock I am going to be up the high road under the shadow of the wood at the back of the kitchen garden with a jingle and pony——'

'A jingle?' asked Harkness.

'Yes, a jingle is Cornish for a pony trap. The obvious thing for me to have had was a car, but after thinking about it I decided against it for a number of reasons. One of them was the noise that it makes in starting, then it might easily stick over the ground that we shall have to cover, then I fancy that it will be the first thing that Crispin will look for if he starts in pursuit. We have only to go three miles anyway, and most of it over the turf of the moor.'

'Only three miles?' Harkness asked.

'Yes, I'll tell you about that in a moment. Crispin Senior is pretty regular in his movements, and just about one o'clock he goes up to his bedroom at the top of the tower with his two Japs in attendance. That is the only time of the day or night that one or another of those Japs isn't hanging about somewhere. They are up there with him on exactly the opposite side of the house from Hesther's room at just that time. That leaves only young Crispin. We shall have to chance him, but, according to Jabez, he has the habit of going to bed between eleven and twelve, and by one o'clock he ought to be sound asleep.

'However, that is one of the things we ought to look out for, one of the things indeed that I want your help about. Meanwhile Jabez is patrolling in the grounds outside.'

'Jabez!' Harkness cried, startled.

'Yes, that is our great piece of luck. Crispin has had some fellow of his own in the grounds all this time, but three nights ago he sent him up to London on some job and Jabez has taken his place. I don't think he trusts Jabez altogether, but he trusts the others still less. He is always cursing the Cornishmen, and they don't love him any the better for it.'

'Well, when you've got safely to your pony cart what happens next?'

'We drive up Shepherd's Lane, down across the moor until we reach the cliff just above Starling Cove. Here I've got a boat waiting, and we'll row across that corner of the bay to another cove—Selton— and just above Selton is Selton Minor where there's a station. At four in the morning there's the first train, local, to Truro, and at Truro we can catch the six o'clock to Drymouth. In Drymouth there are an uncle and aunt of hers—the Bresdins—who have long been fond of her and wanted her often to stay with them. Stephen Bresdin is a good fellow and will stand up for her, I know, once she's in his hands. Then we can get the law to work.'

'Won't Crispin be after you before you reach the Truro train?'

'Well, I'm reckoning first that he doesn't discover anything at all until he wakes in the morning. They are making an early start for London that day, but he shouldn't be aware of anything until six at least. But secondly, if he does, I'm calculating that first he'll think she's catching the three o'clock Treliss to Drymouth, or that she's motored straight into Truro. If he goes into Truro after her or sends young Crispin I'm reckoning that he won't have the patience to wait for that six o'clock or won't imagine that we have, and will be sure that we will have motored direct into Drymouth.

'He'll post after us there. I don't think he knows about the Bresdins in Drymouth. He may, but I don't think so. Of course, it's all chance, but I figure that it is the best we can do.'

'And what's my part in this?' asked Harkness.

'Of course, you're not to do a thing more than you want to,' said Dunbar. 'But this is where you could be of use. The thing that we're mainly afraid of is young Crispin. Hesther can get out of her room easily enough. It is only a short drop on to an outhouse roof, and then a short drop from there again, but if young Crispin is moving about, coming into her room and so on, it may be very difficult. What I suggest is that you stay with the older Crispin looking at his collections and the rest until half-past twelve or so, then bid him a fond goodnight and go. Wait for a quarter of an hour in the grounds. Jabez will be there, and then at about a quarter to one he will let you into the house again.

'Crispin Senior should be up in the tower by then, but if he isn't, you can pretend that you have lost something, take him back into the small library where the prints are, and keep him well occupied until after one. If he *has* gone up to his tower, Hesther will leave a small piece of white paper under her door *if* Crispin Junior is in the way and hanging about. In that case I should knock on his door, apologise, say that you lost your gold matchbox, had to come back for it as they are all leaving early the next day, think it must be in the small library; he goes back with you to look for it and—you keep him there. Do you think you could manage that?'

'I will,' said Harkness.

'There's more than that. One of the principal reasons that Hesther refused to consider any of this was—well, running off alone with me in the middle of the night. But if you are with us—someone, if I may say so, so entirely——'

'Respectable,' Harkness suggested as Dunbar hesitated.

'Well, yes—if you don't mind that word. It alters everything, don't you see. Especially as you've never seen me before, aren't in love with her or anything.'

'Exactly,' said Harkness gravely.

'There you are. The thing's full of holes. It can fall down in all sorts of places, and if Crispin catches us and knows what we are up to, it won't be pleasant. But there's nothing else. No other plan that seems any less dangerous. Are you for it, sir?'

'I'm for it,' said Harkness. At that moment the little marble clock struck the half-hour.

'My God!' Harkness cried, 'I should be at the hotel this very minute. If I miss them there's our plan spoiled.'

He gripped Dunbar's hand once and was off.

9

He went racing through the darkness, the two thoughts changing, mingling, changing incessantly over and over in his brain—that he must catch them at the hotel before they left it, and that he loved, he loved her, he loved her with an intensity that seemed to increase with every step that he ran.

In some way, although Dunbar had said so little about her, his picture of her was infinitely clearer and stronger than it had been before. He saw her in that small village of hers struggling with that drunken father, with insufficient means, with the individualities and rebellions of her two brothers, who, however deeply they loved her (and normal boys are not conscious of their deep emotions), must have kicked often enough against the limitations of their conditions, sneering servants, spying neighbours, jesting and scornful relations, the father in his cups abusing her, insulting her, and for ever complaining—and yet she, through all of this, showing a spirit, a hardihood, a pluck and, he suspected, a humour that only this last fatal intercourse with the Crispin family had broken down.

Harkness was the American man at his simplest and most idealistic, and than this there is nothing simpler and more idealistic in the whole of modern civilisation. The Englishman has too much common sense and too little imagination, the Frenchman is too mercenary, the Southern peoples too sensuous to provide the modern Quixote. In the United States of America today there are as many Quixotes as there are builders of windmills to be tilted at—and that is saying much.

So that, with his idealism, his hatred of cruelty and abnormality, Harkness saw far beyond any personal aggrandisement in this pursuit. He was not thinking now of himself at all, he had danced himself that night into a new world.

In the market-place he had to pause for breath. He had run all the way down the High Street, meeting no one as he went; he had already had considerable exercise that evening, and he was in no very fine condition of training. The market-place was quiet enough, only a few stragglers about; the Town Hall clock told him it was twenty-eight minutes to eleven.

He started up the hill, he arrived breathless at the hotel gates, the sweat pouring down his face. He stopped and tried to arrange himself a little. It would be a funny thing coming in upon them all with his tie undone and lines of sweat running down his face. But, after all, he could make the dance account for a good deal. He pushed his stud through the two ends of his collar and pulled his tie up, finding it difficult to use his hands because they were so hot, wiped his face with his handkerchief, pushed his cap straight on his head.

His face wore an expression of grim seriousness as though he were indeed St. George off to rescue his Princess from the Dragon.

His heart gave a jump of relief when he saw that the Dragon was still there, standing quite unconcernedly in the main hall of the hotel, his son and daughter-in-law quietly beside him. Harkness's first thought at view of him was that Dunbar's story was built up of imagination. The little man was standing, a soft felt hat tilted a little on one side of his head, a dark thin overcoat covering his evening clothes. Because his hair was covered and his face shaded there was nothing about him that was at all startling or highly coloured.

He simply looked to be a nice plump little English gentleman who was waiting, a smile on his face, for his car to arrive that it might take him home. Nor was there anything in the least exceptional in the pair that stood beside him, the man, thin, dark, immobile; the girl, her head a little bent, a soft white wrap over her shoulders, her hands at her side. At once it flashed into Harkness's brain that all the scene with Dunbar had been imagined; there had been no 'Feathered Duck,' no melodramatic story of madness and tyranny, no two-pence-coloured plan for a midnight rescue.

He was about to drive a mile or two to see some beautiful things, to smoke a good cigar and drink some admirable brandy—then to retire and sleep the sleep of the divinely worthy.

The girl raised her head. Her eyes met his, and he knew that whatever else was true or false his love for her was certain and resolved.

Crispin looked extremely pleased to see him. He came towards him smiling and holding out his hand:

'Why, Mr. Harkness, this is splendid,' he said. 'We were just wondering what we should do about you. We were giving you up.'

Harkness was conscious that, in spite of his attempts outside, he was still in considerable disorder. He fingered his collar nervously.

'I'm sorry,' he began. 'But I'm so glad that I've caught you after all.'

251

'Were the revels in the town amusing?' Crispin asked.

Harkness had a sudden impulse, whence he knew not, to make the younger Crispin speak.

'Why didn't you come down?' he asked. 'You'd have enjoyed it.'

The man was astonished at being addressed. He sprang into sudden life like any Jack-in-the-Box.

'Oh!' he said, 'I had to go with my father, you know—yes, to see some old friends.'

He was looking at Harkness as though he were wondering why, exactly, he had done that.

'Are you still willing to come and see my few things?' Crispin asked. 'It's only half-an-hour's drive and my car will bring you back.'

'I shall be delighted to come,' Harkness said quickly. 'I would have been deeply disappointed if I had missed you. But you must not think of sending me back. I shall enjoy the walk greatly.'

'Why, of course not!' said Crispin. 'Walk back at that time of the night! I couldn't allow it for a moment.'

'But I assure you,' Harkness pressed, laughing, 'I infinitely prefer it. You probably imagine that Americans never move a step unless they have a car to carry them. Not in my case. I won't come if I feel that during every minute that I am with you I am keeping your chauffeur up.'

'Well, well—all right,' said Crispin, laughing. 'Have it your own way. You're a very obstinate fellow. Perhaps you will change your mind when the time really arrives.'

They moved out to the doorway, then into the car.

Mrs. Crispin sat in one corner. Harkness was about to pull up the seat opposite, but Crispin said:

'No, no. Plenty of room on the back for three of us. Herrick doesn't mind the other seat. He's used to it.'

They sat down, Harkness between the elder Crispin and the girl. The night was black beyond their windows. Crispin pressed the button. The interior of the car was at once in darkness, and instantly the night was no longer black but purple and threaded with wisps of grey lavender that seemed to hold in their spider filigree all the loaded scent of the summer evening. Again, as the car turned into the long ribbon of the dark road, Harkness was conscious through the open window of the smell of innumerable roses, the late evening smell when the heat of the day is over and the flowers are grateful.

Then a curious thing happened. Through the darkness, Harkness felt one of the fingers of Crispin's left hand creeping like an insect about his knee. They were sitting very closely together inside the car's enclosure. Harkness was conscious that Hesther Crispin was pressed, almost crouching, against the corner of the car, and although the stuff of her dress touched him he was aware that she was striving desperately that he should not be aware of her proximity, and then directly after that, of why she was so striving—it was because she was shivering—shivering in little spasms and tremors that shook her from head to foot—and she was wishing that he should not realise this.

And even as he caught from her the consciousness of her trembling, at the same moment he was aware of the pressing of Crispin's finger upon his knee. He was so close to Crispin, and his leg was pushed so firmly against Crispin's leg, that this movement might have been accidental had Crispin's whole hand rested there. But there was only the finger, and soon it began its movement, staying for an instant, pressing through the cloth on to the bone of the knee, then moving very slowly up the thigh, the sharp finger-nail suddenly pushing more firmly into the flesh, then the finger relaxing again and making only a faint, tickling, creeping suggestion of a pressure. Halfway up the thigh it stopped; for an instant the whole hand, soft, warm, and boneless, rested on the stuff of Harkness's trousers, then withdrew, and the fingers, like a cautious animal, moved on.

When Harkness was first conscious of this he tried to move his knee, but he was so tightly wedged in that he could not stir. Then he could not move for another reason, that he was transfixed with apprehension. It was exactly as though a gigantic hand had slipped forward and enclosed him in its grasp, congealing him there, stiffening him into helpless clay—and this was the apprehension of immediate physical pain.

He had known all his days that he was a coward about physical pain, and that was always the form of human experience that he had shrunk from observing, compelling himself sometimes, because he so deeply hated his cowardice, to notice, to listen, but suffering after these contacts acute physical reactions. Only once or twice in his life had pain actually come to him. He did not mind it so deeply were it part of illness or natural causes, but the deliberate anticipation of it—the doctor's 'Now look out; I am going to hurt,' the dentist's 'I may give you a twinge for a moment,' these things froze him with terror.

During the war, when he had offered his service, this was the thing that from the clammy darkness of the night leapt out upon him. He had done his utmost to serve at the front, and it was in no way his own fault when he was given clerical work at home. He had tried again and again, but his poor sight, his absurd inside that was always wrong in one fashion or another, these things had held him back—and behind it all was there not a faint ring of relief, something that he dared not face lest it should reveal itself as cowardice?

There had been times at the dentist's and one operation. That operation had been a slight one, but it had involved for several weeks the withdrawing of tubes and the probing with bright shining instruments. Every morning for several hours before this withdrawing and probing he lay panting in bed, the beads of sweat gathering on his forehead, his hands clutching and unclutching, saying to himself that he did not care, that he was above it, beyond it . . . . . . .but closer and closer and closer the animal came, and soon he was at his bedside, and soon bending over him, and soon his claws were upon his flesh and the pain would swoop down, like a cry of a discoverer, and the voice would be sharper and sharper, the determination not to listen, not to hear, not to feel weaker and weaker, until at length out it would come, the defeat, the submission, the scream for pity.

The creeping finger upon his knee had the same sudden warning of imminent physical peril. The swiftly moving car, the silence, these things seemed to bear in upon him the urgency of the other—that it was no longer any game that he was playing but something of the deadliest earnest. Once again, the soft hand closed upon his thigh, then the finger once more like a creeping animal felt its way. His body was responsive from head to foot. He was all tingling with apprehension. His hand resting firmly on his other knee began to tremble. Why was he in this affair at all? If Crispin were mad, as Dunbar declared, what was to stop him from taking any revenge he pleased on those who interfered with him?

The tale was no longer one of pleasant romantic colour, the rescuing of a distressed damsel from an enchanted castle, but rather something quite real and definite, as real as the car in which they were sitting or the clothes that they were wearing. He, suddenly feeling that he could endure it no longer—in another moment he would have cried out aloud—jerked his knee upwards. The hand vanished, and at the same moment Crispin's voice said: 'We are almost there. We are going through the gates now.'

Lamps flashed upon their faces and Crispin's eyes seemed to have vanished into his fat white face. He had, in that sudden illumination, the most curious effect of blindness. His lids were closed over his eyes, lying like little pieces of pale yellow parchment under the faint red eyelashes.

'Here we are!' he cried. 'Out you get, Herrick.' And as Harkness stepped out of the car something deep within him whispered: 'I am going to be hurt. Pain is coming——'

Before him swung a cavern of light. It swung because on his stepping from the car he was dizzy, dizzy with a kind of poignant thick scent in the soul's nostrils, deep deep down as though he were at the edge of being spiritually anaesthetised. He paused for a moment looking back into the night piled up behind him.

Then he walked in.

10

It was an old house. The long hall was panelled and hung with the heads of animals. A torn banner of faded red and yellow with long tassels of gold hung above the stone fireplace. The floor was of stone, and some dim rugs of uncertain colour lay like splashes of damp here and there. The first thing of which he was aware was that a strong cold draught blew through the hall. It seemed to come from a wide oak staircase on his right. There were no portraits on the panelled walls. The house gave a deep sense of emptiness. Two Japanese servants, short, slim, immobile, their hair gleaming black, their faces impassive, waited. The outer door closed. The banner fluttered, the only movement in the house.

'Come in here, Mr. Harkness,' Crispin said. 'It is more comfortable.'

His little figure moved forward. Harkness followed him, but he had had one moment with the girl as he entered the hall. The two Crispins had been for an instant back by the car. He had said, his lips scarcely moving:

'I gave him the message. He is coming,' and she had answered without turning her head or looking at him: 'Thank you.'

Only as he walked after Crispin he wondered whether the Japanese could have understood. No. He was sure that no one could have heard those words, but he turned before leaving the hall, and he had a strange impression of the bare, empty, faded place, the staircase running darkly up into mystery, and the four figures, the two servants, Hesther and the younger Crispin, at that moment immobile, waiting as though they were listening—and for what?

The room into which Crispin led him was even shabbier than the hall. It was a large ugly place with dim cherry-coloured paper, and a great glass candelabra suspended from the ceiling. The walls had, it seemed, once been covered with pictures of all shapes and sizes, because the wall-paper showed everywhere pale yellow squares and ovals and lozenges of colour where the frames had been. The wall-paper had indeed leprosy, and although there were still some pictures—a large Landseer, an engraving of a Millais, a shabby oil painting of a green and windy sea—it was these strange sea-sick evidences of a vanished hand that invaded the air.

There was very little furniture in the place, two shabby arm-chairs, a round shining table, a green sofa. The draught that had swept the hall crept here, now come now gone, stealing on hands and feet from corner to corner.

'You see,' said Crispin, standing beside the empty fireplace, 'I am here but little. I have pulled down the pictures from the walls and then left it all shabby. I enjoy the contrast.' At the far end of the room were long oak cupboards. Crispin went to them and pulled back the heavy doors, and instantly in the shabby place there were blazing such treasures as Harkness had never set eyes on before.

Not very many as numbers went—some dozen shelves in all— but gleaming, glittering, shining, flinging out their flashes of purple and amber and gold, here crystalline, now deeply wine-coloured, pink with the petals of the rose, white with the purity of the rising moon. There was jewellery here that seemed to move with its own independent life before Harkness's eyes—Jaipur enamel of transparent red and green, lovely patterns with thick long strips of enamel on a ground of bright gold, over which, while still soft from the furnace, an open-work pattern of gold had been pressed; large rough turquoises set in silver; Chinese work of carved ivory and jade, cap ornaments exquisitely worked, a cap of a Chinese emperor with its embroidered gold dragon and its crown of pearls.

Then the inlaid Chinese feather work, and at the sight of these tears of pleasure came into Harkness's eyes; cells made as though for *cloisonné* enamel, and into these are daintily affixed tiny fragments of kingfisher feather. Colours of blue, green, and mauve here blend and tone one into another miraculously, and the effect of all is a glittering sheen of gold and blue. There was one tiny fish, barely half an inch long, and here there were thirty cells on the body, each with its separate piece of feather. Chinese enamel buttons and clasps, nail-guards beautifully ornamented, Japanese hair combs marvellously wrought in lacquer, horn, gold lac on wood, wood with ivory appliqués, and stained ivory.

Then the Netsukes! Had any one in the world such lovely things! With the ivory and its colour richly toned with age, the metal ones showing a glorious patina. The sword guards—made of various metals and alloys and gold and silver, the metal so beautifully finished that it had the rich texture of old lace.

There was then the Renaissance jewellery, pieces lying like fragments of sky, of peach tree in bloom, of cherry and apple, a lovely pendant parrot enamelled in natural colours, a beautiful ship pendant of Venetian workmanship, an Italian earring formed of a large irregular pear-shaped pearl in a gold setting, a Cinquecento jewel—an emerald lizard set with a baroque pearl holding an emerald in its mouth.

Eighteenth-century glory. Gold studs with little skeletons on silk, covered with glass and set in gold. Initials of fine gold with a ground of plaited hair, this edged with blue and covered with faceted glass on crystal and the border of garnets. A pair of earrings, paintings in gusaille mounted in gold. A brooch set with garnets. A French vinaigrette enamelled in panels of green on a gold and white ground.

Loveliest of anything yet seen, a sixteenth-century cameo portrait of Lucius Verius cut in a dark onyx. The enamel was green, with little white 'peas,' and small diamonds were set in each pod.

'Ah this!' said Harkness, holding it in his hand. 'This is exquisite!'

But Crispin was restless. The eyes closed, the short body moved to another part of the room, leaving all the treasures carelessly exposed behind him. 'That is enough,' he said—'enough of those, I bore you. And now,' turning aside with a deprecatory child-like smile, as though he had been exhibiting his doll's house, 'you must see the prints.'

Harkness turning back to the room saw it as even shabbier than before. It was lit by candle-light, and in the centre of the round shining table there were four tall amber-coloured candlesticks that threw around them a flickering colour as the draught ruffled their power. To this table Crispin drew two chairs. Then he went to a handsome old oak cabinet carved stiffly with flowers and fruit. He stayed looking with a long lingering glance at the drawers, then sharply up at Harkness. Seen there in the mellow light, with the coloured glory of the open cabinets dimly shining in the far room, with the pleasant timid smile that a collector wears when he is approaching his beloved friends, he might have stood to Rembrandt for another 'Jan Six,' short and stumpy though he be.

257

'Now what will you have? Durer, Whistlers, Little Masters, Mery-ons, Dutch seventeenth century, Callot, Hollar? What you will.......
No, you shall have only a few, and those not the most celebrated but perhaps the best loved. Now, here's for your pleasure......'

He came to the table bearing carefully, reverentially, his treasures. He set them down. From one after another he withdrew the paper; there gleaming between the stiff white shining mats they breathed, they lived, they smiled. There was the Rembrandt 'Landscape with a flock of sheep,' there the Muirhead Bone 'Orvieto,' the Hollar 'Sea-sons,' Callot's 'Passion,' Meryon's 'College Henry Quatre,' Paul Pot-ter's 'Two Horses,' a seascape of Zeeman, Cotman's 'Windmill,' Br-acquemond's 'Teal Alighting,' a seascape of Moreau, and Aldegrever's 'Labour of Hercules' to close the list. Not more than thirty in all, but living there on the table with their personal glow and spontaneity. He bent over them caressing them, fondling them, smiling at them. Hark-ness drew near and, looking at the tender wistfulness of the two old Potter's horses, bravely living out there the last days of their broken forgotten lives, he felt a sudden friendliness to all the world, a reassur-ance, a comfort.

Those glittering jewelled things had had at their heart a warning, an alarm; but no one, he was suddenly aware, who cared for these prints could be bad. There are no things in the world so kindly, so simple, so warm in their humanity......

The little man was near to him. He put his hand on his knee.

'They are fine, eh? They know you, recognise you. They are alive, eh?'

'Yes,' said Harkness, smiling. 'They are the most friendly things in art.'

The door opened and one of the Japanese servants came in with liqueurs. They were put on the table close to Harkness, and soon he was drinking the most wonderful brandy that it had ever been his happy fortune to encounter.

He was warm, cosy, quite unalarmed. The prints smiled at him, the dim room received him as a friend.

Crispin was talking, leaning back now from the table, his fat body hugged up like a cushion into his chair.

His red hair stood, flaming, on end. Harkness was, at first, only vaguely conscious that Crispin was speaking, then the words began to gather about him, to force their way in upon his brain; then, as the monologue continued, his comfort, his cosiness, his sense of security slowly slipped from him. His eyes passed from the 'Two Horses' to the high sharp cliffs of the 'Orvieto,' to the thick naked Hercules of the Aldegrever. Then, he was aware that he was frightened, as he had been on the road, in the hotel, in the car. Then, with a flash of awareness, like the sharp contact with unexpected steel, he was on his guard as though he were standing alone with his back to the wall against an army of terrors.

'.....And so, as I like you so much, dear Mr. Harkness, I feel that I can talk to you freely about these things and that you will understand. That has always been my trouble—that I have not been understood sufficiently, and if now I go my own way and have my own fashion of dealing with life I am sure that it is comprehensible enough.

'I was a very lonely child, Mr. Harkness, and mocked at by everyone who saw me. No, I have not been understood sufficiently. The colour of my hair has been a barrier. I realise that I am, and always have been, absurd in appearance, and from the very earliest age I was aware that I was different from other human beings and must pursue another course from theirs. I make no complaint about that, but it justifies, I think, my later conduct.'

Here, as though some wire had sprung taut inside him, he sat forward upright in his chair, staring with his little pale eyes at Harkness, and it was now that Harkness was abruptly aware of his conversation.

'I am not boring you, I trust, but I have taken a sympathetic liking to you, and it may interest you to understand my somewhat unusual philosophy of life.

'My mother died when I was very young. My father was a surgeon, a very wealthy man, money inherited from an uncle. He was a strange man, peculiar, odd. Cruel to me. Very cruel to me. He hated the sight of me, and told me once that it was a continual temptation to him to lay hands on me and cut my heart out—to see, in fact, whether I had a heart. He liked to torment and tease me, as indeed did everyone else. I am not telling you these things, Mr. Harkness, to rouse your pity, but rather that you should understand exactly the point at which I have arrived.'

'Yes,' said Harkness, dragging his eyes with strange difficulty from the pursed white face, the red hair, and glancing about the dim faded room and the farther spaces where the jewels flashed in the candle-light.

'Many people would have called my father insane, did not hesitate to do so. He was a large, extremely powerful man, given to violent tempers. But, after all, what is insanity? There are cases—many, I suppose—where the brain breaks down and is unable to perform any longer its ordinary functions, but in most cases insanity is only the name given by envious persons to those who have strength of character enough to realise their own ideas regardless of public opinion. Such was my father. He cared nothing for public opinion. We led a strange life, he and I, in a big black house in Bloomsbury. Yes, black, that's how it was. I went to Westminster School, and they all mocked me, my hair, my body, my difference. Yes, my difference. I was different from them all, different from my father, different from all the world. And I was glad that I was different. I hugged my difference. Different. . . . . .'

He lent forward, tapped Harkness's knee with his hand, staring into his face.

'Different, Mr. Harkness, different. Different. . . . . .'

And the long draughty room echoed 'Different . . . . . . .different . . . . . .different.'

'My father beat me one night terribly, beat me so that I could not move for pain. For no reason, simply because, he said, he wished that I should understand life, and first to understand life one must learn to suffer pain, and that then, if one could suffer pain enough, one could be as God—perhaps greater than God.

'It was to that night in the Bloomsbury house that I owe everything. I was fifteen years of age. He stripped me naked and made me bleed. It was terribly cold, and I came in that bare room right into the very heart of life, into the heart of the heart, where the true meaning is at last revealed—and the true meaning——'

He broke off suddenly, then whispered:

'Do you believe in God, Mr. Harkness?' and the draught went whispering on hands and feet round the room, 'Do you believe in God, Mr. Harkness?'

'Yes,' said Harkness.

'Yes,' said Crispin, in his lovely, melodious voice; 'but in a good God, a sweet God, a kind, beneficent God. That is no God. God is first cruel, terrible, lashing, punishing. Then when He has punished enough, and the victim is in His power, bleeding at His feet, owning Him as Lord and Master, then He bends down and lifts the wounded brow and kisses the torn mouth, and in His heart there is a great and mighty triumph. . . . . . .Even so will I do, even so will I be . . . . . . .and greater than God Himself!'

There was silence in the room. Then he curled up in his chair as he had done before, and went on with his friendly air:

'Dear Mr. Harkness, it is good indeed of you to listen to me so patiently. Tell me at once when I bore you. My father died when I was seventeen and left me all his wealth. He died in a Turkish bath very suddenly—ill-temper with some casual *masseur*, I fancy.

'I realised that I had a power. The realisation was very satisfactory to me. I married, and during the three years of my married life I collected most of the things that I have shown you this evening. I married a woman whom I was unfortunately unable to make happy. She could have been happy, I am sure, could she have only understood, a little, the philosophy that my father had taught me. My father was a very remarkable man, Mr. Harkness, as perhaps you have perceived, and he had, as I have told you, shown me the real meaning of this strange life in which we are forced, against our wills, to take part. It was foolish of my wife not to benefit by this knowledge. But she did not, and died sooner than I had anticipated, leaving me one child.

'A widower's life is not a happy one, and you will have undoubtedly perceived how many widowers marry again.'

He paused as though he expected some comment, so Harkness said yes, that he had perceived it. Crispin sat forward looking at him inquisitively, and making, with his fingers, a kind of pattern in the air as though he were tracing there a bar of music.

'Yes. I did not marry again, but rather gave myself up to the continuation of my father's philosophy. The philosophy of pain as related to power one might perhaps term it. God—of whose existence no thinking man can truly permit himself to doubt—have you ever thought, Mr. Harkness, that the whole of His power is derived from the pain that He inflicts upon those less powerful than Himself? We conceive of Him as a beneficent Being, and from that it follows that He must have determined that pain is, from Him, our greatest beneficence. It is plainly for our good that He torments us. Should not then we, in our turn, realising that pain is our greatest happiness, seek ourselves for more pain, and also teach our fellow human beings that it is only *through* pain that we can reach the true heart and meaning of life? Through Pain we reach Power.

'I test you with pain, and as you overcome the pain so do you climb up beside me, who have also overcome it, and we are in time as gods knowing good and evil. . . . . . . .A concrete case, Mr. Harkness. I slash your face with a knife. You are so powerful that you take the

261

pain, twist it in your hand and throw it away. You rise up to me, and suddenly I, who have inflicted the pain on you, love you because you have taken my power over you and used it for your soul's advantage.'

'And do I love you because you have slashed my face?' asked Harkness.

Crispin's eyes narrowed. He put out his hand and laid it on Harkness's knee.

'We would have to see,' Crispin murmured. 'We would have to see. I wonder—I wonder......'

They were silent. Harkness's body was cold, but the room was very hot. The candles seemed to throw out a metallic radiant heat. Harkness moved his knee.

'It would not do to prove your theory too frequently,' he said at last.

'No, no, of course it would not. It is, you understand, only a theory that I have inherited from my father. Yes. But I will confess that when an individuality comes close to me and remains entirely outside my influence I am tempted to wonder........Well, to speculate...... I like to see how far one personality *will* surrender to another. It is interesting—simply as a speculation. For instance, you have noticed my daughter-in-law?'

'Yes,' said Harkness, 'I have. A charming girl.'

'Charming. Exactly. But independent, refusing to make the most of the advantages that are open to her. Like my poor late wife, for instance. Unfortunate, because she is young and might benefit so much from my older and more experienced brain.

'But she refuses to come under my influence, remains severely outside it. Now, my son is almost too willing to understand my meaning. Were I to plunge a knife into his arm no blood would flow. I am speaking metaphorically, of course. After a very slight training in his early youth he was all that I could wish. But too submissive—oh yes, altogether too submissive.

'His wife's independence, however, is quite of another kind. It might almost seem as though during these last weeks she had taken a dislike both to myself and my son. However, she is very young and a little time will alter that, I have no doubt—especially as we shall be in foreign countries and to some extent alone by ourselves.'

Harkness pressed his hands tightly together. A little shiver ran, as though it responded to the draught that blew through the room, up and down his body. He was anxious that Crispin should not notice that he was shivering.

'Have you any idea where you will go?' he asked—and his voice sounded strangely unlike his own, as though some third person were in the room and speaking just behind him.

'We have no idea,' said Crispin, smiling. 'That will depend on many things—on Mrs. Crispin herself, of course, amongst others. A young wife must not show too complete an independence. After all, there are others whose feelings must be considered——' He was smiling as it were to himself and as though his thoughts were pleasant ones.

Suddenly he sprang up and began to walk the room. The effect on Harkness was strange—it was as though he were suddenly shut in there with an animal. So often in zoological gardens he had seen that haunting monotonous movement, that encounter with the bars of the cage and the indifferent acceptance of their inevitability, indifferent only because of endless repetition. Crispin, padding now up and down the long room, reminded Harkness of one of the smaller animals, the little jaguars, the half-wolf, half-fox; his head forward, his hands crossed behind his short thick back; his eyes, restless now, moving here, there about the room; his movements soft, almost furtive; every instinct towards escape. As he moved in the room half-clouded with light, the soft resolute step pervaded Harkness's sense, and soon the thick confined scent of a caged animal seemed to creep up to his nostrils and linger there.

Furry—captive—danger hanging behind the plodding step, so that if a sudden release were to come . . . . And he sat there fixed in his seat as though nailed to it while the sweet voice continued: 'And so, my dear Mr. Harkness, I have devoted my later years to the solution of this problem.

'I feel, if I may say so without too much arrogance, that I am intending to help poor human nature along the road to a better understanding of life. Poor, muddled human nature. Defeated always by Fear. Yes, Fear. And if they have surmounted Pain and stand with their foot on its body, what remains? It is gone, vanished. I myself am increasing my power every day. First one, then another. First through Pain. Then through Love. I love all the world, yes, everything in it, but first it must be taught, and it is so reluctant—so strangely reluctant—to receive its teaching. And I myself suffer because I am too tender-hearted. I should myself be superior to the suffering of others, because I know how good it is for them to suffer. But I am not. Alas, no. It is only where my indignation is aroused, and aroused justly, that I can conquer my tenderness, and then—well then . . . . . . .I can make my important experiments. My daughter-in-law, for instance. . . . . .'

He paused, not far from Harkness, and once again his hands made a curious motion in the air as though he were transcribing a bar of music. He stepped close to Harkness. His breath, scented curiously with a faint odour of orange, was in Harkness's face. He leaned forward, his hands were on Harkness's shoulders.

'For instance, I have taken a fancy to you, my friend—a real fancy. I liked you from the first moment that I saw you. I don't know when so suddenly I have taken a fancy to anyone. But to care for you deeply, first—yes, first—I would show you the meaning of pain. . . . . .' Here his body suddenly quivered from the feet to the head. '. . . . . And I could not, liking you so much, do that unless you were seriously to annoy me, interfere in any way with my simple plans'—the hands pressed deeply into the shoulders—'yes, only then could we come really to know one another . . . . . . .after such a crisis what friends we might be, sharing our power together! What friends! Dear me! Dear me!'

He moved away, turning to the table, looking down on the prints that were spread out there.

'Yes, yes, I could show you then my power.' His voice vibrated with sudden excitement. 'You think me absurd. Yes, yes, you do. You do. Don't deny it now. As though I couldn't perceive it. Do you think me so stupid? Absurd, with my ridiculous hair, my ugly body? Oh! I know! You can't hide it from me. You laugh like the rest. Secretly, you laugh. You are smiling behind your hand. Well, smile then, but how foolish of you to be so taken in by physical appearances. Do you know my power? Do you know what I could do to you now by merely clapping my hands?

'If my fingers were at your throat, at your breast, and you could not move but must wait my wish, my plan for you, would you think me then so absurd—my figure, my hair, ridiculous? You would be as though in the hands of a god. I should be as a god to you to do with you what I wished. . . . . .

'What is there that is so beautiful that I, ugly as I am, cannot do as I wish with it? This——' Suddenly he took up the 'Orvieto' and held it forward under the candle-light. 'This is one of the most beautiful things of its kind that man has ever made, and I—am I not one of the ugliest human beings at whom men laugh?—well, would you see my power over it? I have it in my hands. It is mine. It is mine. I can destroy it in one instant——'

The beautiful thing shook in his hand. To Harkness it seemed suddenly to be endued with a human vitality. He saw it—the high, sharp, razor-edged rocks, the town so confidingly resting on that strength, all the daily life at the foot, the oxen, the peasants, the lovely flame-like trees, the shining reaches of valley beyond, all radiating the heat of that Italian summer.

He sprang to his feet. 'Don't touch it!' he cried. 'Leave it! Leave it!'

Crispin tore it into a thousand pieces, wrenching it, snapping at it with his fingers like an animal. The pieces flaked the air. A white shower circled in the candle-light, then scattered about the table, about the floor.

Something died.

A clock somewhere struck half-past twelve.

Crispin moved from the table. Very gently, almost beseechingly, he looked into Harkness's face.

'Forgive me my little game,' he said. 'It is all part of my theory,—to be above these things, you know. What would happen to me if I surrendered to all that beauty?'

The eyes that looked into Harkness's face were pathetic, caged, wistful, longing. And they were mad. Somewhere deep within him his soul, caught in the wreckage of his bodily life like a human being pinned beneath a ruined train, besought—yes, besought—Harkness for deliverance.

But he had no thought at that moment of anything but his own escape. To flee from that room—from that room at any cost! He said something. Crispin did not try to keep him. They moved together into the hall.

'And you won't allow my chauffeur to drive you back?'

'No, no, thank you, I shall love the walk.'

'Well, well. It has been delightful. We shall meet some day again, I have no doubt. . . . . .'

Silence flooded the house. Once more Harkness's hand touched that other soft one. The door was open. The lovely night air brushed his face, and he had stepped into the dim star-drenched garden. The door closed.

PART 3: SEA-FOG

1

In the garden the silence was like a warning, as though the night had her finger to her lips holding back a multitude of breathing, deeply interested spectators.

Harkness, slipping from the path on to the lawn, felt a relief, as though with the touch of his foot on the cool turf there had come a freedom from imprisonment.

The garden was so friendly, so safe, so homely in its welcome. The scent of roses that had seemed to follow him throughout the adventures of that queer evening came to him now as though crowding up to reassure him. The night sky was pieced with stars, but they were thick and dim, seen through a veil of mist. The trees of the garden, like serried ranks of giants in black armour, seemed to stand, in silent attention, on every side of him, waiting his orders. The voice of all this world was the sea stirring, with a sigh and a whisper, below the wall of rock.

His first impulse as he stood on the lawn was to go away as far as he could from that house,—yes, as far as ever he could—miles and miles and miles—China if you like. Ah, no! That was just where that man would be!

He was trembling and shaking and wiping his forehead with his handkerchief; the breeze stroked him with cool fingers. He must run for ever to be clear of that house—and then suddenly remembered that he must not run, because he had his duty to do—and even as he remembered that a figure stepped up to him out of the trees. He would have called out—so wild and trembling were his nerves—had he not at once recognised from his great size that this was Jabez the fisherman.

He might have been an incarnation of the night, with his deep black beard, his grave kindly face, and his simple, natural quiet. He was dressed in his fisherman's jersey and blue trousers, and had no covering on his head.

'Good evening, sir,' he said. 'Mr. Dunbar told me as how you'd be wanting to be back in the house for a moment to fetch something you'd forgotten.

'We'd best be just stepping off the lawn, sir, if you don't mind. They foreigners are always nosing around.'

They turned quietly off the grass and stood closely together under the dark shadow of the house.

'I must go back at once,' said Harkness. 'There's no time to lose. It struck half-past twelve some time ago.'

'I don't know nothing about that, sir,' said Jabez; 'I only know as how you must be going back into the house for something you'd forgotten and I was to let you in.'

'Yes,' said Harkness, his teeth chattering, 'that's right.'

He wasn't made, in any kind of way at all, for this sort of adventure. He had never before realised how utterly inefficient he was. And of all absurdities to go back into the house when he was now safely out of it! Of all Dunbar's mad plan this was the maddest part. What could he do but be seen or heard, and then rouse suspicion when it might so easily have been undisturbed?

Let Crispin find him groping among those dark passages and what was his fate likely to be? There flashed into his consciousness then a sudden suspicion of Dunbar. It might suit the boy's plans only too well that he should be found, and so turn attention to another part of the house, leaving the girl free. But no! There was Dunbar's own steady clear gaze to answer him, and beyond that the certainty that Crispin's suspicions, roused by the discovery of himself, would proceed immediately to the girl.

No, did he return at once, the plan was quite feasible. Seeing him there so soon after his departure, they could do nothing but accept his reasons, and that especially if he returned quite openly with no thought of concealment.

But oh, how he hated to go back! He put his hand on the rough stuff of Jabez's jersey, listened for a moment to the regular, consoling breathing of the sea, sniffed the roses and the cool, gentle night air, then said:

'Well, come along, Jabez; show me how to get back.'

As they moved round to the door the thought came to him as to whether he had given the elder Crispin and his two nasty servants time enough to retire up to their part of the house. A difficult thing that, to hit the precise medium between too lengthy a wait and too short. He could not remember exactly what Dunbar had said as to that.

'Do you think I've waited long enough, Jabez?' he asked.

'Well, if you'd forgotten something, sir,' said Jabez, 'you'd want to be sure of finding it before the house is sleeping. They don't bolt this door, sir,' he continued in a whisper, 'because Mr. Crispin don't like to be bolted in. His fancy. After half-past one or so one of they Japs is around. It's just their hour like from half-past twelve to half-past one that I have to watch this part of the house extra careful. Yes, sir,' he added as he turned the key in the lock and pushed the door quietly open.

267

The hall was very dark. From halfway up the staircase some of the starlit evening scattered mistily through a narrow window, splintering the boards with spars of pale, milky shadow.

A clock chattered cluck-cluck-spin-spin-cluck close to Harkness's ear. Otherwise there was not a sound anywhere. He reflected that several things had been forgotten in his talk with Dunbar; one that there would, in all probability, be no light in the upper passage. How was he then to find the younger Crispin's door, or to see whether or no there were that piece of paper under Mrs. Crispin's? Secondly, it would be in the room on the ground floor where he had had his strange interview with the elder Crispin that he must see the younger, because, of course, that gloomy creature, dumb though he appeared to be, would be at least aware that Harkness had never ventured into the upper floor at all and could not therefore have left his gold match-box there. On the whole, this would be the better for Dunbar's plan, because it would lead the younger Crispin all the farther from his wife's door. But there were, at this point, so many dangers and difficulties, so many opportunities of disaster, that in absolute desperation he must perforce go forward.

He was aware that for himself now the easiest fashion would be to persuade himself that he had indeed lost his match-box and was returning to secure it. He hesitated on the bottom step of the stairs as though he were wondering what he ought to do, how he might find the tiresome thing without rousing the whole house.

He climbed the staircase slowly, walking softly, but not too softly, accompanied all the way by the clock that attended him like a faithful coughing dog. At the turn of the stairs he found the passage that Dunbar had described to him, and he was instantly relieved to find that a wide and deep window at the far end had no curtain, and that through it the long stretch was suffused with a pale, ghostly light turning the heavy old frames, the faded green paper, into shadow opaque.

He hesitated, looking about him, then clearly saw the two doors that must be those of Crispin and his wife; from under one of them, quite clearly, a small piece of white paper obtruded.

He waited an instant, then moved boldly forward, not trying to walk softly, and knocked on the nearer of the two doors. There was a moment's pause, during which the wild beating of his own heart and the friendly chatter of the clock from downstairs seemed to strive together to break the silence.

The door opened abruptly, and the younger Crispin, his white horse-face unmoved above his dark evening clothes, appeared there.

'I really must beg your pardon,' Harkness said, smiling. 'A most ridiculous thing has happened. I left the house some ten minutes ago after wishing your father goodnight, and it was only after going a little way that I discovered that I had lost a gold matchbox of mine that was of very great value to me. I hesitated as to what I ought to do. I guess I should have gone straight back to my hotel, but it worried me to think of losing it. It has some very intimate connections for me. And I knew, you see, that you were leaving early tomorrow morning—or *this* morning as it is by this time, I fancy. So that it was now or never for my matchbox. I came back very reluctantly, I can assure you, Mr. Crispin. I do feel this to be an intrusion. I had hoped that your father would still be about, and that I should simply ask him to give me a light in the room where we were sitting. In a moment I am sure that we would find the thing. Your night porter very kindly let me in, but although I had only been gone ten minutes the house was dark and there was no one about. I would have left again, but I tell you frankly I couldn't bear to leave the thing. I saw a light behind your door, and knew that someone at any rate had not gone to bed. The whole thing has been unpardonable. But just lend me a candle, and in five minutes I shall have found it.'

'I will go down with you myself,' said Crispin, staring at Harkness as though he had never seen him before.

'That's mighty fine of you. Thank you.'

But still Crispin did not move, his eyes fixed on Harkness's face. The eyes moved. They fell, and it seemed to Harkness that they were staring at the small piece of paper underneath the next door. Crispin looked, then without another word went back into his room, closing the door behind him.

Harkness's heart stopped; the floor pitched and heaved beneath his feet. It was all over already, then: young Crispin was now in his wife's room, had discovered her, in all probability, in the very act of escaping. In another moment the house would be aroused.

He prepared himself for what might come, standing back against the wall, his hands spread palm-wise against the paper as though he would hold himself up.

Truly he was shaking at the knees: he could see nothing, only that possibility of being once again in the presence of the elder Crispin, of hearing again that sweet voice, of feeling once more the touch of those boneless fingers, of seeing for another time those mad beseeching eyes. His tongue was dry in his throat. Yes, he was afraid, more utterly afraid than he would have fancied it possible for a grown man ever to be......

The door opened. Crispin appeared holding in his hand a lighted candle.

'Now, let us go down,' he said quietly.

The relief was so great that Harkness began to babble, 'You have no idea .... the trouble I am causing you. .... At this late hour. .... What must you think .....?'

The young man said nothing. Harkness meekly followed, the candle-light splashing the walls and floor with its wavering shadows. Their heads were gigantic on the faded wall-paper, and Harkness had a sudden fancy that the shadows here were the realities and he a mist. The younger Crispin gave that sense of unreality.

A kind of weariness went with him as though he were the personification of a strangled yawn. And yet beneath the weariness and indifference there was a flame burning. One realised it in that strange, absorbed stare of the eyes, in a kind of determination in the movements, in a concentrated indifference to any motive of life but the intended one. Harkness was to realise this with a start of alarmed surprise when, once more in the long shabby room lit now only by the light of one uncertain candle, young Crispin turned upon him and shot out at him in his harsh, rasping voice:

'What are you here for?'

They were standing one on either side of the table, and between them on the floor were the white scattered fragments of the torn 'Orvieto.'

'I told you,' said Harkness. 'I left my matchbox. I won't keep you a moment if you'll allow me to take that candle——'

'No, no,' said the other impatiently, 'I don't mean that. What do I care for your matchbox? You are worrying my father. I must beg you, very seriously, never to come near him again.'

'Indeed,' said Harkness, laughing, 'I don't understand you. How could I worry your father? I have never seen him in my life before this evening. He invited me out here for an hour's chat. I am going now. He is leaving for abroad tomorrow. I don't suppose that we shall ever meet again. Please allow me just to find my matchbox and go.'

But Crispin had apparently heard nothing. He stood, his hand tapping the table.

'I don't wish to appear rude, Mr.—Mr.——'

'Harkness is my name,' Harkness said.

'I beg your pardon. I didn't catch it when my father introduced me this evening. I don't want to seem offensive in any way. I simply thought this a good opportunity for a few words that may help you to understand the situation.

'My father is my chief care, Mr. Harkness. He is everything to me in the world. He has no one to look after him but myself. He is, as you must have seen, very nervous and susceptible to different personalities. I could see at once tonight that your personality is one that would have a very disturbing effect on him. He does not recognise these things himself, and so I have to protect him. I beg you to leave him alone.'

'But really,' Harkness cried, 'the boot's on the other leg. Your father has been very charming in showing me his lovely things, but it was he who sought me out, not I him. I haven't the least desire to push my acquaintance with him, or indeed with yourself, any further.'

Crispin's cold eyes regarded Harkness steadily, then he moved round the table until he was close beside him.

'I will tell you something, Mr.—ah—Harkness—something that probably you do not know. There have been one or two persons as foolish and interfering as to suggest that my father is not in complete control of his faculties, even that he is dangerous to the public peace. My father is an original mind. There is no one like him in this whole world, no one who has the good of the human race at heart as he has. He goes his own way, and at times has pursued certain experiments that were necessary for the development of his general plan. He was the judge of their true necessity and he has had the courage of his opinions—hence the inquisitive meddlesomeness of certain people.' He paused, then added:

'If you have come here with any idea, Mr.—Mr.—Harkness, of interfering with my father's liberty, I warn you that one visit is enough. It will be dangerous for you to make another.'

Harkness's temper, so seldom at his command when he needed it, now happily flamed up.

'Are you trying to insult me, Mr. Crispin?' he asked. 'It looks mighty like it. Let me tell you once again, and really now for the last time, that I am an American travelling for pleasure in Cornwall, that I had never heard of your father before this evening, that he spoke to me first and asked me to dine with him, and that he invited me here. I am not in the habit of spying on anybody. I would be greatly obliged if you would allow me to look for my matchbox and depart. I am not likely to disturb you again.'

But this show of force did not disturb young Crispin in the least. He stood there as though he were a wax model for evening clothes in a tailor's window, his black hair had just that wig-like sleekness, his face that waxen pallor, his body that wooden patience.

'My father is everything to me,' he said simply. 'If my father died I should die too. Life would simply come to an end for me. I am of no importance to my father. He is frequently irritated by my stupidity. That is natural—but I am there to protect him, and protect him I will. We have been really driven from place to place, Mr. Harkness, during the last year by the ridiculous ignorant superstitions of local gossip. Great men always seem odd to their inferiors, and my father seems odd to a number of people, but I warn them all that any spying, asking of questions, and the like, is dangerous. We know how to protect ourselves.'

His eyes suddenly fell on the fragments of the 'Orvieto.' He bent down and picked some of them up. A look of true human anxiety and distress crept into his queer fish-like eyes that gave him a new air and colour.

'Oh dear! oh dear!' he said. 'Did he do this while you were with him?'

'Yes,' said Harkness, 'he did.'

'Ah! it was one of his favourites. He must have been in great distress. This only confirms what I said to you just now about disturbing him. I beg you to go—now, at once, immediately—and never, never return. It is so bad for my father to be disturbed. He has so excitable a temperament. Please, please leave at once——'

'But my matchbox,' said Harkness.

'Give me your London address. I promise you that it shall be forwarded to you.' He held the candle high and swept the room with it, the sudden shadows playing on the walls, like a troop of dancing scarecrows. 'You don't see it anywhere?'

Harkness looked about him, then up at the face of the chattering clock. Time enough had elapsed. She was safe away by now.

'Very well, then,' he said. 'I will give you my address. Here is my card.'

Young Crispin, who seemed in great agitation and, under this emotion, a new and different human being from anything that Hark-

272

ness had believed to be possible, took the card, and with the candle moved into the hall.

He turned the key, opened the door, and the night air rushed in, blowing the flame.

'I wish you goodnight,' he said, holding out his hand.

Harkness touched it—it was cold and hard—bowed, said: 'I must apologise again for disturbing you. I would only reassure you that it is for the last time.'

Both bowed. The door closed, and Harkness was once again in the garden.

3

Jabez was waiting for him. They were both in the shadow; beyond them the lawn was scattered with star-dust mist as though sown with immortal daisies; the stars above were veiled. The world was so still that it seemed to march forward with the rhythm of the sea, that could be heard stamping now like a whole army of marching men.

'They are waiting for you, sir,' Jabez whispered. 'I was terrible feared you'd be too long in there.'

They moved, keeping to the shadows, and reached the path that led to the door in the wall. Here their feet crunched on the gravel, and every step was an agony of anticipated alarm. It seemed to Harkness that the house sprang into life, that lights jumped in the windows, figures passed to and fro, but he dared not look back, and then Jabez's hand was on the door, he was through and out safely in the wide free road.

Then, for an instant, he did look back, and there the house was, dark, motionless, rising out of the trees like part of the rock on which it was built, the high tower climbing pale in the mist above it.

Only an instant's glimpse, because there was the jingle, the pony, Dunbar, and the girl. An absurd emotion took possession of him at the sight of them. He had been through a good deal that evening, and the picture of them, safe, honest, sane, after the house and the company that he had left, came with the breeze from the sea reassuring him of normality and youth.

Jabez, too, standing over them like a protective deity. His whole heart warmed to the man, and he vowed that in the morning he would do something for him that would give him security for the rest of his days. There was something in the patient, statuesque simplicity of that giant figure that he was never afterwards to forget.

But he had little time to think of anything. He had climbed into the jingle, and without a word exchanged between any of them they were off, turning at once away from the road to the right over a turfy path that led to the Downs.

Dunbar, who had the reins, spoke at last.

'My God,' he said, 'I thought you were never coming.'

'I had a queer time,' Harkness answered, whispering because he was still under the obsession of his escape from the house. 'You must remember that I'm not accustomed to such adventures. I've never had such an odd two hours before, and I shouldn't think that I'm ever likely to have such another again.'

They all clustered together as though to assure one another of their happiness at their escape. The strong tang now of the sea in their faces, the freshness of the wide open sky, the spring of the turf beneath the jingle's wheels, all spoke to them of their freedom. They were so happy that, had they dared, they would have sung aloud.

But Harkness now was conscious only of one thing, that Hesther Crispin, a black shawl over her head, only the outline of her figure to be seen against the blue night, was pressed close to him. Her hand touched his knee, the strands of her hair, escaping the shawl, blew close to his face, he could feel the beating of her heart. An ecstasy seized him at the sense of her closeness. Whatever was to come of that night, at least this he had—his perfect hour. The elder Crispin and his madness, the younger and his strangeness, the dim faded house, the jewels and the torn 'Orvieto,' the mad talk, all these vanished into unreality, and, curiously, this ride was joined directly to the dance around the town as though no other events had intervened.

Then he had won his freedom, this sanctified it. Then he had felt his common humanity with all life, now he knew his own passionate share in it.

He wanted nothing for himself but this, that, like Browning's strong peasant, he might serve his duchess, at the last receiving his white rose and watching her vanish into her own magical kingdom. A romantic, idealistic American, as has been already declared in this history; but ten hours ago, both romance and idealism were theoretic, now they were pulsing, living things.

'Hesther's the one for my money,' Dunbar said, some of his happiness at their safety ringing through his voice. 'You should have seen her climb out of that window. She landed on the roof of that toolhouse so lightly that not a mouse could have heard her. And then she swung down the pipe like a monkey. Tell me how you managed with friend Crispin.'

'It wasn't difficult,' Harkness answered. 'He went with me to that long room downstairs like a lamb. He told me that he had been wanting to speak with me to tell me that I was bothering his father and must keep away.'

'That you were bothering his father?'

'Yes. He——Wait. Do you hear anyone coming?'

They listened. The ramp-ramp of the sea was now very loud. They had come nearly two miles on the soft track across the Downs. They stayed listening, staring into the distance. There was no sound but the sea; then a bell ringing mournfully, regretfully, through the air.

'That's the Liddon,' said Dunbar. 'We must be nearly at our cottage. But I don't hear anything. Unless they saw the jingle they never would think of this. Our only danger was the younger Crispin going into Hesther's room after he left you. I believe we're safe.'

They stayed there listening. Very strange in that wide expanse, with only the bell for their company. They drove on a little way, and a building loomed up. This was a deserted cottage, simply the four walls standing.

'I'm to tie the pony to this,' Dunbar said. 'Jabez will fetch it in the morning.'

They climbed out of the jingle and waited while the pony was tied. Having done it, Dunbar raised his head, sniffing the air.

'I say, don't you think the mist's coming up a bit? It won't do if it gets too thick. We'll have difficulty in finding the Cove.'

It was true. The mist was spreading like very thin smoky glass. The pony was etherealised, the cottage a ghostly cottage.

'Well, come on,' Dunbar said. 'We haven't a great deal of time, but the Cove's only a step of the way. Along here to the right.'

He led, the others followed. Hesther had hitherto said nothing. Now she looked up at Harkness. 'Thank you for helping us. It was generous of you.'

He couldn't see her face. He touched her hand with his for a moment.

'I guess that was the least any one could do,' he said.

'Oh! I'm so glad it's over!' She gave a little shiver. 'To be out here free after those weeks, after that house—you don't know, you don't *know* what that was.'

'I can pretty well imagine,' Harkness answered grimly, 'from the hour or two I spent in your father-in-law's company. But don't let's talk about it just now. Afterwards we'll tell each other all our adventures.'

'Isn't it strange,' she said simply, 'we've only exchanged a word or two, we never knew one another before this evening, and yet we're like old friends? Isn't it pleasant?'

'Very pleasant,' he answered. 'We must always be friends.'

'Yes, always,' she said.

They were standing close to the broken wall of the cottage. It had a wonderfully romantic air in the night air. It was so lonely, and so independent as well. The storms that must beat around it on wild nights, the screams of the birds, the battering roar of the waves, and then to sink into that silence with only the voice of the bell for its company. But Dunbar was no poet—a ruined cottage was a ruined cottage to him.

'I don't like this mist,' he said. 'It's made me a little uncertain of my bearings. I wonder if you'd mind, Hesther, waiting here for five minutes while I go and see——'

'Oh no, we'll all stick together,' she interrupted. 'Why should we separate? Why, I'm more sure-footed than you are, David. You're trying to mother me again.'

'No, I'm not,' he answered doggedly; 'but I'm really not quite sure of the way down, and if we got in a mess half-way it would be much worse your being there. Really these paths can be awfully nasty. I want to be *sure* of my way before you come—really, Hesther——'

She saw that it was important to him. She laughed.

'It's stupid, when I'm a better climber than you are. But if you like it—you're the commander of this expedition.'

She seated herself on a stone near the pony. The two men walked off. The sea mist was very faint, blowing in little wisps like tattered lawn, not obscuring anything but rendering the whole scene ethereal and unreal.

Suddenly, however, as though out of friendly interest, the stars, that had been quite obscured, again appeared, twinkling, humorous eyes looking down over the wall of heaven.

'We should be all right,' Dunbar said as the two men set off; 'we are up to time. The boat is bound to be there. It's lucky the fog hasn't come. That's a contingency I never thought of. The path down to the Cove is off here, to the right of the cottage somewhere. I've studied every inch of the country round here.'

The path appeared.

'Tell me, did you have a queer time with Crispin—the elder one, I mean?'

'I've never had so strange a conversation with anyone,' said Harkness. 'Madness is a queer thing when you are in actual contact with it, because we have, every one of us, enough madness in ourselves to wonder whether someone else *is* so mad after all. He talked the most awful nonsense, and *dangerous* nonsense too, but there was a kind of theory behind it, something that almost held it all together; a sort of pathos too, so that you felt, in spite of yourself, sorry for the man.'

But Dunbar was no analyser of human motives. He despised fine shades, and was a man of action. 'Sorry for him! Just about as sorry as you are for a spider that is spinning a nest in your clothes cupboard. Sorry! He wants crushing under foot like a white slug, and that he'll get before I've finished with him. Why, man, he's murderous! He loves torture and slow fire, like the old Spaniards in the Inquisition. There's so little to catch on to—that's the trouble; but I bet that if he had caught us helping Hesther out of that house to-night there would be something to catch on to! Why, if we were to fall into his hands now! Ugh! it doesn't bear thinking of!'

'Oh yes, of course,' Harkness agreed, 'he's dangerously mad. He'll be in an asylum before many days are out. If ever I have been justified in any action of my life it has been this, in helping that poor girl out of the hands of those two men. All the same . . . . . . .oh! it's sad, Dunbar! There is something so tragic in madness, whether it's dangerous or no—something captive, like a bird in a cage, and something common to us all. . . . . .'

'Well, if you think that the kind of things that Crispin Senior is after are common to us all you must have a pretty low view of humanity. The beastly swine! Something pathetic? Why, you're a curious fellow, Harkness, to feel pathos in that situation.'

'You may hate it and detest it, you *must* confine it because it's dangerous to the community, but you can pity it all the same. His eyes—that longing to escape.'

But Dunbar had found the cleft. They were now right above the sea. Although there was so slight a wind, the waves were breaking noisily on the shore. The stars had gone again, but the edge of the cliff was clear, and far below it a thin line of ragged white leapt to the eye, vanished, and leapt again.

'Here's the path down,' said Dunbar. 'There isn't much light, but enough, I fancy. We'll both go down so that we can be sure of our way when we come back with Hesther, and we may be both needed to help her. The path's all right, though. It's slippery after wet weather, but there's been no rain for days. Can you make it out clearly enough?'

'Yes,' Harkness said, but he felt anything but happy. Of all the things that he had done that evening this was the one that he liked least. He had a very poor head for heights, growing dizzy under any provocation; the angry snarl of the sea bewildered him, and little breaths of vapour curled about him changing from moment to moment the form and shape of the scene. He would have liked to suggest to Dunbar that there was no need for him to go down this first time, but, coward though he might be, he had come down to Treliss to beat that cowardice.

Certainly, the adventures of that night were giving him every opportunity. He went to the edge and looked over. The sea banged up to him, and the grey curved shadow of the Cove seemed to be miles below him. The little path ran on the edge of the cliff between two precipitous slopes, and its downward curve was sharp.

He pulled himself together, thinking of Hesther waiting there by the cottage alone. Dunbar had already started; he followed.

When he had gone a little way, his knees began to wobble, his legs taking on a strange life of their own. His imagination had all his days been dangerous for him in any crisis, because he always saw more than was truly there: now the sea breeze blew on either side of him, the path was so narrow that there was not room to plant his two feet at the same time, the dim shadow light confused his eyes, and the roar of the sea leapt at him like a wild animal.

However, he pressed forward, looking neither to right nor to left, and with what thankfulness he felt the wet sand yield beneath him and saw the boat drawn up under an overhanging rock only a few feet away from him!

'There it is,' said Dunbar, eyeing the boat with intense satisfaction. 'Now I think we're all right. I don't see what's going to stop us. We'll be across there in half an hour and then have a good hour before the train.' He held out his hand.

'Harkness, I simply can't tell you what I think of your doing all this for us. Coming down here just to have a holiday, and then taking all these risks for people you'd never seen before. It's fine of you and I'll never forget it.'

'It's nothing at all,' said Harkness, blushing, as he always did when he himself was at all in discussion. 'As a matter of fact, I've had what has been, I suppose, the most interesting evening of my life, and I daresay it isn't all over yet.'

'There's not much fear of their catching us now,' said Dunbar; 'but you've been in more real actual danger than you imagine. As I said just now, anything might have happened to us if he had caught us. You don't know how remote that house is. He could do what he pleased without any one being the wiser, and be off in the morning leaving our corpses behind him. The only servants in that house are those two Japs.'

'There's Jabez,' said Harkness.

'Jabez is outside and is only temporary. He wouldn't have stayed after tomorrow anyway. He hates the man. Fine fellow, Jabez. I don't know how I would have managed this affair without him. He fell in love with Hesther. He'd do anything for her. And then like the rest of the neighbourhood he detested the Japanese.

'They are funny conservative people these Cornishmen. Whatever they may pretend, they've no use for foreigners, and especially foreigners like Crispin.'

They stood a moment listening to the sea.

'The tide's going out,' said Dunbar. 'I was a little anxious lest I'd pulled the boat up high enough this afternoon, and then, of course, someone might have come along and taken a fancy to it. However, I was pretty safe. No one ever comes down into this cove. But we've taken a lot of chances tonight and everything's come off. The Lord's on our side—as He well may be, considering the kind of characters the Crispins have.'

He looked at Harkness. 'Hullo, you're shivering. Are you cold?'

'No,' said Harkness, 'I suddenly got the creeps. Someone walking over my grave, I suppose. I feel as though Crispin had followed us and was listening to every word we were saying. I could swear I could see his horrid red head poking over that rock now. However, to tell you the exact truth, Dunbar, I didn't care overmuch for coming down that bit of rock just now. I'm not much at heights.'

'What! that path!' cried Dunbar. 'That's nothing. However, there's no need for both of us to go back. You can stay by the boat.'

But a sudden determination flamed up in Harkness that it should be he, and none other, that should fetch Hesther Crispin.

'No, I'll go. There's no need for you to come though. We'll be back here in ten minutes. I'll see that she gets down all right.'

'Very well,' said Dunbar. 'But look after her. She's not so good a climber as she thinks she is.'

So, Harkness started off. He waved his hand to Dunbar, who was now busied with the boat, and began his climb. He stumbled over the wet rocks, nearly fell once or twice, and then came to the little path. His thought now was all of Hesther. He played with his imagination, picturing to himself that he was going right out of the world to some unknown heights where she awaited him, having chosen him out of all the world, and there they would live together, alone, happy always in one another's company......

What a fool he was when she was married, and, even if she freed herself from that horrid encumbrance, had that boy down there in the Cove waiting for her. But he could not help his own state. It did no harm. He told no one. It was so new for him, this rich thrilling tingle of emotion at the thought of some other human being, something so different from his love for his sisters and his admiration for his friends. And tonight from first to last there had been all the time this same *tingling* of experience. From his first getting into the train until now he had seemed to be in direct contact with life, contact with all the wrappers off, with nothing in between him and it!

That he must never lose again. After this night he must never slip back to that old half-life with its dilettante pleasures, its mild disappointments, its vague sense of exile. He could not have Hesther for himself, but, at least, he could live the full life that she and her country had shown to him.

'Ours is a great wild country......' Never back to the level plains again!

Full of these fine brave exulting thoughts, he had climbed a very considerable way when—suddenly the path was gone. There was no path, no rocks, no hillside, no Cove, no sea, no stars—nothing. He was standing on air. The fog in one second had crept upon him. Not the thin glassy mist of twenty minutes ago, but a thick, dense, blinding fog that hemmed in like walls of wadding on every side. In the sudden panic his legs gave way and he fell on to his knees and hands, clutching both sides of the narrow path, staring desperately before him. He heard the Liddon bell, as it seemed, quite close to his side, ringing down upon him.

4

His first thought was of Hesther—then of Dunbar. Here they were, all three of them, separated. The fog might last for hours.

He called, 'Dunbar! Dunbar! Dunbar!'

The bell echoed him, mocking him, 'Dunbar! Dunbar! Dunbar!'

Very cautiously he climbed upon his feet, steadying himself. The wind seemed completely to have died, and the sea sent up now only a faint rustle, like the mysterious movement of some hidden woman's dress, but the fog was so thick that it seemed to embrace Harkness ever more tightly—and it was cold with a bitter piercing chill. Harkness called again, 'Dunbar! Dunbar!' listened, and then, as there was no kind of answer, began to move slowly forward.

Once, many years before, when a small boy at his private school, there had been an hour that every week he had feared beforehand with a panic dread. This had been the time of the fire-escape practice, when the boys, from some second-floor window, were pushed down, feet foremost, into a long canvas funnel through which they slipped safely to the ground. The passing through this funnel was only of a moment's duration, but that moment to Harkness had been terrible in its nightmare stifling sense, pressing blinding confinement.

Something of that he felt now. He seemed to be compelled to push against blankets of cold damp obstruction. The Fog assumed a personality, and it was a personality strangely connected in Harkness's confused brain with that little red-headed man who seemed now always to be pursuing him. He was somewhere there in the fog; it was part of his game that he was playing with Harkness, and he could hear that sweet melodious voice whispering: 'Pain, you know. Pain. That's the thing to teach you what life really means. You'll be thankful to me before I've done with you. You shouldn't have interfered with my plans, you know. I warned you not to.'

He tried to drive down his fancies and to control his body. That was his trouble—that every limb, every nerve, every muscle, seemed to be asserting its own independent life. His legs now—they belonged to him, but never would you have supposed it. His arms tugged away from him as though striving to be free. He was not trained for this kind of thing—a cultured American gentleman with two sisters who read papers to women's clubs in Oregon.

He beat down his imagination. He had been crawling on his hands and his knees, and now he put out one hand and touched space. His heart gave a sickening bound and lay still. Which way went the path, to right or to left? He tried to throw his memory back and recapture the shape of it. There had been a sharp curve somewhere as it bent

281

out towards the sea, but he did not know how far now he had gone. He strained with his eyes but could see nothing but the wall of grey. Should he wait there until the fog cleared or Dunbar came to him: but the fog might be there for hours, and Dunbar might never come. No, he must not wait. The thought of Hesther alone in the fog, fearing every moment recapture by the Crispins, filled with every terror that her loneliness could breed in her, spurred him on. He *must* reach her, whatever the risk.

Stretching his arm at full length he touched the path again, but there was an interval. Had there been any break in the path when he came down it? He could not remember any. He felt backwards with his hand and found the curve, crept forward, then his foot slipped and his leg slid over the edge. He waited to stop the hammering of his heart, then, balancing himself, pulled it back, then forward again.

Lucky for him that there was no wind, but again not lucky, because had there been wind the fog might have been blown out of its course: as it was, with every instant it seemed to grow thicker and thicker.

Then he grew calmer. He must soon now be reaching the top, and happiness came to him when he thought that for a time at least he would be Hesther's only protection. On him, until Dunbar reached them, she would have absolutely to rely. She would be cold and he must shelter her, and at the thought of her proximity to him, he with his arm around her, wrapping her with his coat, holding perhaps her hand in his, he was, himself, suddenly warm, and his body pulled together and was taut and strong.

He fancied that he might walk now. Very carefully he pulled himself up, stood on his feet, stepped forward—and fell.

5

He screamed, and as he did so the Fog seemed to put its clammy hand against his mouth, filling it with boneless fingers. This was the end—this death. All space was about him and a roar of air sweeping up to meet him.

Then dimly there came to his brain the message, thrown to him like a life-line, that he was not falling in space but was slipping down a slope. He lurched out with his hands, caught some thick tufts of grass, and held. His legs slid forward and then dangled. With all his forces—and the muscles of his arms were but weak—he pulled himself upward and then held himself there, his legs hanging over space.

While the tufts held, and so long as his arms had the strength, he could stay. How long might that be? Sickness attacked him, a kind of sea-sickness. Tears were in his eyes, and an intense self-pity seized him. What a shame that such an end should come to a man who had meant no harm to any one, whose life had yet such possibilities. He thought of his sisters. How they would miss him! He had been tiresome some-times, and been restless at home, and pulled them up sharply when they had said things that he thought stupid, but now only his good points would be remembered. He had been kind to them; he had a warm heart.

He—and here his brain, working it seemed through his aching, straining arms, began suddenly to whirl like a top, flinging in front of his eyes a succession of the most absurd pictures: days in spring woods gathering flowers, his mother and father laughing at something child-ish that he had said, a bar of music from some musical comedy, Erda appearing before Wotan in *Siegfried*, a night when he had come to a dinner party and had forgotten to wear a dress tie, the moment when once before an operation he had been wheeled into the operating theatre, the day when he had plucked up his courage and decided that he could buy the Whistler 'Little Mast,' the grave, anxious, kindly eyes of Strang as he leant across the etching-table, a morning when he had run for an omnibus up Shaftesbury Avenue and missed it and the conductor had laughed, that hour with Maradick at the club, lights, scents, the cold fog drowning his mouth, his nose, his eyes—then chill space, a roaring wind and silence. . . . . .

How strange after that—and hours afterwards it seemed although it must have been seconds—to find that he was still living, that his arms were aching as though they were one extended toothache, and that he was still holding to those tufts of grass. He had a kind of marvel at his endurance, and now, suddenly, a wonder as to why he was doing this. Was it worthwhile? How stupid this energy! How much better to let himself go and to sleep, to sleep. How delicious to sleep and be rid of the ache, the cold, the clammy fog!

With that, one of the grass tufts to which he was clinging lurched slightly, and his whole soul was active in its energy to preserve that life that but now he had thought to throw away. With a struggle to which he would have supposed he could not have risen, he drew his body up against the slope so that the earth to which he was clinging might the better restrain his weight. Then resting there, his fingers digging deep into the soil of the cliff, his head pressed against the rock, he uttered a prayer:

'O Lord, help me now. I have a life that has been of little use to the world, but I have, in this very day, seen better the uses to which I may put it. Help me from this, give me strength to live, and I will try to leave my idleness and my selfishness and meanness and be a worthier man. O Lord, I know not whether Thou dost exist or no, but, if Thou art near me, help me at least now to bear my death worthily, if it must be that, and to live my life to some real purpose if I am to have it back again. Amen.'

Then he repeated the Lord's Prayer.

After that he seemed to be quieted; a great comfort came to him so that he no longer had any anxiety, his heart beat tranquilly, and he only rested there, passive for the issue. 'If death comes,' he thought to himself, 'I believe that it will be very swift. I shall feel no more than I felt just now when I first tumbled. I shall not have so much pain as with a toothache. I am leaving no one in the whole world whose existence will be empty because I have gone. Hesther after tonight I shall never, in any case, see again, and I am fortunate because, before I die, I have been able to feel the reality of life, what love is, and caring for others more than myself.' He was quite tranquil. The tuft of grass tugged again. His legs were numb, and he had the curious fancy that one of his boots had slipped off, and that one foot, as light as a feather, was blowing loosely in the air.

Then it seemed to him—and now it was as though he were half asleep, working in a dream—that someone was, very gently, pushing him upwards. At least he was rising. His hands, one by one, left their tufts of grass and caught higher refuge, first a projecting rock, then a thick hummock of soil, then a bunch of sea-pinks. In another while, his heart now beating again with a new excited anticipation, his head lurched forward on the earth into space. With a last frantic urge, he pulled all his body together and lay huddled on the path safe once more.

He had now a new trouble because his body refused to move. He had no body, nothing that he could count upon for action. He tried to find his connection with it, endeavoured to rest upon his knees, but it was as though he had been all dissipated into the fog and was turned, himself now, into mist and vapour. Then this passed, and once more he crawled forward.

He turned a corner and met again the Liddon bell. It was strange how deeply this voice reassured him. He had been all alone in a world utterly dead. He had not had, like Hardy's hero, the sight of the crustacean to connect him with eternal life. But this sudden, melancholy, lowing sound like a creature deserted, crying for its mate, brought him once more into reality. The bell was insistent and very loud. It swung through the fog up to him, ringing in his ear, then fading away again into distance. He spoke aloud as men do when they are in desperate straits: 'Well, old bell,' he cried, 'I'm not beaten yet, you see. They've done what they can to finish me, but I'm back again. You don't get rid of me so easily as all that, you know. You can come and look, if you like. Here I am, company for you after all.'

There was a little breeze blowing now in his eyes and this cheered him. If only the wind rose the fog would move and all might yet be well. His clothes were torn, his hands bleeding, his hat gone. He crawled into a sitting position, shook his fist in the air, and cried:

'You old devil, you're there, are you! It's your game all this. You're seeing whether you can finish me. But I'll be even with you yet.' And it did indeed seem to him that he could see through the mist that red head sticking out like a furze bush on fire. The hair, the damp pale face, the melancholy eyes, and then the voice:

'It's only a theory, of course, Mr. Harkness. My father, who was a most remarkable man. . . . . .'

The thought of Crispin enraged him, and the rage drove him on to his feet. He was standing up and moving forward quite briskly. He moved like a blind man, his hands before him as though he were expecting at every moment to strike some hard, sharp substance, but whereas before the fog had seemed to envelop him, strangling him, penetrating into his very heart and vitals, now it retreated from before him like a moving wall.

The incline was now less sharp, and now less sharp again. Little pebbles rolled from beneath his feet, and he could hear them fall over down into distant space, but he had no longer any fear. He was on level ground. He knew that the down was spreading about him. He called out, 'Hesther! Hesther!' not realising that this was the first time he had spoken her name. He called it again, 'Hesther! Hesther!' and again and again, always moving as he fancied forward.

Then, as though it had been hurled at him out of some gigantic distance, the rugged wall of the cottage pierced the sky. He saw it, then herself patiently seated beneath it. In another moment he was kneeling beside her, both her hands in his, his voice murmuring un-intelligible words.

6

She was so happy to see him. His face was close to hers and for the first time he could really see her, her large, grave, questioning eyes, her child's face, half developed, nothing very beautiful in her features, but to him something inexpressibly lovely for which all his life he had been waiting.

She was damp with the fog, and the first thing he did was to take off his coat and try to put it around her. But she stood up resisting him.

'Oh no, I'm not cold. I'm not really. And do you think I'll let you? Why, you! What have you done? Your hands are all torn and your face!'

She was very close to him. She put up her hand and touched his face. It needed to muster everything that he had in him not to put his arms around her. He conquered himself. 'That's nothing,' he said; 'I had some trouble climbing up from the cliff. I was just halfway up when the fog came on. It wasn't much of a path in any case.'

She stood with her hand on his arm. 'Oh, what shall we do? We shall never find the boat now. The fog will clear and we will be caught. We can't move from here while it lasts.'

'No,' he said firmly, 'we can't move. This is the place where Dunbar will expect us. He'll turn up here at any moment. Meanwhile, we must just wait for him. Is the pony all right?'

'I don't know what I'd have done without the pony,' she said. 'When the fog came up I was terrified. I didn't know what I'd better do. I called your names, but, of course, you didn't hear. And then it got colder and colder and I kept thinking that I was seeing Them. His red hair. . . . . .'

She suddenly, shivering, put her hand on his arm. 'Oh, don't let them find us,' she said; 'I couldn't go back to that. I would rather kill myself. I *would* kill myself if I went back. What they are—oh! you don't know!'

He took her hand and held it firmly. 'Now see here, we don't know how long Dunbar will be, or how long the fog will last, or anything. We can't do anything but stay here, and it's no good if we stay here and think of all the terrible things that may happen. The fog can't last for ever. Dunbar may come any minute. What we have to do is to sit down on this stone here and imagine we are sitting in front of our fire at home talking like old friends about—oh well, anything you like—whatever old friends do talk about. Can your imagination help you that far?'

He saw that she was at the very edge of her nerves; a step further and she would topple over into wild hysteria; he knew enough already about her character to be sure that nothing would cause her such self-scorn and regret as that loss of self-control. He was not very sure of his own control; everything had piled up upon him pretty heavily during the last hour; but she was such a child that he had an immense sense of responsibility as though he had been fifteen years older at least.

'I haven't very much imagination,' she said, in a voice hovering between laughter and tears. 'Father always used to tell me that that was my chief lack. And we *are* old friends, as we said a while ago, even though we have just met.'

'That's right,' he said. 'Now we will have to sit rather close together. There's only one stone and the grass is most awfully wet. Every three minutes or so I'll get up and shout Dunbar's name in case he is wandering about quite close to us.'

He stood up and, putting his hands to his mouth, shouted with all his might: 'Dunbar! Dunbar! Dunbar!'

He waited. There was no answer. Only the fog seemed to grow closer. He turned to her and said:

'Don't you think the fog's clearing a little?'

She shook her head. There was still a little quaver in her voice: 'I'm afraid not. You're saying that to cheer me up. You needn't. I'm not frightened. Think how lucky I am to have you with me. You mightn't have come back. You might have missed your way for hours.'

When he thought of how nearly he had missed his way for ever and ever he trembled. He mustn't let his thoughts wander in those paths; he was here to make her feel happy and safe until Dunbar came. They sat down on the stone together, and he put his arm around her to hold her there and to keep her warm.

'Now what shall we talk about?' she asked him.

'Ourselves,' he answered her. 'We have a splendid opportunity. Here we are, cut off by the fog, away from everyone in the world. We know nothing about one another, or almost nothing. We can scarcely see one another's faces. It is a wonderful opportunity.'

'Well, you tell me about yourself first.'

'Ah! there's the trouble. I'm so terribly dull. I've never been or thought or said anything interesting. I'm like thousands and thousands of people in this world who are simply shadows to everybody else.'

'Remember we're to tell the truth,' she said. 'No one ever honestly thinks that about themselves—that they are just shadows of somebody

287

else. Everyone has their own secret importance for themselves—at least, everyone in our village had. People you would have supposed had *nothing* in them, yet if you talked to them you soon saw that they fancied that the world would end if they weren't in it to make it go round.'

'Well, honestly, that isn't my opinion of myself,' Harkness answered. 'I don't think that I help the world to go round at all. Of course, I think that there have to be all the ordinary people in it like myself to appreciate all the doings and sayings of the others, the geniuses—to make the audience, you know. But I'm not even a very good audience. There are so many things I don't care for.'

'What *do* you care for?'

'Oh, different things at different times—not permanently for much. Pictures—especially etchings—music, travel. But never very deeply or urgently, except for the etchings. . . . . . . .Until tonight,' he suddenly added, lowering his voice.

'Until tonight?'

'Yes, ever since I left Paddington—let me see—how many hours ago? It's now about two o'clock, I suppose.' He looked at his watch. 'Ten minutes to two. Nearly nine hours. Ever since nine hours ago, I've felt a new kind of energy, a new spirit, the thrill, the excitement that all my life I've wanted to have but that never came until now. Being really *in* life instead of just watching it like a spectator.'

She put her hand on his. 'I am so glad you're here. Do you know I used to boast that I never could be frightened by anything? But these last weeks—all my courage has gone. Oh, why has this fog come? We were getting on so well, everything was all right—and now I know they'll find us, I know they'll find us. I'm sure he's just behind there, somewhere, hiding in the fog, listening to us. And perhaps David is killed. I can't bear it. I can't bear it!'

She suddenly clung to him, hiding her face in his cloak. He soothed her just as he would his own child, as though she had been his child all her life. 'Hesther! Hesther! You mustn't. You mustn't break down. Think how brave you've been all this time. The fog can clear in a moment and then we'll still have time to catch the train. Anyway, the fog's a protection. If Crispin were after us he'd never find us in this. Don't cry, Hesther. Don't be unhappy. Let's just go on talking as though we were at home. You're quite safe here. No one can touch you.'

'Yes, I'm safe,' she whispered, 'so long as you're here.' His heart leapt up. He forced himself to speak very quietly:

'Now I'll tell you about *myself*. It will be soon over. I grew up in a place called Baker in Oregon in the United States. It is a long way from anywhere, but all the big trains go through it on the way out to the Pacific coast. I grew up there with my two sisters and my father. I lost my mother when I was very young. We had a funny ramshackle old house under the mountains, full of books. We had very long winters and very hot summers. I went to a place called Andover to school. Then my father died and left me some money, and since then—oh! since then I dare not tell you what a waste I have made of my life, never settling anywhere, longing for Europe and the old beautiful things when I was in America, and longing for the energy and vitality of America when I was in Europe. That's what it is to be really cosmopolitan—to have no home anywhere.

'The only intimate friends I have are the etchings, and I sometimes think that they also despise me for the idle life I lead.'

He could see that she was interested. She was quietly sitting, her head against his shoulder, her hand in his just as a little girl might listen to her elder brother.

'And that's all?' she asked.

'Yes. Absolutely all. I'm ashamed to let you look at so miserable a picture. I have been like so many people in the world, especially since the war. Modern cleverness has taken one's beliefs away, modern stupidity has deprived one of the possibility of hero-worship. No God, no heroes any more. Only one's disappointing self. What is left to make life worthwhile? So, you think while you are on the bank watching the stream of life pass by. It is different if someone or something pushes you in. Then you must fight for existence for your own or, better still, for someone else. They who care for something or someone more than themselves—some cause, some idea, some prophecy, some beauty, some person—they are the happy ones.' He laughed. 'Here I am sitting in the middle of this fog, a useless selfish creature who has suddenly discovered the meaning of life. Congratulate me.'

He felt that she was looking up at him. He looked down at her. Their eyes stared at one another. His heart beat riotously, and behind the beating there was a strange pain, a poignant longing, a deep, deep tenderness.

'I don't understand everything you say,' she replied at last. 'Except that I am sure you are doing an injustice to yourself when you give such an account. But what you say about unselfishness I don't agree with. How is one unselfish if one is doing things for people one loves?

I wasn't unselfish because I worked for the boys. I had to. They needed it.'

'Tell me about your home,' he said.

She sighed, then drew herself a little away from him, as though she were suddenly determined to be independent, to owe no man anything.

'Mother died when I was very young,' she said. 'I only remember her as someone who was always tired, but very, very kind. But she liked the boys better. I remember I used to be silly and feel hurt because she liked them better. But the day before she died she told me to look after them, and I was so proud, and promised. And I have tried.'

'Were they younger than you?'

'Yes. One was three years younger and the other five. I think they cared for me, but never as much as I did for them.'

She stopped as though she were listening. The fog was now terribly thick and was in their eyes, their nostrils, their mouths. They could see nothing at all, and when he jumped to his feet and called again, 'Dunbar! Dunbar! Dunbar!' he knew that he vanished from her sight. He could feel from the way that she caught his hand and held it when he sat down again how, for a moment, she had lost him.

'It's always that way, isn't it?' she went on, and he could tell from an undertone in her voice that this talking was an immense relief to her. She had, he supposed, not talked to anyone for weeks.

'Always what way?' he asked.

'That if you love someone very much they don't love you so much. And then the same the other way.'

'Very often,' he agreed.

'I'm sure that's what I did wrong at home. Showed them that I cared for them too much. The boys were very good, but they were boys, you know, and took everything for granted as men do.' She said this with a very old world-wise air. 'They were dear boys—they were and are. But it was better before they went to school, when they needed me always. Afterwards when they had been to school they despised girls and thought it silly to let girls do things for them. And then they didn't like being at home—because father drank.'

She dropped her voice here and came very close to him.

'Do you know what it is to hate and love the same person? I was like that with father. When he had drunk too much and broke all the things—when we had so few anyway—and hit the boys, and did things—oh, dreadful things that men do when they're drunk—then I

290

hated him. I didn't love him. I didn't want to help him—I just wanted to get away. And before—before he drank so much he was so good and so sweet and so clever. Do you know that my father was one of the cleverest doctors in the whole of England? He was. If he hadn't drunk he might have been anywhere and done anything. But sometimes when he *was* drunk and the boys were away at school, and the house was in such a mess, and the servant wouldn't stay because of father, I felt I couldn't go on—I *couldn't!*—and that I'd run down the road leaving everything as it was, into the town and hide so that they'd never find me. . . . . . . .And now,' she suddenly broke out, 'I have run away—and see what I've made of it!'

'It isn't over yet,' he said to her quietly. 'Life's just beginning for you.'

'Well, anyway,' she answered, with a sudden resolute calm that made her seem ever so much older and more mature, 'I've helped the boys to start in life, and I won't have to go back to all that again—that's something. It's fine to love someone and work for them as you said just now, but if it's always dirty, and there's never enough money, and the servants are always in a bad temper, and you never have enough clothes, and all the people in the village laugh at you because your father drinks, then you want to stop loving for a little and to escape anywhere, anywhere to anybody where it isn't dirty. Love isn't enough—no, it isn't—if you're so tired with work that you haven't any energy to think whether you love or not.'

She hesitated there, looking away from him, and said so softly that he with difficulty caught her words: 'I will tell you one thing that you won't believe, but it's true. I wanted to go to Crispin.'

He turned to look at her in amazement.

'You *wanted* to go?'

'Yes. I know you thought that I went for the boys and father. I know that David thinks that too. Of course, that was true a little. He promised me that they should have everything. It was a relief to me that I needn't think of them anymore. But it wasn't only that. I wanted to go. I wanted to be free.'

'To be free!' Harkness cried. 'My God! What freedom! I can understand your wanting to escape, but with *such* men. . . . . .'

She turned round upon him eagerly. 'You don't know what he can be like—the elder Crispin, I mean. And to a girl, an ignorant, conceited girl. Yes, I was conceited, that was the cause of everything. Father had all sorts of books in his room. I used to read everything

I could see—French and German in a kind of way—and secretly I was very proud of myself. I thought that I was more learned than any one I knew, and I used to smile to myself secretly when I overheard people saying how good I was to the boys, and how unselfish, and I would think, "That's not what I am at all. If you only knew how much I know, and the kind of things, you'd be surprised."

'I was always thinking of the day when I would escape and marry. I fancied I knew everything about marriage from the books that I had read and from the things that father said when he was drunk. I hadn't a nice idea of marriage at all. I thought it was old-fashioned to fall in love, but through marriage I could reach some fine position where I could do great things in the world, and always in my mind I saw myself coming one day back to my village and everyone saying: "Why, I had not an idea she was like *that*. Fancy all the time she was with us we never knew she was clever like *this*."'

She laughed like a child, a little maliciously, very simply and confidingly. He saw that she had for the moment forgotten her danger, and was sitting there in the middle of a dense fog on a lonely moor at a quarter past two in the morning with an almost complete stranger as though she were giving him afternoon tea in the placid security of a London suburb. He was glad; he did not wish to bring back her earlier terror, but for himself now, with every moment that passed, he was increasingly anxious. Time was flying; now they could never catch that train. And above all, what could have happened to Dunbar? He must surely have found them by now had some accident not come to him. Perhaps he had slipped as Harkness had done and was now lying smashed to pieces at the bottom of that cliff. But what could he, Harkness, do better than this? While the fog was so dense it was madness to move off in search of any one. And if the fog lasted, were they to sit there until morning and be caught like mice in a kitchen?

And beneath his anxiety, as his arm held the child at his side, there was that strange mixture of triumph and pain, of some odd piercing loneliness and a deep burning satisfaction. Meanwhile her hand rested in his, soft and warm like the touch of a bird's breast.

'When Mr. Crispin came—the elder, the father—and talked to me I was flattered. No one before had ever talked to me as he did about his travels and his collections and the grand people he knew, just as though I were as old as he was. And then David—Mr. Dunbar—was always asking me to marry him. I'd known him all my life, and I liked him better than anyone else in the whole world; but just because I'd always known him he wasn't exciting. He was the last person I wanted to marry. Then Mr. Crispin made father drink, and I hated him for that, and I hated father for letting him do it. I went up to Mr. Crispin's house and told him what I thought of him, and he talked and talked and talked, all about having power over people for their good and hurting them first and loving them all afterwards. I didn't understand most of it, but the end of it was that he said that if I would marry his son he would leave father alone and would give me everything. I should see the world and all life, and that his son loved me and would be kind to me.

'After that it was the strangest thing. I don't say that he hypnotised me. I knew that he was bad. Everyone in the place was speaking about him. He had done some cruel thing to a horse, and there was a story, too, about some woman in the village. But I thought that I knew better than all of them, that I would save father and the boys and be grand myself—and then I would show David that he wasn't the only one who cared for me.

'And so—I consented. From that moment I promised I was terrified. I knew that I had done a terrible thing. But it was too late. I was already a prisoner. That is a hysterical thing to say, but it is true. They never let me out of their sight. I was married very quickly after that. I won't say anything about the first week of my marriage except that I didn't need books any more to teach me. I knew the sin I'd committed. But I was proud—I was as proud as I was frightened. I wasn't going to let anyone know what a terrible position I was in—and especially David. When we went to Treliss, David came too and waited. In my heart I was so glad he was there.

'You don't know what went on in that house. The younger Crispin wasn't unkind. He was simply indifferent. He thought of nothing and nobody but his father. His father mocked him, despised him, scorned him, but he didn't care. He follows his father like a dog. At first you know I thought I could make a job of it, carry it through. And then I began to understand.

'First one little thing, then another. The elder Crispin was always talking, floods of it. He was always looking at me and smiling at me. After two days in the house with him I hated him as I hadn't known I could hate any one. When he touched me I trembled all over. It became a kind of duel between us. He was always talking nonsense about making me love him through pain—and his eyes never said what his mouth said. They were like the eyes of another person caught there by mistake.

'Then one day I came into the library upstairs and found him with a dog. A little fox-terrier. He had tied it to the leg of the table and was flicking it with a whip. He would give it a flick, then stand back and look at it, then give it another flick. The awful thing was that the dog was too frightened to howl, too terrified to know that it was being hurt at all. He was smiling, watching the dog very carefully, but his eyes were sad and unhappy. After that there were many signs. I knew then two things, that he was raving crazy mad and that I was a prisoner in that house. They watched me night and day. I had no money. My only hope of escape was through David, who was always getting word to me, begging me to let him help me. But I still had my pride, although it was nearly beaten. I wouldn't yield until—until the night before you came; then something happened, something he tried to do; the younger Crispin stopped him that time, but another time—well, there mightn't be any one there. That settled it all. I let David know through you that I would go. I *had* to go. I couldn't risk another moment. I couldn't risk another moment, I tell you.' She suddenly sprang up, caught at Harkness's hands in an agony, crying:

'Don't stay here! Don't stay here! They can find us here! We're going to be caught again. Oh, please come! Please! Please!'

She was suddenly crazy with terror. Had he not held her with all his force she would have rushed off into the fog. She struggled in his arms, pulling and straining, crying, not knowing what she said. Then suddenly she relaxed, would have tumbled had he not held her, and murmuring, 'I can't any more—oh, I can't anymore!' collapsed, so that he knew she had fainted.

7

He sat down on the stone, laying her in his arms as though she were his child. He was, himself, not strongly built, but she was so slight in his hold that he could not believe that she was a woman. He murmured words to her, stroked her forehead with his hand; she stirred, turning towards him, and resting her head more securely on his breast. Then her hand moved to his cheek and lay against it.

At last after a long while she raised her head, looked about her, stared up at him as though she had just awoken, turned, and kissed him on the cheek. She murmured something—he could not catch the words—then nestled down into his arms as though she would sleep.

There began for him then, sitting there, staring out into the unblinking fog, his hardest test. As surely as never before in his life had he known what love truly was, so did he know it now. This child in her ignorance, her courage, her hard history, her contact with the worst elements in human nature, her purity, had found her way into the innermost recesses of his heart. He saw as he sat there, with a strange, almost divine clarity of vision, both into her soul and into his own. He knew that when she faced life again he would be the first to whom she would turn. He knew that with one word, one look, he could win her love. He knew that she had also never felt what love was. He knew that the circumstances of this night had turned her towards him as she would never have been turned in ordinary conditions. Yes, he knew this too—that had they met in everyday life she would never have loved him, would not indeed have thought of him twice.

He was not a man about whom anyone thought twice. With the exception of his sisters no woman had ever loved him; this child, driven to terrified desperation by the horrors of the last weeks, had been wakened to full womanhood by those same horrors, and he had happened to be there at the awakening. That was all. And yet he knew that so honest was she, and good and true, that did she once go to him she would stay with him. He saw steadily into the future. He saw her freedom from the madman to whom she was married, then her union with himself. His happiness, and her gradual discovery of the kind of man that he was. Not bad—oh no—but older, far older than herself in many other ways than years, tired so easily, caring nothing for all the young things in life, above all a man in the middle state, solitary from some elemental loneliness of soul.

It was true that tonight had shown him a new energy of living, a new happiness, a new vigour, and he would perhaps after tonight never be the same man as he was before. But it was not enough. No, not enough for this young girl just beginning life, so ignorant of it, so trustful of him that she would follow the path that he pointed out. And for himself! How often he had felt like Nejdanov in *Virgin Soil* that 'everything that he had said or done during the day seemed to him so utterly false, such useless nonsense, and the thing that ought to be done was nowhere to be found . . . . . . .unattainable . . . . . . .in the depths of a bottomless pit.'

Well, of tonight that was not true. What he had done was useful, was well done. But tomorrow how would he regard it? Would it not seem like senseless melodrama, the mad Crispins, his fall from the cliff, this eternal fog? How like his history that the most conclusive and eternal acts of his life should take place in a fog! And this girl whom he loved so dearly, if he married her and kept her for himself would not his conscience, that eternal tiresome conscience of his, would it not for ever reproach him, telling him that he had spoilt her life, and would not he be for ever watching to catch that moment when she would realise how dull, how old, how negative he was? No, he could not . . . . . . .he could not . . . . .

Then there swept over him all the fire of the other impulse. Why should he not, at long last, be happy? Could any man in the world be better to her than he would be? After all he was not so old. Had he not known when he shared in that dance round the town that he could be part of life, could feel with the common pulse of humanity? Did young Dunbar know life better than he? With him she had lived always and yet did not love him.

And then he knew with a flash like lightning through the fog that at this moment, when she was waking to life and was trusting him, he could, by only a few words, lead her to love Dunbar. She had always seen him in a commonplace, homely, familiar light, but he, Harkness, if he liked, could show her quite another light, could turn all this fresh romantic impulse that was now flowing towards himself into another channel.

But why should he? Was that not simply sentimental idealism? Dunbar was no friend of his, he had never seen him before yesterday, why should he give up to him the only real thing that his life had yet known?

But it was not sentimental, it was not false. Youth to youth. In years he was not so old, but in his hesitating, quixotic, undetermined character there were elements of analysis, self-questioning, regret, that would make any human being with whom he was intimately related unhappy.

Sitting there, staring out into the fog, he knew the truth—that he was a man doomed to be alone all his days. That did not mean that he could not make much of his life, have many friends, much good fortune—but in the last intimacy he could go to no one and no one could go to him.

He bent down and kissed her forehead. She stirred, moved, sat up, resting back against him, her feet on the ground.

'Where am I?' she whispered. 'Oh yes.' She clung to his arm. 'No one has come? We are still alone?'

'No,' he answered her gently, 'no one has come. We are still alone.'

8

'What time is it?' she asked.

He looked at his watch. 'Half-past two.'

'We have missed that train now.'

'I don't know. And anyway, there's probably another.'

'And David?'

'He's lost his way in the fog. He'll turn up at any moment.' He stood up and shouted once again:

'Dunbar! Dunbar! Dunbar!'

No answer.

He stood over her looking down at her as she sat with drooping head. She looked up at him. 'I'm ashamed at the way I've behaved,' she said, 'fainting and crying. But you needn't be afraid any more. I shan't give in again.'

Indeed, he seemed to see in her altogether a new spirit, something finer and more secure. She put out her hand to him.

'Come and sit down on the stone again as we were before. It's better for us to talk and then we don't frighten ourselves with possibilities. After all, we can't *do* anything, can we, so long as this horrid fog lasts? We must just sit here and wait for David.'

He sat down, put his arm around her as he had done before. The moment had come. He had only now to speak and the result was certain—the whole of his future life and hers. He knew so exactly what he would say. The words were forming on his lips.

'Hesther dear, I've known you so short a time, but nevertheless I love you with all my heart and being. When you are rid of this horrible man will you marry me? I will spend all my life in making you happy——'

And she, oh, without an instant's doubt, would say 'Yes,' would hide in his arms, and rest there as though secure, yes, utterly secure for life. But the battle was over. He would not begin it again. He clipped the words back and sat silent, one hand clenched on his knee.

It was as though she were waiting for him to speak. Their silence was packed with anticipation. At last she said:

'What is the matter? Is there something you're afraid of that you don't like to tell me? You needn't mind. I'm through my fear.'

'No, there's nothing,' he answered. At last he said: 'There *is* one thing I'd like to say to you. I suppose I've no right to speak of it, seeing how recently I've known you, but I guess this night has made us friends as months of ordinary living never would have made us.'

'Yes, you're right in that,' she answered. He knew what she was expecting him to say.

'Well, it's about Dunbar.' He could feel her hand jump in his. 'He loves you so much—so terribly. He isn't a man, I should think, to say very much about his feelings. I've only known him for an hour or two, and he wouldn't have said anything to me if he hadn't *had* to. But from the little he did say I could see what he feels. You're in luck to have a man like that in love with you.'

She took her hand out of his, then, very quietly but very stiffly, answered:

'But I've known him all my life, you know.'

'That's just why I'm speaking about him,' Harkness answered.

'It's rather strange to have the friend of your life explained to you by someone who has known him only for an hour or two.' She laughed a little angrily.

'But that's just why I'm speaking,' he answered. 'When you've known someone all your life you can't see them clearly. That's why one's own family always knows so little about one. You can't see the wood for the trees. In the first minutes a stranger sees more. I don't say that I know Dunbar as *well* as you do—I only say that I probably see things in him that you don't see.'

They had been so close to one another during this last hour that he felt as though he could see, as through clear water, deep into her mind.

He knew that, during those last minutes, she had been struggling desperately. She came up to him victorious and, smiling and putting her hand into his, said:

'Tell me what *you* think about him.'

'Simply that he seems to me a wonderful fellow. He seems to you, I expect, a little dull. You've always laughed at him a bit, and for that very reason, and because he's loved you for so long, he's tongue-tied when you're there and shy of showing you what he really thinks about things. He has immense qualities of character—fidelity, honesty, devotion, courage—things simply beyond price, and if you loved him and showed him that you did you'd probably see quite new things—fun and spontaneity and imagination—things that he had always been afraid to show you until now.'

Her hand trembled in his.

'You speak,' she said, 'as though you thought that you were so much older than both of us. I don't feel that you are. Can't you——?'

she broke off. He knew what she would say.

'My dear,' and his voice was eloquently paternal, 'I *am* older than both of you—years and years older. Not physically, perhaps, so much, but in every other kind of way. I am an old fogey, nothing else. You've both of you been kind to me tonight, but in the morning, when ordinary life begins again, you'll soon see what a stuffy old thing I am. No, no. Think of me as your uncle. But don't miss—oh, don't miss!—the love of a man like Dunbar. There's so little of that unselfish devoted love in the world, and when it comes to you it's a crime to miss it.'

'But you can't force yourself to love anyone!' she cried sharply.

'No, you can't *force* yourself, but it's strange what seeing new qualities in someone, looking at someone from another angle, will do. Try and look at him as though you'd met him for the first time, forget that you've known him always. I tell you that he's one in a million!'

'Yes, he's good,' she answered softly. 'He's been wonderful to me always. If he'd been less wonderful perhaps—I don't know, perhaps I'd have loved him more. But why are we talking about it? Aren't I married as it is?'

'Oh, that!' He made a little gesture of repulsion. 'We must get rid of that at once.'

'It won't be very difficult,' she answered, dropping her voice to a whisper. 'He hasn't been faithful to me—even during these weeks.'

He put his arm round her and held her close as though he were most truly her father. 'Poor child!' he said, 'poor child!'

She trembled in his arms.

'You——' she began. 'You——? Don't you——?' She could say no more.

'I'm your friend,' he answered, 'to the end of life. Your old avuncular friend. That's my job. Think of your *young* friend freshly. See what a fellow he is. I tell you that's a man!'

She did not answer him, but stayed there hiding her head in his coat.

There was a long silence, then, stroking her hair, he said:

'Hesther dear, I'm going to try once again.' He got up and, putting his hands trumpet-wise to his mouth, shouted through the fog:

'Dunbar! Dunbar! Dunbar!'

This time there was an answer, clear and definite. 'Hallo! Hallo! Hallo!' He turned excitedly to her. She also sprang to her feet. 'He's there! I can hear him!'

'Dunbar! Dunbar!'

The answer came more clearly: 'Hallo! Hallo! Hallo!'

They continued to exchange cries. Sometimes the reply was faint. Once it seemed to be lost altogether. Then suddenly it was close at hand. A ghostly figure was shadowed.

Dunbar came running.

9

He caught their hands in his. He was breathless. He sank down on the stone beside them.

'Give me a minute. . . . . . .I'm done. Lord! this filthy fog. . . . . . Where haven't I been?' He panted, staring up at them with wide distracted eyes.

'Do you realise? I've failed. It's no use our crossing in that boat now even if we could find it. We've missed that train. We're done.'

'Nonsense,' Harkness broke in. 'Why, man, what's happened to you? This isn't like you to lose your courage. We're not done or anything like it. In the first place, we're all together again. That's something in a fog like this. Besides, so long as we stick together we're out of their power. They can't force us, all of us, back into that house again. So long as we're out of that house we're safe.'

'Oh, are we?' said Dunbar. 'Little you know that man. I tell you we're not safe—or Hesther's not safe—until we're at least a hundred miles away. But forgive me,' he looked up at them both, smiling, 'you're quite right, Harkness. I haven't any right to talk like this. But you don't know what a time I've had in that fog.'

'I had a little bit of a time myself,' said Harkness.

'Well, in the first place,' went on Dunbar, 'I was terrified about you. I knew that you didn't know these cliffs well. When the fog started I called to you to come back, but you didn't hear me, of course. I was an idiot to let you start out at all.

'And then, when it came to myself climbing them I wasn't very successful. I was nearly over the edge fifty times at least. But at last when I *did* get to the top the ridiculous thing was that I started off in the wrong direction. There I was only five minutes from the cottage and the pony and Hesther; I know the place like my own hand, and yet I went in the wrong direction.

'God knows where I got to. I was nearly over into the sea twice at least. I kept calling your names, but the only thing I heard in answer was that beastly bell. I never went very far, I imagine, because when I heard your voice at last, Harkness, I was quite close to it. But just to think of it! Every other contingency in the world I'd considered except just this one! It simply never entered my head.'

'Well, now,' said Harkness, 'let's face the facts. It's too late for that train. Is there any other that we can catch?'

'There's one at six, but I don't see ourselves hanging about here for another three hours, nor, if the fog doesn't lift, can Hesther get down into that cove. I'm not especially anxious to try it myself, as a matter of fact.'

'No, nor I,' said Harkness, smiling. 'Then we count the boat out. There aren't many other things we can do. We can take the pony and follow him. He'll lead us straight back to Treliss to whatever stables he came from—a little too close to the Crispin family, I fancy. Secondly, we can wait here until the fog clears; that *may* be in three minutes' time, it may be tomorrow. You both know more about these sea-fogs down here than I do, but, from the look of it, it's solid till Christmas.'

'A heat fog this time of year,' said Dunbar, 'within three miles of the sea can last for twenty-four hours or longer—not as thick as this though—this is one of the thickest I've ever seen.'

'Well, then,' continued Harkness, 'it isn't much good to wait until it clears. The only thing remaining for us is to walk off somewhere. The question is, where? Is there any garage within a mile or two or any friend with a car? It isn't three o'clock yet. We still have time.'

'Yes,' said Dunbar, 'there is. I've had it in my mind all along as an alternative. Indeed, it was the first thing of all that I thought of. Three miles from here there's a village, Cranach. The rector of Cranach is a sporting old man called Banting. During the last week or two we've made friends. He's sixty or so, a bachelor, and he's got a car. Not much of a car, but still it's something. I believe if we go and appeal to him— we'll have to wake him up, of course—he'll help us. I know that he disapproves strongly of the Crispins. I thought of him before, as I say, but I didn't want to involve him in a row with Crispin. However, now, as things have gone, it's got to be. I can think of no other alternative.'

'Good,' said Harkness, 'that settles it. Our only remaining difficulty is to find our way there through this fog.'

'I can start straight,' said Dunbar. 'Left from the cottage and then straight ahead. Soon we ought to leave the Downs and strike some trees. After that it's across the fields. I don't think I can miss it.'

'What about the pony?' asked Hesther.

'We'll have to leave him. He must be there for Jabez in the morning or Jabez will have to pay for both the pony and the cart.'

They started off. The character of the fog seemed now slightly to have changed. It was certainly thicker in some places than in others. Here it was an impenetrable wall, but there it seemed to be only a gauze covering hanging before a multitude of changing scenes and persons. Now it was a multitude of armed men advancing, and you could be sure that you heard the clang of shield on shield and a thousand muffled steps. Now it was horses wheeling, their manes tossing, their tails flying, now secret furtive figures that moved and peered, stopped, bending forward and listening, then moved on again.

All the world was stirring. A breeze ran along the ground rustling the short thin grass. Seagulls were circling the mist crying. A ship at sea was sounding its horn. Figures seemed to press in on every side.

They linked arms as they went, stumbling over the tussocks at every step. It was strange how the sudden vanishing of the cottage left them forlorn. It had been their one sure substantial hold on life. They were in their own world while they could touch those ruined stones, but now they walked in air.

Nevertheless, Dunbar walked forward confidently. He thought that he recognised this landmark and that. 'Now we veer a bit to the left,' he said. 'We should be off the moor in another step.'

They walked forward. Suddenly Hesther pulled back, crying, 'Look out! Look out!' Another instant and they would have walked forward into space. The mist here twisted up into thinning spirals as though to show them what they had escaped; they could just see the sharp black line of the cliff. Far, far beneath them the sea purred like a cat.

They stopped where they were as though fixed like images into the wall of the fog.

Dunbar whispered: 'That's awful. Another moment. . . . . .'

It was Hesther who pulled them together again. 'Let's turn sharp about,' she said, 'and walk straight in front of us. At least we escape the sea.'

They turned as she had said and then walked forward, but in the minds of all of them there was the same thought. Someone was playing with them, someone like an evil Will-o'-the-wisp was leading them, now here, now there. Almost they could see his red poll gleaming through the fog and could hear his silvery voice running like music up and down the scale of the mist.

They were, three of them, worn with the events of the night. They were beginning to walk somnambulistically. Harkness found in himself now a strange kind of intimacy with the Fog.

Yes, spell it with a capital letter. The Fog. The FOG. Some emanation of himself, rolling out of him, friendly and also hostile. He and Crispin were of the Fog together. They had both created it, and as they were the good and the evil of the Fog so was all Life, shapeless, rolling hither and thither, but having in its elements Good and Evil in eternal friendship and eternal enmity.

Every part of his body was aching. His legs were so weary that they dragged with him, protesting; his eyes were for ever closing, his head nodding. He stumbled as he walked, and at his side, step with step in time, the Fog accompanied him, a mountainous grey-swathed giant.

He was talking, words were for ever pouring from him, words mixed with fog, so that they were damp and thick before ever they were free. 'In life there are not, you know, enough moments of clear understanding. Between nations, between individuals, those moments are too often confused by winds that, blowing from nowhere in particular, ruffle the clear water where peace of mind and love of soul for soul are reflected. . . . . . . .Now the waters are clear. Let us look down.'

Yes, he had read that somewhere. In one of Galleon's books perhaps? No matter. It meant nothing. 'A fine sentiment. What it means. . . . . . . .Well, no matter. Don't you smell roses? Roses out here on the moor. If it wasn't for the fog you'd smell them—ever so many.' And so, he tore the 'Orvieto' into shreds. Little scraps flying in the air like goose feathers. What a pity! Such a beautiful thing. . . . . .

'Hold up,' cried Dunbar. 'You're asleep, Harkness. You'll have us all down.'

He pulled together with a start, and opening his eyes wide and staring about him saw only the disgusting fog.

'This fog is too much of a good thing. Don't you think so? I guess we could blow it away if we all tried hard enough. You think Americans always say "I guess," don't you? The English books always make them. But don't you believe it. We only do it to please the English. They like it. It satisfies their vanity.'

He seemed to be climbing an enormous endless staircase. He mounted another step, two, and suddenly was wide awake.

'What nonsense I'm talking! I've been half asleep. This fog gets into your brain.' He felt Hesther's arm within his. He patted her hand encouragingly. 'It's all right, Hesther. We'll be out of this soon. Just another minute or two.'

'By Jove, you're right,' Dunbar cried; 'these are trees.'

And they were. A whole row of them. Crusoe was not more glad to see the footprint on the sand than were those three to see those trees. 'Now I know where we are!' Dunbar cried triumphantly. 'Here's the bridge and here's the lane. What luck to have found it!'

The trees seemed to step forward and greet them, each one tall and dignified, welcoming them to a happier country. They were on a road and had no longer the turf beneath their feet. The fog here was truly thinner, so that very dimly they could see the mark of the hedge like a clothes-line in mid-air.

They moved now much more rapidly, and in their hearts, was an intense, an eager relief. The fog thinned until it was a wall of silver. Nothing was distant, but it was a world of tangible reality. They could kick pebbles with their feet, could hear sheep moving on the farther side of the hedge.

'This is better,' said Dunbar. 'We'll get out of this yet. Cranach is only a mile or so from here. I know this lane well. And the fog's going to lift at last.'

Even as he spoke it swept up, thick and grey, deeper than before. The trees disappeared, the hedges. They had once more to grope for one another's hands and walk close.

Harkness could feel from the way that Hesther leaned against him, and the drag of her feet, that she was near the end of her endurance. She said nothing. Only walked on and on.

They were all now silent. They must have walked, it seemed to them, for miles. An endless walk that had no beginning and no end. And then Harkness was strangely aware—how, he never knew—that Dunbar and Hesther were drawing closer together.

He felt that new relation that he had in a way created beginning to grow between them. She drew away from Harkness ever so slightly. Then suddenly he knew that Dunbar had put his arm around her and was holding her up. She was so weary that she did not know what she was doing—but for that quiet, resolute, determined boy it must have been a moment of great triumph, the first time in their two lives that she had in any way surrendered to him or allowed him to care for her. Harkness was once more alone.

They walked and walked and walked. They did not know where they were walking, but in their minds, they were sure it was straight to Cranach.

Suddenly, after, as it seemed, hours of silence in a dead world, Dunbar cried:

'We're there. Oh, thank God! we're there. This is the rectory wall.'

A wall was before them and an open gate. They walked through the gate, only dimly seen, stumbled where the lawn rose from the gravel, then forward again, down on to the gravel again. The door was open.

Like somnambulists they walked forward. The door closed behind them.

Like somnambulists awakened they saw lights, a dim hall where flags waved.

For Harkness there was something familiar—quite close to him, the chatter-chatter of a clock, like a coughing dog. Familiar? He stared.

Someone was standing, looking at him and smiling.

With sudden agony in his voice, as a man cries in a terrible dream, Harkness shouted:

'Out, Dunbar! Back! Back! Run for your life!'

But it was too late.

That voice of exquisite melody greeted them:

'I had no idea that of your own free-will you would return. My son only a quarter of an hour ago departed in search of you. I welcome you back.'

PART 4: THE TOWER

1

With an instinctive movement both Harkness and Dunbar closed in upon Hesther.

The three stood just in front of the heavy locked door facing the dim hall. On the bottom stair was Crispin Senior, and on the floor below him, one on either side, the two Japanese servants.

A glittering candelabra, hanging high up, was fully lit, but it seemed to give a very feeble illumination, as though the fog had penetrated here also.

Crispin was wearing white silk pyjamas, brown leather slippers, and a dressing-gown of a rich bronze-coloured silk flowered with gold buds and leaves. His eyes were half-closed, as though the light, dim though it was, was too strong for him. His face wore a look of petulant, rather childish melancholy. The two servants were statues indeed, no sign of life proceeding from them. There was, however, very little movement anywhere, the flags moving in the draught the chief.

Hesther's face was white, and her breath came in little sharp pants, but she held her body rigid. Harkness after that first cry was silent, but Dunbar stepped forward shouting:

'You damned hound—you let us go or you shall have this place about your ears!' The hall echoed the words, which, to tell the truth, sounded very empty and theatrical. They were made to sound the more so by the quietness of Crispin's reply.

'There is no need,' he said, 'for all those words, Mr. Dunbar. It is your own fault that you interfered and must pay for your interference. I warned you weeks ago not to annoy me. Unfortunately, you wouldn't take advice. You *have* annoyed me—sadly, and must suffer the consequences.'

'If you touch a hair of her head——' he burst out.

'As to my daughter-in-law,' Crispin said, stepping down on to the floor, and suddenly smiling, 'I can assure you that she is in the best possible hands. She knows that herself, I'm sure. What induced you, Hesther,' he said, addressing her directly, 'to climb out of your window like the heroine of a cinematograph and career about on the sea-shore with these two gentlemen is best known only to yourself. At least you saw the error of your ways and are in time, after all, to go abroad with us today.'

He advanced a step towards them. 'And you, Mr. Harkness, don't you think that you have rather violated the decencies of hospitality? I think you will admit that I showed you nothing but courtesy as host. I invited you to dinner, then to my house, showed you my few poor things, and how have you repaid me? Is this the famous American courtesy? And may I ask, while we are on the question, what business this was of yours?'

'It was anybody's business,' said Harkness firmly, 'to rescue a helpless girl from such a house as this.'

'Indeed?' asked Crispin. 'And what is the matter with this house?'

Here Hesther broke in: 'Look back two nights ago,' she cried, 'and ask yourself then what is the matter with this house and whether it is a place for a woman to remain in.'

'For myself,' said Crispin, 'I think it is a very nice house, and I am quite sorry that we are leaving it today. That is, some of us—not all,' he added softly.

'If you are going to murder us,' Dunbar cried, 'get done with it. We don't fear you, you know, whatever colour your hair may be. But whether you murder us or no I can tell you one thing, that your own time has come—not many more hours of liberty for *you*.'

'All the more reason to make the most of those I *have* got,' said Crispin. 'Murder you? No. But you *have* fallen in very opportunely for the testing of certain theories of mine. I look forward to a very interesting hour or two. It is now just four o'clock. We leave this house at eight—or, at least, some of us do. I can promise all of us a very interesting four hours with no time for sleep at all. I have no doubt you are all tired, wandering about in the fog for so long must be fatiguing, but I don't see any of you sleeping—not for an hour or two, at least.'

Hesther said then: 'Mr. Crispin, I believe that I am chiefly concerned in this. If I promise to go quietly with you abroad I hope that you will free these two gentlemen. I give you that promise and I shall keep it.'

'No, no,' Dunbar cried, springing forward. 'You shan't go with him anywhere, Hesther, by heaven you shan't. Not while there's any breath in my body——'

'And when there isn't any breath in your body, Mr. Dunbar,' said Crispin, 'what then?'

'A very good line for an Adelphi melodrama, Mr. Crispin,' said Harkness, 'but it seems to me that we've stayed here talking long enough. I warn you that I am an American citizen and am not to be kept here against my will——'

'Aren't you indeed, Mr. Harkness?' said Crispin. 'Well, that's a line of Adelphi drama, if you like. How many times in a secret service play has the hero declared that he's an American citizen? Which only goes to show, I suppose, how near real life is to the theatre—or rather how much more theatrical real life is than the theatre can ever hope to be. But you're all right, Mr. Harkness—I won't forget that you're an American citizen. You shall have special privileges. That I promise you.'

Dunbar then did a foolish thing. He made a dash for the farther end of the hall. What he had in mind no one knows—in all probability to find a window, hurl himself through it, and escape to give the alarm. But the alarm to whom? That was, as far as things had yet gone, the foolishness of their position. A policeman arriving at the house would find nothing out of order, only that there two gentlemen had broken in, barbarously, at a midnight hour to abduct the married lady of the family.

Dunbar's effort was foolish in any case; its issue was that, in a moment of time, without noise or a word spoken, the two Japanese servants had him held, one hand on either arm. He looked stupid enough, there in the middle of the hall, his eyes dim with tears of rage, his body straining ineffectively against that apparently light and casual hold.

307

But it was strange to perceive how that movement of Dunbar's had altered all the situation. Before that the three were at least the semblance of visitors demanding of their host that they should be allowed to go; now they were prisoners and knew it. Although Hesther and Harkness were still untouched they were as conscious as was Dunbar of a sudden helplessness—and of a new fear.

Harkness watched Crispin, who had walked forward and now stood only a pace or two from Dunbar. Harkness saw that his excitement was almost uncontrollable. His legs, set widely apart, were quivering, his nostrils panting, his eyes quite closed so that he seemed a blind man scenting out his enemy.

'You miserable fellow,' he said—and his voice was scarcely more than a whisper. 'You fool—to think that you could interfere. I told you . . . . . . .I warned you . . . . . . .and now am I not justified? Yes—a thousand times. Within the next hour you shall know what pain is, and I shall watch you realise it.'

Then his body trembled with a sort of passionate rhythm as though he were swaying to the run of some murmured tune. With his eyes closed and the shivering it was like the performance of some devotional rite. At least Dunbar showed no fear.

'You can do what you damn well please,' he shouted. 'I'm not afraid of you, mad though you are.'

'Mad? Mad?' said Crispin, suddenly opening his eyes. 'That depends. Yes, that depends. Is a man mad who acts at last when given a perfectly just and honourable opportunity for a pleasure from which he has restrained himself because the opportunity hitherto was *not* honourable? And madness? A matter of taste, my friends, decides that. I like olives—you do not. Are you therefore mad? Surely not. Be broad-minded, my friend. You have much to learn and but little time in which to learn it.'

Harkness perceived that the man was savouring every moment of this situation. His anticipations of what was to come were so ardent that the present scene was coloured deep with them. He looked from one to another, tasting them, and his plans for them on his tongue. His madness—for never before had his eyes, his hands, his whole attitude of body more highly proclaimed him mad—had in it all the preoccupation with some secret life that leads to such a climax. For months, for years, grains of insanity, like coins in a miser's hoard, had been heaping up to make this grand total. And now that the moment was come he was afraid to touch the hoard lest it should melt under his fingers.

He approached Harkness.

'Mr. Harkness,' he said quite gently, 'believe me I am sorry to see this. You took me in last evening, you did indeed. I felt that you had a real interest in the beautiful things of art, and we had that in common. All the time you were nothing but a dirty spy—a mean and dirty spy. What right had you to interfere in the private life of a private gentleman who, twenty-four hours ago, was quite unknown to you, simply on the word of a crazy braggart boy? Have you so little to do that you must be poking your fingers into everyone else's business? I liked you, Mr. Harkness. As I told you quite honestly last evening, I don't know where I have met a stranger to whom I took more warmly. But you have disappointed me. You have only yourself to thank for this—only yourself to thank.'

Harkness replied firmly. 'Mr. Crispin, I had every right to act as I have done, and I only wish to God that it had been successful. It is true that when I came down to Cornwall yesterday I had no knowledge of you or your affairs, but, in the Treliss hotel, quite inadvertently, I overheard a conversation that showed me quite plainly that it was some one's place to interfere. What I have seen of you since that time, if you will forgive the personality, has only strengthened my conviction that interference—immediate and drastic—was most urgently necessary.

'Thanks to the fog we have failed. For Dunbar and myself we are for the moment in your power. Do what you like with us, but at least have some pity on this child here who has done you no wrong.'

'Very fine, very fine,' said Crispin. 'Mr. Harkness, you have a style—an excellent style—and I congratulate you on having lost almost completely your American accent—a relief for all of us. But come, come, this has lasted long enough. I would point out to you two gentlemen that, as one of you has already discovered, any sort of resistance is quite useless. We will go upstairs. One of my servants first—you two gentlemen next, my other servant following, then my daughter-in-law and myself. Please, gentlemen.'

He said something in a foreign tongue. One Japanese started upstairs, Harkness and Dunbar followed. There was nothing else at that moment to be done. Only at the top of the stairs Dunbar turned and cried: 'Buck up, Hesther. It will be all right.' And she cried back in a voice marvellously clear and brave: 'I'm not frightened, David; don't worry.'

Harkness had a momentary impulse to turn, dash down the stairs again, and run for the window as Dunbar had done; but as though he knew his thought the Japanese behind him laid his hand on his arm; the thin fingers pressed like steel. At the upper floor Dunbar was led one way, himself another. One Japanese, his hand still on his arm, opened a door and bowed. Harkness entered. The door closed. He found himself in total obscurity.

2

He did not attempt to move about the room, but simply sank down on to the floor where he was. He was in a state of extreme physical weariness—his body ached from head to foot—but his brain was active and urgent. This was the first time to himself that he had had—with the exception of his cliff climbing—since his leaving the hotel last evening, and he was glad of the loneliness. The darkness seemed to help him; he felt that he could think here more clearly; he sat there, huddled up, his back against the wall, and let his brain go.

At first it would do little more than force him to ask over and over again:

'Why? Why? Why? Why did we do this imbecile thing? Why, when we had all the world to choose from, did we find our way back into this horrible house?'

It was a temptation to call the thing magic and to have done with it, really to suggest that the older Crispin had wizard powers, or at least hypnotic, and had willed them back. But he forced himself to look at the whole thing clearly as a piece of real life as true and as actual as the ham-and-eggs and buttered toast that in another hour or two all the world around him would be eating. Yes, as real and actual as a toothbrush, that was what this thing was; there was nothing wizard about Crispin; he was a dangerous lunatic, and there were hundreds like him in any asylum in the country. As for their return, he knew well enough that in a fog people either walked round and round in a circle or returned to the place that they had started from.

At this point in his thoughts a tremor shook his body. He knew where *that* was from, and the anticipation that lying, like a chained animal, deep in the recesses of his brain, must soon be loosed and then bravely faced. But not yet, oh no, not yet! Let his mind stay with the past as long as it might.

In the past was Crispin. He looked back over that first meeting with him, the actual moment when he had asked him for a match, the dinner, the return to the hotel when, influenced then by all that Dunbar had told him, he had seen him standing there, the polite gestures, the hospitable words, the drive in the motor........His mind stopped abruptly *there*. The door swung to, the lock was turned.

In that earlier Crispin there had been something deeply pathetic—and, when he dared to look forward, he would see that in the later Crispin there was the same. So, with a sudden flash of lightening revelation that seemed to flare through the whole dark room he saw that it was not the real Crispin with whom they—Hesther, Dunbar, and he—were dealing at all.

No more than the ravings of fever were the real patient, the wicked cancerous growth the real body, the broken glass the real picture that seemed to be shattered beneath it.

They were dealing with a wild and dangerous animal, and in the grip of that animal, pitiably, was the true struggling, suffering soul of Crispin. Not struggling now perhaps anymore; the disease had gone too far, growing through a thousand tiny, almost unnoticed stages to this horrible possession.

He knew now—yes, as he had never, never known it, and would perhaps never have known it had it not been for the sudden love for and tenderness towards human nature that had come to him that night—what, in the old world, they had meant by the possession of evil spirits. What it was that Christ had cast out in His ministry. What it was from which David had delivered King Saul.

Quick on this came the further question. If this were so, might he not perhaps when the crisis came—as come he knew it would—appeal to the real Crispin and so rescue both themselves and him? He did not know. It had all gone so far. The animal with its beastly claws deep in the flesh had so tight a hold. He realised that it was in all probability the personality of Hesther herself that had urged it to such extremes. There was something in her clear-sighted, simple defiance of him that had made Crispin's fear of his powerlessness—the fear that had always contributed to his most dangerous excesses—climb to its utmost height.

He had decided perhaps that this was to be the real final test of his power, that this girl should submit to him utterly. Her escape had stirred his sense of failure as nothing else could do. And then their return, all the nervous excitement of that night, the constant alarm of the neighbourhoods in which they had stayed, so that, as the younger Crispin had said, they had been driven 'from pillar to post,' all these things had filled the bowl of insanity to overflowing. *Could* he rescue

Crispin as well as themselves?

Once more a tremor ran through his body. Because if he could not——Once more he thrust the anticipation back, pulling himself up from the floor and beginning slowly, feeling the wall with his hand like a blind man, to walk round the room.

His eyes now were better accustomed to the light, but he could make out but little of where he was. He supposed that he was on the second floor, where were the rooms of Hesther and the younger Crispin. The place seemed empty, there was no sound from the house. He might have been in his grave. Fantastic stories came to his mind, Poe-like stories of walls and ceilings growing closer and closer, of floors opening beneath the foot into watery dungeons, of fiery eyes seen through the darkness. He repeated then aloud:

'I am Charles Percy Harkness. I am thirty-five years of age. I was born at Baker, Oregon, in the United States of America. I am in sound mind and in excellent health. I came down to Cornwall yesterday afternoon for a holiday, recommended to do so by Sir James Maradick, Bart.'

This gave him some little satisfaction; to himself he continued, still walking and touching the wall-paper with his hand: 'I am shut up in a dark room in a strange house at four in the morning for no other reason than that I meddled in other people's affairs. And I am glad that I meddled. I am in love, and whatever comes out of this I do not regret it. I would do over again exactly what I have done, except that I should hope to do it better next time.'

He felt then seized with an intense weariness. He had known that he was, long ago, physically tired, but excitement had kept that at bay. Now quite instantly, as though a spring in the middle of his back had broken, he collapsed. He sank down there on the floor where he was, and all huddled up, his head hanging forward into his knees, he slept. He had a moment of conscious subjective rebellion when something cried to him: 'Don't surrender. Keep awake. It is part of his plan that you should sleep here. You are surrendering to *him*.'

And from long, misty distances he seemed to hear himself reply:

'I don't care what happens any more. They can do what they like. . . . . They can do what they like. . . . . .'

And almost at once he was conscious that they were summoning him. A tall thin figure, like an old German drawing, with wild hair, set mouth, menacing eye like Baldung's 'Saturnus,' stood before him and pointed the way into vague misty space. Other figures were moving about him, and he could see, as his eyes grew stronger, that a vast multitude of naked persons were sliding forward like pale lava from a volcano down a steep precipitous slope.

As they moved there came from them a shuddering cry like the tremor of the ground beneath his feet.

'Not there! Not there!' Harkness cried, and Saturnus answered, 'Not yet! You have not been judged.'

Almost instantly judgement followed—judgement in a narrow dark passage that rocked backward and forward like the motion of a boat at sea. The passage was dark, but on either side of its shaking walls were cries and shouts and groans and piteous wails, and clouds of smoke poured through, as into a tunnel, blinding the eyes and filling the nostrils with a horrible stench.

No figure could be seen, but a voice, strong and menacing, could be heard, and Harkness knew that it was himself the voice was addressing. His naked body, slippery with sweat, the acrid smoke blinding him, the voices deafening him, the rocking of the floor bewildering him, he felt desperately that he must clear his mind to answer the charges brought against him.

The voice was clear and calm:

'On February 2, 1905, your friend Richard Hentley was accused in the company of many people, during his absence, of having ill-treated his wife while in Florence. You knew that this was totally untrue and could have given evidence to that effect, but from cowardice you let the moment pass and your friend's position was seriously damaged. What have you to say in your defence?'

The thick smoke rolled on. The walls tottered. The cries gathered in anguish.

'On March 13, 1911, you wired to your sisters in America that you were ill in bed when you were in perfect health, because you wished to stay for a week longer in London in order to attend some races. What have you to say in your defence?

'On October 3, 1906, you grievously added to the unhappiness of Mrs. Harrington-Adams by asserting in mixed company that no one in New York would receive her and that all Americans were astonished that she should be received at all in London.'

Here at any rate was an opportunity. Through the smoke he cried:

'There at least I am innocent. I have never known Mrs. Harrington-Adams. I have never even seen her.'

'No,' the voice replied. 'But you spoke to Mrs. Phillops, who spoke to Miss Cator, who then cut Mrs. Adams. Other people followed Miss Cator's example, and you were quoted as an authority. Mrs. Adams' London life was ruined. She had never done you any harm.

'On December 14, 1912, you told your sisters that you hated the sight of them and their stuffy ways, that their attempts at culture were ridiculous, and that, like all American women, they were absurdly spoilt.'

Through the smoke Harkness shouted: 'I am sure I never said——'

The voice replied: 'I am quoting your exact words.'

'In a moment of pique I lost my temper. Of course, I didn't mean——'

'On June 3, 1913, you went secretly into the library of a friend and stole his book of Rembrandt drawings. You knew in your heart that you had no intention of returning it to him, and when, some months later, he spoke of it, wishing to lend it to you, and wondered why he could not find it, you said nothing to him about your own possession of it.'

Harkness blushed through the rolling smoke. 'Yes, that was shameful,' he cried. 'But I knew that he didn't care about the book and I——'

'What have you to say against these charges?'

'They are all little things,' Harkness cried, 'small things. Everyone does them. . . . . .'

'Judgement! Judgement! Judgement!' cried the voice, and suddenly he felt himself moving in the vast waters of human nudity that were slipping down the incline. He tried to stay himself; he flung out his hands and touched nothing but cold slimy flesh.

Faster and faster and faster. Colder and colder and colder. Darker and darker and darker. Despair seized him. He called on his friends. Others were calling on every side of him. Thousands and thousands of names mingled in the air. The smoke came up to meet them—vast billowing clouds of it. He knew with a horrible consciousness that below him a sea of upturned swords were waiting to receive them. Soon they would be impaled. . . . . With a shriek of agony he awoke.

He had not been asleep for more, perhaps, than ten minutes, but the dream had unnerved him. When he rose from the ground he tottered and stood trembling. He knew now why it was that his enemy had designed that he should sleep; he knew *now* that he could no longer ward off the animal that on padded feet had been approaching him—the pain! The pain! The pain!

The sweat beaded his forehead, his knees gave way, and he sank yet again upon the floor. He was murmuring: 'Anything but that. Anything but that. I can't stand pain. I can't *stand* pain, I tell you. Don't you know that I have always funked it all my life long? That I've always prayed that whatever else I got it wouldn't be *that*. That I've never been able to bear to see the tiniest thing hurt, and that in all my thought about going to the war, although I didn't try to escape it, it was even more the pain that I would see than the pain that I would feel.

'And now to wait for it like this, to know that it may be torture of the worst kind, that I am in the power of a man who can reason no longer, who is himself in the power of something stronger and more evil than any of us.'

Then dimly it came through to him that he had been given three tests tonight, and, as it always is in life, the three tests especially suited to his character, his strength and weakness, his past history. The dance had stripped him of his aloofness and drawn him into life, his love for Hesther that he had surrendered had taken from him his selfishness— and now he must lose his fear of pain.

But that? How could he lose it? It was part of the very fibre of his body, his nerves throbbed with it, his heart beat with it. He could not remember a time when it had not been part of him. When he had been five or six his father had decided that he must be beaten for some little crime. His father was the gentlest of human beings, and the beating would be very little, but at the sight of the whip something had cracked inside his brain.

He was not a coward; he had stood up to the beating without a tear, but the sense of the coming pain had been more awful than anything that he could have imagined. It was the same afterwards at school. He was no coward there either, shared in the roughest games, stood up to bullies, ventured into the most dangerous places.

But one night earache had attacked him. It was a new pain for him and he thought that he had never known anything so terrible. Worse than all else were the intermissions between the attacks and the warnings that a new attack was soon to begin. That approach was what he feared, that terrible and fearful approach. He had said very little, had only lain there white and trembling, but the memory of all those awful hours stayed with him always.

Any thought of suffering in others—of poor women in childbirth, of rabbits caught in traps, of dogs poisoned, of children run over or accidentally wounded—these things, if he knew of them, produced an odd sort of sympathetic pain in himself. The strangest thing had been that the war, with all its horrors, had not driven him crazy as he might have expected from his earlier history. On so terrible a scale, was it that his senses soon became numbed? He did the work that he was given to do, and heard of the rest like cries beyond the wall. Again, and again he had tried to mingle, himself, in it; he had always been prevented.

A dog run over by a motor car struck him more terribly than all the agonies of Ypres.

But these things, what had they to do with his present case? He could not think at all. His brain literally reeled, as though it shook, tried to steady itself, could not, and then turned right over. His body was alive, standing up with all its nerves on tiptoe. How was he to endure these hours that were coming to him?

'I must get out of this!' someone, not himself, cried. It seemed to him that he could hear the strange voice in the room. 'I must get out of this. How dare they keep me if I demand to be let out? I am an American citizen. Let me out of this. Can't you hear? Bring me a light and let me out. I have had enough of this dark room. What do you mean by keeping me here? You think that you are stronger than I. Try it and see. Let me out, I say! Let me out!'

He tottered to his feet and ran across the room, although he could not see his way, blundering against the opposite wall. He beat upon it with his hands.

'Let me out, do you hear! Let me out!'

He was not himself, Harkness. He could no longer repeat those earlier words. He was nobody, nothing, nothing at all. They could not hurt him then. Try as they might they could not hurt him, Harkness, when he was not Harkness. He laughed, stroking the wall gently with his hand as though it were his friend.

'It's all right, do you see? You can't hurt me because you can't find me. I'm hiding. *I* don't know where to find myself, so that it isn't likely you will find me. You can't hurt nothing, you know. You can't indeed.'

He laughed and laughed and laughed—gently enjoying his own joke. There was a sudden knocking on the door.

'Come in!' he said in a whisper. 'Come in!'

His heart stood still with fear.

The door opened, splashing into the darkness a shower of light like water flung from a bucket. In the centre of this the two Japanese were standing.

'Master says please come. If you ready he ready.'

At sight of the Japanese a marvellous thing had happened. All his fear had on the instant left him, his beastly physical fear. It fell from him like an old suit of clothes, discarded. He was himself, clear-headed, cool, collected, and, in some strange new way, happy.

Harkness followed them.

3

Harkness followed, conscious only of one thing, his sudden marvellous and happy deliverance from fear. He could not analyse it—he did not wish to. He did not consider the probable length of its duration. Enough that for the present Crispin might cut him into small pieces, skin him alive, boil him in a large pot like a lobster, and he would not care. He followed the sleek servants like a schoolboy.

The Tower? Then at last he was to see the interior of this mysterious place. It had exercised, all through this adventure, a strange influence over him, standing up in his imagination white and pure and apart, washed by the sea, guarded by the woods behind it, having a spirit altogether of its own and quite separate from the man who for the moment occupied it. This would be perhaps the last building on this world that would see his bones move and have their being; he had a sense that it knew and sympathised with him and wished him luck.

Meanwhile he walked quietly. His chance would still come and with Dunbar beside him. Or was he never to see Dunbar again? Some of his new-found courage trembled. The worst of this present moment was his loneliness. Was the final crisis to be fought out by himself with no friends at hand? Was he never to see Hesther again? He had an impulse to throw himself forward, attack the servants, and let come what will. The silence of the house was terrible—only their footsteps soft on the thick carpet—and if he could wring a cry or two from his enemies that would be something. No, he must wait. The happiness of others was involved with his own.

The men stopped before a dark-wooded door.

They went through and were met by a white circular staircase. Up this they passed, paused before another door, and crossed the threshold into a high circular brilliantly lit room. For the moment Harkness, his eyes dimmed a little by the shadows of the staircase, could see nothing but the gayness and brightness of the place, papered with a wonderful Chinese pattern of green and purple birds, cherry-coloured pagodas, and crimson temples. The carpet was a soft heavy purple, and there

317

were a number of little gilt chairs, and, in front of the narrow barred window, a gilt cage with a green and crimson macaw.

All this, standing by the door shading his eyes from the dazzling crystal candelabra, he took in; then suddenly saw something that swept away the rest—Hesther and Dunbar standing together, hand in hand, by the window. He gave a cry of joy, hurrying towards them. It was as though he had not seen them for years; they caught his hand in theirs. Crispin was there watching them like a benevolent father with his beloved children.

'That's right,' he said. 'Make the most of your time together. I want you to have a last talk.'

He sat down on one of the gilt chairs.

'Won't you sit down? In a moment I shall leave you alone together for a little while—in case you have any last words. . . . . .' Then he leaned forward in that fashion so familiar now to Harkness, huddled together, his red hair and little eyes and pale white soft hands alone alive. 'Well, and so—in my power, are you not? The three of you. You can laugh at my ugliness and my stupidity and my bad character, but now you are in my hands completely. I can do whatever I like with you. Whatever . . . . . . .the last shame, the last indignity, the uttermost pain. I, ludicrous creature that I am, have absolute power over three fine young things like you, so strong, so beautiful. And then more power and then more and then more. And over many finer, grander, more beautiful than you. I can say crawl and you will crawl, dance and you will dance . . . . . . .I who am so ugly that everyone has always laughed at me. I am a little God, and perhaps not so little, and soon God Himself . . . . .'

He broke off, making the movement of music in the air with his hands.

'You a little overestimate the situation,' said Harkness quietly. 'For the moment you can do what you like with our bodies because you happen to have two servants who, with their *Jiujitsu* and the rest of their tricks, are stronger than we are. It is not you who are stronger, but your servants whom your money is able to buy. I guess if I had you tied to a pillar and myself with a gun in my hand I could make you look pretty small. And in any case, it is only our bodies that you can do anything with. Ourselves—our real selves—you can't touch.'

'Is that so?' said Crispin. 'But I have not begun. The fun is all to come. We will see whether I can touch you or no. And for my daughter-in-law'—he looked at Hesther—'there is plenty of time—many years perhaps.'

Nothing in all his life would ever appeal more to Harkness than Hesther then. From the first moment of his sight of her what had attracted him had been the exquisite mingling of the child and of the woman. She had been for him at first some sort of deserted waif who had experienced all the cruelty and harshness of life so desperately early that she had known life upside down, and this had given her a woman's endurance and fortitude. She was like a child who has dressed up in her mother's clothes for a party and then finds that she must take her mother's place.

And now when she must, after this terrible night, be physically beyond all her resources she seemed, in her shabby ill-made dress, her hair disordered, her face pale, her eyes ringed with grey, to have a new courage that must be similar to that which he had himself been given. She kept her hand in Dunbar's, and with a strange, dim, unexpected pain Harkness realised that that new relation between the two of which he had made the foundation had grown through danger and anxiety the one for another already to a fine height. Then he was conscious that Hesther was speaking. She had come forward quite close to Crispin and stood in front of him looking him calmly and clearly in the eyes.

'Please let me say something. After all I am the principal person in this. If it hadn't been for me there would not have been any of this trouble. I married your son. I married him, not because I loved him, but because I wanted things that I thought that you could give me. I see now how wrong that was and that I must pay for doing such a thing. I am ready to do right by your son. I never would have tried to run away if it had not been for you—the other night. After that I was right to do everything I could to get away. I begged your son first—and he refused. You have had me watched during the last three weeks—every step that I have taken. What could I do but try to escape?'

'We've failed, and because we've failed and because it has been all my fault I want you to punish me in any way you like but to let my two friends go. I was not wrong to try to escape.' She threw up her head proudly, 'I was right after the way you had behaved to me, but now it is different. I have brought them into this. They have done nothing wrong. You must let them go.'

'You must let all of us go,' Dunbar broke in hotly, starting forward to Hesther's side. 'Do you think we're afraid of you, you old play-acting red-haired monkey? You just let us free or it will be the worse for you. Do you know where you'll be this time tomorrow? Beating your fancy-coloured hair against a padded cell, and that's where you should have been years ago.'

'No, no,' Hesther broke in. 'No, no, David. That's not the way. You don't understand. Don't listen to him. I'm the only one in this; I tell you—can't you hear me?—that I will stay. I won't try to run away, you can do anything to me you like. I'll obey you—I will indeed. Please, please—Don't listen to him. He doesn't understand. But I do. Let them go. They've done no harm. They only wanted to help me. They didn't mean anything against you. They didn't truly. Oh! let them go! Let them go!'

In spite of her struggle for self-control her terror was rising, her terror never for herself but now only for them. She knew, more than they, of what he was. She saw perhaps in his face more than they would ever see.

But Harkness saw enough. He saw rising into Crispin's eyes the soul of that strange hairy fetid-smelling animal between whose paws Crispin's own soul was now lying. That animal looked out of Crispin's eyes. And behind that gaze was Crispin's own terror.

Crispin said:

'This is very comforting for me. I have waited for this moment.'

Then Harkness came over to him and stood very close to him.

'Crispin, listen to me. It isn't the three of us who matter in this, it is yourself. Whatever you do to us we are safe. Whatever you think or hope you can't touch the real part of us, but for yourself tonight this is a matter of life or death.

'I may know nothing about medicine and yet know enough to tell you that you're a sick man—badly sick—and if you let this animal that has his grip on you get the better of you in the next two hours you're finished, you're dead. You know that as well as I. You know that you're possessed of an evil spirit as surely as the man with the spirits that cleared the Gadarene swine into the sea. It isn't for our sakes that I ask you to let us go tonight. Let us go. You'll never hear from any of us again. In the morning, in the decent daylight, you'll know that you've won a victory more important than any you've ever won in your life.

'You talk about mastering us, man. Master your own evil spirit. You know that you loathe it, that you've loathed it for years, that you are miserable and wretched under it. It is life or death for you tonight, I tell you. You know that as well as I.'

For one moment, a brief flashing moment, Harkness met for the first and for the last time the real Crispin. No one else saw that meeting. Straight into the eyes, gazing out of them exactly as a prisoner gazes from behind iron bars, jumped the real Crispin, something sad, starved, and dying. One instant of recognition and he was gone.

'That is very kind of you, Mr. Harkness,' Crispin said. 'I knew that I should enjoy this quarter of an hour's chat with you all, and truly I *am* enjoying it. My friend Dunbar shows himself to be quite frankly the young ruffian he is. It will be interesting to see whether in—say an hour's time from now—he is still in the same mind. I doubt it; quite frankly I doubt it very much. It is these robust natures that break the easiest. But you other two—really how charming. All altruism and unselfishness. This lady has no thought for anything but her friends, and Mr. Harkness, like all Americans, is full of fine idealism. And you are all standing round me as though you were my children listening to a fairy story. Such a pretty picture!'

'And when you come to think of it here, I am quite alone, all defenceless, one to three. Why don't you attack me? Such an admirable opportunity! Can it be fear? Fear of an old fat ugly man like me, a man at whom every one laughs!'

Dunbar made a movement. Harkness cried: 'Don't move, Dunbar. Don't touch him. That's what he wants.'

Crispin got up. They were now all standing in a little group close together. Crispin gathered his dressing-gown around him.

'The time is nearly up,' he said. 'I am going to leave you alone together for a little last talk. You'll never see one another again after this, so you had best make the most of it. You see that I am not really unkind.'

'It is hopeless.' Harkness turned round to the window. 'God help us all.'

'Yes, it is hopeless,' Crispin said gently. 'At last my time has come. Do you know how long I have waited for it? Do you know what you represent to me? You have done me wrong, the two of you, broken my hospitality, betrayed my bread and salt, invaded my home. I have justice if I punish you for that. But you stand also for all the others, for all who have insulted me and laughed at me and mocked at me. I have power at last. I shall prick you and you shall bleed. I shall spit on you and you shall bow your heads, and then when you are at my feet stung with a thousand wounds I will raise you and care for you and love you, and you shall share my power——'

He jumped suddenly from his gilt chair and strutted, waving his hands as though he were commanding an army, towards the macaw, who was asleep with his head under his crimson wing. 'I shall be king in my own right, king of men, emperor of mankind, then one with the gods, and at the last I will shower my gifts. . . . . .'

He broke off, looking up at a red-lacquer clock that stood on a little round gilt table. 'Time—time—time nearly up!' He swung round upon the three of them.

Dunbar burst out:

'Don't flatter yourself that you'll get away tomorrow. When we're missed——'

'You won't be missed,' Crispin answered with a sigh, as though he deeply regretted the fact. 'The hotel will receive a note in the morning saying that Mr. Harkness has gone for a coast walk, will return in a week, and will the hotel kindly keep his things until his return? Of course, the hotel most kindly will. For Mr. Dunbar—well, I believe there is only an aunt in Gloucester, is there not? It will be, I imagine, a month at least before she makes any inquiry. Possibly a year. Possibly never. Who knows? Aunts are often extraordinarily careless about their nephews' safety. And in a week. Where can one not be in a week in these modern days? Very far indeed. Then there is the sea. Anything dropped from the garden over the cliff so completely vanishes, and their faces are so often—well, spoilt beyond recognition. . . . . .'

'If you do this,' Hesther cried, 'I will——'

'I regret to say,' interrupted Crispin, 'that after eight this morning you will not see your father-in-law of whom you are so fond for six months at least. Ah, that is good news for you, I am sure. That is not to say you will never see him again. Dear me, no. But not immediately. Not immediately!'

Harkness caught Hesther's hand. He saw that she was about to make some desperate movement. 'Wait,' he said; 'wait. We can do nothing now.'

For answer she drew him to her and flung out her hand to Dunbar. 'We three. We love one another,' she cried. 'Do your worst.'

Crispin looked once more at the clock. 'Melodrama,' he said. 'I, too, will be melodramatic. I give you twenty minutes by that clock—a situation familiar to every theatre-goer. When that clock strikes six I shall, I'm afraid, want the company of both of you gentlemen. Make your *adieus* then to the lady. Your eternal *adieus*.'

He smiled and gently tiptoed from the room.

4

'And so, the curtain falls on Act Three of this pleasant little drama,' said Dunbar huskily, turning towards the window. 'There will be a twenty minutes' interval. But the last act will be played *in camera*. If only one wasn't so beastly tired—and if only it wasn't all my fault. . . . . .' His voice broke.

Harkness went up to him, put his arm around him and drew him to him. 'Look here. I'm older than both of you. I might almost be your father, so you've got to obey my orders. I'll be best man at your wedding yet, David, yours and Hesther's. There's nobody to blame. Nothing but the fog. But don't let's cheat ourselves either. We're shut up here at half-past five in the morning miles from any help, no way out, no telephone, and two damn Japs who are stronger than we are, in the power of a man who's as mad as a hatter and as bloodthirsty as a tiger.

'It's going to be all right, I tell you. I know it. I feel it in my bones. But we've got to behave for these twenty minutes—only seventeen of them now—as though it won't be. It's of no use for us to make any plan. We'll have to do something on the spur of the moment when we see what the old devil has up his sleeve for us——

'Meanwhile, as I say, make the best of these minutes.'

He put out his arm and drew Hesther in.

'I tell you that I love you both. I've only known you a day, but I love you as I've never loved any one in my life before. I love you as father and brother and comrade. It's the best thing that has happened to me in all my life.'

The three, body to body, stood looking out through the gilded bars at the sky, silver grey, and washed with shifting shadows.

'After all,' he went on, 'if our luck doesn't hold, and we are going to die in the next hour or so, what is it? It's only what millions of fellows passed through in the war and under much more terrible conditions. Imagination is the worst part of that I fancy, and I suggest that we don't think of what is going to happen when this time is over—whether it goes well or ill—we'll fill these twenty minutes with every decent thought we've got, we'll think of every fine thing that we know of, and every beautiful thing, and everything that is of good report.'

'All I pray,' said Dunbar, 'is that I may have one last dash at that lunatic before goodbye. He can have a hundred Japs around him but I'll get at him somehow. Harkness, you're a brick. I brought you into this. I had no right to, but I'm not going to apologise. We're here. The thing's done, and if it hadn't been for that rotten fog——But you're right, Harkness. We'll think of all the ripping things we know. With me it's simple enough. Because the beginning and the middle and the end of it is Hesther. Hesther first and Hesther second and Hesther all the time.'

He didn't look at her, but stared out of the window.

'By Jove, the sun's coming. It's been up round the corner ever so long. It will just about hit the window in another ten minutes. It seems kind of stupid to stand here doing nothing.'

He stepped forward and felt the bars. 'Take hours to get through that, and then there's a drop of hundreds of feet. No, you're about right, Harkness. There's nothing to be done here but to say goodbye as decently as possible.'

He sighed. 'I didn't want to kick the bucket just yet, but there it is, it can happen to anybody. A fellow can be as strong as a horse, forget to change his socks and next day be finished. This is better than pneumonia anyway! All the same I can't help feeling we missed our chance just now when we had him alone in here——'

'No,' said Harkness, 'I was watching him. That's what he wanted, for us to go for him. I am sure that he had the Japs handy somewhere, and I think he wanted to hurt us in front of Hesther. But his brain works queerly. He's formulated a kind of book of rules for himself. If we take such and such a step, then he will take such and such another. A sort of insane sense of justice. He's worked it all out to the minute. Half the fun for him has been the planning of it, and then the deliberate slowness of it, watching us, calculating what we'll do. Really a cat with, mice. There's nothing for deliberate consecutive thinking like a madman's brain.'

Hesther broke in:

'We're wasting time. I know—I feel as you do—that it's going to be all right, but however he fails with you he *can* carry me off somewhere, and so it *is* very likely that I don't see either of you again for some time. And if that's so—*if* that's so, I just want to say that you've been the finest men in the world to me.

'And I want you to know that whatever turns up for me now—yes, whatever it is—it *can't* be as bad as it was before yesterday. I can't ever again be as unhappy as I was now that I've known both of you as I've known you this night.

'I didn't realise, David, how I felt about you until Mr. Harkness showed me. I've been so selfish all these years, and I suppose I shall go on being selfish, because one doesn't change all in a minute, but at least I've got the two best friends a woman ever had.'

'Hesther,' Dunbar said, turning towards her, 'if we get free of this and you can get rid of that man—I ask you as I've asked you every week for the last ten years—will you marry me?'

'Yes,' she said. But for the moment she turned to Harkness. He was looking through the bars out to the sky, where the mist was now very faintly rose like the coloured smoke of far-distant fire. She put her hand on his shoulder, keeping her other hand in Dunbar's.

'I don't know why you said you were so much older than we are. You're not. Do you promise to be the friend of both of us always?'

'Yes,' he said. Something mockingly repeated in his brain, 'It is a far far better thing that I do——'

He burst out laughing. The macaw awoke, put up his head and screamed.

'You are both younger by centuries than I,' he said. 'I was born old. I was born with the Old Man of Europe singing in my ears. I was born to the inheritance of borrowed culture. The gifts that the fairies gave me at my cradle were Michael Angelo's "David," Rembrandt's "Goldweigher's Field," the Temples at Paestum, the Da Vinci "Last Supper," the Breughels at Vienna, the view of the Jungfrau from Mürren, the Grand Canal at dawn, Hogarth's prints, and the Quintet of the *Meistersinger*. Yes, the gifts were piled up all right. But just as they were all showered upon me in stepped the Wicked Fairy and said that I should have them all—on condition that I didn't touch! Never touch—never. At least I've known that they were there, at least I've bent the knee, but—until last night—until last night . . . . .'

He suddenly took Hesther's face between his two hands, kissed her on the forehead, on the eyes, on the mouth:

'I don't know what's coming in a quarter of an hour. I don't like to think. To tell you the truth, I'm in the devil of a funk. But I love you, I love you, I love you. Like an uncle you know, or at least like a brother. You've taken a match and set fire to this old tinder-box that's been dry and dusty so long, and now it's alight—such a pretty blaze!'

He broke away from them both with a smile that suddenly made him look young as they'd never seen him:

'I've danced the town, I've climbed rocks, I've dared the devil, I've fallen in love, and I know at last that there's such a hunger for beauty in my soul that it must go on and on and on. Why should it be there? My parents hadn't it, my sisters haven't it, no one tried to give it to me.

I've done nothing with it until last night, but now when I've needed it it's come to my help. I've touched life at last. I'm alive. I never can die anymore!'

The macaw screamed again and again, beating at the cage with its wings.

'Hesther, never lose courage. Remember that he can't touch you, that no one can touch you. You're your own immortal mistress.'

The red-lacquered clock struck the quarter, and at the same moment the sun hit the window. Strange to see how instantly that room with the coloured pagodas, the fantastic temples, the gilt chairs, and the purple carpet shivered into tinsel. The dust floated on the ladder of the sun: the blue of the early morning sky was coloured faintly like a bird's wing.

The sun flooded the room, wrapping them all in its mantle.

'Let's sit down,' said Dunbar, pulling three of the gilt chairs into the centre of the room, where the sun shone brightest. 'I've a kind of idea that we'll need all the strength we've got in a few minutes. That's fine what you said, Harkness, about being alive, although I didn't follow you altogether.

'I'm not very artistic. A man who's been on the sea since he was a small kid doesn't go to many picture galleries and he doesn't read books much either. To tell you the truth, there's always such a lot to do, and when I've finished the *Daily Mail* there doesn't seem time for much more, except a shocker sometimes. The sort of mess we're in now wouldn't make a bad shocker, would it? Only you'd never be able to make Crispin convincing. All I know is, if I wrote a book about him I'd have him tortured at the end with little red devils and plenty of pincers. However, I get what you mean, Harkness, about being alive.

'I felt something of the same thing in the war sometimes. At Jutland, although I was in the devil of a funk all the time, I was sort of pleased with myself too. Life's always seemed a bit unreal since the armistice, until last night. And it's a funny thing, but when I was helping Hesther climb out of that window and expecting Crispin Junior to poke his head up any minute I had just that same pleased-all-over feeling that I had at Jutland. So that's about the same as you feel, Harkness, only different, of course, because of your education. . . . . . . .Hesther, if we win out of this and you marry me I'll be so good to you—so good to you—that——'

He beat his hands desperately on his knees.

'Here's the time slipping and we don't seem to be doing anything with it. It's always been my trouble that I've never been able to say what I mean—couldn't find words, you know. I can't now, but it's simple enough what I mean——'

Hesther said: 'If we only have ten minutes like this it's so hard to choose what you would say, but I'd like you to know, David, that I re-member everything we've ever done together—the time I missed the train at Truro and was so frightened about father, and you said you'd come in with me, and father hadn't even noticed I'd been away; and the time you brought me the pink fan from Madrid; and the time I had that fever and you sat up all night outside my room, those two days father was away; and the day Billy fell over the Bring Rock and you climbed down after him; and the time you brought me that Sealy-ham and father wouldn't let me have him; and the time just before you went off to South Africa and I wouldn't say goodbye. I've hurt you so many times and you've never been angry with me once—or only that once. Do you remember the day I struck you in the face because you said I was more like a boy than a girl? I thought you were laughing at me because I was so untidy and dirty and so I hit you. And do you remember you sprang on me like a tiger, and for a moment I thought you were going to kill me? You said no one had ever struck you with-out getting it back. Then suddenly you pulled yourself in—just like going inside and shutting your door.

'I've never seen you until tonight, David. I've been blind to you. You've been too close to me for me to see you. It will be all right. We'll come out of this and then we'll have such times—such wonder-ful times——'

She came up to him, drew his head to her breast. He knelt on the floor at her feet, his arms round her, his head on her bosom. She stroked his hair, looking out beyond him to the blue of the sky.

Harkness felt a mad wildness of impatience. He went to the win-dow and tugged at the bars. In despair his hands fell to his side.

'The only chance, Dunbar, is to go straight for him the moment we're out of this room, even if those damned Japs are with him. We can't do much, but we may smash him up a bit first. Then there's Jabez. We've forgotten Jabez. Where's he been all this time?'

Dunbar looked up. 'I expect he went home after we went off.'

'No,' said Harkness, 'he was to be there till six. He told me. What's happened to him? At any rate he'll give the alarm if we don't turn up.'

'No, he'll think we got safely off.'

'Yes, I suppose he will. My God, it's five to six. Look here, stand up a moment.'

They stood up.

'Let's take hands. Let's swear this. Whatever happens to us now, whether some of us survive or none, whether we die now or live happily ever afterwards, we'll be friends for ever, nothing shall ever separate us, for better or worse we're together for always.'

They swore it.

'And see here. If I don't come out of this don't have any regrets either of you. Don't think you brought me into this against my will. Don't think that whichever way it goes I regret a moment of it. You've given me the finest time.'

Dunbar laughed. 'I sort of feel we're going to have a chance yet. After all, he's been probably playing with us, trying to frighten us. There'll be nothing in it, you see. Anyway, I'll get a crack at his skull, and now that I've got you, Hesther, I wouldn't give up this night for all the wealth of the Indies. I don't know about life or death. I've never thought much about it, to tell you the honest truth, but I bet that anyone who's as fond of anyone as I am of you can't be very far away, whatever happens to their body.'

'There goes six.'

The red-lacquer clock struck. Hesther flung her arms around Harkness and kissed him, then Dunbar.

They all stood listening. Just as the clock ceased there was a knock at the door.

5

Harkness went to the door and opened it; not Crispin, as he had expected, but one of the Japanese. For the first time he spoke:

'Beg your pardon, sir. The master would be glad you see him up-stairs.' Harkness did not look back. He knew that Dunbar and Hesther were clasped tightly in one another's arms. He walked out, closing the door behind him. He stood with the Japanese in the small space waiting. It was a dim, subdued light out here. You could only see the thick stone steps of the circular staircase winding upwards out of sight. Harkness's brain was working now with feverish activity. Whatever Crispin's devilish plan might be he would be there to watch the climax of it. If Harkness and Dunbar were quick enough they could surely have Crispin throttled before the Japanese were in time; without Crispin it was likely enough that the Japanese would be passive. This was no affair of theirs. They simply obeyed their master's orders.

He wondered why he had not attempted something in that room just now—why, indeed, he had prevented Dunbar; but some instinct had told him then that Crispin was longing to shame them in some way before Hesther. He had then an almost overpowering impulse to turn back, run into that room, fling his arms about Hesther and hold her until those devils pulled them apart. It was an impulse that rose blinding his eyes, deafening his ears, stunning his brain. He half turned. The door opened and Dunbar came out. Harkness sighed with relief. At the sight of Dunbar, the temptation left him.

They mounted the stairs, one Japanese in front of them, the other behind. At the next break in the flight the Japanese turned and opened a door on the left.

'In here, gentlemen, if you please,' he said, bowing.

They entered a small room with no windows, quite dark save for one dim electric light in the ceiling, and without furniture save for two wicker chairs.

They stood there waiting. 'The master,' said the Japanese, 'he much obliged if you gentlemen will kindly take your clothes off.'

For a moment there was silence. They had not realised the words. Then Dunbar broke out: 'No, by God, no! Strip for that swine! Harkness, come on! You go for that fellow, I'll take this one!' and instantly he had hurled himself on the Japanese nearest the door.

Harkness flung at the one who had spoken. He was conscious of his fingers clutching at the thin cotton stuff of the clothes, and, beneath the clothes, the cold hard steel of the limbs. His arms gripped upwards, caught the cloth of the shirt, tore it, slipped on the smooth, hairless chest. Then in his left forearm there was a pain, sharp as though some ravenous animal had bitten him there, then an agony in the middle of his back, then in his left thigh.

Against his will he cried out; the pain was terrible—awful. Every nerve in his body was rebelling so that he had neither strength nor force. He slipped to the floor, writhing involuntarily with the agony of the twisted muscle and, even as he slipped, he saw sliding down over him, impervious, motionless, fixed like a shining mask, the face of the Japanese.

He lay on the floor; panic flooded him. His helplessness, the terror of what was coming next, the fright of the dark—it was all he could do at that moment not to burst into tears and cry like a child.

He was lying on the floor, and the Japanese, kneeling beside him, had one arm under him as though to make his position more comfortable.

'Very sorry,' the Japanese murmured in his ear; 'the master's orders.'

As the pain withdrew he felt only an intense relief and thankfulness. He did not care about what had gone before nor mind what followed. All he wished was to be left like that until the wild beating of his heart softened and his pulse was again tranquil.

Then he thought of Dunbar. He turned his head and saw that Dunbar also was lying on the floor, on his side. Not a sound came from him. The other Japanese was bending over him.

'Dunbar!' Harkness cried in a voice that to his own surprise was only a whisper, 'wait. It's no good with these fellows. We'll have our chance later.'

Dunbar replied, the words gritted from between his teeth: 'No—it's no good—with these devils. It's all right, though. I'm cheery.'

Harkness saw then that the Japanese had been stripping Dunbar, and he noticed with a curious little wonder that his clothes had been arranged in a neat, tidy pile—his socks, his collar, his braces, on his shirt and trousers. He saw the Japanese move forward as though to help Dunbar to his feet; there was a movement as though Dunbar were pushing him away. He rose to his feet, naked, strong, his head up, swung out his arms, pushed out his chest.

'No bones broken with their monkey tricks. Hurry up, Harkness. We may as well go into the sea together. I bet the water's cold.'

But no. The Japanese said something. Dunbar broke out:

'I'm damned if I will.' Then, turning to Harkness: 'He says I've got to go on by myself. It seems they're going to separate us. Rotten luck, but there's no fighting these two fellows here. Well, cheerio, Harkness. You've been a mighty fine pal, if we don't meet again. Only that rotten fog did us in.'

Harkness struggled to his knees. 'No, no, Dunbar. They shan't separate us. They shan't——' but there was a touch of a hand on his arm and instantly, as though to save at all costs another pressure of that nerve, he sank back.

Dunbar went out, one of the Japanese following him. The door closed.

Now indeed Harkness needed all his fortitude. He had never felt such loneliness as this. From the beginning of the adventure there had been an element so fantastic, so improbable, that except at certain moments he had never believed in the final reality of it. There was something laughable, ludicrous about Crispin himself; he had been like a child playing with his toys. Now absolutely Harkness was face to face with reality.

Crispin did mean all that he had threatened. And what that might be———!

The Japanese was beginning to take off his clothes, very lightly and gently pulling his coat from under him. Harkness sat up and assisted him. This did not matter. Of what significance was it whether he had clothes or no? What mattered was that he should be out of this horrible room where there was neither space nor light nor company. Anything anywhere was better. The Japanese's cool hard fingers slipped about his body. He himself undid his collar and mechanically dropped his collar-stud into the right-hand pocket of his waistcoat, where he always put it when he was undressing. He bent forward and took off his shoes.

The Japanese gravely thanked him. There was a small hole in his right sock and he slipped it off quickly, covering it with his other hand. He was ashamed for the Japanese to see it.

His clothes were piled as neatly as Dunbar's. He stood up feeling freshened and cool.

Then the Japanese, bowing, moved to the door. Harkness followed him.

They climbed the stairs once more, the stone striking cold under Harkness's bare feet. They must now be reaching the very top of the Tower. There was a sense of space and height about them and a stronger light.

The Japanese paused, pushed back a door and sharply jerked Harkness forward. Harkness nearly fell, but was caught by someone else, closed his eyes involuntarily against a flood of light into which he seemed, with a curious sensation as though he had dived from a great height, to be sinking ever deeper and deeper, then to be struggling up through bursting bubbles of colour. His eyes were still closed against the sun that pressed like a warm palm upon the lids.

He felt hands moving about him; then that he was held back against something cold; then that he was being bound, gently, smoothly; the bands did not hurt his flesh. There was a pause. He still kept his eyes closed. Was this death then? The sun beat upon his body, warm and strong. The cool of the pillar to which he was bound was pleasant against his back. There were boards beneath his feet, and on their dry, friendly surface his toes curled. A delicious soft lethargy wrapped him round. Was this death? One sharp pang like the pressure of an aching tooth and then nothing, sinking into dark silence through this shaft of deep and burning sunlight. . . . . .

He opened his eyes. He cried aloud with astonishment. He was in what was plainly the top room of the Tower, a high white place with a round ceiling softly primrose. One high window went the length from floor to ceiling, and this window, which was without bars, blazed with sun and shone with the colours of the early morning blue. The room was white—pure virgin white—round, and bare of furniture. Only—and this was what had caught the cry from Harkness—three pillars supported the ceiling, and to these three pillars were bound by white cord, first himself, then Dunbar, then, naked as they, Jabez.

The fisherman stood there facing Harkness—a gigantic figure. Yesterday afternoon on the hill, last night in the garden, Harkness had not recognised the man's huge proportions under his clothes. Now, bound there, with his black hair and beard, his great chest, the muscle of his arms and thighs, the sunlight bathing him, he was mighty to see.

His eyes were mild and puzzled like the eyes of a dog who has been chained against reason. He was making a strange restless motion from side to side as though he were testing the white cords that held him. His face above his beard, his neck, the upper part of his chest, his hands, his legs beneath the knees, were a deep russet brown, the rest of him a fair white, striking strangely with the jet blackness of his hair.

He smiled as he saw Harkness's astonishment.

'Aye, sir,' he said. 'It wasn't me you was expectin' to see here, and it wasn't myself that was expectin' to be here neither.'

They were alone—no Japanese, no Crispin.

'I've been in here half an hour before you come,' he went on. 'And I can tell you, sir, I was mighty sorry to see them bringin' both you gentlemen in. Whatever happens to me, I said, they've got clear away. It never kind of struck me that the fog was going to worry you.'

'Why didn't you get away yourself, Jabez?' Harkness asked him.

'They was down on me about an hour after. The fog had come on pretty thick and I was walkin' up and down oat there thinkin'. I hadn't no more than another hour of it and pleasin' myself to think how mad that old devil would be when he'd found out what had happened and me safe in my own house with the mother, when all of a sudden I hear the car snortin'. "Somethin' up," I says, and three seconds later, as you might say, they was on me. If it hadn't been for that fog I might of got clear, but they was on me before I knew it. I had a bit of a struggle with they dirty stinkin' foreigners, but they got a lot of dirty tricks an

Englishman would be ashamed of using. Anyway, they had me down on the ground pretty quick and hurt me too.

'They trussed me up like a fowl, carried me into the hall, and didn't the old red-headed devil spit and curse? You've never seen nothing like it, sir. Sure, raving mad he was that time all right. And he came and kicked me on the face and pulled my beard and spat in my eyes. I don't know what's coming to us right now, but I pray the Almighty Father to give me just one turn with my fist. I'll land him.

'Then, sir, they carried me upstairs and tumbled me into a dark room. There I was for I wouldn't like to say how long. Then they came in and took my things off me, the dirty foreigners. It's only a foreigner would think of a thing like that. I struggled a bit, but what's the use? They put their thumb in your back and they've got you. Then they tied me up here. I had to laugh, I did really. Did you ever see such a comic picture as all three of us without a stitch between us tied up here at six in the morning?

'When I tell mother about it she'll laugh all right. Like the show down to St. Ives when they have the boxing. I suppose we'll be getting out of this all serene, sir, won't we?'

'Of course, we will,' said Dunbar. 'Don't you worry, Jabez. He's been doing all this to frighten us. He daren't touch us really. Why, he'll have the county about his ears as it is. Don't you worry.'

'Thank you, sir,' said Jabez, still moving from side to side within the bands, 'because you see, sir, I wouldn't like anything to happen to me just now. Mother's expectin' an addition to the family in a month or so and there's six on 'em already, an' it needs a bit of doing looking after them all. I wouldn't have been working for this dirty blackguard here if it hadn't been for there being so many of us—not that I'd have one of them away, if you understand me, sir.'

'You needn't be afraid, Jabez,' Dunbar said. 'When we get out of this Mr. Harkness and I will see that you never have any anxiety again. You've been a wonderful friend to us tonight and we're not likely to forget it.'

'Oh, don't you mistake me, sir,' said Jabez. 'It wasn't no help I was asking for. I'm doing very well with the boat and the potatoes. It was only I was thinking I wouldn't like nothing exactly to happen to me along of this crazy lunatic here, if you understand me, sir. . . . . . . .I'm not so sure if they give me time I couldn't get through these bits of rope here. I'm pretty strong in the arm, or used to be—not so dusty even now. If I could work at them a bit——'

333

The door opened and Crispin came in.

He appeared to Harkness as he stepped in, quietly closing the door behind him, like some strange creature of a dream. He seemed himself, in the way that he moved with his eyes nearly closed, somnambulistic. He was wearing now only his white silk pyjamas, and of these the sleeves were rolled up, showing his fat white arms. His red hair stood on end like an ill-fitting wig. In one hand he carried a curved knife with a handle of worked gold.

In the room, blazing with sunlight, he was like a creature straight from the boards of some neighbouring theatre, even to the white powder that lay in dry flakes upon his face.

He opened his eyes, staring at the sunlight, and in their depths Harkness saw the strangest mingling of terror, pathos, eager lust, and a bewildered amazement, as though he were tranced. The gaze with which he turned to Harkness had in it a sudden appeal; then that appeal sank like light quenched by water.

He was wrung up on the instant to intensest excitement. His whole body trembled. His mouth opened as though he would speak, then closed again.

He came close to Harkness. He put out his hand and touched his neck.

'We are alone,' he said, in his soft, beautiful voice. He stroked Harkness's neck. The soft, boneless fingers! Harkness looked at him, and, strangely, at that moment their eyes were very close to one another. They looked at one another gently. In Harkness's eyes were no malice; in Crispin's that strange mingling of lust and unhappiness.

Harkness only said: 'Crispin, whatever you do to us, leave that girl alone. I beg you leave her. . . . . .'

He closed his eyes then. God helping him he would not speak another word. But a triumphant exultation surged through him because he knew that he was not afraid.

There was no fear in him. It was as though the warm sun beating on his body gave him courage.

Standing behind the safeguard of his closed eyes his real soul seemed to slip away, to run down the circular staircase into the hall and pass happily into the garden, down the road to the sea.

His soul was free and Crispin's was imprisoned.

He heard Crispin's voice: 'Will you admit now that I have you in my hand? If I touch you here how you will bleed—bleed to death if I do not prevent it. Do you remember Shylock and his pound of flesh?

"Oh! upright Judge!" But there is no judge here to stay me!'

The knife touched him. He felt it as though it had been a wasp's sting—a small cut it must be—and suddenly there was the cool trickle of blood down his skin. Then his right shoulder—a prick! Now a cut again on his arm. Stings—nothing more. But the end had really come then at last? His hands beneath the bonds moved suddenly of their own impulse. It was not natural not to strive to be free, to fight for his life.

He opened his eyes. He was bleeding from five or six little cuts. Crispin was standing away from him. He saw that Dunbar, crimson in the face, was struggling frantically with his cords and was shouting. Jabez, too, was calling out. The room, hitherto so quiet, was alive with movement. Crispin now stood back from him watching him. The sight of blood had completed what these weeks had been preparing.

With that first touch of the knife on Harkness's body Crispin's soul had died. The battle was over. There was an animal here clothed fantastically in human clothes like a monkey or a dog at a music-hall show. The animal capered, stood on its hind legs, mowed in the air with its hands. It crept up to Harkness and, whining like a dog, pricked him with the knife point now here, now there, in a hundred places.

Harkness looked out once more at the great window with its splash of glorious sky, then ceased to struggle with his cords. His lips moved in some prayer perhaps, and once more, surely now for the last time, he closed his eyes. He had a strange vision of all the moving world beyond that window. At that moment at the hotel the maids would be sweeping the corridors, people would be stirring and rubbing their eyes and looking at their watches; in the town, family breakfasts would be preparing, men would be sauntering down the narrow streets to their work, the connection with the London train would be running in with the London papers, already the men and women would be in the fields, the women would be waiting perhaps for the fishing-fleet to come in, Mrs. Jabez would be at the cottage door looking up the road for her husband. . . . . .

His heart pounded into his mouth; with a mighty impulse he drove it back. Crispin was laughing. The knife was raised. His face was wrinkled. He was running round the room, round and round, making with the knife strange movements in the air. He was whispering to himself. Round and round and round he ran, words pouring from his mouth in a thick unending stream. They were not words, they were sounds, and once and again a strange sigh like a catch of the breath, like a choke in the throat. He ran, bending, not looking at the three men, bending low as though as he ran he were looking for something on the floor.

Then quite suddenly he straightened himself, and with a growl and a snarl, the knife raised in one hand, hurled himself at Jabez.

All followed then quickly. The knife flashed in the sunlight. It seemed that the hands caught at Jabez's eyes, first one and then another; but there had been more than the hands, because suddenly blood poured from those eyes, spouting over, covering the face, mingling with the beard.

With a great cry Jabez put forth his strength. Stung by agony to a power that he had never known until then his body seemed to rise from the ground, to become something superhuman, immortal. The great head towered, the limbs spread out, it seemed for a moment as though the pillar itself would fall.

The cord that tied him to the pillar snapped and his hands were free. He tottered, the blood pouring from his face. He moved, blindly, staggering. Not a sound had come from him since that first cry.

His hands flung out, and in another moment Crispin was caught into his arms. He raised him. The little fat hands fluttered. The knife flashed loosely and fell to the ground. The giant swung into the middle of the room, blinded, but holding to himself ever tighter and ever tighter the short fat body.

Crispin, his head tossed back, his legs flung out in an agony now of terror, screamed with a strange, shrill cry like a rabbit entrapped.

Jabez turned, and now he had Crispin's soft chest against his bleeding face, the arms fluttering above his head. As he turned his shoulder touched the glass of the window. He pushed backward with his arm and the window swung open, some of the broken glass tinkling to the ground. There was a great rush of air.

That strange thing, like no human body, the white silk, the brown slippers, the red hair, swung. For one second of a time, suspended as it were on the thread of that long animal scream, so shrill and yet so thin and distant, the white face, its little eyes staring, the painted mouth open, hung towards Harkness. Then into the air, like a coloured bundle of worthless junk; for a moment a dark shadow across the steeple of sunlight, and then down, down, into fathomless depths of air, leaving the space of sky stainless, the morning blue without taint......

Jabez stood for a moment facing them, his chest heaving in convulsive pants. Then crying 'My eyes! My eyes!' crumpled to the floor.

6

First Harkness was conscious of a wonderful silence. Then into the silence, borne in on the back of the sea breeze, he heard the wild chattering of a multitude of birds. The room was filled with their chatter, up from the trees, crowding the room with their life.

Straight past the window, like an arrow shot from a bow, flashed a seagull. Then another more slowly wheeled down, curving against the blue like a wave released into air.

He recognised all these things, and then once again that wonderful blessed stillness. All was peace, all repose. He might rest for ever.

After, it seemed, an infinity of time, and from a vast distance, he caught Dunbar's voice:

'. . . . . Jabez! Jabez! Jabez, old fellow! The man's fainted. Harkness, are you all right? Did he hurt you?'

'No,' Harkness quietly answered. 'He didn't hurt me. He meant to, though. . . . . .' Then a green curtain of dark thick cloth swept through the heaven and caught him into its folds. He knew nothing more. The last thing he heard was the glorious happy chattering of the birds.

7

He slowly climbed an infinity of stairs, up and up and up. The stairs were hard to climb, but he knew that at their summit there would be a glorious view, and, for that view, he would undergo any hardship. But oh! he was tired, desperately tired. He could hardly raise one foot above another.

He had been walking with his eyes closed, because it was cooler that way. Then a bee stung him. Then another. On the chest. Now on the arm. Now a whole flight. He cried out. He opened his eyes.

He was lying on a bed. People were about him. He had been climbing those stairs naked. It would never do that those strangers should see him. He must speak of it. His hand touched cloth. He was wearing trousers. His chest was bare, and someone was bending over him touching places here and there on his body with something that stung. Not bees after all. He looked up with mildly wondering eyes and saw a face bending over him—a kindly bearded face, a face that he could trust. Not like—not like—that strange mask face of the Japanese. . . . . That other . . . . .

He struggled on to his elbow, crying: 'No, no. I can't any more. I've had enough. He's mad, I tell you——'

A kind rough voice said to him: 'That's all right, my friend. That's all over. No harm done——'

My friend! That sounded good. He looked round him and in the distance, saw Dunbar. He broke into smiles, holding out his hand.

'Dunbar, old man! That's fine. So, you're all right?'

Dunbar came over and sat on his bed, putting his arm around him.

'All right? I should think so. So are we all. Even Jabez isn't much the worse. That devil missed his eyes, thank heaven. He'll have two scars to the end of his time to remind him, though.'

Harkness sat up. He knew now where he was, on a sofa in the hall—in the hall with the tattered banners and the clock that coughed like a dog. He looked at the clock—just a quarter to seven! Only three-quarters of an hour since that awful knock on the door.

Then he saw Hesther.

'Oh, thank God!' he whispered to himself. '*Nunc dimittis* . . . . .'

She came to him. The three sat together on the sofa, the bearded man (the doctor from the village under the cliff, Harkness afterwards found) standing back, looking at them, smiling.

'Now tell me,' Harkness said, looking at Dunbar, 'the rest that I don't know.'

'There isn't much to tell. We were only there another ten minutes. When you fainted off I felt a bit queer myself, but I just kept together, and then heard someone running up the stairs.

'I thought it was one of the Japs returning, but there was a great banging on the door and then shouting in a good old Cornish accent. I called back that I was tied up in there and that they must break in the door. That they did and burst in—two fishermen and old Possiter the policeman from Duntrent. He's somewhere about the house now with two of the Treliss policemen. Well, it seems that a fellow, Jack Curtis, was going up the hill to his morning work in the Creppit fields above the wood here when he heard a strange cry, and, turning the corner of the road, finds on the path above the rocks, Crispin—pretty smashed up, you know. He ran—only a yard or two—to the Possiter's cottage. Possiter was having his breakfast and was up here in no time. They got into the house through a window and saw the two Japanese clearing off up the back garden. Curtis chased them, but they beat him and vanished into the wood. They stopped two other men who were passing, and then came on Hesther tied up in the library. She sent them to the Tower.'

'Well—and then?' said Harkness.

'There isn't much more. Except this. They got up the doctor, had poor old Jabez's face looked to and cleared him off down to his cottage, were examining your cuts—all this down here. Suddenly a car comes up to the door and in there bursts—young Crispin! The two Treliss policemen had turned up three minutes earlier in *their* car and were here alone except for Possiter examining Crispin Senior—who was pretty well smashed to pieces I can tell you.

'Crispin Junior breaks through, gives one look at his father, shouts out some words that no one can understand, puts a revolver to his temple, and blows the top of his head off before anyone can stop him. Topples right over his father's body. The end of the house of Crispin!

'I saw all this from the staircase. I was just coming down after looking at you. I heard the shot, saw old Possiter jump back, and got down in time to help them clear it all up.

'No one knows where he'd been. To Truro, I imagine, looking for all of us. He must have cared for that madman, cared for him or been hypnotised by him—*I* don't know. At least he didn't hesitate——'

'And now, sir, would you mind telling me .....?' said the stout red-faced Treliss policeman, advancing towards them.

8

He was free; it was, from the moment that the red-faced policeman, smiling upon him benevolently, had informed him that, for the moment, he had had from him all that he needed, his one burning and determined impulse—to get away from that hall, that garden, that house, with the utmost possible urgency.

He had not wished even to stay with Hesther and Dunbar. He would see them later in the day—would see them, please God, many many times in the years to come.

What he wanted was to be alone—absolutely alone.

The cuts on the upper part of his body were nothing—a little iodine would heal them soon; it seemed that there had come to him no physical harm—only an amazing all-invading weariness. It was not like any weariness that he had ever before known. He imagined—he had had no positive experience—that it resembled the conditions of some happy doped trance, some dream-state in which the world was a vision and oneself a disembodied spirit. It was as though his body, stricken with an agony of weariness, was waiting for his descent, but his soul remained high in air in a bell of crystal glass beyond whose surface the colours of the world floated about him.

He left them all—the doctor, the policeman, Dunbar, and Hesther.

He did not even stop at Jabez's cottage to inquire. That was for later. As half-past seven struck from the church tower below the hill he flung the gate behind him, crossed the road, and struck off on to the Downs above the sea.

By a kind of second sight he knew exactly where he would go. There was a path that crossed the Down that ran slipping into a little cove, across whose breast a stream trickled, then up on to the Down again, pushing up over fields of corn, past the cottage gardens up to the very gate of the hotel.

It was all mapped in his mind in bright, clear-painted colours.

The world was indeed as though it had only that morning been painted in green and blue and gold. While the fog hung, under its canopy the master-artist had been at work. Now from the shoulder of the Down a shimmer of mist tempered the splendour of the day. Harkness could see it all. The long line of sea on whose blue surface three white sails hovered, the bend of the Down where it turned to deeper green, the dip of the hill out of whose hollow the church spire like a spear steel-tipped gesticulated, the rising hill with the wood and the tall white tower, the green downs far to the right where tiny sheep like flowers quivered in the early morning haze.

All was peace. The rustling whisper of the sea, the breeze moving through the taller grasses, the hum of tiny insects, a lark singing, two dogs barking in rivalry, a scent of herb and salt and fashioned soil—all these things were peace.

Harkness moved a free man as he had never been in all his life as yet. He was his own master, and God's servant too. Life might be a dream—it seemed to him that it was—but it was a dream with a meaning, and the events of that night had given him the key.

His egotism was gone. He wanted nothing for himself any more. He was, and would always be, himself, but also, he had lost himself in the common life of man. He was himself because his contact with beauty was his own. Beauty belonged to all men in common, and it was through beauty that they came to God, but each man found beauty in his own way, and, having found it, joined his portion of it to the common stock.

He had been shy of man and was shy no longer; he had been in love, was in love now, but had surrendered it; he had been afraid of physical pain and was afraid no longer; he had looked his enemy in the eyes and borne him no ill-will.

But he was conscious of none of these things—only of the freshness of the morning, of the scents that came to him from every side, and of this strange disembodied state, so that he seemed to float, like gossamer, on air.

He went down the path to the little cove. He watched the ripple of water advance and retreat. The stream of fresh water that ran through it was crystal clear, and he bent down, made a cup with his hands, and drank. He could see the pebbles, brown and red and green like jewels, and thin spires of green weed swaying to and fro.

He buried his face in the water, letting it wash his eyes, his forehead, his nostrils, his mouth.

He stood up and drank in the silence. The ripple of the sea was like the touch on his arm of a friend. He kneeled down and let the fine sand run, hot, through his fingers. Then he moved on.

He climbed the hill: a flock of sheep passed him, huddling together, crying, nosing the hedge. The sun touched the outline of their fleece to shining light. He cried out to the shepherd:

'A fine morning!'

'Aye, a beautiful morning!'

'A nasty fog last night.'

'Aye, aye—all cleared off now, though. It'll be a warm day.'

The dog, his tongue out, his eyes shining, ran barking hither, thither. They passed over the hill, the sheep like a cloud against the green.

He pushed up, the breeze blowing more strongly now on his forehead.

He reached the cottage gardens, and the smell of roses was once more thick in his nostrils. The chimneys were sending silver skeins of smoke into the blue air. Bacon smells and scent of fresh bread came to him.

He was at the hotel gates. Oh! but he was weary now! Weary and happy. He stumbled up the path, smelling the roses again. Into the hall. The gong was ringing for breakfast. Children, crying out and laughing, raced down the stairs, past him. He reached his room. He opened the door. How quiet it was! Just as he had left it.

Ah! there was the tree of the 'St. Gilles,' and there the grave friendly eyes of Strang leaning over the etching-table to greet him.

Just as they were—but he!—not as he had been! He caught his face in the glass, smiling idiotically.

He staggered to his bed, flung himself down, still smiling. His eyes closed. There floated up to him a face—a little white face crowned with red hair, but not evil now, not animal—friendly, lonely, asking for

341

something. . . . . .

He smiled, promising something. Lifted his hand. Then his hand fell, and he sank deep, deep, deep into happy, blissful slumber.